Diana Appleyard is a writer, broadcaster and freelance journalist for a number of national newspapers and magazines. Until three years ago she was the BBC's Education Correspondent in the Midlands, before deciding to give up her full-time job and work from home – a decision which formed the basis of her first novel, *Homing Instinct*, published by Black Swan in June 1999. She lives with her husband, Ross, and her two young daughters in an Oxfordshire farmhouse.

Also by Diana Appleyard

HOMING INSTINCT

and published by Black Swan

A CLASS APART

Diana Appleyard

BLACK SWAN

A CLASS APART
A BLACK SWAN BOOK : 0 552 99822 2

First publication in Great Britain

PRINTING HISTORY
Black Swan edition published 2000

1 3 5 7 9 10 8 6 4 2

Set in 11pt Melior by
County Typesetters, Margate, Kent.

Black Swan Books are published by Transworld Publishers,
61–63 Uxbridge Road, London W5 5SA,
a division of The Random House Group Ltd,
in Australia by Random House Australia (Pty) Ltd,
20 Alfred Street, Milsons Point, Sydney, NSW 2061, Australia,
in New Zealand by Random House New Zealand Ltd,
18 Poland Road, Glenfield, Auckland 10, New Zealand
and in South Africa by Random House (Pty) Ltd,
Endulini, 5a Jubilee Road, Parktown 2193, South Africa.

Printed and bound in Great Britain by
Cox & Wyman Ltd, Reading, Berkshire.

To Mum and Dad

Many thanks to my agent Jo, to Linda
and all at Transworld

Chapter One

Lucy woke first. Rob's arm lay over her, like a dead weight. Slowly, she pushed it off and he grumbled in his sleep, humped the pillow into two and turned over, stretching his long legs away from her. Despite the open window, against which Lucy's new cream curtains billowed, one side of his dark hair — still long, resting on his shoulders just as it had when they first met — was darkened and sticky with sweat. Lucy stretched out her feet, feeling her knees tighten, and laid her hands flat against the white pure cotton sheets Rob insisted were a complete extravagance. But Lucy needed these little luxuries, and the one thing she had insisted on, having moved into the house nine months before, was the complete redecoration of their bedroom from flowery hell to a white and cream oasis of calm. Rob said it was rather like sleeping in a lunatic asylum.

In the pale morning light — through the curtain she could just see the thick indigo of the autumn night sky seeping into a watery, almost ghostly sunlight — the oak tree at the bottom of the garden where Rob was building a tree house for the girls was silhouetted in its increasingly bare clothes, like a child's drawing. Lucy glanced at the alarm clock. Seven. Thank God, it was Saturday, no school. Any moment Olivia would rise, creep from her bed, wee as silently as possible without flushing the loo and tip-toe down the stairs to put on the banned Cartoon Network. Laura would slumber on, nine going on nineteen, a sweaty mound under her new Habitat duvet, clutching the fluffy kangaroo she claimed she no longer needed.

Lucy's mind ran idly through the day, kaleido-scoping events into a swift stream of consciousness. Leisurely breakfast in dressing gowns, someone had to go to the supermarket – she was sure it was Rob's turn – tidy up everything, stuff the washing machine, sort those clothes currently on the rack into iron and non-iron. Lunch – she really would make some soup, not just give them Heinz – and then the girls' riding lesson. Just the second time they had been, wildly excited, despite Rob's misgivings. Laura looked like she really might be quite good. Rob thought it was a silly, snobby – and dangerous – sport for them to take up. Tough. Then this evening, a drinks party for one of Rob's staff leaving, in the pub, not a smart do. Lucy grimaced in the semi-darkness. She'd have to drive, as it was his party. Great. Standing in the pub nursing a Diet Coke and a forced smile while everyone else got pissed. And she knew they all found it hard to talk to her, thinking she was posh and stand-offish. Which she wasn't. Mostly, she was just bored. It wouldn't matter so much if Rob noticed she was uncomfortable and drew her in, but he rarely did. She curled her fingers against the soft white sheet. Shit. Was there nothing else? Against any form of conscious will, a tear brimmed like a rain-drop and slid out of the corner of her eye, down into her ear. She reached up a hand to brush it away. How stupid. With the pads of her fingers, the nails she always meant to paint but never had the time, she brushed the translucent trail away. Come on. Time to face the day.

'Lucy! Come and sort these two out before I plant them in the bloody garden!'

A shrill and persistent noise could be heard floating up the stairs, like a kettle coming to the boil. It was the sound of a small child who had been heftily thumped by her older sister for the sneaky purloining of a hair-clip. Not a hanging offence in most people's book, admittedly, but vitally important when you are nine and your most *absolutely precious* possession is your treasure trove of glittery hairclips. Rob, however, had no truck with the pettiness of his children's arguments. He had child intolerances like other people had food intolerances.

His broad Lancashire accent, which Lucy felt he hung onto like a fashion accessory, cut through her dreamy reverie. She was leaning, half dressed, with her elbows on the top of her antique pine chest of drawers, peering intently in the swing mirror at the bags under her eyes. Age was such an insidious thing, she mused, one minute you had skin which fitted your face, the next it had taken up origami without even asking you first. She pulled her mouth down into a grimace. That was better, the bags disappeared. Then she smiled, and there they were again. Lord. She looked like Fred Basset. In her bra, she held her arms out from her sides. Christ. She used to wear batwing jumpers. Now she had batwing arms. How come her face and body spoke of age, when she didn't *feel* age? But it was true age was sneaking up on her – she'd recently passed the two greatest yardsticks of getting older – thinking a canteen of cutlery was an excellent present and becoming genuinely excited at the thought of visiting a teashop.

'If you don't do something about these two I am *leaving*. Jesus!' he called. 'Is it too much to ask for five minutes' peace? I've given them breakfast.'

Yes, thought Lucy, ruefully, and wished she had stayed in bed. With two children who appeared to have inherited the extremes of both their parents' personalities, it was. But then, Saturday mornings were always tricky. Rob managed to avoid the full force of child guerrilla warfare during the week, with what Lucy thought was the underhand tactic of leaving for work very early and returning very late, normally just in time to read bedtime stories when they had been lulled into a soporific trance like the Flopsy Bunnies, through exhaustion and a hot bath. At weekends, there were no such mitigating factors.

'What the *hell* are you doing up there? Your coffee's getting cold.' Rob, despite having been last out of bed, had attacked the day like a tornado, sweeping a protesting Olivia away from the television, dragging Laura out of bed and singing a loud and tuneless song in the shower as the girls spat toothpaste into the sink. Lucy, although up first, felt as if she was moving underwater. Everything seemed a huge effort, today.

'Looking for something,' Lucy called back. Then she said more quietly, staring at herself, 'I seem to have carelessly mislaid my youth.'

Sighing, she wandered down the stairs, running her hand down the dado rail as she went. They really would have to change almost the entire decoration – the people before obviously had shares in Laura Ashley. Every inch of wall which could accommodate a swagged flowery border or spriggy wild poppies, did so. It was like living in an Interflora van. On the stairs, beneath the dado rail, were legions of small pink roses on a creamy background. Above, in a masterpiece of riotous bad taste, were bright pink and white candy stripes which would adorn the sort of hatbox normally swung by a Southern belle called Mary-Lou. If Lucy had the energy she would have stripped the lot, as she had done in her bedroom, and replaced it with a deep flat colour from the Farrow and Ball range of paints, but at the moment with work and the girls and everything, she just couldn't be arsed. The one thing which had to go were the ruched curtains in the living room – or the lounge, as Rob insisted on calling it, which made Lucy wince even after twelve years of marriage. They were like looking at a hen's bum.

Jackie from next door had popped in the day after they'd moved – when Lucy was ready to lie down on the floor and sob at the impossibility of ever making this house feel like home – and said, admiringly, 'Isn't it *super*. You don't need to change a thing, do you? It's just like a show house.' Lucy looked at her in horror, and opened her mouth to say no, it was absolutely vile and she had to change everything, when she intercepted a sharp look from Rob. Jackie, in fact, did live in the former show house on the estate and, as she found out later, worshipped at the altar of pink. She was also gazing admiringly at Rob, but then he always had this effect on women when they first met him. Lucy now hardly noticed that he looked like a sexily dissolute rock star, and it amazed her how other women's mouths hung open with longing. It was all very well looking at him. They ought to try living with him.

Lucy wished Rob wouldn't swear so freely in front of the children. She knew it was probably the legacy of her own seriously repressed childhood and totally anal, but whenever he let fly – which he frequently did – she had to fight the urge to clap her hands over the children's ears. She had visions of her mother coming to tea and Laura saying casually, 'Pass the fucking salt.' Lucy's parents had never sworn in front of her and her sister Helen. Once a small 'bugger' had slipped past her mother's lips in a moment of extreme emotion, and she looked like she'd farted in front of the Pope. They'd fallen about, laughing hysterically like hyenas.

They were both at boarding school at the time and had all the fluency of abuse of foul-mouthed navvies, but, like most teenagers, had perfected the art of swearing copiously in front of their friends, and employing an inbuilt safety valve in the company of their parents or teachers. It was like being bilingual. When Lucy met Rob at university, she was secretly excited by the fact that he had no such inhibitions and refused to modify his language for anyone. Now, she minded. What had seemed daring and free-thinking and radical sixteen years ago now seemed simply bloody-minded and uncouth.

It was funny, being a parent, Lucy mused. You thought so many things were silly and irrelevant as a child: no eating sweets in the street, no bad language, no chewing gum, no elbows on the table, always saying 'pardon me' if even the tiniest burp was emitted, asking 'please may I leave the table', and, God forbid, no spitting – if Lucy or Helen had spat her mother would have had a coronary and been carted off to hospital in a bundle of trembling cashmere. Yet now she found herself repeating the same things, like a mantra, to her own children. Rob thought she was appallingly fussy to care so much what other people thought. He was incredibly strict about discipline – far more so than Lucy, with what Rob said were her woolly liberal middle-class ideals – but he didn't care about any of the surface stuff that he thought obsessed Lucy, the desire to constantly impress people, whether through clothes or car or home. Here was a man who would happily answer the door in slippers. He hadn't been brought up to trip the high wire between what was acceptable, and what was not, which Lucy thought she didn't care about but which had clearly been deeply implanted like some kind of identity tag and was now worming its way to the surface. She knew this was the case because the other day Laura had tried to buy bubblegum in the village shop. 'You can't have that!' Lucy said in horror. 'It's comm—' She only just stopped herself in time.

'Ow! Olivia, do look where you're going.'

Running full pelt, Olivia hit her amidships at the bottom of the stairs. She was still clutching the hairclip in a small, determined fist, like pirates' booty. Laura, close behind, lunged forward and grabbed her round the waist. Olivia let out a high-pitched squeal as Laura flung her to the floor. Sitting astride her, pinning her down, she tried to prise her fingers open while Olivia wriggled and shrieked. 'Stop it!' Lucy said firmly, standing over them. 'Just stop it!' As usual, they ignored her. Rob emerged from the kitchen at the din, brandishing his newspaper.

'That's enough Laura!' he said. 'Get off *now*!' Hearing her father's voice so close, Laura jumped off Olivia, who lay stock-still on the beige fitted carpet, like the mortally wounded. She sensed that if she kept a very low profile, she could lay claim to being the injured party, *and* keep the hairclip. Laura burst into noisy sobs. 'That's not fair!' she shouted. 'She started it. You always take her side. You love her much more than me. I hate you! I hate you both!' Sobbing, she turned and pounded up the stairs. Lucy moved to go after her.

'Leave her,' Rob said. 'And you can get up,' he said to Olivia, who was rubbing an imaginary hurt with the mortified air of The Deeply Wronged.

'I said up. Now,' Rob added, sharply. 'There's nothing wrong with you.' Olivia looked pleadingly at Lucy. 'My hand's poorly.' She held out a little hand like an injured paw. Lucy picked her up and cuddled her, hoping to goodness this wouldn't prove the flash-point for their favoured argument *du jour*, that Lucy spoilt the children and they were growing up without any appreciation of the lifestyle they enjoyed and they took everything for granted. If Rob said, 'When I was young I didn't even have a . . .' once more Lucy thought she would scream. This argument made her want to go back to bed and sit under the white pure cotton duvet like an inert mound.

'Put her down,' Rob said. 'She isn't a baby. You,' he said sternly to Olivia, who was now pressing herself against Lucy's legs, whining, 'can go and tidy your room or there's no riding. Not today, not for weeks. Go on.' Olivia opened her mouth to protest, saw how set her father's face was, and shut her mouth again. She knew her father very well. You couldn't get round him, not like her mum.

Olivia ran up the stairs, her progress hampered slightly, Lucy now saw, by her own new black suede platforms. On the top step, she turned, and stuck her tongue out. Rob groaned. Lucy fought back an urge to laugh. Then Olivia started to sing a little song, her sense of injustice vanished. That was the great thing about being five, Lucy thought. You existed in a little five-year-old bubble. Laura, on the other hand, felt everything very deeply. Very, very deeply indeed. If this was the level of hysteria she had reached at nine,

Lucy reckoned Rob would have to leave home as she approached thirteen, because he wouldn't be able to get through the front door for massed ranks of female hormones.

As Olivia disappeared into the sanctity of her bedroom, Rob turned to Lucy. 'Why the hell,' he said, patiently, 'is it so difficult to make them behave? I come home at the weekends and there's clearly been no discipline at all during the week. Why do you let them get away with it? They're in danger of turning into two little spoilt brats. It's appalling how Laura speaks to you.'

'What about how she speaks to you?' Lucy retorted angrily. 'Why is it always my fault? Why can't you take responsibility for them too? And please, please don't swear in front of them – what kind of image does that give them? It's like living in a council house.' As soon as she said the words, she wanted to swallow them. Rob's expression, which had simply been miffed, became cold.

'I think you need to examine your own values before you start slinging insults about living in a council house. Not, of course,' he added icily, 'that you would know. If I'd spoken to my parents like that they'd have bloody leathered me. Just because your parents were always so *nice* to each other – or so you claim – doesn't mean our children can grow up thinking they can get away with anything. If that's how they're going to behave then there will be no more *riding lessons* and all that bollocks.'

'Rob, please,' Lucy said, rubbing her hand over her forehead. 'Don't start that again. Look, why don't you come with me to watch them? You've never been yet. Laura's really good, and they *love* it.'

'Watching them riding,' Rob said, starting to laugh,

'would be marginally less pleasurable than having my toenails pulled out. Anyway, I want to watch the rugby.'

'Well, that's marvellous, isn't it!' She tried to keep her voice low so the children wouldn't hear. 'Please. Why don't we do more things together? It would make it much more fun. I don't have a wild time, you know. I'm not doing it for me.'

'Really?' said Rob. 'Look, let's stop arguing.' He pulled her towards him. 'Let's go back to bed,' he said, nuzzling her neck.

'Rob, please,' Lucy said, pulling away from him. 'Not now. There's far too much to do.'

'Of course,' he said, looking down at her through dark, slanting eyes. 'There's the kitchen table to be tidied, which is far more important, isn't it? I'll just go and finish my coffee, if that's all right with you. Doesn't mess up your plans does it? I would hate to get in the way.'

Lucy willed herself to be calm. He was always doing this. Starting a row, exploding like a firecracker, getting her worked up, and then retreating, so she felt she was the one who'd started the argument in the first place. He was brilliant at making her feel in the wrong. And why was he always so sodding *confrontational*, so that even the smallest issue seemed like a battleground? Polite calm. That was what she wanted around her. Why shouldn't problems be swept neatly under the carpet? Made life a lot easier. The last thing she wanted was a long-running argument because they'd had one the previous weekend, as Rob had refused point blank to go to her parents' house for Sunday lunch. Lucy knew her mother drove him mad, with her little well-meant offers of financial help for private education, the girls would benefit *such* a lot and they'd meet lots of other nice children. Rob, however, was of the entrenched opinion that anything his family achieved he and Lucy would pay for, thank you very much. Lucy knew her mother didn't mean to wind him up, but she did have a tendency to harp on about Lucy's old friends and how well Miles or whoever was doing in the City. The problem was that both of her parents had a bit of a thing about journalists, it wasn't somehow the *right* sort of profession. Her father, frankly, regarded them as one step up the evolutionary ladder from the amoeba.

Following him into the kitchen and banging the white Formica cupboards she yearned to replace with old pine butcher blocks and a big dresser, Lucy searched for a clean cup.

'Could you pass me the *Telegraph*?' Without looking up from the sports pages of the *Mail*, Rob pushed the unopened paper across the table. Lucy opened up the style section. '"Minimalist chic is back,"' she read. '"Smooth limed oak floors teamed with the whitest of white walls in your living areas . . ."' Yeah right, Lucy thought, looking despairingly at the patterned lino floor and green and orange flowery wallpaper. In the cottage, she'd spent a fortune pulling up the wool fitted carpet upstairs and installing a neutral sea of sisal. But Rob was constantly being stabbed in the toe by reedy splinters and claimed it was like wearing a hair shirt on your feet. What she really wanted to do, she thought, looking around, was put a wooden floor down throughout, but it would cost an absolute fortune, and putting a wide-boarded wooden floor into a Seventies redbrick box would look just a smidgen pretentious.

Folding the paper neatly, she began to clear up the debris of breakfast, spilt Rice Krispies, a slug-like

19

trail of sticky honey and the remains of Rob's fried egg and bacon, with a half-eaten slice of processed white bread at the side of the plate. She could not make him eat granary, and now the girls professed they liked white sliced best. Lucy was constantly fighting a losing battle on the food front, trying to slide 'I Can't Believe It's Not Butter' into the fridge, while Rob insisted on real butter. She shuddered to think about the state of his arteries. Furry as a herd of alpacas. A full-cream milk bottle stood on the table. Lucy grimaced, picked it up, and poured the contents into a jug for later. Then she cleared the plates into the dishwasher, and wiped the surface of the table around Rob. It amazed her how he could sit in complete chaos and not even notice.

Squeezing out the J-cloth in the sink, she gazed out of the window. It was a bright autumn day, the sort of day which made you want to go outside wrapped in a scarf and kick about in leaves. Not that you'd find any leaves on this estate, she thought, as soon as a little red leaf had the courage to flutter in a downward trajectory, it would be grabbed and stuffed into a bright green gardening tidy, or sucked up into an outside Hoover. Lucy and Rob's was the only lawn which wasn't mown into a crew cut, with edges like a geometric drawing. Even the plants were set in serried rows. In next door's garden, the begonias and busy Lizzies were wilting, ready to be pulled up and thrown away until it was time to plant new ones next spring. Lucy had had the only garden that summer which hadn't looked like Technicolor vomit. She favoured instead drifts of lavender and a herbaceous border full of soft, pastel colours – or at least she would, if she could persuade Rob that gardening was a stimulating thing to do with your weekends, instead of slumbering on the sofa or taking the kids to the pub for Sunday lunch.

Rob seemed quite happy with the house, but she couldn't whip up any enthusiasm for it at all. Their three-bedroom cottage had clearly got too small – once Lucy and Rob had tried to exit different rooms at the same time and got jammed together in the hallway so tightly Lucy thought she was going to have to dial the fire brigade – and Lucy had wanted to buy another cottage in the same village which had an extra bedroom but a tiny garden. Rob, however, had been seduced by this 'small but select' development of four-bedroomed 'executive' homes on the edge of the neighbouring village, which had bigger gardens and a garage. To Lucy, the house was completely soulless, like living in a block of Lego. And all the other houses were so exactly the same it reminded her of Trumpton. She also had an inbuilt antipathy to living anywhere which had two big flags flying at the entrance. That was so typical of Rob – he was the first to mock anyone else's pretentious aspirations, but he had been determined to buy a house they couldn't really afford primarily because it was the type of house which would have impressed his parents.

Thank God this afternoon there was a ray of cheer at the thought of seeing Martha again. She had met Martha the previous week at the girls' first riding lesson. Lucy was aching with boredom with an increasingly numb bum after just ten minutes, as Laura and Olivia's two half-dead ponies – the equine equivalent of three-toed sloths – ambled their way on lead reins round the gloomy indoor school. If any of the children's whirlwind flapping legs ceased even momentarily, all the ponies fell into a coma, like the film *Awakenings* in reverse. The door had burst open,

21

and a tall woman in dark glasses shot inside, tripped up, and uttered a sharp 'fuck.' The two women in front of Lucy, who had been earnestly discussing the merits of boarding, turned and looked appalled. Sliding her glasses onto the top of her head, the woman spotted Lucy's sympathetic gaze, grinned, and came and sat down next to her.

'Hi,' she hissed. 'I'm Martha. We're always fucking late. I know this is going to be a nightmare. I can never hit a deadline, especially on a Saturday.'

Hannah, the incredibly strict teacher who had already put the fear of God into both Laura and Olivia, glared at the small girl now hastily pulling her reluctant pony through the enormous sliding wood doors at the side of the indoor school.

'I'm Lucy,' she hissed back. 'Is this your daughter's first lesson?'

'Yup – we've only just moved in. Holly Farm in Lower Winchborough.'

Lucy looked at her in surprise. 'I didn't know it was for sale. We live in the village, too. Well, on the outskirts, anyway.'

'It was a private sale,' Martha said, dismissively. 'Friends of my parents. And you? Where are you?'

'Cherry Orchard Close,' Lucy said. She winced as she said it. All the names on the estate were just as toe-curlingly aspirational to 'proper' country addresses – Horseshoe Lane, Apple Barrow Avenue.

'Lovely and near,' Martha said. 'Excellent.' She betrayed no sign this was the wrong end of the village.

Lucy was glad she'd put on her new country-mud-coloured Nubuck jacket and the grey cashmere scarf her mother had given her for her last birthday. Martha was wearing a slightly battered long Drizabone coat, black jeans and a really lovely pair of ankle-length deep brown leather low-heeled boots. Lucy mentally toyed with the idea of asking her where she'd got them, and then thought it was too soon.

'Is it always this boring?' said Martha in a stage whisper. In the gloom, Lucy grinned. 'This is better than last week,' she whispered back. 'They've been allowed to trot.'

'Jesus,' Martha groaned, and flung herself against the hard wooden back on the bench. 'Does anyone ever fall off?'

'Not so far,' Lucy said. 'They don't go fast enough.'

'How old are yours?'

'Five and nine. Yours?'

'Emily is eight, and I have Sophie, who's five.'

'Where are they going to school?'

'Radlett. And you?'

'Winchborough C of E,' Lucy said. 'It's very near to us,' she added.

'I've heard it's very good. Can't say I'm fantastically impressed by Radlett, it seems to be full of tarts in convertibles. But Sebastian insists . . .'

'My husband insisted on Winchborough.' It was a very sore point with Lucy. They could – just – have afforded to send the girls to Radlett, an independent prep school set in the leafy countryside between Lower Winchborough and the nearest village, Stanton Harcourt, where they used to live, but Rob had put his foot down and said there was absolutely nothing wrong with state education, it hadn't done him any harm and if you were bright you rose to the top anyway. At the time, weighed down by the pressures of a new job and yet another house move, Lucy hadn't had the energy to disagree, and she knew she was a snobby cow for wincing at some of the children's accents and

23

the fact that their uniform consisted of a sweatshirt. Both Laura and Olivia seemed to be getting along fine, but oh, it didn't make a very glamorous start to the day. Lucy, if she was honest with herself, longed for glamour. The most exciting social events she seemed to enjoy these days were parties for overexcited five-year-olds with a serious cake habit.

'You must come round, once I've unpacked some of the bloody boxes.'

'I'd love to,' Lucy said.

'What does your husband do? Does he work near here?'

'He works in Oxford,' Lucy said. 'He's a journalist – the editor of the paper. I do an odd bit at the radio station. And yours?'

'Stockbroker,' Martha said. 'He commutes to London, which means it keeps him out of my hair most of the time. And keeps me in DKNY, anyway.'

Lucy laughed. 'Do you work?'

'Are you mad, darling? Why?'

Lucy looked at her sharply, and saw she was grinning. 'I'm not trained for anything. Thick as a brick. You career women scare me rigid.' Martha, Lucy thought, was unlikely to be scared by Darth Vader with a migraine. 'No, I'm fit for nothing. Actually, that's a lie. I'm pretty good at drinking. You and your husband must come over for dinner. Sebastian would love to meet him. I can't promise food, but there'll be loads of booze.'

'That would be lovely,' Lucy said, with a sinking heart. Rob was unlikely to agree. Friends that Lucy found he always presumed to be hideously boring, and whenever he met people like Martha – who did sound very Cheltenham Ladies – his vowels didn't just flatten, they lay down and died. His politics also, when

24

confronted by undoubted Conservatives like Sebastian, moved marginally to the left of Lenin.

'Are you OK to do the shopping?'

Rob raised his eyes from his newspaper and made a pathetic, hangdog face. 'Do I have to?'

Lucy swiftly weighed up staying at home with the children, tidying up and forcing Laura to emerge from the cocoon of a deep sulk, against steering a trolley round Waitrose on her own. Solo shopping won. 'OK, OK, I'll do it.' She made it sound like a big favour. Fetching her jacket, she picked up the soft straw two-handled basket she used as a handbag, and checked it had her purse and mobile. Rob said it made her look like Little Red Riding Hood, but Lucy felt it added at least a touch of country class to her existence. At the door, she paused.

'Could you do a bit of tidying up? And you'll need to find their hats because we'll have to get straight off when I get back. Their jodhpurs are in the ironing pile.'

Rob put the paper down and looked at her pointedly. 'Just *go*,' he said.

Lucy reversed her diesel hatchback swiftly out of the drive, narrowly avoiding a small boy on a bike ridden with the velocity of a scud missile. It was colder outside than she had thought, and she turned the car heater up, slipping in a Van Morrison tape. Driving out of the wide tarmac entrance to the estate, she turned left into the centre of the village, past what she always thought of as the real houses, the old deep golden stone higgledy-piggledy cottages and bigger stone detached houses set back from the road, and out towards the new industrial estate which lay two miles to the west, conveniently located but a bit of an eye-sore. Van Morrison's soothing, wailing voice made her

25

think of holidays, and travel, and being eighteen when anything was possible and being grown-up was going to mean freedom and adventure. It hadn't turned out like that, she thought. It turned out like work and mortgages and children being cheeky and rows about whose turn it was to stack the dishwasher. The question passed through her mind, as it often did, as to what would happen if she just kept going, if she just kept on driving, away from the house and the family and into a future where there was just her and limitless possibilities. But then, they would definitely run out of kitchen towel and Rob would never be able to find Olivia's school sweatshirt which only Lucy knew was currently making a bed for Ponytail Barbie.

Turning into the supermarket car park, she wasn't looking where she was going. A dark green Range Rover cut across her, and she glanced up, about to toot the horn angrily. Fucking *men*. She caught a glimpse of a tanned face, a fag hanging out of the corner of his mouth and thick blond hair swept back. An electric shock ran through her. Bloody hell. He looked incredibly like Max.

Chapter Two

The single piece of advice Caroline Beresford ever ventured to give her teenage daughter Lucy on the subject of marriage was 'Look for a man with potential.' Lucy retorted sharply that girls of her generation no longer needed to live their lives vicariously through men, thank you very much. Her generation, she said, rolling over on her green candlewick bedspread, were not going to be defined by their husband's professional status. They were going to change the world, never mind caring about washing whiter than white and worrying about Keeping Their Man.

'It doesn't matter what your husband does,' said Lucy angrily, picking at her dark brown nail varnish – with four coats you could peel the whole lot off in one go – 'what matters is what you achieve in life. I shall marry – if I bother to get married – the man I love, not on the basis of what he might achieve. That "potential" stuff,' she continued, 'is an anachronism designed to make people of the same class marry each other and perpetuate the whole cycle of marital entrapment. The belief that women are incapable of fulfilling their own potential without a man is what has kept women in harness for generations. Look at you. A university degree, and what have you got to show for it? What's your life's work?'

'My daughters,' Caroline said. 'You're my life's work. Now *get up.*'

Lucy reluctantly heaved herself off the bed and, still wearing the boy's rugby shirt she had slept in every night since being given it by the captain of the first eleven at the neighbouring boys' school to hers in a bid to make her sleep with him (it failed) wandered into the bathroom, her painted toenails lost in the thick chocolate-coloured shagpile carpet. The new bathroom was her parents' pride and joy and contained the very latest word in style, a bidet.

In the bathroom Lucy peered at herself, brushing back her flicked-out fringe, and then ferreted around in the cupboard. Another bloody spot from God's spot factory. Where the hell was the Clearasil? Sodding Helen must have nicked it. Her vile sister only got spots on her forehead, which she could hide with her fringe. Lucy's spots, on the other hand, were of the exhibitionist variety and liked to be seen – either on the side of her nose or in the middle of her chin, surrounded by flashing lights and pointy arrows.

Lying in the bath, radio perched precariously on the edge, Radio One turned up loudly against the sound of their cleaner hoovering outside the door like a relentless wasp, Lucy reflected that what she wanted from life was something far, far different from her mother's experience. Not for her the gin-and-tonic-and-bridge parties, and coffee mornings in which the subtle art of one-upmanship was played out amongst the Wedgwood china and the home-made chocolate cake, prestige dependent on husband's career, the size of one's home and the school one's children attended. Getting a child into Oxford was far better than sex, and having two children away at school, like Caroline, put her mother several notches above her closest friends, who could only manage a private day school. It allowed her to toss the phrase 'of course with the girls away, I have so much more time . . .' into the conversation on a casual, but regular, basis.

Nor, thought Lucy, turning up *The Golden Hour* on Simon Bates, did she intend to fill her adult days with her mother's good works – all that pointless schlepping about with hot meals for ungrateful smelly pensioners, stuck in high-rise flats in the nearby town, and selling ghastly woolly lampshades for a few pence in the charity shop in their Cotswold village. Since there were hardly any genuine poor in their village anyway, Lucy thought all it meant was an endless recycling of useless tat among the well-heeled residents, who hid the offending vases, lampshades and bowls under the stairs until the next church bring and buy.

Lucy had already mapped out her future career. She desperately wanted to get into television, and when, or rather if, she had children, she would become a writer and tap out deathless prose on the kitchen table. Or she would seamlessly continue her rise up the career ladder, causing her father to gasp with admiration at her ruthless ambition, and simply hand her kids over to a nanny. She didn't much fancy bringing up children anyway, certainly not on her own. Caroline, concerned that Lucy might just fudge her A levels and trying hard at that time to give her a sense of purpose – after all, they had spent an *awful* lot of money on her education – was giving her little tips about possible suitable careers. What about a nice secretarial college after A levels? Or maybe Daddy could run to a finishing school, if she didn't want to go straight to uni? It drove Lucy mad: presumably her mother must have had some kind of interesting, vaguely rebellious streak because in her day very few women, comparatively speaking, did go on to university. When she quizzed her mother about boyfriends and suchlike when she was at university, and whether she'd even been on any protest marches, the most alternative and daring thing her mum could come up with was being vice-president of Arts Soc. And, her mother said, some of her friends 'did' but it was so different in those days. Nice girls simply didn't.

Her mother, she mused, seemed to think that the only possible careers for women were those of a sec-retary or a teacher – but all of it was only a handy form of filling in until she met Mr Right. And, her mother, added, it would help that Lucy was very pretty. Lucy howled, but her mother said, 'You may laugh, Lucy, but it does make a difference.' Whenever Caroline referred to someone in authority it was always as a 'him' – she automatically assumed it would be a man, and Lucy drove her mad by constantly saying, 'How do you know it's a he?' Why on earth did her mother's generation always defer to men? If she and her sister were having a meal in a restaurant and there were businessmen on the next table, Caroline would tell the two girls to keep their voices down. The implication was that they shouldn't interrupt an important conver-sation with their silly, girly chatter. It irritated Lucy so much how much her mother ran around her father, but then, she supposed, it was her chosen career.

Lucy believed her father was too spoilt for his own good. When she and Helen were young, they were pre-sented to their father on his return from work only when they were clean-smelling, pink and shiny from their bath. All the toys would be tidied away, and the house warm and welcoming for the lord and master. It was absurd how her mother panicked if Archie's dinner wasn't absolutely ready for his return. Being married was like being sold into slavery, she thought.

It also made Lucy fume that the main aspiration her parents had for her – hide it as they might – was to marry 'well'. When Lucy pressed her father on how pointless it was for her mother just to look after the family, he simply replied that her mother's degree was useful in that it served to make her a more intelligent companion for *him*.

Soaping carefully between her toes, Lucy decided that what she wanted was a marriage – a 'partnership' was far better, she was definitely going to live with her husband before marriage anyway – based on true equality, with a partner equally at home pushing a supermarket trolley, or giving a bottle of warm milk to a damp-bottomed baby at three o'clock in the morning, as he was setting off in the morning clutching a brief-case, with 'Breadwinner' stamped on his forehead.

And all this virginity stuff that her parents' generation went in for. Pointless. To Lucy this was rubbish – it was only the sad types who wanted to remain virgins, the ones with long spindly pale blonde plaits who sewed cushion covers, stayed in the Guides, never used peel-off eyeliner or shaved their legs.

At sixteen, however, although Lucy was loath to admit it, she was still a virgin. Well, technically, anyway – she'd done most things with boys at the neighbouring school but the actual act – and most of her detailed information about sex came from Harold Robbins' novels, stolen from her parents' bedroom and read in the toilet with the door locked during the holidays, or under the bedclothes with a torch. Oddly, the fiction of Harold Robbins didn't seem to correlate very well to her own experience of sex. The heroine in a

Harold Robbins novel – always blonde and golden-skinned – was usually ravished by an Arab sheik or a motor-racing champion. It didn't really equate to being squashed up against the captain of the junior eleven, his packet of Number Six digging painfully into your chest while he transferred half a pint of saliva into your mouth. But she dutifully took the novels to school where the margins became full of notes like 'Cor!!!' and 'What????' It was not possible, as a teenager, to communicate with friends unless heralded by an army of !!! or ??? Their life was one long exclamation mark.

But if Max had his way, so to speak, her virginity was not long for this world. RIP, Virtue. She'd been going out with Max for six months now, who told her if she didn't give in soon he would physically explode and burst all the buttons off his Brutus jeans. She'd known Max as a childhood friend – he was the son of one of her mother's sleekly groomed coffee-morning cronies, and they were at private prep school together. Her mother was greatly chuffed at their friendship as his father was the local Conservative MP, and thereby holder of much social cachet. Caroline would never do anything as shameless as fawn over anyone socially superior, but she did enjoy the connection. At the age of ten, Lucy and Max had lost touch – Max went off to boarding school, and Lucy too had been parcelled off to a boarding school which would turn her into a young lady and where hopefully she would meet some 'nice' girls who had 'nice' brothers.

Lucy had expected to enjoy it, but instead felt like a small, uprooted plant. It was like Colditz, with the guards not steely-eyed men, but ancient warty lesbians. Outwardly far more confident and articulate than her shyer younger sister, it was she, who felt the pain of separation from home, dog and parents most acutely. She knew it was seen by many as a badge of privilege, but, honestly, how could anyone think that being banged up in an institution full of warty lesbians was a privilege? Nightly she sobbed under the thin covers of her narrow school bed, sympathy available on a limited basis from the girl in the next bed, who only saw her parents twice a year as they ran a tea plantation in Kenya. 'At least your parents are in the same country,' she whispered to Lucy. 'Imagine how I feel. My parents don't even live in the same *time zone*.' When Lucy and Max met, they had the misery of a privileged upbringing in common.

Thank God she met Max when she did. Her life up till then at home had been aching with boredom. Days in the holidays were spent listlessly brushing her hair, longing to look like Alexandra Bastedo from *The Champions*, staring in the mirror at her spots and listening to her David Cassidy LPs over and over again. Between the ages of nine and thirteen, David Cassidy was her *idol*.

Helen preferred Donny Osmond, but personally Lucy thought his teeth were far too big and she hated his hair. It looked like a wig. The only reason anyone thought he was good-looking was in comparison to his brothers. Muppets, or what? How could you take any-one seriously who sang about 'Puppy Love?' David Cassidy was far more sophisticated. With his centre-parted hair and breathless voice, when he sang 'I'm just – huh – daydreamer' she swooned. Most nights in the holidays were spent lying with her head next to the record player, listening to his LPs. Her walls at home were covered with his posters, her favourite being the one with him standing next to a beautiful palomino horse. In her head she endlessly composed letters to him telling him how much she loved him, and fervently believed that, were they to meet, he would fall instantly in love with her and recognize her as his true soulmate. The fact that she was twelve at the time and he eighteen never entered her head as a problem. He was singing to her, and when she saw films of him, wandering through lush cornfields on *Top of the Pops* – he never seemed to actually turn up in person – she thought she would die of love. She hated Susan Dey with a passion, because she was sure she and David had a thing going behind the scenes of *The Partridge Family*.

Max was her first serious boyfriend. The boys at school didn't count, because all you ever did was say, 'My friend fancies you,' snog for an hour at a time on a park bench so you lost all feeling in your lips, and then giggle about it with your friends once you'd regained your ability to breathe unaided. You didn't talk about anything, God no, that was far too embarrassing. Anyway, what would you say? Max was different in that she actually went out on dates with him – he had a car, which made him impossibly glamorous in Lucy's eyes. They met – ironically, considering the determined onslaught he was currently making on her virginal status – at a party Caroline forced her to attend.

It was the middle of the holidays, and Lucy was sitting staring listlessly out of her bedroom window. The phone rang, and her mother took the call. Lucy heard, 'Really? Yes, she's home. No, I'm sure she'd be delighted. She hardly knows anyone at home any more. Isn't it, yes, such a big problem when they're away at school. I know.' Lucy winced. Did her mother have to make her sound such a sad case to complete strangers?

'About eight? That'll be lovely.'

'Delighted about what?' said Lucy suspiciously, wandering down the stairs, her jeans four inches too long without platforms.

'Rupert Jackson's invited you to a party. That was his mother. She is delightful, I must arrange—'

'Yes, yes,' said Lucy impatiently. 'Rupert who? Do I know him?'

'Of course you do. You were at school together, he was in the year above. You must remember him, lovely family.'

Lucy had a fleeting memory of a small creepy person in a bottle-green cap who might have pushed her over in the park playing kiss chase. 'He was awful. You don't really expect me to go?'

'Of course you must. There might be some nice people there. Do make an effort, darling.'

Lucy spent the next few days affecting cool while panicking inside. What should she wear? Rupert went to Harrow. She wouldn't know anyone. She had a big spot, and she'd run out of Anne French cleansing milk.

On the night Caroline tried desperately to usher her into a pretty dress to impress Rupert's mother. After all, they had a swimming pool. But there was no way Lucy would be seen dead in a dress. A short but exhilarating argument followed, until Lucy won the day with a brown cheesecloth shirt, love beads and impossibly tight blue jeans. Spraying on Cachet, she peered at her face in the bathroom mirror. She had plastered the spot in Clearasil, but you could still see it. She hoped it would be dark.

The red light had come on, which meant her curling tongs were hot enough. Squatting on the floor of her bedroom, she carefully flicked out each side of her fringe. Her blonde hair used to be long enough to sit on, but now it was shoulder-length, dead straight and parted in the middle. Thank goodness that awful feather cut had finally grown out. One of the boys at the neighbouring public school had told her she looked like the blonde from Abba, which Lucy thought was a double-edged compliment because she had a *huge* bottom.

'Come on, darling!' Caroline stood at the bottom of the stairs, tapping her foot, immaculate in soft olive cashmere twinset, pearls and navy Jaeger slacks. Waiting for Lucy, she reapplied a deft slick of red lipstick in the hall mirror, brushing her sleek blonde bob into place so it swung just beneath her chin. She hoped Lucy would look smart. She really *ought* to wear a dress for a party.

'Com-ing!' Lucy shouted irritably, with the rising note of sarcasm she knew inflamed her mother. One final flick of mascara, and a nervous hand smoothing out the pale blue eyeshadow Lucy painted not only on her upper lids but in an arch rising to her eyebrows. She filled in the gap with white highlighter which apparently 'accentuated your eyes', according to *Jackie* magazine, Lucy and Helen's bible.

She walked down the stairs very carefully. Her jeans were so tight she had to lie flat on her back to get them on when they'd just been washed, and pull the zip up with a coat hanger. Going to the loo took about an hour. Sometimes when she wore this particular pair – size eight, she thought proudly – she went numb from the waist down.

'Bye.' She stuck her head round the living-room door. Helen was sprawled out on the floor in front of the television watching *The Dukes of Hazzard* (Lucy died for the legs of Barbara Bach), sulking madly because she hadn't been invited, and her father was apparently asleep on the tan leather sofa, Ben the loopy red setter curled up in the L made by his legs. Ben and her father were inseparable, united against a house full of women. Her father opened one eye.

'Going out? Not going to get changed?' Lucy picked up a cushion from the nearby armchair, and threw it at him. He caught it and threw it back, but Lucy had deftly closed the door so it thumped against the panelling. Caroline sighed. They were always indulging in this kind of horseplay, which made *such* a mess.

In the car Lucy fiddled with the L she always wore on a chain round her neck. She was actually quite worried – it was the first 'real' party she'd gone to at home. Her mother clicked on Radio Four, which to Lucy was like listening to voices from beyond the grave.

'Can't we have Radio One on?'

Her mother groaned, but Lucy twiddled the knob until she found the right wavelength. As they edged down the long drive in the Volvo, Lucy tried to mentally will her mother to change out of first gear. She gave up. 'Mum, please change gear. You're killing the car.'

Behind them, the lights of the house receded. Lucy felt her stomach flip slightly in panic, just as it did when she was leaving home to go back to school. Then, she would twist round in the car, desperate for one last glance. As they drove slowly down the drive, she would drink in every detail – the solid square frame of the old stone house with its soft honey-coloured walls which seemed to glow, warm to the touch in summer. The Virginia creeper which covered most of the front, tapping with russet feathery fingers in the autumn against her bedroom window, the spidery outhouses which lay to the side, full of gardening equipment and the boxes of cooking apples Caroline religiously picked each year, and turned into apple pies, apple crumbles, apple tortes, until Lucy wanted to scream at the sight of anything apple-y coming towards her. Once her family were completely satiated, Caroline then began to make pies for the rest of the village, and left a big box of those that remained at the bottom of the drive, with a sign saying 'Please Take'.

The party was being held in a large garage at the side of Rupert's ostentatiously large house. Fairy lights had been draped around the garden, and inside Lucy could see a big glittering silver ball swinging from the ceiling and a medley of red, yellow and green lights flashing from the disco at the far end. Blondie's rhythmic bass line drowned any attempt at conversation within, and Lucy could see as yet no-one was dancing, which for some reason made her feel a bit better.

By the door, Rupert's mother hovered.

'Don't come in with me,' Lucy hissed at her mother. She even wished she had Helen for moral support, but Helen had been deemed too young.

'You must be Lucy,' said Rupert's mother, effusively. Oh God, thought Lucy. She's going to kiss me. Lucy stuck out her hand. She sensed the presence of her mother behind her, and the next moment she felt Caroline's hand on her shoulder, propelling her into the room. 'Darling, do go in. They won't bite. She's a little bit shy because she doesn't know anyone,' she confided, turning to Rupert's mother.

Lucy shot her mother a look of pure loathing, but Caroline was engaged in two-cheek kissing, murmuring, 'You look *wonderful.*'

'Rupert! That music,' she sighed. 'I can't hear myself think.' As she spoke, Lucy saw a tall youth with dark hair reluctantly disengage himself from a small huddle of young men, all dressed identically in corduroy trousers and stripy shirts with the collars turned up. He wandered nonchalantly towards them. His eyes swept languidly over Lucy, registering a flicker of interest in her prettiness, but then dismissing her, primarily because he didn't know her. He didn't need to know anyone else, he had quite enough friends.

'Hi,' he said, his eyes not meeting hers. Lucy realized he was already exceedingly pissed. 'Rupert,' his mother twittered nervously, 'this is Lucy. Lucy Beresford. Do you remember? You were at Sunnybank together. She came,' she added triumphantly, 'to your fifth birthday party. Can you imagine?' She laughed, and Rupert looked at her blankly. 'Oh yah?' he said, his face revealing a complete lack of interest. The chances of the appropriate brain cells colliding to spark the memory were pretty slim, Lucy thought.

'Do introduce Lucy to some people,' his mother said, turning away to a group of new arrivals.

'D'you know anyone?' Rupert weaved slightly as he led her towards the drinks table.

'Not really,' Lucy said, longing and longing to be anywhere else. 'The 'rentals will go in a minute,' he said, leaning forward and peering owlishly at her. She *was* quite pretty. Sounded OK, too. Lucy caught him as he lunged forward. 'Whoops,' he said, swinging back onto his heels, unabashed. 'D'you smoke?' He fished a packet of black Sobranie out of his back pocket, peering to see if his mother had disappeared.

'Thanks,' said Lucy, taking one out of the packet, carefully holding his hand steady as she did so. She took the box of matches out of his hands. He was likely to set fire to her hair.

'There's the booze,' said Rupert, pointing her at a trestle table groaning with cider, beer and a punch in which bits of apples and oranges floated.

'Thanks,' said Lucy, turning to him. He'd gone. Minutes later she heard a roar of laughter from his group, and she felt six pairs of eyes home in on her. Blushing furiously, she poured herself a paper cup of punch. She would have to get pissed. This was going to be *agony*, and she was sure she was already sweating rings on her shirt.

Lucy was working out how she could slide away and make some excuse about why she had to urgently ring her parents, when the door burst open. In walked a group of boys, the first of whom looked vaguely familiar. He stood out from the crowd, not only by dint of the fact he was extremely good-looking, with thick long wavy blond hair, dark brown eyes and a deep suntan, but because he was wearing a huge, hairy Afghan coat, as if surprised from behind by a yak. He shrugged off the coat, which fell like a pelt to the floor, revealing a white collarless shirt and very tight faded blue jeans. In one hand swung a bottle of Canadian Club whisky, the other held a packet of Gitanes.

Why was he familiar? As he turned to laugh with one of his friends, a blinding flash ran through Lucy. Jesus Christ – it was Max! Little Max, Max the pest, Max she'd had long-jump competitions with in her back garden at the age of six and played endless table tennis with and eek – had baths naked together with until they were found by a shocked Caroline. Max was the first boy she'd willingly shown her knickers to. Should this be her opening gambit?

She was beginning to turn away in a flurry of agonized indecision when he caught her eye. Oh *no*. What if he didn't recognize her? What should she do? She could feel a deep blush growing from around her shoulders, sizzling up her cheeks. He smiled a delighted grin, and walked towards her. 'Lucy – it is you, isn't it? All grown up,' he said, grinning and looking her up and down. Rupert weaved over, intercepting him. 'Max, mate, how are you? How were the Yanks?' He leant forward to clap Max on the shoulder, missed, and executed a perfect one hundred and eighty degree turn. Max stepped deftly aside. 'Piss off, Rupert,' he said. 'You're legless.'

'Hello – Max, isn't it?' Lucy said with desperate coolness, the beastly blush beating under her cheeks. This cheesecloth shirt showed every stain and she just knew she had sweaty marks. She kept her arms firmly clamped to her side.

'What's that shit you're drinking?' he said, peering into her cup, which contained the foul punch. 'Have some whisky,' he said, reaching over for a clean paper cup. Lucy had never tasted whisky before. But she had somehow to convey to Max that she was the kind of girl who would try anything. So she dogged it in several gulps, and then felt very dizzy. Max looked at her admiringly.

'How do you know Rupert?' Lucy shouted over the disco beat of Chic's 'Le Freak'.

'Went skiing with him last year,' Max shouted back. 'He's a complete wanker, but his pool's pretty useful in summer.'

He then told Lucy all about the year he'd just spent on an exchange visit to a high school in America, how he'd nearly been expelled for drinking and smuggling girls into his dorm, how his parents had just given him a really neat car. His voice had a faintly American twang, and Lucy did have to admit he seemed a teeny bit fond of himself. But he was so good-looking. She mentally began to compose the phone call to her best friend the next day.

'Do you want to dance?' he said, as the quavering tones of Bryan Ferry slid out of the stereo. 'Let's Stick Together,' he crooned as Max and Lucy danced with intense concentration a foot apart, not looking at each other. 'Good dancer, too,' Lucy thought as he rolled his shoulders back confidently, moving only from the waist up. Being a good dancer was just about the most important attribute in a boyfriend – no-one wanted a boy who danced like a dad. Max's friends, she could see, were gesturing and laughing at him, pointing at Lucy and making thumbs-up signs. 'Ignore them,' said Max. 'Complete tossers. They're just jealous.' Lucy's cheeks glowed.

After half an hour's dancing in the room, the temperature was approaching boiling point from the gyratory bodies and the hot breath of teenage passion unleashed by the cider punch, which Max had spiked with whisky. Holding firmly onto her hand, he pulled her out into the chilly night air. Walking along a garden path, Max slid his arm round her.

'Are you going out with anyone?' he asked, very casually.

'No-one special,' said Lucy, determined not to seem too available.

'Good,' he said, turning her face up to his. They bumped noses. Then tried again. This time the offending facial features slid parallel. Good dancer, great kisser, Lucy thought, trying to remember to breathe. Lucy had quite got used to French kissing by this time, and enjoyed it as long as there wasn't too much slobber. Boys at school seemed either to be too dry, so it was like being kissed by your gran, or it was like kissing a washing machine. Max's mouth was warm, just right.

They were just getting passionate – Max was deftly sliding his leg between Lucy's – when Lucy, to her horror, spotted Rupert's mother bearing down on them. She pushed Max, who had closed his eyes, away.

'Do come back in,' Rupert's mother said, politely, as if she hadn't seen a thing. 'You'll catch your death.' Lucy saw she had a torch in her hand. Presumably designed to root snogging couples out of the shrubbery.

Back inside, the dance floor was heaving, everyone having completely lost their urge to be cool. In the middle lay one of Rupert's mates, out cold, with girls dancing round him like a large handbag. Max pulled Lucy down onto one of the beanbags by the wall. The next moment, there was a retching sound. A boy close to them, who appeared to have gone to sleep, lurched forward. Lucy jumped aside just as the boy was sick, copiously and brownly, down the crack between the cushions.

'Yuch.' Lucy leapt up.

The DJ, glancing down at his watch, realized it was almost midnight and time to pack up. Thank God. Time for Nilsson. 'I can't live . . . if living is without you . . .' Max held Lucy tight, as they swayed about, holding each other up. Those who hadn't managed to pull stood at the edge trying to look as if they didn't care and heckling their friends. As the last notes died away, there was a flash of harsh neon. Lucy hastily ducked her head so her hair swung over her face, and headed for the door. All that kissing would have rubbed off her spot cover, and she really didn't want to put Max off this early.

Outside, the driveway was full of cars. The couples Rupert's mother had managed to miss were emerging from bushes, picking off bits of twigs and clutching damp patches caused by squirming about on soggy earth. Max and Lucy, holding hands, came out to find their mothers standing by matching Volvo estates, deep in conversation, Max's mother knowing from bitter experience he would be too drunk to drive. Lucy tried to drop Max's hand, but Max hung on.

'Say goodbye to me now,' she hissed. Max, abruptly, pulled her into a rhododendron bush. 'Ow,' said Lucy, as he held her face tightly in his hands, and kissed her, hard.

'Give me your number. I'll buzz you tomorrow.'

'It's in the book,' Lucy said, jumping out of the bush as she heard footsteps on the path.

'Hi Mum. This is Max, Max do you—' Max gave Lucy's mother a huge, winning smile.

'Mrs Beresford, of *course* I remember you,' he said effusively, holding out his hand. 'You make the most wonderful chocolate cake!' Lucy looked at him in astonishment. He does mothers, too. Caroline, completely charmed and not used to Lucy's friends being so forthcoming, held out her hand in return, smiling. Lucy sidled round the back of her mother, and, looking down, realized the top six buttons of her cheesecloth shirt were undone.

Saying her goodbyes, Lucy saw her mother had her polite, society smile on, the one which didn't quite reach her eyes, and was usually accompanied by vigorous nodding. Max's mother, Annabelle, whom she hadn't met for over a year, always made her feel slightly ill at ease. They were so *glamorous*, the Yorkes. He was a rising star of the Conservative party and she was terrifyingly stylish and hosted the most absolutely fabulous dinner and drinks parties, although they did have a housekeeper who was also a gourmet cook, which helped, Caroline thought. Archie, though generous in most ways, baulked at the thought of a full-time housekeeper so Caroline had to make do with a cleaner.

Caroline opened the car door for Lucy, who slid her hand out of Max's. 'I'll ring you,' he hissed into her ear. As Lucy bent to get in the car, he ran his hand over her bottom. Lucy hastily pulled the car door shut. As they drove away, Lucy turned to see Rupert's mother gesticulating at Max and Annabelle. Rupert's mother was barely visible behind Max's huge, hairy coat, as if wrestling a bear. She'd come upon it, quite by chance, as she sadly surveyed the mess of squashed paper cups and cigarette packets, harshly illuminated by the strip lighting. Thank goodness they'd booked contract cleaners. Lifting the coat, she found the boy who'd been sick, sleeping peacefully.

In the car, Lucy wriggled down in her seat, blissful with happiness. 'Max,' she thought to herself. 'Max, Max.' It was like being given the present you'd always wanted at Christmas. She closed her eyes and saw his face, eyes closed with passion, so near to hers. She shivered.

'Are you cold, darling?' Caroline asked. 'I'll put the heating on. You should have taken a coat, it's much colder than you think . . .'

Lucy let her mother witter on, deep in her own private fantasy. They were on the beach, Max was leaning over her, her back was against the warm sand and . . .

'Lucy! I asked you if you thought Max was nice. I must say, he seems a very polite boy.' If only you knew, Lucy thought. Then she thought – and the thought was like being doused in cold water – maybe he won't ring. Maybe he's forever chatting up girls at parties and promising to ring them and then not. Maybe she should have written out her number, maybe he wouldn't bother looking in the book. Maybe she'd blown it. Maybe he had seen her spot and been repulsed. She must lose some weight and stop eating sweets. She made a secret promise to herself that if Max rang her, she would never eat a Mars bar again. If she had Max, she didn't need chocolate.

The next day, Lucy hopped every time the phone rang. In the morning, there was a succession of the dullest calls Lucy had ever taken for her mother. Eventually her friend Jo rang and Lucy bit her head off, then apologized and said she'd ring back. She was so desperate to keep the line clear. By lunch time, she was frothing with misery, and offered to take Ben out for a walk. As he goofily leapt up and down in front of her at the sight of his lead, the phone rang. 'Yes, hullo,' said Lucy listlessly, ready to hear the well-bred tones of yet another of her mother's bridge friends. 'Lucy?'

Lucy was suddenly aware of a loud beating noise. It was her heart. Her hand was slippery with sweat and she had to concentrate hard on not dropping the phone.

'Yes?' she said, determined not to say, 'Max.'

'It's Max. How are you? I had a hell of a headache this morning. That bloody awful punch. Only consolation is that wanker Rupert will feel much worse. Did you see him fall over?' Lucy laughed, remembering the sight of Rupert, who went down very suddenly, as if he'd been hit over the head with a pole.

'Fancy a drink tonight?' Lucy forced herself to hesitate. Then, casually, 'OK.'

'Great. I'll come for you at eight. I can remember where you live.'

'Great.' There was a long pause. 'Bye,' she said.

'Bye.' Lucy could still hear him breathing. 'Bye,' she

said again. She didn't want to put the phone down. 'Bye,' he said. 'We could stay on the phone until tonight, but I don't think my dad would be too pleased.' 'No,' said Lucy, mortified, and crashed the receiver down. She leant, panting, against the wall. He'd phoned. He'd phoned and he was coming here tonight. Oh my God. What could she wear? She ran upstairs. She had nothing to wear. Within half an hour, every item she possessed was on the floor of her bedroom. 'Mum,' said Helen, wandering past Lucy's door, 'I think we've been burgled. Either that or Lucy's got a date.'

When the doorbell rang, accompanied as usual by frantic howling from Ben, who always performed vertical leaps until the door was finally opened and then hurled himself forward so you needed to be standing squarely on both feet to withstand two hundred pounds of enthusiastic setter, her mum ran off to put on lipstick. Lucy, holding Ben in a firm stranglehold by his collar, opened the door several inches.

'Dog,' she hissed. 'Stand back.'

'No probs,' said Max, grinning. 'We've got a Labrador, only he's a bit past the leaping stage.' Lucy opened the door and Ben hurled himself forward. Max caught him expertly under his front legs. Overcome with joy, Ben twisted his face round to comprehensively lick this accommodating new visitor. Max laughed. Most people would be making disgusted faces and reaching for their handkerchiefs, Lucy thought, but Max just wiped away the worst of the slobber and pushed Ben off, who then stuck to him like glue.

He looked, if possible, even more attractive than the previous night. The yak coat had been left behind, for which Lucy was truly thankful, as her father and

Afghan coats were unlikely to be mutually appreciative. Tonight he was wearing a blue denim shirt, the deep tan of his face contrasting perfectly with the faded colour, and a pair of cream chinos. He wore no socks, and slightly scuffed brown deck shoes. He somehow managed to look casual, as if he'd made no effort at all, and yet deeply glamorous. Lucy found she couldn't look at him, for fear of going bright red. 'Shall we go straight out?' she said, anxious not to involve him in a potentially embarrassing parent situation. 'I better say hi to your folks first,' he said. There was a rustle behind Lucy, and before she knew what was happening she'd been elbowed aside and her mother was kissing Max on both cheeks, exclaiming, 'Max, how lovely! Come and meet Lucy's father. I'm sure he'll remember you.' Caroline was smiling, with her head coquettishly on one side. Pass the sick bag, Lucy thought. Why couldn't her mother be more cool?

Max was willingly led into the big drawing room, the windows overlooking a sweep of lawn.

Archie was pouring himself an early G and T and turned with some irritation at the thought of a visitor.

'Archie, darling, this is Max. Do you remember, Max Yorke? Annabelle and George's boy?' she said, smiling at Max, who was holding out his hand to Archie.

Lucy could see her father eyeing him up and down. He had an innate suspicion of most young men, because he remembered all too well what he'd been like at their age. But this boy certainly looked a decent sort. Very confident, anyway. 'Max,' he said, holding out his hand, which Max shook. 'I know your father well. Good golfer, don't suppose he gets much time now, though. Would you like a drink?'

'I'd love one, sir,' Max said. Sir? Lucy looked at Max covertly. Was he joking? No, there was no trace of subtle irony on his open face – he was merely being polite.

'Lovely evening,' Archie said. 'Can I show you round the garden?' Oh Lord, Lucy thought, glancing beseechingly at her mother. He'd take Max to see his tomatoes. Even Max couldn't appear interested in tomatoes. Her mother caught the glance and said, 'Archie, really, I'm sure these young people want to be on their way.'

'Nonsense,' said Lucy's father. 'Come on, Max.'

For twenty minutes Max trotted dutifully around the acres of their estate and into the greenhouses, Ben always at his heels. Lucy and her mother hung back, astonished at the sight of Archie and Max getting on like a house on fire. Archie rarely took to people on first meeting them, and the family had a secret theory that, if possible, he would have built a moat around their house and pulled up the drawbridge, only allowing people in he knew well and liked, all others repelled by boiling oil. When they returned, Max had clearly seen enough tomatoes to last him a lifetime, but was still going strong. 'Fine,' Lucy heard her father saying as they walked slowly down the path towards them, feet scrunching on the golden gravel. 'I'll see about a game then?' 'Game?' said Lucy, desperate to get Max on his own. 'Golf,' said Max. 'I didn't realize your father was a member at the Royal Cotswold.'

As they climbed into Max's Golf GTi, he said enthusiastically, 'Aren't your parents ace?' 'Wonderful,' said Lucy, ruefully, thinking, what about me?

Max drove the car fast and expertly down the drive. At the bottom he stopped, out of sight of the house. 'But not,' he said, 'as great as you. You look fantastic.' He pulled on the handbrake, and turned to look at her. His hand reached out and touched her face. Lucy felt her pulse racing so fast her whole body was vibrating like an overstrung harp. Any minute she'd go twang and fly out the window.

'Come here, you gorgeous creature,' he said. Lucy, who'd never been called a gorgeous creature before, was mesmerized. He pulled her towards him – Lucy squeaked as she encountered the handbrake – and kissed her very thoroughly. 'I'm so glad I went to that party,' he said. Lucy's happiness would have been complete if she hadn't got her interlocking ring caught in his hair. 'You can let go of me now,' he said, laughing, pulling back from the kiss. 'No, I can't,' said Lucy. 'My hand's stuck.'

Chapter Three

Two hundred miles away, Rob Atkinson wheeled his bike down the path at the side of the house, at the end of his evening paper round. It was a pain in the neck doing it twice a day, but the newsagents paid him well, comparatively, as well as all the free sarsaparilla and pear drops he could consume. Closing the door of the shed carefully, he heard his mum's voice calling to him through the side door.

'Is that you, Rob? Come and get your tea before it goes cold.'

'No,' he called back. 'It's the Milk Tray man.'

'Get on with you,' replied his mother's disembodied voice. Then she appeared in the doorway, pinny tied round her middle, hands in pink Marigolds, smiling. 'You won't be told, will you?' she added, looking at his pullover. 'Where's your new anorak? You'll catch your death. Come on. Your dad's sitting down. And mind them shoes.'

Obediently, Rob reached down and pulled off his muddy training shoes. His mother thoroughly disapproved of them as a form of footwear, and drove Rob mad by calling them pumps. His father, when he first saw them, roared with laughter. 'What are you in training for? Staying in bed the longest? Having the muckiest bedroom?' His dad was always like that, making jokes, teasing him. When he was little, his dad's favourite trick was to switch all the lights off when Rob was watching something spooky on television, like *Dr Who*, go outside and scratch on the window.

In the front room, a fire blazed in the grate, and Rob's grandma sat in her armchair as close to the heat as possible, flicking through the *TV Times*. 'Not eating, Gran?' Rob said, loudly.

'I had some cake before,' she said. 'I'm not hungry,' she added, pressing her stomach. 'It's not agreed.'

'Going anywhere exciting tonight, Gran? Off down the disco, or is it your night for wrestling?'

'What does he say?' she asked, looking in a bewildered fashion at Rob's mother, who walked in carrying a tray holding a big tureen of hotpot.

'Just ignore him,' she said, loudly. 'He's being daft.'

'I don't know,' she said, shaking her head at Rob. 'You're just like your father.'

Rob grinned, and picked up his dad's newspaper. 'Win anything?' he said, scanning the football results.

'Bugger all.'

'Rob,' his mum said. 'Put that down now. It's teatime. Now where's Claire?'

'I'll get her,' said Rob, jumping up. He knew where Claire would be. Lying on her bed, mooning over the Bay City bloody Rollers, who to Rob were about as spastic a group as you could get. Rob – who had just paid out most of his hard-earned paper-round money for his first-ever electric guitar – favoured instead real groups. Groups that made a noise like a multiple pile-up, like Black Sabbath and Led Zeppelin. He was currently trying to persuade his mum to let him go to see Whitesnake at St George's Hall in Blackburn, but she thought it would be full of yobs and she didn't like him getting the late bus back, even though they were only a quarter of an hour from Blackburn.

When he was little Rob deeply minded the way his mum fussed over him, but he could see now it was because she loved him so much. Half of his mates' mothers never seemed to know or care where they were – usually hanging around the chip shop at the top of the road, roaring around on their bikes or trying to cadge fags from each other. And, just recently, to Rob's disgust, there had been much talk of trying to get into Blackburn's one and only nightspot to pick up girls. Girls, Rob thought, were more trouble than they were worth and they were forever following him round at school, saying stupid things like, 'My mate Suzanne fancies you. Will you go with her?' To which the only response was a glowering stare. They were also always coming out with daft statements like, 'You look dead like David Essex, you do.'

No, girlfriends were far too much trouble, and they were likely to be expensive too. Not only would there be the cost of the pictures, but chips afterwards. Rob was now saving up for a motorbike, but he hadn't told his mum because she'd be absolutely horrified.

Most of the time at school, Rob kept his head down. He was popular, with a big circle of friends, but he was more quiet than most, and, unlike many of his friends who reckoned they'd only end up on the dole as there seemed to be sod-all industry left in the town, he had his heart set on university. His dad wanted him to go straight into the newspaper from school – after all, he was father of the print chapel and stood a bloody good chance of getting him a job, even if only as a teaboy at first in the reporters' room, but he was a bright boy, he'd work his way up. Rob had grown up with the smell of hot metal – he loved going in to see his dad as a special treat in the holidays, sitting on a high stool, watching what went on in the hot, smoky production room. But most of all he liked to see the presses rolling, it was almost unbearably exciting to watch the hot metal flanges being fixed to the heavy roller, and then to see the pages flying round, tomorrow's news today. He had always wanted to be a journalist, as his dad said that was where the real money was.

Sure enough, Claire was lying flat out on her bed, the Rollers on her record player at a deafening level. 'Tea-time!' he yelled. 'Come on. Mum's in a bate.'

After tea, Rob's father, Jack, leant back in his chair and wiped his mouth with his handkerchief. 'That was very tasty,' he said. Peggy smiled at him. She knew what was coming. 'I'm just going to get a bit of fresh air.' Standing up, he whistled for the dog, which emerged from under the settee. 'Coming, Rob?'

'No thanks, Dad. I've homework.'

'You and your books. It's like living with Einstein. Claire?'

'I'm washing my hair,' she said, grinning. This was an evening ritual.

'I'll just have to go on my own.' Sighing, he fetched his jacket, and set off for the pub.

After he'd finished his homework, Rob went out for a walk. At the back of their row of terraced houses – theirs was on the end, and so was slightly bigger than the rest, which Rob teased his mum made them a cut above – lay a large reservoir. At night, there was something slightly eerie about the vast expanse of water. So still, so deep. Last summer, a kid had drowned, and now there were warning notices everywhere. Rob stood on the path which ran all the way round, and skimmed stones across the silent blackness. From the woods at the back, an owl hooted. He heard footsteps behind him. He turned, unperturbed. It was his mum, wrapped in her warm winter coat.

'I thought I'd find you up here. It's a bit nippy, isn't it?' she said, looking out over the water.

'It's all right. Dad back yet?'

'Is he heck,' she said. Rob laughed. His mum never minded his dad going out like some of his friends' mums did – Peggy just said he worked so hard he deserved a bit of pleasure. They were funny, his mum and dad. He'd come into the front room and find them sitting holding hands, and they chatted to each other all the time – teasing, mostly – in a way his friends' parents never seemed to. But then his mum was clever, as his dad always said. She was the clever one of the family. She worked as a secretary at the local primary school, and his dad said she had a real head for figures. Within her, there was a steely determination that Rob and Claire would make, as she said, 'something out of' their lives.

'Mum?' Rob said, suddenly. 'Are you happy?'

'Happy?' she said. 'That's a funny question.' She thought for a moment. 'Yes,' she said. 'Yes, I am. Why?'

'Just wondered.'

'You are an odd one. Come on, let's go home. It's brass monkeys up here.' And, with her cuddling him, they walked together back down to the house.

Chapter Four

Lucy, lying with her head on Max's chest one early summer evening, watching the pale evening light filtering down through the leaves of the old sycamore tree in the field at the back of her house, felt completely happy. Max, his head resting on one arm, was smoking, the smoke curling upwards like a signal and then disappearing as it rose gently towards the just-visible moon. Lucy's blonde hair lay like a curtain over his soft blue flannel shirt, and the fingers of her left hand played idly with its tortoiseshell buttons.

'Max,' she said, lifting her head from his chest and, rolling over, rested her face on her clasped fingers. 'What?' he said lazily, examining the top of his cigarette before flicking it high with two fingers, so it flew in a faintly glowing arc into the middle of the field.

'Don't do that,' said Lucy. 'You'll start a fire. What are you thinking about?' Max, who had been thinking about absolutely nothing save the fact his arm was going numb, grinned. Why did women always want to know what you were thinking? 'You,' he lied, rolling over so he rested on one arm and his face was level with Lucy's. 'I'm thinking,' he said, 'how much I want to make love to you. All this waiting is driving me *crazy*.' He made a pathetic face. Lucy eyed him beadily. He had been going on and on about this all year, as if she was somehow causing him physical pain by refusing to sleep with him. But then it was all right for him, he'd didn't have to sidle into the Brook Advisory Clinic with a face like a beetroot to try to get the pill, and then smuggle the capsules home, like ticking timebombs. If her mum found she'd gone on the pill she'd ban Lucy from ever seeing Max again – charm or no charm. Having a daughter on the pill would be roughly the social equivalent of catching leprosy.

'D'you fancy coming down to Devon?'

'What?'

'Coming to the house. We're going next week, all of us. Well, Mummy's already down there, opening up, all that stuff. Come on,' he said, rolling over. 'It'll be a laugh. You'll love everyone down there, they're a seriously good crowd.'

'Will your parents definitely be there?'

'Of course,' Max said, reaching over to tickle her nose with a piece of long grass. 'Why? Do you think I'm only asking you so I can have my wicked way?'

'Yes,' said Lucy.

Max laughed. 'Chance would be a fine thing. No, just come. Mummy suggested it, actually.'

It would be worth it, he mused as he drove home. There was a girl he was supposed to be seeing down there, but that was OK, he'd sort it. And his parents went out all the time, he was sure that Lucy would finally have to give in. Either that, or he really would have to think about chucking her. There was only so long a man could wait.

*　　*　　*

57

Wearing her new drainpipe jeans and a white short-sleeved skinny-rib jumper, sunglasses perched on her head, Lucy felt the epitome of glamour as they sped down the motorway towards Devon. The Doors blared out of the stereo. Lucy thought the fact that he liked The Doors was very cool. No-one at school even knew who they were, and although Jim Morrison did whinge on a bit, he was excruciatingly gorgeous. Shame he was dead. Lucy lit two cigarettes, and handed one to Max. Max drove with one hand on the wheel, the other on her thigh. As he drove, Lucy sneaked covert glances at his profile. She had tried to draw him on the back of her jotter, but it was hard to reproduce that aquiline nose, the way his thick blond hair stood up from his forehead, his soulful Labrador-brown eyes, curving, almost girlish full mouth, and dimply chin. She liked to look at him when he didn't know she was watching, and noted how other girls reacted to him – when he walked into a pub, the heads of almost every girl in the room would swivel. Which, of course, he knew. Then there was his effortlessly stylish walk – almost a lope. He moved with something of the dancer about him.

'I bet we could persuade Ma and Pa to go out,' he said, turning his head to look at Lucy. She shivered slightly at the thought. What if she was useless in bed? Max now had half the sixth form at Lucy's school in love with him, and Lucy was pretty determined he must never visit, as several girls were far more glamorous than her. Every day she ripped open the one newspaper they were allowed, to read his stars, which she then read out to the rest of the class, who palpitated and swooned.

Lucy was almost asleep by the time they got there, after mile on mile of long, winding roads only wide enough for one car. Max swore copiously as he met a tide of estate cars coming the other way, surfboards tied to roofs, boots stuffed with duvets and wind-breaks, sleepy children in the back. The sound of the stereo going off jerked Lucy awake as they stopped.

Night lights illuminated the white, weathered front of the house. Max led her round the back, and Lucy could see far below them, dimly, the sweeping curve of the beach, littered with the hulls of upturned boats. In front of the house was a wooden deck, with two rock-ing chairs covered in rugs and a swinging bench. Damp towels left on the railings flapped in the evening breeze, and a surfboard belonging to Max's younger brother, Henry, was propped up against the steps, alongside the detritus of beach holidays – an old cricket bat, a snorkel and a pair of new-looking water-skis. Classical music floated out from the open veranda doors. Max draped his arm around Lucy's shoulder, and led her inside.

Annabelle, wearing a navy guernsey, beige shorts and no shoes, dark hair hooked behind one ear, was chopping lettuce at a big central wooden table in the kitchen. She put down the knife as they came in.

'Darlings!' She gave Max a huge bear hug and then kissed Lucy. Lucy felt a bit shy – her family weren't really the kissy sort, whereas Max's went in for a lot of Continental-type hugging and kissing. 'The troops finally here?' said Max's father George, wandering in, large gin and tonic in hand. Like Annabelle, he was deeply tanned.

'Drinkies?' he said, waggling his glass.

'Yes please,' said Lucy, breathing in the smell of damp towels and sea, mixed with the aroma of a wine-soaked beef casserole bubbling in a large stockpot on the top of the Aga.

*   *   *

Unloading of the car over, each clutching a large glass of chilled Sauvignon, she and Max sat out on the veranda. Across the bay, the lights of the nearest town became glowing blobs which dipped and flickered in their reflection in the slowly moving dark mass of water. A warm breeze blew across her face and she eased her sore feet out of her new deck shoes. Max had his old ones on, crusted with salt. His feet were already brown, and the hairs on his toes bleached gold. They sat on the swinging seat, his arm around her shoulders, hers round his waist against his navy and white stripy T-shirt. Max bent his head to kiss her.

'Sorry!' George emerged from the door, his large frame silhouetted by the light from the kitchen. He was quite unembarrassed. 'Fancy a spot of sailing tomorrow? The boat's on the water.' Lucy, glad the dark covered her puce face, followed his pointing arm and could just see, about two hundred yards from the shore below them, the outline of what was clearly some kind of racing boat, shrouded in a cover. Max had told her all about it in the car, thrilled with his and his father's new toy.

That night she slept deeply in a wide oak bed, on pure cotton sheets under a thick goosedown duvet. Annabelle had put her in a room directly opposite Max, which Lucy felt was tempting fate somewhat. Annabelle and George's bedroom was down the hall. There was no carpet, just wooden floorboards which creaked alarmingly when Lucy got out of bed in the middle of the night to go to the loo. She put on the big jumper of her father's she'd brought, rather than wandering out in her nightie as she would at home, because she had visions of meeting George in the corridor, which would be too hideous for words. She'd left Max up drinking with his father, and when she'd bent to kiss him goodnight, he'd whispered he would 'see her later'. Lucy had lain awake for half an hour, watching the door handle to see if it would slowly slide down. It didn't, and the only sound all night was the tick-tick of claws on the wooden floor of the family's ancient black Labrador, William, in his nightly perambulations.

Lucy came down the next morning to the smell of frying bacon and coffee. Annabelle, she was to discover, always rose early to cook for 'the boys', as she called Max, Henry and George. It was such a difference, to Lucy, to be in a house full of men, and she sensed that Annabelle had wanted her to be there because she simply wanted another female around. Annabelle, who hardly ever cooked at home, enjoyed this little touch of domesticity, although she drew the line at cleaning. They had a lady who came in and cleaned and did the washing during the holidays, and looked after the house when the family were away. Annabelle surrounded herself with 'treasures'.

Lucy and Annabelle quickly formed a conspiracy. Annabelle took her off for expensive shopping trips into Salcombe, buying her sailing jumpers and scarves and even a waterproof jacket because Lucy's denim jacket was not the right kind of outer gear for windy boat trips. Max loved the fact that Annabelle and Lucy got on so well, and all through their first week Lucy could sense she was growing constantly in his esteem, fitting into his family like a piece of Rubik's cube.

After a boozy night midway through the week at the powerboat club, they weaved their way home up the hill from the harbour, with loud disco music still ringing in their ears like tinnitus and legs wobbly from too much beer.

'I'll make some tea.'

'Don't bother.' Max stood close behind her as she lifted the heavy aluminium Aga kettle. She pulled the hotplate lid down, and turned to him, the rail pressing into her back. Max's mouth tasted of French cigarettes and beer, mixed with Ambre Solaire and fresh sea air. 'I love you, you know,' he said.

Silently, he took her hand and led her out onto the veranda. On the creaking seat, they kissed. After a while, Lucy started to pull away. 'We'd better go—'

'Shush,' said Max. His voice was thicker and deeper than usual, and Lucy could feel his face was very warm. He held her tight, while she tried to move away from him.

'Let's go upstairs,' he said, his voice muffled against her neck.

'We can't,' Lucy said. 'Your mum and dad . . . Henry . . .'

'They're asleep.'

Lucy longed to say no. She dreaded the thought of Max seeing her naked, felt hideously embarrassed about seeing *him* naked, but most of all, she couldn't bear the thought of his parents waking up. But – how long could she put him off? Max wasn't the kind of boy who would wait – he had girls queuing up to go out with him. Just that night, a girl called Camilla, barf, had made a major play for him when Lucy was in the loo – she'd come back and seen Camilla had her hand on his leg, and they'd both jumped back, embarrassed. Lucy hadn't said anything, but she had serious doubts about Max's ability to be faithful. Especially if she wouldn't sleep with him.

'OK.'

As they started to creep up the stairs, Max holding onto to one of Lucy's fingers, William trotted happily up to them, his feet clacking loudly on the floor.

'SHUSH, William,' said Max, as the dog's tail thumped against the heavy oak banisters. 'Bed!' he said sternly. William smiled happily up at them, jumping up and down as far as his arthritic limbs would allow. Lucy stifled a giggle.

'You go on up,' hissed Max, trying to lead William back to his basket. The dog stuck his front feet straight out ahead of him like brakes, and sat down heavily. This was an exciting night-time bonus, and he wasn't going to give up on company quite so easily. Max had to drag him, bottom sliding along the floor, towards the kitchen, while William twisted his head frantically in a bid to get his collar off and escape. Eventually Max resorted to getting behind him and shoving him in front of him like a trolley. William yelped in protest.

Lucy tiptoed up the stairs to her room. Mostly she was petrified, but she did also feel a weird kind of elation. Maybe she was finally going to 'do it'. In the bathroom, she examined herself naked in the full-length mirror. The deep tan of her shoulders contrasted vividly with the whiteness of her breasts, and there was a vee of white tracing the line of her bikini bottoms. She sucked her stomach in. She could see her ribs. Face not so great – blotchy from too much booze and her mascara was running. She splashed her face, and then put on some more mascara. She cleaned her teeth quickly, then wrapped a towel round herself and, carrying her clothes, hopped down the passageway to her room.

Max was lying in her bed. From downstairs, she could hear the frantic whimpering of William, who had been firmly locked in the kitchen, and who was scrabbling at the door with his paws. 'Bloody dog,' muttered Max, smiling. Against the brilliant white of the sheets, his shoulders were deep brown. He didn't seem shy at all, but Lucy didn't quite know what to do – she didn't want to just drop the towel, because that would make her look such a floozy, but then she could hardly get into bed wrapped in it. Blimey. The etiquette of bonking.

She opted for a quick drop and immediate slide into the sheets.

'Uh-uh,' said Max. 'I want to look at you.'

He pulled the sheet gently back from her shivering body. Despite the warm air blowing in through the window Annabelle had left open so Lucy wouldn't be uncomfortably hot in the night, Lucy felt a chill running through her. She was *sure* she didn't want to do this. It was much too grown-up. It was like mortgages, and bank accounts, and possessing your own washing machine. Something for the future, not now.

'You're beautiful,' said Max, staring at her trembling body in wonder. Lucy tried to smile, but she found her lips had stuck to her teeth. Max moved towards her and she felt how warm his skin was, radiating all that heat absorbed from the sun, and she felt too as if the blood was pumping very near to the surface of her own skin, every nerve jumping about like iron filings at an approaching magnet. Stroking her hair, Max looked at her. They stared at each other, astonished by the enormity of their emotions. He dropped his head to her shoulder. Rhythmically, the headboard of the old bed began to bang against the wall as Max tried to make love to her.

'Shit.' Lucy felt him leave her, a creaking of floorboards, and then he was beside her. As he started again, the noise ceased. 'What did you do?' she whispered. 'A towel against the headboard,' he whispered back. Then a sharp pain made her almost sit up. 'Ow,' she yelped.

'It's OK,' said Max. 'Relax.' She tried to relax, but her thighs wanted to clamp themselves together. It felt awfully undignified, like a frog being laid out for dissection . . .

Gradually, the pain ceased. She was not exactly on the point of passionate ecstasy, but the movement was reassuring and, if she closed her eyes, she felt herself begin to spin gently into a dark world where there was nothing but their movement and the smell of his skin.

A loud yowl brought them sharply back to earth. Max stopped abruptly. 'What the f—?' Then there was a loud crash. It came from the kitchen. Max and Lucy froze at the sound of his parents' door opening.

'Max? Is that you?'

Annabelle's voice floated down the corridor. Lucy, terrified, was horrified at having to fight an urge to snort. Max, frozen above Lucy, looked at her in disbelief. The door to Lucy's room, which he was sure he'd closed firmly, creaked open.

It opened towards his parents' bedroom. There was no way Max could get out of Lucy's bed without being seen by Annabelle, and as soon as she walked down the corridor she would see them in flagrante. Even worse, the moon, which had been previously covered by a cloud, now shone brilliantly, filling the room with a sharp white light.

'I'll go.' Lucy heard George's voice, thick with sleep, and Annabelle retreated into her room, saying, 'They're out very late. Do you think we should . . .' Then George's footsteps came along on the landing. Max collapsed against Lucy's body, and they lay together, trembling like aspen leaves. Lucy didn't dare look up. She waited for the sound of her door being pushed open more widely.

Instead, she heard George's footsteps pause by her door. Very firmly, it was pulled close. Looking at each other in wonder, they then heard George's heavy tread on the stairs, and a loud 'Bloody dog!' A sharp whack, and a high-pitched yelp. George came back upstairs.

'Dog's had the plates off the table,' they heard him say to Annabelle. 'We should have cleared up.'

'Are they in yet?'

'No sign,' said George. His door banged shut and Lucy and Max could hear the creak of bedsprings as he got back into bed.

Next morning, William looked very sorry for himself. He sat pointedly on his hurt bottom, and flattened his ears pathetically whenever George went near him. The smashed plate had been brushed up and put in the bin, and Annabelle had had the thankless task of clearing up elderly-dog diarrhoea caused by the unexpected ingestion of Béarnaise sauce.

Lying next to Max, listening to his quiet breathing and feeling quite unlike herself, Lucy had been unable to sleep. When they slowly – and very, very quietly, like mice in bedroom slippers – resumed love-making, Max was slower, far more gentle. Lucy began to feel a hint of rapture. Not a full-blown orchestra of passion, maybe just the string section. Max fell asleep immediately afterwards, and Lucy lay awake, watching his face, the freckles on the bridge of his nose, the way his lashes swept onto his cheek and the way his mouth twitched. She'd never slept next to anyone before, and it was something of a revelation. Eventually she'd drifted off for an hour or so, before waking with a numb arm. Peering at the clock, she realized it was five in the morning.

'Max,' she whispered, nudging him awake. 'You'd better go.' He woke slowly, blinking, and smiled sleepily. 'Not yet,' he said. '"Twas the nightingale, and not the—"' 'Oh *fuck off*,' said Lucy, grinning too. 'You have to. Go!' Slowly, and grumbling quietly, he slid from the bed. The light illuminated his broad bare back as he bent over to pull on his jeans. Lucy watched him, carefully. He really was very beautiful. And it wasn't so bad, after all.

'I love you,' he said. Then the door softly opened, and closed. Lucy reached out a hand and touched the warm hollow left by his body. Then she slept.

At breakfast, she slid down the stairs feeling as if 'SEX' was written all over her forehead. She couldn't meet Max's eyes, and hopped when George put his hand on her shoulder. 'Sleep well?' he asked. There was no trace of irony in his voice.

'Yes, thank you,' she squeaked, pulling out a chair as quietly as she could and sliding into it in a sinuous eel-like gesture. Reaching out for the coffee pot, her hand met Max's. She looked up, and caught his eye. Neither could look away. They stared at each other, as if they had become quite different people, sharing a huge secret. Annabelle, bending over to give Henry some bacon from the griddle pan, intercepted the glance. Goodness, she thought. They really are in love. George, also observing the intensity of their gaze, thought, lucky bastard.

Chapter Five

On the last day of the holiday, the weather turned. Clouds massed in the open sky above the bay, and the boats rose and fell on the choppy steely-grey water. Lucy had risen glumly, feeling that somehow today was the end of an era. So many changes loomed – A-level results, university, Real Life. With Max's family, she felt protected. They had all been so kind, George taking her out on the boat, Henry trying to teach her to waterski and Annabelle so delighted to have such a pretty girl to spend money on, which, Lucy had surmised, was Annabelle's mission in life. Spending money on herself, on the house, on the boys – it frittered away from her like confetti at a windy wedding.

Annabelle wanted to pack the house up and get off early, to try to avoid the motorway crowds. It was also the end of a bank holiday weekend, which meant the motorway would be jam-packed with carloads of depressed families perched on soggy towels, mothers glum in anticipation of the mounds of washing to be done, fathers suicidal at the thought of the Monday morning office. Annabelle, ever the organizer, was up early, putting everything into neat piles, even separating wet swimming costumes into plastic bags. William sat on a neatly folded towel, his tail thumping in the hope someone would notice him and give him a pat. He hated change of any kind, and he'd got used to the smells around this house and his daily walks on the beach. As everyone was ignoring him, he went to lie down in his basket under the table. Only when he got there, he found it had been packed. Dispiritedly, he circled four times and lay down on the hard floor, sighing like a punctured tyre.

Lucy tried to be useful, but found she was getting in the way more than helping. She'd already packed her small bag, denim shorts crusty with salt water – it had seemed a good idea to swim in them at the time – yellow bikini baggy from being worn every day. Looking at herself in the mirror, she was very pleased with her appearance – her face was golden brown, her hair almost white-blonde.

Max wandered about, restlessly. His mother had packed his bag for him, which Lucy felt was massively indulgent. But then Max seemed incapable of even putting the kettle on, on his own. When Lucy started to lift the breakfast plates from the table – Max was standing looking out to sea, and George was sitting with his legs sideways over the arm of a chair, reading *The Times* with irritated sweeps of pages – Annabelle swiftly took them away from her.

'Henry hasn't come down yet,' she said. 'It's all right darling, leave it.'

Maybe Lucy should go and wake up Henry – he really was a lazy little tyke, who needed cattle-prodding out of bed. Most of the mornings in the holiday he'd come downstairs, later than everyone else, in his pyjamas, yawning, with his hair sticking up at the back like a cockatoo. His bedroom always looked like it had been vigorously burgled. Annabelle cleared it up every morning, saying happily, 'Boys! Honestly, Lucy, don't ever have boys!' Lucy was wise enough not to point out that they could, actually, tidy up after themselves.

'Why don't you go for a walk?' Annabelle suggested, desperate to get the house to herself so she could finish off properly.

'Good idea,' said George, heaving himself out of the chair. He liked being with Max and Lucy. 'Come on, William.' William sighed even more pointedly. Did they not realize it was very *cold* outside today and he was a Labrador of a certain age?

'Not you,' Annabelle said sharply. 'I need you to load up the car.' George subsided back into his chair, with an expression like William's.

Lucy pulled on a big jumper of Max's. She loved wearing his clothes, and had already pinched several of his T-shirts and sweatshirts.

They walked down the beach slowly, the wind whipping their hair, their jumpers flapping like flags against their bodies. Max stopped, and pulled Lucy down on top of him. Putting out her hands to stop her fall, she felt the warm grit of the damp sand against her fingers, her face inches above his. On the bridge of his nose the dark brown skin was beginning to peel away, the sharp white crust contrasting with the deep pink skin underneath. His eyes seemed darker than ever in his tanned face, which for once was deadly serious.

'I love you,' he said. She relaxed her body on top of his, but supported herself on her elbows, so she didn't seem too heavy.

'How would you feel about marrying me?'

Lucy rolled off, howling with laughter.

'Don't be ridiculous!'

Looking away from her, he scooped up a handful of sand, and then let it run slowly through his fingers.

'I don't mean *now*,' he said crossly, picking at a stick poking up through the sand. 'After university.'

Lucy stopped laughing and looked hard at him. He had to be joking. Make a promise like this at their age? Spooky.

'We can't make plans,' she said, rolling over on her back. Of course he was joking, he had to be joking, but had he really said that? Wow. 'Who knows what will happen? I'm going to Manchester, you're going to Bristol . . . anything could happen.' This was how he liked her to be. He hated it if she was clingy. He and his mates had a description for girls like that – leechy.

Looking at him carefully, she reached out and pulled his sleeve, playfully. He jerked away. Exasperated, Lucy got to her feet and walked off down the beach. After a few minutes she stopped, expecting to be grabbed round the waist from behind. He wasn't there. She turned and saw him still lying flat out, like a stroppy piece of driftwood. She walked back. 'Stop sulking,' she said, looking down at his prone, sandy form. He rolled over away from her. 'I'm not.' His voice was muffled in the folds of his woolly jumper. 'I don't think you love me at all,' he said, petulantly.

'How can you say that? I let you . . . we've . . .'

'I know!' Max hit the sand angrily with the flat of his hand. 'But how do I know you aren't going to go off to university and sleep with loads of other blokes? Who knows what can happen up there?'

Lucy looked at him crossly. This was a side to Max she hadn't seen before. It wasn't massively attractive. 'Look,' she said, calmly. 'I have no intention of going out with anyone else. You can come up and see me whenever you want. We aren't splitting up, are we?

Why should it mean we go off and sleep with other people?'

'Well, I know I won't. But how do I know about you?'

'And how do I know about you?' Lucy pointed out, reasonably.

'That's not fair!' he blazed, staring angrily at her.

'Oh, stop being so bloody *childish*,' Lucy said. 'What do you want me to say?'

'I want you to say you won't go out with anyone else.'

'OK,' said Lucy, repeating it like a mantra, 'I won't go out with anyone else. And presumably, neither will you.'

'Oh *shut up*,' Max said. 'Stop qualifying everything.'

Lucy looked at him in amazement. 'You're not making a lot of sense,' she said. But, not wanting to spoil what had been such a great holiday, she smiled at him, and reached down to give him a hug. He pulled away, jumped up and walked off. Lucy looked after him in bewilderment. How could you ever know what men were going to do? She thought about running after him, but then thought, sod it. She sat back, the dampness of the sand seeping through her jeans, and pulled the roll-neck of his jumper up over her chin. She sniffed. It smelt of his aftershave and cigarettes, and she closed her eyes.

After several minutes, she stood up, slowly.

The clouds, which had previously been simply grey and pregnant, now let their burden fall. The rain dropped sharply and suddenly, visible slivers of sharp arrows which stung Lucy's face. Her clothes were soon sopping wet, and her hair darkened into brown tendrils which snaked down her face and dripped onto Max's jumper.

She walked slowly back along the beach, trailing her feet in the wet sand, resting her hand briefly on the green hull of one of the sailing boats, the season coming to an end, its purpose redundant. The beach was deserted, and the fronts of the houses on the cliff above already looked closed, shuttered and empty.

Lucy reached the end of the sand, where the stones were hard to walk over and littered with thick black clumps of slimy seaweed and lumps of rusty brown metal and hooks. Behind, wooden slatted steps, cracked in places from years of use by deck shoes and flip-flops, stretched up to Max's house.

She sank down on the bottom step and turned her face to the wind, enjoying its cold, sharp presence.

'Lucy . . .' Annabelle's voice floated down, a tiny wisp of sound, almost lost.

'Here!' she yelled back, and, reluctantly, trotted up the steps.

'Look at the state of you!' Annabelle exclaimed as she got to the door of the house. The kitchen was empty, all the bags neatly placed in the boot of the Volvo. William, wearing a displaced expression, was just visible through the car's back window, surrounded by suitcases. The Aga had been switched off, slowly seeping out its heat, armchairs in the big kitchen covered in white sheets.

'Max is already in the car,' Annabelle said. 'I put your bag in. He seems a little . . . is everything all right?'

'Yes, fine,' said Lucy, leaning forward to kiss Annabelle on the cheek. 'Thank you so much. It's been lovely. You've all been so kind.' She just stopped herself from saying, 'Thank you very much for having me,' which was the mantra dinned into her by her mother after parties. 'What do you say?' 'Thank you very . . .'

in her best party dress, itchy with ruched stitching on the front, tights drooping from energetic musical chairs and small hand clutching a going-home party bag with the cake she never ate.

'Time for off,' said George, wandering back into the room, clutching the car keys. 'Come on, darling. We've got the Hendersons for dinner tonight. Bye Lucy,' he said, wrapping his arms around her, heedless of the wet jumper. Lucy let out a slight 'oof' as he crushed her ribs. 'We'll see you soon, no doubt. Now don't let that son of mine drive too fast.'

'I won't,' she said with a small smile and followed them out to the cars. Annabelle locked the back door with the preoccupied air of a woman who is running through a mental checklist of several hundred tasks. Lucy could hear Max revving the Golf's engine.

She ran past his parents' car, and, waving at Henry, blew him a kiss. Henry, through the rainswept window, could be seen to blush. Lucy would be his secret fantasy for many years to come and he resolved there and then he would marry a blonde.

Max didn't look at her as she got in.

'I'm soaked,' she said, heaving the wet wool of his jumper over her head. Her T-shirt underneath clung. 'Put the heating on, you're soaked too.'

Rain dripped down from his hair over his face. A tic was beating next to his eye.

Lucy pulled a soggy packet of cigarettes out of her back pocket and lit one for both of them. He took it without looking at her. They shot off in a screech of tyres which caused George to exclaim in the car behind, 'Steady on!' Annabelle looked at him. 'I think they . . .' she said. 'It's none of our business,' George said.

Max turned the music in the car up very loud. Lucy

reached out to touch his arm, but he pulled it away. Really, he was being very childish.

'This isn't fair. Don't do this. Don't spoil everything.'

There was a long silence, and then he suddenly pulled the Golf over into a lay-by. Behind them, the Volvo swept past, with three quizzical faces turned towards them. Lucy hoped to God they wouldn't stop, thinking they'd run out of petrol.

To her horror, Max buried his face in his arms on the steering wheel, and began to weep.

'Max . . .' she reached out a tentative hand.

'Say you will marry me,' he murmured, intensely, into the folds of his arms. 'Now. Say it. I don't care where, or when, just say it.'

'OK, OK,' said Lucy. 'I'll marry you. But not,' she added hastily, 'for ages. This is just a secret promise, isn't it? We don't have to tell anyone or anything like that?'

'Yes,' he said. 'I just wanted to know you *could* say it.'

'You're completely mad,' she said, starting to laugh. He began to laugh too. He raised his face to hers and they hugged hard, while cars full of tired holiday-makers streamed past.

'Love me for ever,' said Max, winding his fingers in Lucy's still-wet hair. 'I need you, Lucy.'

'I will,' she promised. And knew she'd never see him this vulnerable again.

Chapter Six

'Now.' Caroline was standing in the middle of Lucy's tiny room in her halls of residence. 'Are you sure you have everything you need? Let me put your duvet cover on. I'll have a go at making some better curtains than that.' She fingered the polyester see-through brown curtains with disdain, and began to flap the duvet into the neatly ironed cover. Lucy had felt deeply humiliated walking into the entrance hall with Caroline – all around her were parentless travel-stained girls with enormous backpacks, like hippie snails.

Her mother, with her navy pleated on-the-knee skirt and Ralph Lauren blazer, stood for a moment be-wildered, a little island of clean in a sea of grunge. This wasn't quite how she'd envisaged university – and it wasn't how she remembered it *at all*. When she'd asked the one student outside who looked reasonably with-it if there was such a thing as a porter, he looked at her as if she was totally mad. Not only that, but Lucy was standing next to him with an enor-mously heavy bag and he didn't even offer to help carry it up the steps. Used to the organization of board-ing school, where Matron was always there to greet you, Caroline found this situation anarchic. No wonder Archie had said he'd stay in the car.

'Mum, just go.' Lucy tried not to sound impatient, aware that a number of decent-looking girls had already filed past her open door to see her mother opening and shutting drawers, testing the light in the Anglepoise lamp and pulling the curtains to and fro to make sure they closed properly. They didn't.

Lucy had wanted to travel on her own by train, but even she had been defeated by the enormous pile of things she needed to take with her, not to mention the huge cheese plant she'd been nurturing ever since it was little. It was now the size of a small barn door, and Lucy secretly hoped it would die because she was fed up with having to water it. Eventually she agreed that it made more sense to let her mother and father bring her.

Archie kissed her goodbye in the car, his face taut with suppressed emotion. Lucy leant in from the passenger side and hugged him. Closing her eyes she breathed in his familiar smell of cigars, warm cashmere and a faint tang of Old Spice. Whenever she smelt this smell, she always felt six, and safe from the bogeyman.

'You don't want us in there. Ring if you need any money. I'll probably agree the first time but then the purse is closed.' He smiled, the lines around his eyes crinkling.

'Don't eat too much.' Lucy patted him on his prodigious stomach. 'And you make sure you eat,' he replied. 'You're much too thin. And work hard – it's not all about fun.' Lucy groaned, and hugged him harder.

Lucy was amazed at how bereft she felt, which was nuts because, at eighteen, one really should have got over missing one's parents. For the first time in her life, she felt quite alone. Everything seemed an awesome responsibility. She would have to run her own life, there was no-one there to look after her. It was like plunging over the precipice of adulthood in a barrel.

She had an awful urge to cry, but walking into your new halls of residence with blotchy eyes and a red nose would not look deeply cool. She swallowed hard. 'Give Ben a kiss from me,' she said to her father. He hadn't been allowed to come because Lucy's cheese plant took up all of the boot, laid flat, so she'd had to hug him goodbye on the back step of home, while Helen hung onto his collar and he gazed at her with the mournful brown eyes of the deeply abandoned dog. She'd even felt sad saying goodbye to Helen, which was mad. She knew damn well that as soon as their car pulled out of the drive Helen would be into her bedroom like a ferret, ripping open her wardrobe to see which clothes Lucy had left behind. She would then wear them immediately, stretch them and imbue them with the stink of her awful perfume.

Caroline had enrolled Lucy in an all-girls halls of residence. Lucy was livid to discover this, but she'd been in Devon when all the stuff came through. It was only when she got back that she discovered her mother had enrolled her in a place more suitable for apprentice nuns. Looking at the glossy brochures the university provided, she saw there were a number of much smaller mixed-sex self-catering halls, but no, her mother had swooped on St Margaret's Hall, no doubt home for the type of girls who thought an all-female hall would be *fun*. Lucy just couldn't *wait* to meet them.

Max was very pleased when she told him where she would be living. He'd offered to drive her up to

Manchester, but Lucy had felt very strongly this wasn't a good idea. This was a new start for her, and she couldn't cope if Max began to lay an even heavier guilt trip on her. That he should do so at all was pretty rich, because whenever she mooted the idea of him staying faithful, he was remarkably reticent and changed the subject quickly. Lucy pondered in private moments that Max would have been far happier if she'd stayed at home and sat by a window stitching tapestry cushions and sighing. It was almost as if he wanted to try to control her, by foot-stamping displays of petulance such as the one on the beach. A few months away would do them both good — after all, he was off to Bristol where he was far more likely to have a wild social life, as most of their friends had plumped for either Bristol or Exeter. Very few were headed up north. If their relationship stood this litmus test, maybe they did have a future.

'OK darling, I'll go.' Her mother reached forward and hugged her. Lucy felt an overwhelming urge to cry. Instead she swallowed hard and bent over her trunk, fiddling with the locks. 'Bye, darling,' said her mother. 'Are you sure you've got everything that you need?'

'MUM!'

Her mother waltzed out and a few seconds later Lucy could hear her chatting with a girl further down the corridor. Lucy stuck her head out of the door.

'We're from the south too,' she could hear her mother saying. 'Dorset? What a lovely part of the world. We're from the Cotswolds. I know, it is pretty. But awfully touristy in summer. Which way did you come? Really? Wasn't the motorway busy? My daughter's Lucy — that room down there, on the left. She's reading English . . . Are you? Isn't that marvellous?'

Lucy, groaning, withdrew her head and waited a few

seconds. Sure enough, her mother's neat blonde head popped back round the door. 'I've met *such* a nice girl. She's reading English too. Why don't you just—'

'I can manage!' Lucy almost shouted. 'Please, Mum, I can introduce myself. Let me get sorted out.'

'All right,' Caroline said. 'There's no need to bite my head off. And remember,' she added, 'the best way to meet people is to join masses of societies.' Lucy grinned. 'You've told me, Mum.' They smiled at each other. 'I'll miss you so much,' said Caroline, reaching forward and giving her a warmly scented hug. Lucy, her head against her mother's shoulder, sniffed. 'Go on,' she said. 'Dad'll be waiting.' Caroline turned, and with a final tweak of the duvet cover to straighten it, she left.

Alone, Lucy discovered that, if she stood in the middle and stretched her arms out, she could comfortably touch each side of her room. The bed took up sixty per cent of the available space. The rest was taken up by a minute desk at the end of the bed, a tiny bedside cupboard and a fitted wardrobe with shelves. Lucy looked at her trunk and suitcases, and the cupboard. There was no way all her stuff was going to fit in here. She'd brought far too much, and there was also a huge box containing her record collection, which had to go somewhere. Maybe under the bed? And what about the new hi-fi her dad had bought for her? Sod it – it would have to go on the desk.

But here. At last. On her own. She could lie in bed all day. She could play music deafeningly loud. She could buy her own bottle of Martini Extra Dry and drink it all in one go. She could sleep with anyone and no-one would know. What *fantastic* freedom. A tear trickled down her face. What loneliness. Brushing away the tear, angry at being so pathetically juvenile, she took out the photos of her mum and dad, Helen and Ben, and one of Max on his speedboat looking gorgeous and brown, and Blu-Tacked them to the wall by her bed. Then she began to unravel her posters, and stood for a while, wondering where the Monet water-colour should go. Perhaps above the bed.

As she stuck the posters to the wall, she began to cheer up. She had made the right decision. Everyone at school had thought she was completely mad in choosing Manchester, because she'd been predicted to do so well in her A levels, as she had, straight As in all three subjects, and could have taken Oxbridge. But somewhere, in the back of her mind, was a determination to try something different. All her friends were applying for Bristol, or Exeter, or the London unis like Goldsmith's. Lucy was made to feel she was being deliberately perverse. She wasn't sure why, but, having decided she was going to read English, she defiantly put down Manchester. It had an excellent course and a really good reputation, and it annoyed her intensely that everyone seemed to regard wanting to go there as a big joke. Her friends teased her about becoming a Lefty, and said she'd be joining CND next. But Lucy, having visited in the autumn term, loved the vibrancy and energy of the city – having got over the initial shock that people actually talked like that. Never having been north of Cheltenham, apart from a couple of holidays in Scotland when her father went salmon-fishing, she'd assumed that northern accents were exaggerated on the TV. When she'd tried to get a cab from the station, she had to ask the taxi driver three times to repeat what he was saying.

Leaving the motorway, she'd seen her father almost wincing as they drove through an estate of grey high-rise tower blocks. Unfortunately it was raining, so the outlook was perhaps even more bleak and depressing. Her father and mother hadn't said anything, but Lucy could see they weren't impressed at all, and perhaps even a little fearful for her. Lucy knew her mother would have much preferred it if she'd followed Max to Bristol, where Caroline had several friends, and they could have had lovely shopping trips.

As they drove through the centre of the city, all the shops were closed apart from a couple of newsagents, their fronts like blank faces shuttered in iron. Lucy remembered just the year before there had been riots nearby, in Moss Side. To Lucy, even now there seemed a slight feel of the aftermath of a riot about the city – it was unnaturally quiet, deserted and vaguely threatening. Lucy shivered at the alien landscape. The only riot they'd have in Burford would happen if the local authority tried to set up a home for young offenders, when all the forceful tweedy ladies with their wicker shopping baskets would sit outside the site on shooting sticks holding up polite banners saying, 'I don't think that's an awfully good idea'.

There was a sharp knock on the door. Lucy, who was now trying to stick a poster of a Frenchman wearing a sweeping black cloak and carrying a bottle of wine to the wall above the desk, shouted 'Come in!' Turning round, she saw an extraordinary-looking girl. She was wearing a long beaded skirt and no shoes, coupled with a brightly coloured striped jumper full of holes, cropped bleached-blonde hair and thick black eyeliner which made her eyes look huge in her tiny, tanned elfin face. Lucy swiftly deduced this was not the 'nice girl' her mother had encountered.

'I'm Annie.' Her voice was surprisingly cut-glass, emerging from such Bohemian apparel. Lucy jumped down from the bed so vigorously the poster slid down behind the desk. 'Lucy. Are you first year too?'

'I think we all are on this corridor. New inmates. Isn't it fucking awful? I've been here a day already,' Annie said, picking at half-varnished nails. 'Just come back from a kibbutz so I thought I'd rather come straight here than go home and get grief from the parents.'

'Have you met anyone else? Are they OK?' Lucy was thinking of the girls she'd seen so far on the corridor.

'Bleedin' mice,' Annie said. 'The ones I've met so far spend all their time scampering about putting up posters of bloody rabbits and arranging their shampoos in the bathroom. I even caught one putting her name on the label of a piece of cheese before she put it in the fridge. I ate it,' she added, with some satisfaction.

Lucy snorted. 'What's your course?'

'English and Philosophy. Total doss. I won't stick it. I'm only doing it to get the grant and so I can do some more travelling. Who's that?' she said admiringly, looking at the photo of Max.

'Boyfriend,' said Lucy. 'Max.'

'Wouldn't kick him out of bed. Has he got any friends?'

'Not sure you'd like them,' said Lucy. 'He's just starting at Bristol.'

'Hoorays?'

'Hoorays.'

'No Hoorays here,' said Annie. 'They shoot them in the north.'

'Where are you from?'

'London. Chelsea. Don't ask. My dad's a judge. My mother's career is social climbing. I'm not their favourite person at the moment.'

There was something quite lost about her, Lucy thought, a funny mixture of outrageous confidence and

83

foul language, coupled with a defensive vulnerability. She liked her at once.

'Do you like punk?' Annie said.

'Some of it,' said Lucy carefully. There was enough of the Caroline in her to find punks a bit grubby and scary, and Max hated both the music and the people.

'Great. There's a brilliant band on at the union tonight, I've seen the posters. Better than all that freshers crap. Unless,' she said mischievously, 'you came here bursting to join Dram Soc and go around kissing everyone. Come with me. It'll be a riot. Check out the talent, if there is any. Haven't seen any yet.'

'I don't think . . .' Lucy began. 'Max and I . . .'

'Oh Gordon Bennett,' said Annie. 'What did you come here for?'

After that first night, spent frantically pogoing in a sea of black-clad students, the walls of the room dripping with sweat, to emerge, shivering, into the cold autumn air to buy a doner kebab, Lucy felt truly initiated into life in the city. Then she was sick all over her new knee-length boots.

After just a few weeks, Lucy felt like she'd never lived anywhere else. There was a mad energy about the place. Most of the students – apart from the engineers, of course – wore a weird and wonderful mix of clothes, mostly bought from an Aladdin's cave of individual stalls called Affleck's Palace. Lucy went out and bought almost an entire new wardrobe for twenty quid, of long Indian skirts, collarless grandad shirts, and a fabulous long white lace skirt which she guessed had originally been a petticoat but which looked brilliant with her brown leather boots, and the slightly mothy long fur coat she'd picked up for £5. Every night there was a different type of band to see, from punk to indie to the last of the New Romantics. Annie forbade Lucy to like Adam Ant, but she did, really. Annie was into far more obscure music, including African reggae, and tried to make Lucy listen to and appreciate singers with names like Prince Nico Mbarga. She was witheringly scornful of Lucy's populist tastes. Annie's only concession to pop was a sneaking admiration for Teardrop Explodes, Echo and the Bunnymen and The Cure, but they were all pretty street cred.

Annie and Lucy wore their CND badges with pride. Every night they sat up late, sorting out the problems of the world, from Third World debt to the imperative need for nuclear disarmament. Annie was the driving force in assembling a group of perhaps the strangest people from their courses, people Lucy would never normally have been friends with but whom she found fascinating as their life experiences were so dramatically different from hers. She did have a couple of girlfriends on her English course who didn't look like refugees from a peace camp, but she had to keep them separate from Annie. Almost every night about eight of them would cram into either Lucy or Annie's room after the bar closed, music blaring from the hi-fi, smoke fogging the window and fags being dropped into half-drunk cups of coffee as they righted the wrongs of humanity.

Annie was the most stimulating friend Lucy had ever had. The only subject over which they disagreed – apart from Annie's perpetual taunt that Lucy was totally repressed – was the amount of drugs Annie took. She was constantly looking for a means of escape, as if always on the run from something inside her.

Used to the rigid constraints of life at boarding school and then at home with her parents, Lucy found

Annie's way of life, which had absolutely no boundaries and the normal pattern of awake during the day and asleep at night did not apply, incredibly energizing and liberating. But it was also completely exhausting. All too often she and Annie whooped into halls at five in the morning after clubbing all night, fully intending to get up for their ten o'clock lecture, but never quite making it. Lucy felt she was becoming quite a different person, much freer, more tolerant of so many other different types of people. Perhaps – she felt herself carefully – she really was becoming a socialist. Nope. She couldn't be. Her hair was too clean, and she had not, as yet, purchased a copy of *Socialist Worker*.

Annie also slept with lots of people. She was quite indiscriminate in her sexual habits, picking up a number of dull-looking and weedy men for the purposes of experimentation, she said, in the belief that men who looked so dull had to be good at *something*. There was no contact with her parents, while all that first term Caroline kept up a string of letters to Lucy, the occasional food parcel and bottles of multi-vitamins. Her letters were full of chatty, breezy facts about home, the garden, how hard Archie was working, their plans to go skiing after Christmas – did she want to come? Kitzbühel, Caroline thought. So pretty. Did she have enough money for clothes? They comforted and irritated Lucy by turn – her mother's life seemed so inconsequential. Lucy, on the other hand, felt she had passed through her phase of innocence and was now entering experience. With a bang.

Lucy and her friends totally disregarded the small band of rather lost-looking Hoorays who had been displaced by the random nature of the clearing system onto undersubscribed courses in chemistry and physics at Manchester. They also steered well clear of the great mass of be-anoraked engineers. The university was thronged with them, mooching about like one great living, breathing kagoul.

Lucy rapidly discovered that by attending a couple of lectures a week and all her tutorials, she could convey the impression of diligence without any real active participation. The only students who appeared to do any work at all were the engineers, and they were too dull to do anything else, and the law undergrads. The philosophy students seemed to do the least of anyone. They just wandered about looking troubled and trying to buy drugs.

Lucy spoke to Max quite often on the phone, but, as the term went on, they seemed to have less and less to say to each other. Lucy found their phone calls quite excruciating, and in between times she forgot what Max actually sounded like, so when she spoke to him, his accent annoyed her intensely, as if he was putting it on. Max had enrolled himself in an all-male hall, mainly because it had traditional dining-in nights and its own wine cellar. He liked all that kind of stuff – the legacy of public school, Lucy supposed.

It was purely by chance she was passing the phone on the ground floor of her halls when it rang.

'Hullo,' she said, wishing she hadn't picked the damn thing up. It would be for one of the mice.

'Lucy?'

'Max!' She held the phone slightly away from her ear. How odd to hear his voice. She felt immediately irritated. It had that arrogant, booming tone she hadn't noticed before.

'Lucy, is that you? You don't sound like yourself.'

Lucy wasn't aware her voice had changed. But she had, subconsciously, begun to drop her boarding-school tones and the first time she'd unthinkingly said,

'OK, yah' all her friends had fallen about and mimicked her for days. Annie had almost immediately dropped her own accent and had rapidly adopted the flat, faintly camp Mancunian drawl. Lucy hadn't gone quite so far, but it was a long time since she'd said 'absolutely'.

'Of course it's me,' she said, rather crossly.

'By 'eck,' said Max. 'Mind the whippet, lass.'

'Very funny,' said Lucy, much more in her old voice. 'How are you?'

'Fine Well, not fine really. Bloody awful hangover. Pissed as a rat last night. Anyway,' he continued, brightening, 'I'm thinking of driving up to you next weekend. Jules wants to come too, he's got some friends at the poly.'

There was a pause. Lucy suddenly thought, I don't want him here, everyone will take the mick. Annie will kill him. Or sleep with him. She'd have to keep him hidden. 'Brilliant,' she said.

'Talk about dark satanic mills,' Max said, climbing out of the Golf and stretching his long legs. Christ, what the hell was he wearing? Oh bloody hell – a stripy bow tie.

'Where's Jules?' she said, ushering him quickly into the entrance hall of her block.

'Dropped him off at his mate's flat. Sad place, Lucy. Really grim, like Coronation Street.'

'It's not all like that,' Lucy said, crossly.

'Isn't it? You really must come to Bristol. I'm moving into a *serious* flat next year – Cat's parents are buying it for her. Have I told you about Cat? She's on my course, a bloody good girl. The flat's on Royal York Crescent. Clifton.' He paused, waiting for Lucy to be impressed. She wasn't. She thought, you pretentious git.

Concentrate on his beauty, she told herself sternly. He's far better-looking than anyone here. He looked so healthy, despite his claims of yet another hangover. Most of her mates had acquired the deathly pallor which went with no sleep, too much drink and a diet of crisps and takeaway pizza. They always seemed to miss the meals in halls – Lucy was finding it increasingly difficult to meet any kind of deadline at all. The thought of catching a train scared her rigid. It took her an hour to get out of bed in the morning – or afternoon. She and her friends kept planning trips, like going to the Peak District in the beaten-up Ford Anglia van belonging to Rebecca on her course, but it took them five hours just to achieve any kind of motion.

'Is this your room?' Max peered into the tiny space unbelievingly.

'All the rooms are like this,' she said.

'Spooky,' he said. As they'd walked down the passageway to Lucy's room, there'd been an orchestration of opening and closing doors behind them, as the mice, by mouse telegraph, heard Lucy had a very good-looking unknown man with her. Once in the room, he chucked down his leather bag and collapsed full-length on the bed, suede brogues hanging over the edge.

'Come here,' he said.

'Do you want a coffee?' Lucy said, rather desperately. Why didn't she want him to touch her? This was very weird. This was Max, allegedly her boyfriend, and the man for whom she'd resisted the advances of loads of blokes here – but then most of them were either too cool to try very hard or just too pissed to concentrate. Lucy amazed herself by thinking, I don't want him here, in my room. He looks totally out of place and if he criticizes just one more thing he's out. He felt like an appalling liability, and how she was going to get him out without meeting Annie or any of her friends was going to be incredibly tricky. He was the epitome of everything they despised.

'No, I don't want a coffee,' he said, irritably. 'I've been driving for four hours on a fucking horrible motorway, the heater's packed up on the car and one of the windscreen wipers fell off. I want you, and then I want a good strong drink. OK?'

Lucy suppressed her irritation, and went to lie down beside him. This was very difficult, as her bed was only just wide enough for her. Occasionally when she turned over in bed, she fell out.

Max scooted onto one side and Lucy lay on her side, facing him. He stroked her cheek.

'Have you missed me, Lucy-Luce?'

No, she thought. 'Yes, of course I have.'

His smile slowly vanished, and his face took on the serious expression with which he conveyed lust. Orchestrated passion, Lucy thought, suddenly and perhaps uncharitably. He kissed her, and, reaching down, began to pull off her jumper.

'I'm stuck,' she squealed, as the T-shirt she was wearing underneath jammed on her ears. Max gave it a heave, they both spun round, knocked a cup full of congealed coffee off the bedside cabinet and bounced onto the floor.

'This is ridiculous.' Max looked deeply annoyed. 'Shall we go to a hotel?'

'We can't afford it,' said Lucy, appalled.

'My dad's given me a *gold* American Express card,' he said. 'He won't care.' Lucy looked at him in amazement. 'You can take me out for a meal,' Lucy said, climbing back onto the bed and pulling her T-shirt over her head, remembering too late she wasn't wearing a bra. She felt very shy, and slid under the duvet.

Max, without taking his eyes off her, pulled his thick navy sweater over his head, pulled off his bow tie and unbuttoned his shirt. It looked ironed. Lucy hadn't ironed anything for months. Turning away from her, he pulled off his trousers. She'd forgotten what a lovely body he had. He slid in beside her, so she could feel the warmth of his skin.

'I've missed you,' he breathed. Lucy had a terrible urge to laugh. Why was he being so serious? She closed her eyes and told herself to concentrate. She was just beginning to let go when the door burst open.

'What the fuck—' Max said, twisting round.

'Hi,' said Annie.

Lucy peered out from underneath Max.

'Annie, do you mind?'

'Not at all,' said Annie, quite unabashed. 'I need your notes on Coleridge. I've got to get that essay done or the prof will fucking kill me. Are they on here?' She rooted about on Lucy's desk.

'Er – Annie, this is Max,' squeaked Lucy. Max had eased himself out of her and was turning over with extreme difficulty, trying to keep the duvet over both of them.

'Pleased to meet you,' she said. 'I won't shake your hand, if you don't mind.'

Max laughed. 'I'll see you guys later,' she added. 'Are you on for a bevvy?' Then she disappeared through the door. 'Tarra.'

'Who in God's name was that?' Max asked. 'And what the hell is a bevvy?'

'Annie,' she said. 'A friend. You'll meet her later.'

'Everyone up here,' he said, 'is barking mad.'

Much later, they emerged. Lucy still felt faintly hysterical from the moment when Max, deciding he needed a shower, had wandered off down Lucy's corridor wearing only a towel. He hadn't bothered to lock the bathroom door. One of the miciest of the mice, Fiona, had unfortunately at that moment decided she, too, would like a shower. Opening the door, she was confronted by the glorious vision of a stark naked Max.

'Oooh,' she squealed. Max gave her his most charming smile, his *Cosmopolitan* centrefold splendour marred only by the fact he was wearing Lucy's flowery bathcap.

'Won't be a minute,' he said. 'You can wait if you want.'

'I wouldn't have minded,' a quivering Fiona told her friend Emily later. 'But he was using *my soap.*'

As Lucy wielded her hairdryer, tipping her head forward to make her hair stand out – big hair was very in, Annie had just had a root perm which made her look like a cockatoo in a state of permanent surprise – Max said casually, 'I said we'd meet Jules and his crowd later.' He was lying on Lucy's bed, naked apart from a pair of stripy boxer shorts, reading *Beowulf.* 'Awful crap,' he said, tossing it to the floor. 'Why isn't it in English?'

'It is English,' Lucy said, exasperated. 'Old English. Oh shut up,' she said, as she saw through strands of blonde hair that Max was laughing at her.

'You've got awfully earnest, Lucy-Luce,' said Max, tugging at the elastic on her knickers. Lucy reached down, and began to pull on her favourite long lacy white skirt. Max looked at her quizzically. 'Are you going out like that?'

She looked at him defiantly. 'Of course,' she said. 'Why?'

There was a thump on the door. This was now firmly

locked. The door handle rattled, then an irritated Annie's voice said, 'Lucy, we're going down the uni bar, then we thought we'd hit the Dug-Out. Shall we see you there?'

Max made an agonized 'no' face at her. 'Great!' Lucy called back. 'See you later.'

'And stop bonking,' was Annie's parting shot. 'I'll tell the warden.'

They heard her stilettos clack away down the lino of the corridor, followed by a muffled 'fuck' as she dropped something.

'Charming friends,' said Max. 'Are they all like that?'

'God no,' said Lucy. 'Annie's the refined one.'

Inevitably, Lucy found herself being dragged off to meet Jules and his cronies in a new wine bar which had just opened on Deansgate. She and her gang avoided it because drinks there were three times the price of those at the union bar, and it was the hang-out of the beleaguered band of Hoorays, who capered about trying to pretend they were at Oxford.

Lucy heard Jules's group before she could see them. There was a loud braying and shouting of laughter, and then Lucy saw them, lounging back on their chairs, feet on the table, which was already littered with numerous glasses and crumpled cigarette packets.

Max sneaked up and kicked the legs of Jules's chair away. He crashed to the ground. 'You bastard!' he yelled. The waitress, who was a second-year student, rolled her eyes in despair. Lucy made a sympathetic face.

'Jules, you know Lucy.' Lucy smiled down at the prostrate figure on the floor, rubbing his leg. 'Hi,' she said. Jules heaved himself up and looked her up and down appreciatively. 'Lucy, meet the gang – Jonno,

Sebastian, Michael and Sophie,' he said. Four not entirely friendly pairs of eyes turned towards her.

'Yah, hi,' they chorused.

'You're all at the poly?' Lucy said. She hadn't meant it to sound like a criticism, but it came out like that. They all ignored her. 'Drink?' said Max.

'Pint of beer,' Lucy said. Max looked horrified. 'It lasts longer and it's much cheaper,' she said.

After an hour of listening to tales of how Jules, Sebastian, Jonno and Max had got magnificently arse-holed in varying ways that term – hilarious anecdotes involving crashed parents' cars, fully-clothed leaps into swimming pools, broken conservatory windows and people being left asleep in bizarre places – Lucy was ready to lie down and die. As Jules was relating the story of how his brother, who'd just been given a job as an Aston Martin salesman in London, had trashed his new car after an all-night party, got out, surveyed the wreckage and said simply, 'It's OK mates, company car,' while the others shouted with laughter, Lucy cut in.

'Max, I did say we'd meet Annie . . .'

Max turned to her with a look of irritation, which mellowed when he saw Lucy's furious expression. 'Point taken,' he said. 'Come on, you guys, we're going to experience some northern culture.'

They heaved themselves to their feet, and spilled out onto the pavement. The waitress student, wiping glasses, watched through the window with relief as they departed. Just what made them think they were so special they could disrupt everyone else's lives?

In contrast to the wine bar, the union bar seemed dark and grungy. Lucy spied Annie and her group sitting in their usual corner, huddled over pints.

94

'I'll get the beers,' said Max. Lucy stood awkwardly at the edge of the seated group, Jules and his mates ranged behind her. 'Annie, Flo, Nick, Pete, Simon – this is Jules and . . .' They introduced themselves, eyeing the other group warily. There was much shuffling about as they tried to make room for them all to sit down. Moss-green corduroys squeezed in next to faded black jeans. Sophie, in her piecrust Laura Ashley white blouse with pearls, slid her legs in burgundy velvet pedal-pushers next to Annie's junk-shop silk skirt teamed with an extremely beaten-up black denim jacket of Pete's, with whom she was currently sleeping. Pete was a lovely bloke, Lucy thought, but she wasn't sure if she could bring herself to sleep with him – he was incredibly tall and thin and always dressed from head to toe in spidery black. His hair was dyed jet black which combined with his extreme pallor to give the overriding impression of a young melancholic undertaker. Pete ingested a mind-boggling amount of hallucinatory substances, including, on one occasion for lack of anything else, a jar of Potter's Asthma Inhaler which had resulted in a brief trip to Casualty last week.

Max came back carrying four pints in outstretched fingers. Immediately there was a rattling of pockets as everyone in Lucy's group turned out handfuls of small change onto the table. 'No,' said Max, bewildered. 'My round.' They looked at him as if he was mad. Everyone always bought their own beer.

Max squeezed in next to Lucy. 'So,' he said pleasantly to Annie, 'Lucy tells me you were at Cheltenham. You must know . . . ?'

It was not the best opening gambit. Annie, desperate to play down her background, had by now almost made herself believe she had been at a comprehensive in Moss Side. She ignored him completely and turned back to Pete. 'Of course I didn't mean it like that, you idiot, I was being ironic, of course he didn't sell his soul . . .' Pete, who was already well into orbit thanks to a cheapish cube of Moroccan gold, nodded owlishly and knocked the ash from his roll-up into the Manchester United ashtray. Jules, next to him, drew heavily on a Benson and Hedges.

'I'm talking seriously bollocksed, and this bloody copper said . . .'

'But if you're talking existentially . . .'

'Naked! Stark bloody naked on the bonnet of the Alfa!'

Lucy looked at them all in despair. Annie and her friends obviously thought Jules's group were a bunch of complete wankers. She gave Pete a nudge with her foot and glared at him. Sighing, he turned to Jules. 'Where are you at?'

'Bristol,' said Jules, proudly.

'Didn't get into Oxford, then?' Pete replied, and turned away.

Lucy had to fight hard not to snort at Jules's outraged face. This had been a *big* mistake.

'Max,' Lucy tapped him on the shoulder. 'Are you sure you want to go to a club? I'm really tired.'

'No, I'm on for it,' he said, having downed five pints.

They had to queue in the freezing night air to get in. A large black man with a shaved head, hands clasped in front of him, loomed in the doorway. As Lucy passed, he looked her slowly up and down. Lucy tugged at her lacy skirt, which was rather tight and clinging.

'Sign in,' said the bouncer, impassively. The crumpled page, covered in scribbled joke names, was streaked with blood. Sophie, who had now downed about twelve spritzers, was being supported between Jules and Jonno, who were also swaying. They all signed in, and showed their student cards. Max paid for Lucy, which made Pete very nervous, glancing over at Annie, but she'd already paid for herself.

As they clattered down the stairs, the noise and the heat hit them like a wall. Inside, there was a mass of heaving bodies. 'I need the loo,' said Sophes. 'I wouldn't,' Lucy said. Some minutes later, Sophes emerged wearing a look of outraged horror. 'There was something awful all over the floor, and all the doors were locked for ages,' she said. 'I don't know what they were doing in there, then three girls came out together.' Annie shot her a pitying look. 'Come on Pete,' she said. 'Let's dance.' Annie danced frenziedly, while Pete stood stock-still with his eyes closed, his only concession to the art of dance a vague waving of the fingers.

The rest of their party stood in a tight group, unable to speak as the music was so loud. They held tightly onto their beer, as every time someone pushed past a drink was spilt. Lucy felt her sides running with sweat, made hotter by the fact she was clutching onto her fur coat, which appeared to be moulting. 'Can we sit down?' Max bellowed in her ear. 'Where?' Lucy yelled back helplessly. There were only a few seats, on old beer barrels around sticky sloping tables, each barrel holding at least two people. Eventually Lucy could bear it no longer and dragged Max out into the freezing night air. Outside, he took off his jumper and gave it to her to put on her fur coat. Lucy was amazed. None of her friends would have dreamt of doing that, in case it was interpreted as a sexist gesture.

Back in her room, they made love without words,

Max much more thoughtful and restrained than before. Lucy woke earlier than him, as the thin morning light began to seep through her curtains. In sleep, he looked so like a child, almost helpless. But even so, in the intimacy of the moment, she felt she was no longer the person he wanted her to be, and amazed herself by still wishing him gone.

Chapter Seven

'Leave me alone . . .'

'Annie, please. You haven't eaten for days.'

Lucy crouched next to Annie's bed in her dim, mouldy-smelling room. Clothes were piled up in a huge mound on her chair, the floor littered with ash-trays and dirty coffee cups. On the table next to her bed was a half-drunk glass of red wine, in which a fag end floated. Lucy winced, and put it on the floor. She was proffering a plate of baked beans on toast, stolen from the mice and prepared in the common room.

'You have to get up. You haven't been to a lecture all week and the prof cornered me this morning and asked if I'd seen you. You missed our tutorial on Tuesday with sexy Dr Ashworth – and you know how you look forward to seeing his bum – and that essay on Coleridge was due in last week. Come on,' she said, tiying to lift the edge of the duvet.

'No!' squeaked Annie, stapling it down with her fingers. 'I don't fucking care.'

'You're being stupid,' Lucy said. 'He's not worth it. You told me you didn't like him much anyway. You said he was hopeless in bed.'

'He is,' said Annie's muffled voice. 'That's not—'

'Well what is it then?' asked Lucy, exasperated. Standing up, she opened the curtains for the first time in several days. Annie pulled the duvet cover higher over her head.

'Don't!'

Daylight flooded into the room, remorselessly tracing the varying stages of decay on plates in which cigarettes had been stubbed out, and mice-owned mugs now grimy and ringed. Records out of their sleeves littered the top of her desk, and a page of A4, where Annie had started to write her essay and then aborted, was stained with wine. Lucy began to clear up.

'Come on. You can come to the lecture this afternoon and then we'll go to the library. I'll bloody well stand over you until that essay's finished. It has to be in by the end of term.'

'Stop bullying me.'

'Someone has to. Look Annie, please. It isn't like you to give up. Once you get it finished we can go out. *Eraserhead*'s on at the arts centre. You really wanted to see that.'

Annie made a groaning noise and turned to face the wall. 'That'll finish me off,' she said, smiling faintly.

'Look, Annie, is Pete all that's wrong?' Lucy noticed that next to the ring left by the glass of red wine was a letter, written on expensive-looking cream notepaper in a neat, flowing hand.

Annie emerged from the duvet and, leaning forward, reached out a hand to snatch it away.

'I'm not interfering,' said Lucy, 'I'm just worried.'

'Oh Christ.' Annie sat up in bed, tucking the duvet round her waist. She was wearing a mottled purple baggy T-shirt. 'It's my mother.' She lifted the letter. 'Listen to this. "In the light of your conduct,"' Annie read in a drop-dead imitation of her old voice, '"Daddy does not think it would be appropriate for you to come home just yet."' She screwed it up.

'What did you do?' Lucy said, gently.

'Why I went to Israel,' Annie shrugged. 'I got caught with some dope at school. They let me take my A levels but then I pushed off straight away. Mum and Dad came to pick me up but they'd made such a song and dance about the whole bloody thing I couldn't face them. I couldn't go home. My darling father managed to hush it all up, not good for the old career, you know. I've got some money in a trust fund and I managed to get at some of that and spent all summer bumming around. Then Mum rang last week and it was OK but then she started on about how upset Dad was and how I'd let the family down, so fucking predictable, so I put the phone down. Look, Lucy, let's leave it. It doesn't matter.'

'You could come home with me,' Lucy said, not entirely sure how her parents would cope. But she knew they would, Caroline wouldn't be able to bear the thought of someone temporarily homeless, no matter how bizarre they might look.

'No thanks,' said Annie. 'I don't think I'd bring much comfort and joy at the moment. I can doss down here – Nick's offered me a space on the floor in his flat.' She smoothed out the crumpled cotton of her duvet with trembling, pale hands. 'I dunno yet if I'm going to come back next term, the course is so fucking boring. Full of wankers. I fancy going off again.' She ran her fingers nervously through her spiky and slightly greasy blonde hair. Then she smiled at Lucy, a smile of brilliant purity and charm. 'Will you come with me?' Lucy grinned back at her. 'You know I can't.' 'Conformist,' said Annie, flopping back down onto her pillow. 'Are you ever going to do anything remotely exciting in your life, Lucy Beresford?'

'Fuck off,' Lucy said. 'And get up.'

It hadn't been the best time for Pete to finish with her, Lucy reflected, as she heaved herself to her feet and began stacking the filthy plates. He'd told Annie he needed to get his head sorted out, which Lucy felt was an aim verging on the wildly optimistic.

'Have a bath,' she said. 'It'll make you feel much better.' Annie shouted with laughter for the first time in days.

'That's it,' said Lucy, gloomily. 'I am my mother.'

Annie seemed to cheer up over the next few days. She went to lectures, she finished her essay under Lucy's stern gaze in the library and they went to see *Eraserhead*. It was awful. One of the main characters was doing something unspeakable with a chicken and a pencil when Annie hissed, 'Sod this. Let's go and get pissed.'

They bought a bottle of gin and several bottles of tonic at the late-night offie and walked back to halls, clinking. On the way they met Nick, whose eyes brightened perceptibly at the gin. 'No way,' said Annie. 'Girls' night.'

Leaning with her back against Annie's bed, Lucy heard the unexpurgated story of Annie's life. It was very chaotic. She was the middle one, with a clever older brother, Sebastian, now in his final year reading law at Cambridge, and a beautiful younger sister, Alexandra, still at Cheltenham. She heard about the abortion in the last year at school. By the end, both she and Annie were in gin-soaked tears.

'I love you,' Annie said, leaning forward to hug Lucy.

'I love you too. You're my best friend.' They clung helplessly to each other.

'I better go t'bed,' Lucy said, trying to heave herself upright. The floor came up to meet her. 'Whoops,' she said, kneeling on all fours and crawling towards the door. 'G'night,' she said, falling out onto the corridor. She lay on her back and tried to work out which way was her room.

'Good night,' shouted Annie through the door. 'I can't get up,' Lucy hissed back, giggling weakly. 'I'll have to sleep out here.'

The next morning Lucy woke with a head like a cement mixer. She could hardly bear to open her eyes, and her body felt like lead. She tried to move her legs. Good. Not totally paralysed, then. She squinted at her bedside clock. Jesus wept, it was midday. Two lectures missed. She groaned, and realized she was lying fully clothed on top of her duvet. Her vision was very blurry too, she'd slept in her contact lenses.

It took her half an hour just to change, splash her face with water and trudge down the corridor to go to the loo. She'd better wake Annie.

She banged on the door; there was silence. It was locked, so Annie must be in there. 'Annie!' she hissed through the door, her head throbbing. 'You have to get up. I feel bloody awful. Are you all right?' There was no response. 'Annie,' she yelled. 'Wake up.' Still silence. They were on the third floor, so she couldn't go and look in at the window.

Clutching her head, she trailed down the stairs. Outside, she counted along to Annie's window. It was partially open, but the curtains were closed. She looked around for a stone. Picking up a biggish pebble, she lobbed it at the window. It missed. 'Annie!' she

103

shouted. Picking up another, she managed to hit the target. There was still no sign of life.

Lucy was beginning to panic. Annie was obviously in there, but only a corpse could have slept through the row she'd made. But there wasn't anyone around she could ask for help. She ran back inside, and began banging on doors. Everyone was out at lectures. She ran outside again, and headed for the all-male hall down the road. Maybe there'd be a security guard or cleaner or someone who might have some keys.

In her panic, she didn't look where she was going.

'Watch it!' Lucy felt a hand catch her arm just as a car whizzed past, inches from her.

'Are you OK?'

'I'm fine, it's just—' She looked up to see a tall youth with long dark hair. His face was very pale and his eyes almost black. He was holding a folder of notes in one hand, Lucy with the other.

'Could you help?' she said, desperately. 'It's a friend, she's, I don't know if she's all right, her room's locked and I can't wake her up.'

'Doesn't sound like a crisis to me,' said the youth, smiling. 'Sounds like most of my friends.'

'No, really,' said Lucy, trying not to cry. 'She was really upset and I think she . . .'

'Where is she?' he said. He had a lovely deep voice, calm and unhurried, brushed with something northern, but not Manchester. More rural than that.

'St Margaret's,' Lucy said. 'I know it sounds stupid but could you hurry?'

Turning, she ran back down the road.

'This is the room,' she said, breathlessly, after they'd both run up the stairs. 'Annie!' she shouted, rattling the handle. 'Annie, please wake up!' There was no sound.

'Could you break the door down?' she said, turning to the dark youth.

'I should think so. Are you sure she's in there? We're going to look a bit stupid if she isn't.'

'I'm sure,' said Lucy. 'She never locks the door when she goes out.'

'OK,' he said. 'Your decision.'

Bracing himself, he put his shoulder against the door. He tried a hard shove, holding on to the handle. The door didn't budge.

'We're going to have to go for it,' he said, and, leaning back, he crashed against the door with all his strength.

It remained resolutely closed. 'Ow! Bloody hell,' he said, rubbing his shoulder. The wood around the lock had begun to splinter. 'Try again,' said Lucy.

He leant back, and thumped his side into the door. There was a crashing sound as it gave way and they both catapulted into the room. It was dark, the curtains blowing slightly in the breeze. Under the duvet was a mound. Lucy ran to the bed and yanked back the covers.

Annie lay, her head tipped slightly backwards, her mouth open, eyes closed. She was as pale as death.

'Oh Christ,' Lucy moaned, seizing her by the shoulders, shaking her gently. 'Annie, wake up.' She was as limp as a rag doll. There was sick on the pillow, and next to her bed was a small opened brown bottle.

The youth pushed Lucy aside, urgently feeling for Annie's wrist. 'She's OD'd. Go and ring for an ambulance. NOW.' Lucy was standing, horror-struck. She felt like she couldn't move, Annie's face, the smell in the room, her head began to spin. 'GO!' he shouted. Willing herself to move, Lucy ran down the stairs to the payphone in the hall. She dialled 999, and in as controlled a voice as she could muster she told them where to come. 'Come quickly,' she pleaded, tears rolling down her face. 'We will, love,' came the flat reassuring Manchester voice.

Lucy ran back up the stairs. The youth was carefully lifting Annie up, wrapping her body in the grubby duvet. 'Mind,' he said, pushing past Lucy. Lucy could only see the whites of Annie's eyes. 'Oh God,' she said, wrapping her arms around herself. 'What have you done?'

Hurrying past a couple of astonished students in the hallway, they headed outside, to hear the sound of the sirens. Without even thinking, both Lucy and the youth climbed into the ambulance beside Annie. Lucy gave details of what had happened as they raced through the streets, outside so much life, Annie so lifeless.

'She's still breathing,' said the paramedic, strapping an oxygen mask gently to her face. Lucy held Annie's hand tightly.

At the hospital they lost sight of Annie, raced away on a stretcher. Lucy and the boy slumped down on orange plastic chairs in a waiting room. 'Do you want a coffee?' he asked, reaching in his pocket for change. 'Please,' Lucy said. She felt awful. Hungover, exhausted, scared, as if real life had been turned on its head. She looked at her watch. She should be in a lecture now. None of their other friends knew, they'd all be sitting there yawning, taking notes, doodling, while Annie lay dying. It didn't seem possible. Life had gone mad.

'Thanks.' She reached up for the steaming plastic cup. 'Do you take sugar?' he said. 'Yes, no – I don't know,' Lucy said, bursting into tears. 'God, I'm sorry.' Placing his cup down next to his chair, the boy knelt in front of her. Gently, he put his arms around her. 'She'll be OK,' he said. 'She didn't take the whole lot.' Lucy leant against him, his hair against her face. 'Thank you,' she said, lifting her eyes to his, only a few inches away as he crouched in front of her. They were extraordinary eyes, dark and slanting. His skin was deathly pale, under a dark growth of stubble. What a lovely face, Lucy was alarmed to find herself thinking, as they stared at each other.

'Excuse me?'

A nurse stood at the door. 'Did you come in with the young girl?' She consulted her clipboard. 'Anna Rosco?' Lucy started. 'Yes,' she said, getting up. 'How is she? What's happening?'

'Do you have a number for her parents?'

'No,' Lucy said, 'but I know it's Chelsea, her father's a judge.'

'Ring the Law Society,' said the youth. 'They'll be able to contact him.'

'Can we see her?'

'Not just yet.'

'I'm sorry,' Lucy said. 'You must want to go.'

'Gets me out of a tutorial,' he said, sitting down in the seat next to her. Turning, he gave her a lopsided grin. 'I'm Rob. Rob Atkinson.'

'Lucy,' Lucy said, smiling through her exhaustion. 'Lucy Beresford.'

'I'll wait with you,' he said. 'If you don't mind.'

'No,' said Lucy. 'I don't mind.'

Chapter Eight

They waited for what felt like hours in the grim little room, drinking chemical coffee. Aware that she must look awful, Lucy wandered off to find the loo. Even the air in the corridor tasted metallic and sharp, and the bright neon lights were making her headache worse. What a horrible place to be ill in, she thought.

In the loo, she splashed her face with water and, ignoring the sign which said, 'Do Not Drink The Water', she swilled it round her mouth and then felt panic-stricken about legionnaires' disease. Or did you get that from air conditioning?

Looking at herself, things were as bad as she feared – huge dark circles under her eyes, her hair greasy at the roots because she hadn't had time to wash it, and mascara smudged under one eye. Her mouth tasted vile because she hadn't even cleaned her teeth. She'd better not breathe on him. She put her hand over her mouth, and sniffed. Yuch. Her skin looked translucent, and the only thing she could do with her hair was finger-comb it. Unwashed, it hung at the side of her face like spaniel's ears. He must just feel sorry for me, she thought.

Returning, she saw he was flicking through one of

the weekly magazines you'd never ever buy, which lay ripped and scattered over the low yellow Formica table. 'Did you know,' he said, looking up when Lucy closed the door carefully behind her, 'a hamster can eat its own body weight in food every day?' 'Never,' she said, smiling for the first time in what felt like hours.

'Hello – ' a nurse put her head around the door. 'Could I have a word?'

'Yes?'

'Your friend will be fine. We've given her a stomach pump so she isn't feeling wonderful but she is conscious now. Would you like to see her?'

'I'll stay here,' Rob said. Lucy flashed him a 'thank you' look. Even in the space of an hour, she felt enormously dependent on him. There was something very still and calm about him.

'Have you managed to get in touch with Annie's parents?' Lucy asked the nurse as they marched down the corridor. Why do nurses always walk so fast? Lucy thought as she puffed after her, head still throbbing.

'Yes,' the nurse said, turning to her as she pushed open the swing door of the ward. 'They're on their way here, I think. At least her mother is. I'm not sure we've made contact with the father.'

Annie was in the bed at the end, screens still partially hiding her from the rest of the ward. In the other beds, ancient women sniffed, groaned and snored. 'We only had a bed on geriatric,' the nurse said. Wonderful, thought Lucy. An old woman shuffled up to them, her yellowing scalp visible through thin strands of grey hair. Her cheeks were sunken, without teeth. The old woman placed a hand bent like a claw on Lucy's arm. 'Do you know who I am?' she said. 'Don't worry, Margaret,' said the nurse, patting her 'Back to bed, now.'

Lucy approached Annie's bed, hesitatingly. She had no idea what to say. Annie's face was turned away from her. She was still wearing the purple T-shirt. There was an overpowering smell of vomit and antiseptic.

'Annie,' Lucy said, softly. Slowly, Annie turned to her. Her face was alabaster, with a thin film of sweat. A tear welled in the corner of her eye and then slowly rolled, like a raindrop on a windowpane, down her cheek, onto the frayed white sheet. Lucy sat down carefully on the bed, on the yellow criss-crossed blankets, like baby blankets, she thought.

Annie said nothing, simply looked at her. Lucy reached up to stop another tear, which brimmed, then fell.

'I've seen you look better,' she said, quietly. Annie's hand moved, in slow motion, to wipe her eyes. 'Did they . . .' Her voice was barely audible, dry. She swallowed.

'Your mother's coming . . .' Lucy said. Annie grimaced. 'Here?' she said, looking at the row of hawking and spitting old dears. 'I can hardly wait.' Lucy laughed gently, and, reaching down, took Annie's hand. 'How do you feel?'

'How do you think I feel?' Annie whispered. 'I've had a tube like a garden hose down my throat and I've thrown up all the takeaways I've eaten for the last week. That pizza tasted bad enough first time round.' Lucy laughed. 'Why did you do it?' she said, softly.

Annie turned her face away and said nothing. 'I'm sorry,' Lucy said. 'I shouldn't have left you.'

'Did you sleep on the corridor?' Annie whispered.

'No, I made it to my room although God knows how. More ammunition for the mice, though. They'll get us drummed out.'

'Good,' said Annie. 'I hate that place. I'd love to have an excuse to leave.'

'We'd have to eat everything in the fridge first,' Lucy said. 'And use their shampoos.'

'And rip the labels off their coffee jars.'

'And fill the showers with naked men.'

'And kidnap their teddies.'

'And burn their fluffy slippers.'

'Put amphetamines in their sponge bags.'

'Stop,' said Lucy, giggling. Annie was giggling too, then suddenly she stopped. From down the corridor they could both hear the sharp tap, tap of high heels, and then a woman's loud voice, high-pitched, dominating and officious.

'Where is my daughter?'

'Oh fuck,' said Annie. 'Hide me.'

'How?' said Lucy. The next moment, the remaining screens were pulled away from the bed. Lucy was overwhelmed by a sharp gust of perfume. She got up.

'Darling!' Lucy moved slightly away. The woman bent over Annie, and Lucy saw an expensively navy-blue-suited back, a wing of sleek brown hair tucked behind one ear and large gold hooped earrings. Lucy moved to the end of the bed. 'Annie, I'll wait outside.'

'Don't go,' Annie said. The woman turned to Lucy.

It was Annie's face, perfectly made up, with just a hint of lines around the eyes. Her navy-blue Chanel suit was edged in cream, her legs silk-stockinged, long and thin like a racehorse, and her shoes navy leather with gold buckles. A black leather bag with a hooped 'C' clasp was leant against one of the legs of the bed. 'What an awful place,' she said loudly, looking round. Her voice was sharp enough to slice through paper. 'Couldn't they give you a private ward, darling? I'll

111

ask. You're so . . . exposed.' Her bony shoulders shivered.

'I'm not a priority,' said Annie.

'Well you should be, darling. Daddy will sort it out. He's coming up later, he's got a big case on today. Thank God Christianne said I could use their plane.' She brushed non-existent hairs off her skirt. 'Now, who's the consultant. Nurse,' she called loudly down the ward. Lucy could see Annie wince. 'Nurse! I need to speak to someone.' She turned back to Annie, smoothing her hair away from her forehead. 'That was so silly. What were you thinking of?'

'I'll go,' Lucy said. Annie reached up and grabbed her jumper. 'No, please, please don't. Mum, this is Lucy.' Annie's mother turned headlamp eyes on her, a thick line of black on her upper lids. Her deep red lipstick looked freshly applied.

'I'll come with you,' Annie's mother said. 'I need to find the person in charge around here. Darling, Daddy wants you to be flown to London. You can't stay here.'

'No!' Annie was horrified. 'I'm fine now, really, they've said I can go home later.'

'That's what I mean,' her mother said. 'You can come home. Where we can keep an eye on you.'

'You can't just parcel me up,' Annie said. 'I don't want to come to your house.'

'Darling,' Annie's mother's voice had taken on a dangerous edge. 'Let's not discuss it here, shall we, in front of strangers?' And, taking Lucy's arm, she led her off down the ward.

'Are you her special friend?' she said. Lucy wanted to take her arm away, but it was held in a vice-like grip. 'I suppose so,' she said slowly. 'Tell me,' Mrs Rosco said. 'Is it drugs? Again? You've no idea what we've been through with that girl. I can't face it all over again.

Her father will be furious – we're due in Meribel in two weeks. It couldn't have come at a worse time. Now someone will have to look after her. Really, she is so selfish. It's so inconvenient.'

Lucy looked at her in astonishment. She could have been talking about a traffic jam on the motorway. If this had happened to her, Caroline would have been sitting, holding her, and they would have both been crying. There wasn't a flicker of grief to disturb the made-up mask. 'And Alexandra, our youngest, she's due home from school tomorrow. What am I going to tell her? Her sister's a drug addict?'

'She isn't,' Lucy said. 'It just all got too much, I suppose.' She had to firmly resist the urge to add, 'Your letter didn't help.'

'Some boy,' her mother retorted. 'We've been there before, too.'

Lucy wanted to shake her clasping hand off, run back and drag Annie out of bed, yell for Rob, and run away.

As they reached the swing doors, Annie's mother suddenly stopped. Turning, Lucy saw the shuffling Margaret had a firm hold of her expensive leather handbag. 'Do you know who I am?' she whispered, her mouth, sticky with spit at the corners, only inches away from Mrs Rosco's face. 'Frankly, I have no idea, nor do I wish to. Please let go,' she said, and, pushing the doors firmly, they walked out of the ward, leaving the old woman staring at them through the window, further confusion flooding a world already awash with bewilderment. The lady had looked so nice. She was sure she could help. If only she could remember her name, they might let her go home.

Rob was walking down the corridor towards them. Lucy sighed with relief.

'Who's this person? The boyfriend?'

'He saved her,' Lucy said. 'He broke down the door.'

Mrs Rosco grimaced with distaste and, without even acknowledging Rob, turned away from them both, marching off down the corridor in search of authority.

'Who's the rich bitch?' Rob said, watching her streamlined figure disappear.

'Annie's mother,' said Lucy, sadly.

'No wonder she took an overdose. Could I see her?'

'Sure,' said Lucy. 'I don't think they'll mind.'

Lucy put her head round the door of the ward. 'Could I bring another friend in to see Annie?' she asked.

'Fine, as long as you're not long. She needs to rest.'

Rob and Lucy tiptoed up to the bed. The old women, at the sight of a man, drew their blankets tightly up to their chests. Rob grinned at them. 'Hello,' he said, cheerfully, to one old lady tucked up in bed wearing a pink woolly bedjacket. She raised a hand, darkened in patches with age spots, and waved at him.

Annie was lying with her back to them.

'Annie, this is Rob. He wanted to say hi. He found you. We bust your door.'

She heard Annie laugh, and then she turned over. Her face was still streaked with tears but her expression was interested. 'What a scandal I'll cause,' she said, not unhappily. She pushed herself into a sitting position. 'I don't quite know how to thank someone for saving my life. It's not something I've done before. Is there some kind of etiquette to it?'

Rob grinned, quite unembarrassed. 'You can do the same for me one day. But I warn you, it makes your shoulders hurt like bloody hell. Find an axe, if you can.'

'I'll remember,' Annie said, nodding gravely.

'Well,' he said, 'I'd better go. As long as you're OK. I'll leave you to it. See you again, maybe,' he said, looking at Lucy. 'Maybe,' Lucy said, feeling her face redden.

Lucy and Annie watched him lope off down the ward.

'I'm dying, and you're meeting amazing men?' Annie said. 'He is *stunning*. Why haven't we found him before? So deliciously dirty. What does he do?'

'History and Philosophy,' said Lucy, dreamily.

'Why haven't I seen him?' Annie demanded.

'Dunno. I don't think he goes out much. He plays in a band.'

At the bottom of the ward, Rob had paused. Annie and Lucy saw him engaged in earnest conversation with Margaret. Then, putting his arm round her, he led her back to her bed.

She sat down, a delighted smile like a sunflower on her lined face. She reached up for him, and kissed him on the cheek. They saw him smile and walk away. At the end of the room, he looked back at Lucy and Annie. Seeing they were watching him, he grinned. 'I'm in there,' he mouthed at Lucy, nodding in Margaret's direction.

'Wow,' Lucy said, sinking onto Annie's bed. 'Sod off,' said Annie, wriggling down under the sheets. 'I think I've just found the will to live.'

115

Chapter Nine

'I'd never been on a bus before I came to Manchester,'
Lucy said, peering down through the rain-drenched
window, as the wet streets of the city disappeared
beneath her in a grey blur of slippery pavements and
upturned umbrellas, people huddled underneath, bent
double like paper clips against the chill wind.

'How the hell,' Rob said, turning to face her, his arm
draped along the metal rim of the seat behind her
shoulders, 'have you lived your whole life without
sampling the delights of the double-decker?'

'Mum drove us everywhere,' Lucy said, grinning.

'You really haven't lived, have you?' he said, catching hold of the ends of the big red scarf which was
currently all the rage – when it rained you draped it up
over your head, flicking one end over your shoulder.
Slowly, he pulled her towards him, his dark eyes still
mocking. She closed hers in anticipation of a kiss.
When nothing happened, her eyes flew open – to see
he'd stopped just a few inches from her face. Her heart
was beating so wildly she had visions of it flying out of
her chest, like a budgie out of a cage. He stared at her,
not saying anything. Even sitting on a bus with him felt
exciting.

Rob didn't seem to live by normal rules, the rules she'd been taught to observe. She'd never met anyone who cared so little about what other people thought. Brought up to be acutely aware of what other people thought and conscious from an early age of all the little pitfalls and traps of society, she was thrilled by the fact he genuinely didn't give a toss. He ate in the streets. He usually met Lucy with hair which had plainly enjoyed a night of wild excess. He spat (which Lucy didn't like) and he talked to everyone in exactly the same way, from his professor to the street cleaner who asked him for a light. He had time for everyone, like the speaking clock.

Rob stared at her intently for a while, and then slumped back against the seat. He held up one hand, theatrically ticking off the points on his fingers. 'Let me get this straight. You've never been on a bus. You've never been in a betting shop. You've never eaten fish and chips – how can that be true? – and you've never had a Saturday job. Not even at Woollies? You,' he said, pulling her back against him, 'are spoiled rotten. What are you?' 'Spoiled rotten,' Lucy said obediently.

Rob had left a note pinned to the door of her halls which she found on returning from the hospital. It said, 'Meet me in the union bar at eight. Margaret has stood me up.' There was no name. She pulled the note off, and stood holding it for a while, before pushing open the door of her room. There she sank down onto her bed, exhausted. Most of her was full of worry for Annie, but, inside, there was a tiny glow-worm of happiness.

The hospital had said that Annie would need to stay in for the night, but Lucy could come and help her get home the next day. She'd thought about ringing the ward to tell Annie about the note, but reflected this would be a bit unfair.

Walking into the union bar, she saw Rob standing engaged in animated conversation with the barman. He was wearing faded black Levi's, big brown boots and a navy jumper with an enormous hole in the elbow. Over his arm was a scuffed black leather biker's jacket. He didn't look up until she was almost at his elbow. 'Hi,' she said, rather nervously. He took a long draught of his beer.

'I'm sorry, do I know you?' he said. 'I've never seen this woman before. Have you?' he enquired of the barman, who shook his head, grinning. 'Hang on,' he said, slapping his forehead. 'Now I remember. You ordered me to break a door down, didn't you?' Lucy smiled. 'That's me.' 'I told you she looked like trouble,' he said confidingly to the gay barman, who gazed back at him, quite besotted. Having bought Lucy a pint, he wheeled her round and they found somewhere to sit.

'How's your friend?' he asked, as they sat down.

'She was OK when you left,' said Lucy slowly, 'but then her bloody mother came back and started ordering everyone around and I think she's arranged to take Annie home the day after tomorrow. Don't know if she'll go – her family seem the pits. I just wish I could have done something more. I felt awful leaving her lying there.'

'Nothing you could have done,' Rob said briskly. 'I may be wrong, but I suspect your friend is a bit of a drama queen herself. Drink up. I've got free tickets for the Hacienda.'

She had thought Rob's biker jacket was purely for effect but no, he really did have a bike. It was very old, smelled strongly of oil and chunks of its paintwork seemed to be missing, but it was definitely a motor-bike. 'Put this on,' he said, as they reached it, their breath crystallized in the chilly December air. 'Do I have to?' said Lucy. He grinned at her. Putting the helmet on, Lucy felt like a spaceman. It felt very hot and smelt rather sweaty. 'Sorry if it pongs a bit,' Rob shouted over his shoulder. 'My mate Eddie had it on last and he's not great on personal hygiene. You OK?' Lucy nodded, through the thick visor. 'You have to take the . . .' He reached over and tapped her visor. 'You have to lift this up to talk.' 'What?' she shouted.

On the bike, he took hold of her arms and wrapped them firmly round his waist. Nervously, she shuffled up the bike until she was pressed close up against him. It was all a bit intimate, but thoughts of embarrassment shot out the window once he'd fired the engine up. 'Bloody hell,' Lucy found herself shouting into her helmet, as they whipped off through the wet streets. It was terrifying. After a few minutes she found it was best not to look and buried her astronaut head in his shoulder. He had nice shoulders for such a purpose. They arrived in what felt to Lucy like ten seconds. He abruptly screeched to a halt, and, gently leaning the bike onto its rest, he climbed off. Lucy sat for a moment, dazed. The experience had been rather like being sucked out of an aeroplane window at ten thousand feet. As she climbed off, she found her legs were extremely wobbly, and she hung onto Rob's arm for support. She slowly pulled off her helmet, and shook out her hair, which felt sticky and sweaty at the front. Her skirt had ridden up so high the gusset of her tights was plainly visible. Hastily, she tugged the hem down. Stilettos, she decided, were not the thing to wear on a motorbike. She hadn't noticed while they were hurtling through the dark streets at the speed of sound, but one of her heels had been pressed up against the hot exhaust and had now melted into a stump. Oh, brilliant. Now she would have to hobble about like Jake the Peg with his extra leg.

The club was hot, sweaty, and incredibly exciting. But not the place for an intimate conversation. Whenever Rob spoke to her, Lucy yelled 'What? Sorry?' and had to lean close to his mouth to hear anything. Rob seemed to know masses of people, and after a wander round the club they ended up in the bar with a group of his mates, who Lucy discovered were all in the same band. Because she couldn't hear anything she spent all night nodding and smiling. They must have thought she was a deaf mute, she decided. It was also hard in that they were all so tall, they had to bend down to hear anything she said. It was almost more effort than it was worth. She was happy standing there hearing what she could of their banter, but Rob kept trying to get rid of them.

Eventually, at midnight, she and Rob were sitting on a bench eating Kentucky Fried Chicken, Lucy wearing Rob's jacket on top of her own. In the relative quiet, she discovered Rob came from a small town in Lancashire called Darwen. His father had just lost his job as a printer after a row between the unions and the newspaper bosses, who had sacked almost everyone from Rob's dad's department overnight, and moved the printing to a non-union firm. Rob was extremely bitter about it, and Lucy sensed he idolized his father. A month after the sackings, his father had had a stroke. His mum, who had worked as a school secretary, had given up her job to care for him. Rob had one sister, Claire, still at his former comprehensive. He wanted to be a journalist if he couldn't be a rock star. He played guitar and sang lead vocals with a student punk band called Rubbish.

'We're playing a gig tomorrow at Rafters on Deansgate. D'you want to come?' he said.

'What about Annie?' Lucy said.

'Bring her,' he said, shrugging.

At one, he delivered her back to St Margaret's. Lucy felt a bit queasy from the fried chicken and the smell of bike oil. She also felt a tiny bit in love.

'D'you want to come then, tomorrow?' he asked casually, running his hands through his thick dark hair after taking off his helmet. Lucy, whose thighs were burning as if clamped around hot coals, urgently needed a bath. But she didn't want to say goodnight. 'Don't expect anything. We're really useless,' he said, grinning. Lucy said, 'I'll come. We'll come. Goodnight, then.' She paused. He made no move to kiss her. 'See you,' he said, getting back onto his bike. 'By the way, your hair suits you like that.' Lucy's hand flew up to her forehead. Oh God. Part of her fringe was sticking up like TinTin.

At ten the next morning Lucy went in to collect Annie. She pushed through the swing doors, to be met immediately by Margaret. 'I'm Margaret,' she said, happily. 'Look.' Lucy saw a large name tag had been pinned to her mothy dressing gown. 'I'm going home next week, now I know who I am.' She shuffled off, twittering contentedly, her worn mules slapping on the lino floor. 'Great,' Lucy called after her. 'I'm so pleased.'

Annie was not in her bed. It was neatly made, with new, frayed but clean sheets tucked under the blanket. 'Your friend's gone,' said the woman in the opposite bed. 'Her mother took her home.' Oh shit. It was the last thing Annie wanted.

Presumably her mother had just overpowered her. Lucy pressed her hand against the newly made bed, which now bore no sign of Annie's drama. The crisis of life and death became just another bed to be made up. Hospitals were weird places. Turning, she wandered back down the ward in search of a nurse. She found one, bending over a sheaf of notes at the desk by the door.

'Um,' Lucy began, not quite sure what to say. 'My friend, Annie, Anna Rosco, she was in the end bed, she isn't here? Do you know where she's gone? I was supposed to bring her home this morning.'

The nurse looked up, sharply. 'Her father came first thing. They were flying her back to London for specialist treatment.'

'Oh.' Lucy hopped from foot to foot. 'Did they say which hospital?' 'I have no idea,' said the nurse, brusquely. 'Are you family?' 'No,' said Lucy. 'Just a friend.'

She started to leave, and then turned. 'I'm so pleased about Margaret,' she said.

'What?' said the nurse, looking puzzled. 'Margaret, over there,' Lucy said, nodding in the old woman's direction, who was now piling the contents of her locker onto her bed. 'Going home.' The nurse looked at Lucy kindly. 'She isn't going home,' she said.

Three days later, Lucy's parents arrived to take her home for Christmas. The night before she was due to leave, she and Rob slept together. It was after another of his gigs, where Lucy had stood, squashed and immensely hot, at the side of the stage while Rob belted out incomprehensible, shouty lyrics and the rest of the band hopped around the slippery stage on one leg. Lucy could not perceive any particular notes or even a tune of any sort, but Rob had undeniable charisma. She noticed that the front row of frantically pogoing students was primarily girls. The concert was punctuated by ear-splitting feedback howls, and after an hour Lucy staggered out into the fresh air, not sure she could take any more. Maybe she wasn't cut out to be a groupie.

Thankfully, she heard the last painful note die away, like a wounded cat being dragged off into the distance. She pushed the fire door of the hall open, and the heat of the concert hit her once more. Rob jumped off the stage, pushed through the crowd, looking for her.

'Rob!' she yelled from the corridor. 'Here.' He walked towards her, dripping. He was wearing a black ripped T-shirt, which was wringing with sweat, and his hair was soaked. He shook it out of his eyes, and smiled at her. Even in such a state, he was heart-stopping. 'How were we?' he asked. 'Awful,' said Lucy, smiling. 'Haircut One Hundred you were not. It was like listening to a road accident.' 'Excellent,' he said. 'Exactly the effect I was aiming to achieve. Can I use your shower?'

They rode on Rob's bike back to Lucy's halls. So far, in one week, Rob had kissed her precisely twice. The first time was on their second date, when on saying goodbye he'd leaned silently forward, and, without touching her, kissed her softly on the lips. She had leaned forward, wanting more, but he'd pulled back and sped off. Either he didn't fancy her, he was playing very hard to get or he was having an affair with the fat barman. The second time, they were walking together through the quad after Rob had met her from a lecture. Chatting casually about their mornings, he'd suddenly stopped and, holding her shoulders, swivelled her round to face him. 'Give us a snog,' he said, and then, bending his head in front of an assorted crowd of fellow students, kissed her full on the mouth. But then nothing else. It was all very confusing.

When they got back to the halls, Lucy hustled Rob in through the door. There was a rule that men weren't allowed to stay in your room overnight, which obviously she had flouted with Max, but thought she'd better not push her luck by making a song and dance about it. They scooted up the stairs, Lucy pushing Rob ahead of her. He burst loudly into 'London's Burning'. Lucy shushed him furiously. In her room, she handed him a pink bath towel and her soap. He sniffed it. 'I am going to be popular down the gents' bogs,' he said, and, with a wink, disappeared with Lucy's floral sponge bag over one arm.

She sat on the bed in a fever of indecision. What now? Tomorrow she was due to go home and face Max and presumably be Max's girlfriend, but she couldn't bear the thought of sleeping with him when her heart was too full of Rob, but what if Rob didn't really want her? Then she'd end up with no-one. Max's photo beamed out from the wall. She hastily peeled it off. Goodness, he did look healthy. And good-looking. Next to Max, Rob seemed so dissolute. But sexy, with his long dark hair, white skin and eyes almost black in colour. And his earring. Normally, Lucy didn't like men with earrings but on Rob it just looked right, like a punk gypsy.

There was a soft knock on her door. 'I've had a bit of an incident,' he hissed, as he slid back inside, Lucy's pink towel tied precariously round his hips. His body was long, pale and damp with thick dark hair on his chest, descending in a dark line into the towel. Max, with his blondness, was almost hairless. She could think of going to bed with Rob as a kind of anthropological experiment. 'What kind of incident?' Lucy said, feeling laughter bubble up inside her. 'I forgot to close the shower curtain.' He held up his clothes, which were now a sodden black mess.

'That's OK,' said Lucy, carefully. 'You can stay here.'

'Are you sure?' He looked at her seriously.

'Yes, I'm sure,' she said, sliding Max's photo under the duvet.

'Have you got any cards?' he asked.

'What?'

'Cards,' he said. 'Or games? Monopoly, Cluedo? I like Cluedo.'

'Funnily enough,' said Lucy, 'I haven't.'

'Shame,' he said. 'We'll have to think of something else to do. Could you lend me a jumper? I'm freezing.' Lucy, without looking at him, handed him her biggest sweatshirt. It was Max's.

'Thanks.' He lay down on her bed.

'Can I ask you something?' Lucy said.

'Sure,' Rob said, his eyes closed.

'Do you find me attractive?'

'I quite fancied you with your hair sticking up,' he said.

She punched him on the arm. 'It's just, you haven't, you don't seem . . .' She wriggled with embarrassment.

'What?' he said, enjoying her discomfort. 'All over you? Why should I be? You've got a silly name and you've never been on a bus. And you think Haircut One Hundred are better than us.'

Lucy reached out to light a cigarette.

'I've got a bottle of wine in the wardrobe.'

'But have you got a corkscrew?'

'No,' she admitted. 'Can you push the cork in?'

Rob sat up on the bed, took firm hold of the neck of the bottle and pushed hard. Nothing happened. He pushed harder. The cork suddenly gave way and a stream of red wine exploded over Lucy's duvet. 'What will my mother say?' she said, trying to sponge it up with the towel Rob had dropped. He caught hold of her hands. 'OK,' he said. 'I give in. You can ravish me.'

'Not sure I want to now,' said Lucy. 'You're all sticky.'

Making love with Rob was a quite different experience from sleeping with Max. With him, Lucy felt she had to perform in some way, as if she had to appear more sexy than she really was. With Rob, she didn't have to pretend. He was incredibly intense, and far more concerned with pleasing her than Max ever was. It meant much more. It felt like the beginnings of a dangerous addiction.

Chapter Ten

'Lucy!' Helen called up the stairs. 'It's for you. I think it's Max.'

Lucy, who'd been sitting at the desk in her bedroom trying to think of something original to say about Swift and failing – she thought *Gulliver's Travels* was the silliest book she'd ever read, matched only in the boredom factor by Milton's *Paradise Lost* – started guiltily. She'd meant to ring him soon after she got home for Christmas, but every time she picked up the phone she had the most vivid mental picture of herself in bed with Rob, and thought this might inhibit her conversation somewhat so she gave up.

Helen had been insufferable ever since she came home, having acquired some aphid of a boyfriend at the boys' school near to her school, who by chance also lived in the vicinity. He rang her all the time, unlike the silent Rob, and arrived to take her out in his daddy's Austin Princess. Lucy wouldn't have been seen dead in a car that looked like a slice of chocolate cake. He was called Will and he had lots of teeth. It was Donny Osmond all over again, in a tweed jacket.

Caroline had swathed the thick oak banisters in natural foliage from the garden – in fact the whole house looked like an upmarket version of Santa's grotto, with lots of white candles, tartan bows and greenery. Ben was in disgrace because he'd chased the cat up the Christmas tree and Caroline's perfect *Homes and Gardens* edifice had toppled over.

'Darling!' Max's confident tones oozed down the phone. 'Thank God you're home. I'm bored fucking stiff. If I have to accompany my mother around any more shops I will scream. Fancy a night of wild excess down the pub?'

Lucy mentally sighed. She wasn't sure she could cope with seeing him, but anything was better than sitting next to a silent phone. For the first time in her life, she felt obsessively jealous. Who was Rob with? Who were his friends? She knew literally nothing about his life at home, although he questioned her endlessly about hers, primarily for the purpose of taking the mick.

When her parents arrived to pick her up, she'd lugged all her stuff down into the front hall because he was still in her bed, smoking a roll-up and reading Wordsworth. He'd kissed her goodbye almost absent-mindedly. 'Will you ring?' Lucy said. 'My number's on the table.' 'Mm,' he said, not looking up.

'I'm going,' she said.

'Bye,' he said.

'Bye,' said Lucy, lingering by the door, clutching a heavy suitcase full of washing.

'Great sex,' he murmured. He looked at her over the top of his book. 'We must do it again, if you're free.'

'That would be lovely,' Lucy said, politely.

'Merry Christmas,' he said, and, putting the book down, snuggled himself back down under the duvet.

'Merry Christmas to you,' said Lucy, smiling as he pulled the duvet up so that only tufts of his hair were visible.

She was halfway down the stairs when she heard him call out, very loudly for the benefit of her entire corridor, 'I hope you still respect me.'

When Max rang the old pull doorbell, Lucy had to swallow hard and steel herself before she opened it. She smoothed her hands down her long black velvet skirt. The goth look was just coming in, and towards the end of term everyone had been going round like the cast of *Zombie: The Living Dead*.

Cautiously, she opened the door. Max was standing in a pool of light, the snow, which was just starting to fall, resting gently on his hair. He looked like a Christmas card. All he needed was a big white ruff and a chorister's outfit. Lucy, although she felt quite prepared to resist him, was taken aback by his golden beauty. What the hell was she doing? Why was she lusting after a mad biker who played in an awful punk band and swore all the time? And not only did he swear, he made her feel constantly wrong-footed and he was exceedingly cheeky about her hair.

'Can I come in? It's freezing out here.'

'Of course.' Lucy shook herself out of her reverie. He stepped into the dim light of the porch, brushing aside a branch of the wisteria, which framed the heavy oak door in its bare winter clothing. He reached out and gently put his hand under her chin, lifting her face to his. 'I've missed you so much,' he said. And, putting his arms round her, he kissed her gently on the mouth. Lucy felt that her deceit must be written all over her face.

'Come in,' she said, and, attempting to hold back a

delirious Ben with one hand, she ushered him into the hall. Caroline had brought out the heavy pewter candle stands, which illuminated the hall like a cathedral. The oak floor, buffed to a gleaming finish by their daily, reflected the amber glow of the flickering candles. Every time she walked down the stairs, Lucy felt she ought to burst into 'Ave Maria'.

Caroline, on hearing the door close, emerged silkily from the drawing room.

'Max, darling,' she said. 'How lovely to see you. How is your mother?'

'Equalling the national debt of Brazil,' said Max, smiling. 'Santa won't need a sleigh to deliver our presents, he'll need a lorry.'

'Don't be naughty,' said Caroline, looking fondly at him. Why did Lucy look so stricken? 'How's your father?' Caroline enquired, brightly. 'We saw him on *Newsnight* last night. He was marvellous. That interviewer was so rude.'

'Was he?' said Max, politely. If possible, he tended to ignore his father's career, only bringing it out like a trump card when absolutely essential. When he'd been going through his rebellious sixth-form years with the long hair and Afghan coat, he had always played down the fact that his father was a Tory MP, and now seemed likely to become a Minister. At Bristol, however, he found it gave him quite a bit of kudos. Lucy had always previously just taken it for granted that that was what George did. When Max had come up to Manchester, she'd been terrified that the truth would be somehow revealed, as being the son of a Tory MP was just about equivalent among her friends to being the son of the anti-Christ.

'Come and have a drink with Archie,' Caroline said. Lucy's father greeted Max with the same air of beaming bonhomie. Lucy tried to picture Rob in the same situation and failed. Oh where was he, what was he doing? She felt like a train which had comfortably trundled down a certain set of tracks for years, and now someone had flicked a switch and sent her careering off into the sidings.

Lucy, studying Max closely, watched as he charmed her parents with carefully edited tales of his university term, the occasional self-deprecating remark about how little work he was doing, and comments specifically designed to please. He told Caroline how beautiful the house looked, and asked Archie about the state of the stock market. He was so effortless, Lucy thought, looking at him lounging elegantly on their black leather sofa, one hand clasped round a glass of red wine, asking Caroline if she minded him smoking, laughing at Archie's jokes and absent-mindedly stroking Ben. He looked so comfortable, so absolutely right, she asked herself what the hell she was doing. Her parents so clearly adored him, he was perfect in every way, so why on earth was she finding him so irritating? Why did she see his charm as being somehow synthetic, manufactured, as if he was really bored stiff but going effortlessly through the motions? I don't know you, she thought, suddenly. I don't know what's underneath all that charm and nice-ness. And I don't know if there's anything real at the centre of you, as if everything is on the surface, chip the veneer and there's nothing underneath. But then she told herself she was being unfair. He was really good company, she almost always had a good time with him. But he seemed so *conventional*. Just think-ing about Rob made her want to faint with a kind of dark longing.

*   *   *

131

The next morning, two days before Christmas, she was lying in bed at midday, groaning, with a hangover so intense she felt she was wearing an iron hat. She'd been out with Max the night before to a party at one of his friends' houses, which had ended up with them all swimming at midnight in an indoor pool. This had seemed a good idea at the time but, as Lucy discovered, when you hit the water drunk you came out drunker, and Max, who'd also been pissed as a rat, had driven her home and then literally poured her through the door. She knew Max would have slept in his car, pretending to have stayed over because if Annabelle knew he'd driven she would have been furious. The family, now George was getting to be a big noise, was extremely sensitive about such matters and Max had been given endless lectures about not letting them down. The old Max would have said 'bollocks' and carried on, but the new Bristol Max took grave note.

Lucy lay in bed, quite still, knowing that if she lay here long enough Caroline, exasperated at her inactivity, would bring her up a cup of tea. Then she heard an unfamiliar sound, like the humming of a thousand angry bees. Not a car engine, she thought, more like a – motorbike. A bike? She sat up in bed. Downstairs, she heard the doorbell ring. Heaving herself out of bed, she padded to the door, wearing only an old shirt of her father's. She heard her mother's voice saying, 'But we're not expecting a delivery.'

Then a voice, just a low murmur, saying something in return which clearly made her mother hesitate. Who? Lucy ran into the bathroom, which overlooked the front of the house. There, leaning against one of their outhouses, was a familiar sight, its paint dropping off to reveal bare metal patches, oil dripping onto the immaculate gravel drive. Lucy fell back from the window and leant against the wall, feeling dizzy.

'You're what?' Lucy could hear floating up the stairs the polite tones her mother reserved for strangers. 'A friend of Lucy's?' Lucy ran back into her bedroom, clutching her throbbing head, and hastily pulled on a pair of jeans. Peering in the mirror, she groaned at the sight of her face, pale and slightly sweaty, with great black panda-eyes because she'd forgotten to take off her mascara. She splashed water on her face in the sink in her bedroom, and dragged a brush through her hair. No time to clean her teeth – her mother could well have frogmarched Rob out of the house by then. Grabbing a jumper, she tore down the stairs and through the kitchen.

Her mother was standing with her back to Lucy, holding the door ajar. One hand, pale and perfectly manicured with pink nail varnish, her ruby engagement ring nearly as big as a quail's egg, glittered against the rim of the door. Lucy almost ran into her.

'Lucy! Be careful,' her mother said. 'This – person – says he's a friend. Were you expecting anyone?'

'I didn't think I was,' said Lucy, smiling. Over her mother's shoulder she saw Rob, clutching his helmet. He was dressed from head to toe in black leather.

'Hi,' she said

'I'm sorry,' Caroline said, carefully. 'I don't think we've been introduced.'

'Mum,' said Lucy, as Caroline stood aside so they were both framed in the doorway. 'This is Rob, a friend from university.'

'Hello,' said Caroline, giving Rob one of her charming smiles. 'I'm sorry I wasn't more welcoming. It's just, Lucy hadn't told us to expect . . .' 'It's OK,' said Rob. 'She didn't know I was coming.'

'Do come in,' said Caroline. Lucy, who was fighting back a desperate urge to laugh, reached forward to take his helmet. They had a brief tussle, which Lucy won. Rob pulled off his long gloves, which Lucy also took. He stepped heavily into the porch. 'You'd better take off your boots,' Lucy hissed. Rob reached down and unzipped them, leaning back against the door frame to pull them off. He had a large hole in the toe of one of his socks, through which a long pale toe protruded.

'Would you like a coffee?' said Caroline, with her back to them, reaching up to take a couple of mugs down from the hooks on the dresser.

'I'd love a beer,' Rob said.

'A beer. Lucy, do you think you could look in the drinks cupboard? I think Daddy bought some for the Christmas Eve party. They'll be at the back. The beer glasses are on the top shelf.'

'A can will be fine,' said Rob. 'I just want something to cool me down. It gets really hot on the bike, even though it's so cold.'

'Really,' said Caroline, looking at the heavy scuffed jacket Rob was now unzipping.

'May I use your toilet?'

'The loo,' said Lucy, 'is just through the door.'

'I'll pop off to the *loo*, then,' Rob said, and, draping his jacket over one of the stripped-pine kitchen chairs surrounding the old refectory table, he brushed past Lucy. As he walked out, she caught a gust of his smell. He smelt of hot leather, the outside air and cigarettes. It made her quite sick with longing.

Her mother turned, her entire face a question. 'Really, Lucy,' she said, very quietly. 'You know I'm up to my ears at the moment, with this party tomorrow and then Christmas Day drinks and the family coming.

I can't,' she lowered her voice even further, 'cope with having people to stay. Especially people I don't know. It was very thoughtless of you.'

'I didn't invite him,' Lucy whispered back. 'I had no idea he was coming. Just be nice,' she pleaded.

'I've never even heard you mention him,' Caroline said. 'What's his name?' 'Rob,' Lucy hissed, as she heard the sound of the loo flushing and the door opening and closing.

'Thanks,' Rob said, taking the cold beer out of Lucy's hand. He removed the ring pull, flicked it onto the table and sat down contentedly, taking a long draught. 'That's better.' Lucy saw her mother staring at the ring pull. Ring pulls didn't just lie on tables, they were put immediately in waste bins. Lucy reached forward and snatched it up. 'Have you come far?' said Caroline, lifting the heavy Aga kettle off its ring and making coffee for herself and Lucy.

'Lancashire,' Rob said.

'Lancashire?' Caroline said. 'This morning?'

'Yeh,' said Rob, leaning back in his chair. 'I was bored at home so I thought I'd visit Lucy.'

'I didn't know you knew where I lived,' Lucy said, astonished. 'Asked the warden,' said Rob, casually. 'They always have forwarding addresses for post. I spoke to him on the day you left.' Lucy's eyes flew up and caught Rob's gaze. He looked steadily at her, grinning. 'You don't mind, do you?'

'Not at all,' said Lucy. 'Not at all. It's – super – to see you.'

'And it's *super* to see you,' he said, holding her gaze. Caroline, standing by the sink, intercepted the look. Goodness, she thought. Then she shook herself. He couldn't be a boyfriend. What about Max?

'Do you mind if I smoke?' Rob said, reaching into the

pocket of his jacket, slung over the back of the chair, for his tin.

'No,' said Caroline. But she flicked on the air-conditioning switch above the Aga, which hummed loudly.

Rob placed his old battered yellow and green tin on the table and took off the lid. Inside was his usual litter of Rizla papers, a red packet of tobacco, and, Lucy could see, a small decaying lump of dope.

Caroline, carrying two steaming cups of coffee, placed one in front of Lucy and sat down with hers. She glanced nervously at the clock. She was due at the hairdresser's in half an hour, but for some reason she felt loath to leave Lucy alone. There had been enough electricity in that gaze to light Burford High Street. Even with his hair damp with sweat and that awful old sweatshirt he was wearing, he exuded a sexuality so potent Caroline could almost smell it.

'Which part of Lancashire are you from?' she asked pleasantly.

'Darwen,' Rob said. Caroline looked blank, then recovered swiftly.

'I've heard parts of Lancashire are very pretty. We know some people in Lancashire, don't we, darling?' Caroline said, turning to Lucy. 'The Chambers, they live near Clitheroe. That's not far from you, is it? Do you know them? They're a lovely family.'

'No,' said Rob, smiling. 'I don't believe I do.'

Caroline, whose antennae told her she was being very gently mocked, blushed. She floundered slightly. 'Which course are you doing? Lucy seems very impressed with the university.'

'History and Philosophy,' Rob said. Lucy saw her mother wince slightly at the 'philosophy'. Philosophy scared her a bit, and, in her day, joint honours were rather second best.

'And your family?' she continued. 'Does your father work in Darwen?' She pronounced the name of the town as if it were in Outer Mongolia.

'Not any more,' Rob said bluntly. 'He was sacked. He's been ill, too.'

'Oh,' said Caroline, trying to be bright. 'Well, Lucy's daddy's pretty near to retirement, isn't he, darling? I don't know what we'll do with him under our feet all day.'

'Now,' she added, getting up, 'I had better be going. Hairdresser's.' She ran her hand through her immaculate hair. 'Darling, can you make sure the dog's in if you go out and tell Mrs Hodges her money's on the dresser, and she needn't come tomorrow. There's some quiche in the fridge and fresh bread and cheese in the larder if you're both hungry.' She disappeared and then came back a few moments later, pulling on her camel coat. She held out her hand to Rob. 'It was lovely to meet you,' she said. 'I'd love to be able to ask you to stay but I'm afraid we're a bit hectic at the moment. Perhaps another time?'

Rob stubbed out his roll-up. Without getting up, he held out his hand. 'I'm sure we'll meet again.' Caroline, looking up, caught the mirth in his eyes. He's very sure of himself, she thought. Glancing back, she intended to say goodbye to Lucy. But she saw that her daughter, normally so laid-back and unruffled, was gazing at him with a passionate intensity Caroline had never seen on her face before.

After the front door had slammed shut, Rob leant forward across the table.

'You don't mind me turning up?' he said, softly. 'I

was just bored at home and I fancied a spin on the bike.'

'From Lancashire to here?' Lucy said, laughing.

'Not far down the motorway,' Rob countered, 'with a prevailing wind.'

'Be honest,' Lucy said. 'You missed me.'

'Might have,' said Rob, grinning. 'Or maybe I just wanted to see how the other half live.'

'And how do we?'

'Dunno,' he said. 'I've only seen the servants' quarters so far. Can you take me to the dungeons?'

Mrs Hodges wandered in, untying her blue and yellow floral pinny. 'I'll just put away the Hoover, Mrs B.,' she said, not looking round. 'And then I'll be off, if you don't mind. We've got an afternoon do at the village hall. Thanks so much for the lovely cake. You shouldn't have bothered.'

'Your money's on the dresser,' Lucy said. 'Mum's gone out. She said don't bother to come tomorrow with it being Christmas Eve. We can manage.'

Mrs Hodges walked over to the dresser, and picked up the envelope. 'But she's paid me double,' she said, opening it. 'Lucy, your mother's a one and no mistake. Oh,' she said, seeing Rob for the first time. 'I'm sorry. I didn't know you had company. I'll get off.' She started to pull on her grey mac.

'I'll give you a lift,' Rob said.

'What, dear?'

'I'll give you a lift,' he repeated more loudly. 'On my bike.'

Mrs Hodges walked over to the window and, looking out, saw the sorry lump of metal. 'On that thing?' she said. 'I don't think so!'

'Are you sure?' Rob said. 'I'm quite happy.'

'Thanks, love,' she said. 'I'll walk. I'm only halfway through the village. The exercise will do me good.'

She opened the door, and with a cheerful 'Bye-bye, Lucy, love', she disappeared.

Lucy and Rob could hear her chuckling down the drive. They looked at each other and burst out laughing.

'What is it with you and older women?' Lucy said.

'Dunno,' Rob said. 'Just a knack.'

'What am I going to do with you?'

'I can think of a few things,' he said. 'How long's your mum going to be at the hairdresser's?'

'Why?' said Lucy, feigning innocence.

'I fancy a quick game of Cluedo,' he said.

'I'll go and look in the old toy box,' Lucy said. But she didn't get that far.

Chapter Eleven

'Annie?' Lucy knocked hesitantly on the door of her room. Lucy had been back two days but there was no sign of Annie, just a new door with shiny metal hinges. Lucy sighed. Maybe she wasn't coming back. She'd tried to ring Annie several times in the holidays but had only got the Filipina maid. Surely Annie would have let her know if she wasn't coming back?

'She's still not back,' she said to Rob, who was lounging on her bed. He'd more or less moved into her room this term. It was lovely to have him there, but the room, designed for half a person, did not comfortably accommodate two. They could both only stand upright if one of them stood in the wardrobe. Fortunately Rob brought with him almost no possessions save his bike helmet.

Annie eventually returned a week after the beginning of term. Lucy, glancing out of her window, caught sight of her unmistakable hair. She raced down the stairs two at a time.

'Where have you been?' she demanded, angrily. 'I've been worried sick. Did you get my messages?'

'Nope,' said Annie. She seemed somewhat subdued, as if someone had turned out the light. 'We only got back from Meribel yesterday.'

'How was it?' said Lucy, alarmed at Annie's lack of spark.

'White,' said Annie. 'White and cold and full of my parents' friends. I have been toted around like a freak for the past three weeks and if anyone else asks me how I'm feeling I'll be sick on their shoes. I think it's become a badge of privilege, to have a reformed drug-addict daughter. No upper-class family is complete without a child in rehab,' she added, savagely. 'At least I haven't disappointed them in one way.'

'I'm glad you're back. I've missed you.' Annie flashed a grateful look. 'At least someone cares,' she said, bitterly.

'I need a good strong drink,' she said, as she lugged her bags up the stairs. 'My bloody mother has been watching me like a hawk every time I've poured myself a drop of wine, despite the fact that she swills gin like the Queen Mother.'

'I've got some vodka in my room.'

'Lead on.'

Lucy pushed open the door of her room, and Rob, who had been lying dozing on the bed as usual – he did an alarming amount of sleeping – started.

'Hi,' Annie said, clearly surprised.

'Annie, you remember Rob,' said Lucy, like a society hostess.

'How could I forget? I see you two got it together,' she added, dumping one of her bags on the floor.

'You could say that.' Lucy and Rob exchanged looks of pure intimacy. After Rob had roared off on his bike, she'd spent the rest of Christmas in a sea of bliss. Max, fortunately, had been whisked off to Verbier skiing

141

with his parents, protesting, but not very much, soon after Christmas. He asked Lucy if she wanted to come, but she said she had too much work to do.

Annie took a big swig of vodka, and coughed. 'I'm going to give this up,' she said, holding the glass away from her and peering at its contents. 'It's poison. I've decided to become a teetotaller vegan.' Rob and Lucy looked at her in astonishment. 'Who is he?' Lucy said.

Annie grinned at her. 'Rollo,' she said.

'Rolo?' said Rob. 'The chocolates?' Lucy sighed. Annie ignored him.

'I met him in Meribel,' she said. 'He's a ski guide – well, he will be eventually. At the moment he's cleaning chalets. He's a health-food nut, won't put anything poisonous in his body. He's a former addict – he went to Eton,' she explained, as if the two were synonymous. 'So we have something in common, which is nice,' she added, ironically.

'But is *he* nice?' said Lucy, handing Rob a glass of vodka and orange juice, poured straight from the carton and full of orangey bits.

'Not really,' said Annie, quite happily, resting her feet on one of her bags. 'He's still pretty screwed-up and my mum hates him, so that's fine.'

'We have to go to this.'

Rob was standing with his arm round Lucy, in front of a poster on the door of the students' union. 'Anti Poll Tax Federation Demo,' it said. 'Coaches leave at 7 p.m., Friday.'

'Why?' said Lucy. She wasn't very sure that demonstrations were really her. She wasn't a great one for public demonstrations – she felt embarrassed doing the hokey-cokey.

'Because it matters,' Rob said. 'We can't just let

142

Maggie walk all over everyone. My mum and dad would have to pay four times what they're paying now on the rates. They just can't afford it. It isn't fair, is it, that your mum and dad and my mum and dad should have to pay the same amount?'

'No,' Lucy admitted. 'But where will we sleep?'

'There's not much of the gypsy in you, is there?' said Rob, laughing.

'OK,' said Lucy, stung. 'I'll go. What about asking Annie?'

'Mrs Macrobiotic?' said Rob. 'I suppose if we can get her away from the lentils long enough, she might come,' he said.

Annie, true to her word, had given up drugs and alcohol. She said it was for ever, but Rob and Lucy were laying bets about how long it would last. Always one to go the whole hog, she'd also given up eating white bread, meat, dairy products and wearing anything that could be remotely linked to the animal kingdom. Lucy now knew when Annie was approaching her room because of the slap, slap of her raffia sandals. She existed on a disgusting mixture permanently bubbling and seething to itself on the hob in the common room of orange lentils, soya beans and tofu. It looked, and smelt, like dog sick. Her clothes, always Bohemian, were now entirely composed of woolly jumpers from a craft stall in the open market and floor-length batik-print skirts. A miasma of joss sticks floated out from under her bedroom door, like the Great Fog of London. She had also had one ear pierced five times and was the first person, she claimed, in the entire city of Manchester to have her nose pierced. Small children pointed at her in the street.

* * *

On the Saturday morning Lucy woke cramped, stiff and very cold. She, Annie, Rob and a group of their friends had kipped down on Euston station. They'd been moved on about four times in the night, and now Lucy was desperate for a hot bath and a steaming cup of coffee. Every joint ached, and she knew that drinking extra strong lager had been a bad idea at the time. Even worse, in retrospect, as the pale light of the spring dawn filtered through the windows.

'I need to wash,' she moaned to Rob. 'Bogs over there,' he said.

'You *do* know how to show a girl a good time,' Lucy said, sliding her cramped legs out of her sleeping bag. She wrapped her second-hand suede jacket more tightly around her. The loos were full of girls, cleaning their teeth and splashing their faces with water. There was an air of cheerful comradeship, and everyone in sight sported 'No to the poll tax' badges.

By about eleven, the protesters had begun to gather in Kennington Park. The day, after a misty start, was now sunny and there was the air of a festival, with vendors selling ice creams and hot dogs from vans and stalls.

'Bloody hell,' said Rob. 'I never thought there'd be this many people. Look, if we get lost, we'll meet up at Euston at about eight. OK?' 'Sure,' said Annie, looking about her with excited eyes. This was much more thrilling than the demo she'd arranged against animal experimentation outside Piccadilly station.

'Maggie, Maggie, Maggie, out, out, out!' began the cry, which rippled out into the crowd like the circles on a pond. Lucy held tight to Rob's hand. He smiled down at her, his face too alight with excitement. 'You'll be fine,' he said. 'Just stick close to me.'

During the morning, the air of festivity prevailed.

Steel bands played, and people were dancing, or lying about in the park getting stoned in the warm sunshine. Lucy began to think protesting was quite a lark. It was nice to be part of a such a large, peaceful demonstration. If they weren't prepared to take a stand, as students, then who would? She felt her breast swelling with righteous pride. What a social conscience she had.

At about one, the march set off. Rob and Lucy had already lost Annie, sucked away amidst the swirling maelstrom of people. The cries among the crowds had now changed to 'We won't pay the poll tax! Na na na na!' A man dressed as Mrs Thatcher harangued the crowds with a megaphone. The atmosphere was still relatively light-hearted, and Lucy enjoyed bowling towards Trafalgar Square, chanting along, smiling at the people with children. All along the route, there were earnest-looking people selling *Socialist Worker*. Rob took a copy and stuffed it into his jacket.

By three, most of the crowd had arrived in Trafalgar Square. Lucy and Rob were miles away from the stage, but the speeches by Tony Benn and another left-wing MP were loud enough to bring roars of approval from the crowd. Lucy cheered too. Everything they said made perfect sense. She felt so proud to be supporting such a just cause. Some ten minutes later, rumours began to ebb and flow through the crowd. There was trouble in Downing Street. Some protesters had pulled down the barriers and started to hurl bricks and stones. Arrests had been made.

'Rob,' Lucy said hesitantly, 'do you think we ought to stay?' 'What?' Rob shouted back, over the swell of the crowd's noise. 'Don't be daft. We'll be fine.' Just then there was a surge of people towards the square, from Whitehall. It caught Lucy up, lifting her off her feet. She glanced round desperately for Rob, managing to catch hold of his hand before she was swept away. The whole crowd began to move back towards Whitehall, up against a police cordon. Lucy, looking up, saw the ranks of police officers, many on horseback, lined up behind the barriers.

'Rob,' she shouted. 'I don't like this. I think we should go.'

Near to her, a child began to cry noisily. The mother, holding a 'No To The Unfair Poll Tax' placard, bent down to soothe him. The father, Lucy saw, was glancing nervously about him. 'Do you know,' he said, in a strong northern accent, 'how we can get out?'

'No, sorry,' Lucy shouted back, but her words were lost as the crowd erupted.

On scaffolding erected around the platform, youths wearing army combat trousers and with dreadlocked hair, began taunting the police. First one, and then many bricks and bottles were thrown. They rained down on the crowd, who tried to scatter, like ants from an upturned stone. The force of the crowd moved inexorably towards the police cordon, with some of the protesters trying to push their way to the front, shouting obscenities, gesticulating, families trying to find a way out. A mother next to Lucy covered her child's ears. Tears were pouring down her face. As the crowd surged, the child went down. 'Rob!' Lucy screamed, frantically tugging at his jacket. He turned, saw what had happened and snatched up the child, just as the crowd toppled forward. The mother turned a frantic face to Rob. 'Please,' she shouted. 'Please, can you help?' Rob, the boy in his arms, Lucy and the child's mother tried to push their way forward. They were now only feet from the cordon. Over their heads flew bricks, bottles, debris, anything that could be picked up and hurled. The sun was blotted out by the projectiles and all around them was the roar of the crowd, cries for help mingling with taunts and obscenities.

Suddenly, in front of them, the barriers parted. 'This way!' Rob shouted, trying furiously to elbow his way through the mass of people. But then an armoured van appeared through the gap, and began, unbelievably, to drive into the crowd. 'Look out!' yelled Rob, as he and Lucy were forced apart. Lucy reeled backward after being struck by the wing of the van, as it pushed, like a boulder, into the depths of the angry and frightened people. 'My son!' the woman next to her shouted. 'Michael! Where are you?'

Lucy held onto her arm, and dragged her to the side of the square. If they could get higher up, they'd stand a chance of trying to find Rob. Gesticulating at the woman, Lucy turned and tried to push her way out. It was hopeless. The crowd now, jammed in so tight, had formed an immovable phalanx, impenetrable and unyielding. 'Please,' Lucy sobbed, tears running down her face too. 'This woman has lost her child! Please.'

Above the noise of the crowd came a new sound – horses' hooves. In the gap made by the armoured van, the mounted police pushed into the crowd, and Lucy watched aghast as batons began to rain down on the protesters' heads. It was completely arbitrary: fathers bent over children to protect them from the blows, mothers snatched terrified toddlers into their arms. But still the chants came, louder and louder, more and more provocative. Next to Lucy, a youth with thick matted blond hair, his face an arrow of hate, lifted his arm. In his hands a car battery. 'No!' shrieked Lucy, as he lobbed it with violent force towards the police lines. It struck one of the charging horses on the face, cutting it deeply underneath the eye. Blood streamed through the sweat.

From the scaffolding down rained all kinds of objects – scaffolding poles, paint drums, fire extinguishers. Among the chaos of shrieks, sirens, chanting and frantic neighing of the terrified police horses was the sound of breaking glass. A horse moved up next to Lucy, so close she could almost touch its steaming flanks. 'Please,' she shouted up to the police officer. 'Let us through.' He looked down at her impassively and said nothing.

Just then, a gap appeared ahead of them. Lucy and the mother fell through, and, turning, ran to St Martin-in-the-Fields. They clambered up the steps. Tears were streaming down the woman's face. Lucy put her arm round her. 'Don't worry,' she said. 'Rob will look after your child. We'll find them.' Even as she said it, she knew this was an impossible task. At least they seemed relatively safe here. All around them parents and children huddled, dazed, astonished at the way the demonstration had turned. 'You're supposed to be *protecting* us!' shouted one of the mothers as more police in riot gear swept past.

'Come on,' Lucy said. 'We'll head towards the cordon from the other side. Breathing heavily, they ran down the steps. As they rounded the corner into the far end of the square, they gazed with horror at the buildings. South Africa House in particular looked like it had been attacked by a band of guerrillas. All the windows were smashed in, and, as they watched, protesters were clambering in through the windows. It was impossible to think this was London, on a sunny Easter day. This was anarchy.

For over an hour Lucy and the woman, Helen, searched backward and forward amongst the crowd.

Eventually, they both decided it was hopeless. The family had come by coach from Halifax, and Lucy told Helen of their plan to meet up back at Euston. 'I think it's our only chance,' she said. Dispiritedly, the pair pushed their way out of the square. It was now 5.30, the rally supposedly over. But around them was chaos. The violence had spilled over from the square into Charing Cross Road. Barricades had been made from Westminster's green litter bins. Fires had been started in waste bins.

Ahead of them a nervous-looking man in a Porsche edged forward. He'd been working in the City, was trying to get home. The mob closed in on him. Lucy and Helen watched aghast as a group of youths ripped open the car door and dragged him out. In his suit and tie, he looked so incongruously clean against the combat uniform of many of the youths. They threw him to the ground. He stood up, open-mouthed, as they ripped off his windscreen wipers. He made a move of protest, but was pushed flat on his back. Struggling up, he snatched the keys from the ignition, grabbed his brief-case and turned and ran. The mob howled, and then stood back as someone opened the petrol cap and lobbed in a match. There was a mushroom of smoke, and then the petrol tank ignited. Within seconds, the entire car was ablaze. The heat hit the two of them like a furnace, and grabbing Helen's hand, Lucy turned and fled. As they ran down towards Oxford Circus, they were surrounded by a sea of mayhem. Windows were being smashed in, shops looted, people dragged from their cars. One man was walking casually along hold-ing a television. 'Excuse me,' he said, as he politely manoeuvred it down the street. Lucy could not believe it. These were the people, presumably, who had surrounded her so peaceably in Kennington Park, who had sat and clapped and danced to the bands. They had turned into a baying, looting mob. It didn't seem possible that English people could behave like this.

They reached Euston on foot by half seven. Helen by now was almost hysterical. Lucy reasoned that her husband would be able to find his own way home, and Rob would bring Michael back to their meeting spot. At least, that was what she hoped to God would happen. They sat in the cafe, drinking coffee with trembling hands. All around them were people shell-shocked, too dazed even to recount the day's events. They had stumbled from a known world into the abyss.

At eight, Lucy and Helen began a search of the main concourse. Crowded with people frantic to get home, tannoys blaring, it was a scene from hell. They stood under the main display unit, eyes flicking backward and forward. Suddenly, through the crowd, Lucy saw Michael. Riding high on Rob's shoulders, he was clutching a burger in one hand and Rob's baseball cap in another. 'Over there!' Lucy grabbed Helen and pointed. Lucy shouted and shouted to get Rob's attention. Like a circus double act, they pushed their way through the crowds. Near to Helen, Rob dropped his shoulders and gently lifted the child to the floor. Helen, sobbing, fell to her knees and hugged him. Michael looked quite unperturbed. 'I had a burger!' he said. 'And Rob's given me this!' He twirled the cap around his fingers. 'Did you have a nice time?' Rob, reaching forward, wrapped his arms around Lucy's neck. 'Next time you take me for a day out in London,' she said, 'could we go to the zoo instead?'

Helen tapped Lucy on the sleeve. 'We'd better be off,' she said. 'I'll get the train from here. Thanks so much for your help.'

'I didn't do anything,' said Lucy. 'Well, thank your

friend,' she said. 'He's a bloke in a million.'

Rob bent down to give Michael a big hug. 'See you, champ,' he said. 'Can I have an earring like yours?' Michael asked. 'Not at seven,' his mother said, leading him briskly away.

Caroline and Archie were drinking gin in the snug, watching the news on television. They'd spent the day dead-heading roses and pruning, and Archie had mown the lawns using his new sit-on tractor. The Yorkes had been coming for dinner, but Annabelle had rung in an annoyed state an hour ago saying George had been called to London to 'deal with' something. 'Such a bore,' she said.

'Just look at them,' Archie said in disgust, as a group of youths hurled bricks and stones from their scaffolding positions. 'It's appalling. This will cost millions to clear up. Do they ever think about that when they set off rioting? That ordinary people will have to foot the bill for their day out?'

The ugly noise of the riot filled the calm, still air of the television room. A shaft of evening sunlight held millions of dancing fragments of dust in its glow. Ben circled and yawned in front of the unlit fire, before flopping at Archie's feet.

Amongst the crowd the camera zoomed in on a small group, cowering back from a charging horse.

'My God!' shouted Caroline. 'It's Lucy!'

'What?' said Archie, spilling his drink as he leant forward. 'There, there, by the horse with that woman and the child and – oh Lord. Rob.'

'Who's Rob?'

'He came to visit while you were at work, just before Christmas. What on earth is Lucy playing at?'

'I have no idea,' said Archie. 'We just need to know

151

that she is safe.' He rose swiftly from his chair.

'What are you doing?' asked Caroline, as Archie reached for the phone. 'Ringing the police,' he said grimly. But before he could dial the number, the phone rang. It was Annabelle.

'Did you see Lucy? Isn't it awful?' Caroline took the phone from Archie. 'What?' 'Lucy, on the television. One of the protesters.' Annabelle was horrified. 'I don't mean to be rude but what on earth is a girl like Lucy doing amongst all those people? What if the press find out she's Max's girlfriend? It'll be all over the papers.'

'We have no idea,' said Caroline coolly. 'But at the moment we're more concerned with making sure she's safe. A lot of the protesters were peaceful, you know.'

'I know,' Annabelle said. 'I'm really just worried. Do you think she's all right?'

'I'm sure she is,' Caroline said. 'Archie's just about to ring the police.'

'Darling, I hope you don't think I'm being rude, but you won't mention George, will you?'

'Why should we?' Caroline said. 'Of course we won't.' Putting the phone down, she grimaced at Archie. Lucy could get them into more hot water than she realized. Archie began to dial, but she put her hand over his.

'Leave it. Lucy will ring.'

But Lucy didn't ring. It took them over six hours to get back to Manchester, standing on a hot, crowded train, buffeted by drunks. When they got back to the halls, Lucy keeled over in exhaustion. Rob, exhausted too, gently eased her out of her jacket, and pulled off her shoes. Then he lay down on the floor, carefully, on his back, so as not to put any weight on the shoulder hit by a brick.

Chapter Twelve

'Have you heard?' Annabelle's voice was pleasant and polite, but Caroline could sense she was upset about something.

'What?' she said, carefully.

'Our silly children,' Annabelle said, in a voice which ended with a nervous laugh.

'Apparently, they've split up. Max is at home. He's really rather upset.'

'Oh no.' Caroline was profoundly shocked. Why hadn't Lucy told her? 'I really didn't know, you know what they're like at university, they never get in touch unless they run out of money. I'm really very surprised, they seemed so keen.'

'Exactly,' Annabelle said. 'I just feel very sad. I don't suppose you could have a word with her, could you? It seems so *sudden*.'

'I'll try,' Caroline said. 'But Lucy's old enough to make up her own mind, I'm not sure how much I can help. But do send my love to Max. He's such a wonderful boy, we're all very fond of him.'

'I know,' Annabelle said. Caroline could sense she was close to tears. 'And Lucy was like a daughter to me. I shall really miss her, Caroline, if it's true.'

*　　*　　*

Lucy hadn't meant to finish with Max quite so brutally. Of course it had been in the offing ever since she'd slept with Rob, but one of Lucy's less attractive traits was her inability to face unpleasant situations head on. She'd far rather ignore them and hope they went away of their own accord. So when Max turned up unexpectedly at her halls of residence halfway through the summer term, she was horrified. He arrived clutching a huge bouquet of flowers. It was the supreme romantic gesture which backfired, as Lucy was in bed with Rob.

When he knocked on the door, she shouted, 'Go away!' thinking it was Annie or another friend. There was a long pause, and then Max's voice said, 'Lucy!' in shocked tones. It wasn't what he'd expected after turning up with flowers and having made the noble gesture of driving up the M6 for four hours in pouring rain.

'Oh my God,' said Lucy, looking in horror at Rob, who, God rot him, started to laugh. He had found out about Max after finding his picture, now stuffed at the back of Lucy's desk. 'Who's this then?' he said, holding the picture aloft. Lucy, furious, tried to grab it off him and was then forced to explain that Max had been her boyfriend and still was, a bit. Sort of. 'Aha,' said Rob, knowingly. 'No wonder your mother looked at me as if a bad smell had crept under the door.' He looked at the photo more carefully. 'Is that his boat he's sitting on?' he said. 'Yes,' said Lucy, trying to sound careless.

'Let me get this straight,' said Rob calmly, lying back on the bed. 'You're going out with him – *and* you're going out with me? Bit of a contradiction in terms there? Or am I missing something?'

'He isn't *really* a boyfriend,' she said. 'More of a

friend.' She tried to sound careless, but her heart was beating fast.

'So why have you hidden his picture?'

'Just hand it over, Inspector Clouseau,' Lucy said.

'I will,' Rob said, holding it away behind his head. 'If you faithfully promise me you will never sleep with this man again. Do you hear me? Never!' he said, putting on a fake German accent.

'I promise,' Lucy said, giggling. 'Now give me it back. You'll squash it.'

'He's got a very girly face,' Rob said.

'Shut up.'

'Lucy?' Max knocked on the door again. Lucy, who by now was feeling completely hysterical, shoved Rob to get out of bed. Thank God she'd locked the door. 'Get *out*,' she hissed. 'Where?' said Rob. 'Would you like me to fly out of the window like Peter Pan?' 'Just get in the cupboard,' she said. Rob, who was completely naked, hopped over to the wardrobe. 'I'm only doing this,' he whispered, 'because I've always wanted to hide in a wardrobe. Naked.'

'Hang on,' shouted Lucy through the door. 'I was asleep.'

She looked around the room frantically for her jeans. They were hooked over the back of her chair. Standing on one leg, she pulled them on. Then she heaved a jumper over her head, and opened the door a crack. She affected bleariness.

'Max,' she said. 'What are you doing here?'

'What the hell d'you think I'm doing here?' he said. 'Visiting the girl with the face like a frog who found me in the shower? For God's sake, Lucy, let me in.'

'I can't,' she said, frantically. 'Annie's in here. She's just — been sick. It's all over the floor.' From the cupboard there was the sound of a large snort.

This was not the romantic meeting Max had planned. All the way up from Bristol – and it was a bloody long way, he thought.

'Well, come out then,' he said.

'I can't,' said Lucy desperately. 'I can't leave her.'

'Fuck this,' said Max, angrily. 'I'll be in the bar.'

He turned on his heel and stomped off, leather brogues clattering down the stairs. Lucy drew her head wearily back into the room. How was she going to get out of this one? Slowly, she opened the door of the wardrobe. Rob was standing there with his hands folded across his chest. He made a completely ludicrous sight. 'These,' he said portentously, 'Are the wages of sin. Can I come out now? My bollocks are cold.'

Lucy, despite herself, giggled. She sat down heavily on the bed, put her head in her hands, and laughed. But even as she laughed, she felt the first stirrings of despair. She would have to make a decision.

Rob began pulling on his Levi's.

'For someone,' he said carefully, 'who is much more of a *friend* than a *boyfriend*, you seem to be making an awful fuss. I'll see you later.' Without looking at her, he was gone. Oh *balls*, Lucy thought.

Somewhere, in the back of her mind, there was a tiny flicker of doubt about whether choosing Rob over Max was the right thing to do. She loved him passionately, she fancied him rotten, he made her howl with laughter, he was so clever, so deep – but he wasn't, oh bugger, inside herself there was a little voice saying, 'He might not be the man for you. He isn't like you. He doesn't care about the things you care about. What will your mum and dad think? Would he fit in with your friends at home? What does he want to do with his

156

life?' Questions Rob would think were laughable, as if any of that stuff mattered. Stop trying to *plan*, he always said. You're so bloody *sensible*. Who knows what's going to happen? What mattered to him was being in love, and having fun, and seeing a bit of the world, not panicking about whether you'd fit into the society you saw as your future. The future with Rob would be an enormous question mark. Exhilarating, no doubt, but a completely unknown quantity. The future with Max was territory she'd trodden all her life. A land she knew. But she couldn't lose Rob. The thought of him making love to anyone else made her feel physically sick.

Lucy walked down to the bar and bought a pint. She carried it carefully to the table where Max was sitting, every fibre of his being registering outrage and hurt. When she put it down, a little beer slopped onto the table.

'Well?' he said. 'Tell me what's really the matter. All that stuff,' he said, 'about Annie was bollocks, wasn't it? Please, Lucy, don't lie to me.' His face was pained, and all the irritation Lucy had felt about him turning up so thoughtlessly out of the blue drained away. He seemed genuinely upset, and Lucy had never seen him before look so unconfident about himself She wanted to hug him. The flowers he'd been carrying were now lying on the floor, wilting as if told off.

'Max,' Lucy said hesitantly. In the spilt beer, she traced a circle with her finger. 'I don't know how to tell you this but I think we should cool . . .'

As soon as she said it, she knew it was a mistake. Everyone in the entire universe knew that 'I don't know how to tell you this' was *the* chuck phrase. Max looked at her, horrified. Without saying a word, he jumped up. He walked, quickly, out of the bar, pushing through the double swing doors. Lucy leapt up and ran after him. A youth at the next table, noting her sudden departure, stood up, looked about him and then took her beer.

'Max, wait!' Lucy yelled after him. It was a cold evening, and her words were lost in the chill wind swirling round the square hall buildings. He didn't stop. 'Please Max!' she shouted. 'I'm sorry!' She started to run to try to catch him up, and there he was, standing by his car, trying to get the key in the lock. She caught hold of his arm. 'Don't go like this.' He turned, furiously. 'You want me to stay?' he said. His face, so beautiful, was contorted by tears. Lucy couldn't bear to see him like that. 'I don't know . . .'

'Don't,' he said, turning away, as she reached up for his face. 'Don't touch me. How could you? How could you end it?' He looked at her with genuine grief. She suddenly felt like they were children again. She knew him, she really knew him, inside out. More than anyone else. And she did love him. It was like a dose of cold water. Lucy grabbed his jacket, but he'd got the door open, and he ducked into the car. She fell back, her heel banging painfully against the pavement.

He revved the engine, hard, and began to drive away. 'I loved you,' he screamed out of the window.

Lucy wrapped her arms tight around her body. The rational part of her looked down and said, 'Why? Why are you so upset? You love Rob more,' while the irrational side – a tiny voice, a siren call from deep within, said 'You are wrong.'

Chapter Thirteen

'And this,' said Caroline, carefully holding out a slightly tattered picture of Lucy sitting on a golden retriever stark naked, beaming seraphically at the camera, 'is Lucy at three years old.'

Peggy, terrified to move on Caroline's exquisite Wesley-Barrell sofa in case she knocked off the cup of tea perched on a spindly table just next to her ample knee, edged forward very slightly and smiled nervously at Caroline. The tea was Earl Grey, which she'd never tasted before and thought was awful, like drinking hot perfume. But she didn't want to offend Caroline and ask if she had any real tea.

'Isn't she lovely,' she said, as Lucy groaned. In return Peggy handed Caroline a picture of Rob aged eighteen months, looking like a potato with ears.

It had not been Peggy's idea to get together at the Beresford home once the engagement had been announced, rendering it imperative that both sets of parents meet. When Lucy had first mooted the suggestion to Jack and Peggy, they'd thought perhaps they could meet halfway on the motorway, on neutral territory – perhaps a Little Chef? Since his stroke, Jack disliked long journeys in the car, in fact he became nervous about any trip out which took them away from home. It broke Peggy's heart to see a man who had been so confident, so full of himself, reduced to this. He could still walk unaided, and his speech was relatively unaffected. But it had knocked the stuffing out of him in the cruellest way and he'd come to rely on her for almost everything. On hearing the words 'Little Chef', Caroline made frantic 'no' gestures at Archie when he repeated the words on the phone, and turned to her, eyebrows raised quizzically.

'A Little Chef? Darling – do you know if there's a Little Chef just off the M6 where we could meet?' He was being very carefully polite, and he liked the sound of Peggy – she had a forthright, no-nonsense way of talking that made him immediately warm to her, even though he had to listen very hard to get past the accent.

'Surely there must be a nice hotel?' Caroline whispered. 'Somewhere quiet, and pretty. Shall I check the Egon Ronay?'

'Perhaps we could find a hotel?' Archie said. 'Somewhere a little more jolly?'

There was a pause on the other end of the phone. Peggy didn't know how to say this, but they couldn't afford to stay overnight at a hotel, living as carefully as they had to on Jack's pension. The redundancy money had lasted no time at all. Archie sensed the pause, and quickly said, 'I'm being ridiculous. You must come here, of course. For dinner.'

Peggy's voice was slightly puzzled.

'Dinner?' she said. 'I'm not sure we could manage to get down to you by then.' There was a long pause while she held the phone away from her mouth and said, quietly, 'Dad? Could we get to the Cotswolds by dinner?' 'Pushing it a bit,' Archie could hear a quiet, muffled voice. 'It isn't so far,' said Archie, confused. 'Shouldn't take you much more than four hours or so from Lancashire, and of course,' he continued, 'you must stay the night.'

'I suppose we could set out at about six in the morning,' Peggy said.

Archie held the phone away from him and looked at it curiously. 'It really won't take so long.'

'But I thought you said dinner,' Peggy said.

The penny dropped. 'You mean lunch,' Archie said. 'I'm so sorry, I meant an evening meal, I do apologize . . .'

Peggy paused, and then said, calmly, 'We'd love to come – for tea. Thank you very much.'

After graduating, Rob had found a job almost immediately on his father's old newspaper, who at least had some conscience about the way they'd treated Jack, who'd given them years of unswerving loyalty until his brutal sacking. Lucy, who'd um-ed and ah-ed about her career – with some subtle pressure from her parents to apply for a graduate media-training course, ideally in London – had finally had her mind made up for her by being offered, quite out of the blue, a reporter's job on the local radio station in the same town as Rob's newspaper. She'd fired off her CV to masses of stations, and hadn't really expected a response. Glamorous it was not, but it was one way to earn a living, if not exactly a lucrative one. They were comfortably ensconced – if one could be comfortably ensconced in a damp cold cottage where the ratio of mice to people was about 35:2, making picking up items of clothing in the bedroom an exercise involving a certain amount of unnecessary risk – in a small village, just a short drive from where they worked.

161

It would have been more convenient to have lived in the town itself, but Lucy at this point put her foot down. Rob was moving her even further into the frozen north, whilst most of their contemporaries were either staying on in Manchester after graduating, or taking up graduate traineeships in Birmingham or London. Moving to Blackburn did seem to be something of a deliberately ironic statement, for which both Lucy and Rob received much stick. Annie, who had scraped a third class degree to Lucy's two two and Rob's amazing top second (Lucy could not recall him ever doing any kind of academic work whatsoever), was shooting off to stay in Verbier with Rollo, who had graduated from cleaning chalets to working in a pub. It hardly seemed to either Lucy or Rob to be a positive career move, but Annie, as ever, was neutral to the point of unconsciousness about the need for any kind of career. She'd even said – which had alarmed Lucy greatly – that she'd quite like to have a baby, because they were quite portable, weren't they? She could take it travelling with her. It would be nice to have the company.

Lucy, with her unerring ability to sniff out the 'nice' in her surroundings, settled them in Clitheroe. A small market town, nestling in the Ribble Valley, it was undeniably scenic and even verging on the genteel. Even Caroline was remarkably impressed on her first visit, looking about her at the Barboured-and-green-wellied women with wicker shopping baskets, saying it was almost like home. Lucy guessed she'd expected something out of a Lowry painting, their cottage crouched under glowering dark satanic mills. Instead Caroline found an excellent butcher, friendly people and a quite wonderful wine shop. She even gave it the ultimate accolade, 'I might bring Daddy next time and we'll have a little holiday.'

On Rob and Lucy's combined salaries, however, they could only afford to rent this two-bedroom cottage with a downstairs bathroom, no central heating and an immersion heater which sounded like it was about to blast them into orbit. The living room was warmed by an open fire, so Lucy, who usually got in before Rob, had to light it nightly like the tweeny maid. Rob claimed he'd seen mice wearing balaclavas.

The only thing that saved Lucy from despair was that it was, at least, several steps up from the truly awful terraced house she and Rob had shared in the final year with Annie and Nick, who was on Rob's course, played in his band and had quite remarkably green hair. Under the green hair he was a lovely, gentle bloke, but he did look a bit alarming. Lucy had introduced him to Caroline and Archie on graduation day, and she had taken a huge amount of secret pleasure in watching Caroline coping. But amazingly – as Nick was normally a man of few words, usually related to the purchase of illegal substances – Lucy found them getting on ten minutes afterwards like a house on fire, and Caroline remarked later he was 'a lovely boy'. Her mother never ceased to amaze her.

Not only was their student house not in the most salubrious area of the city, it also had an impressive range of structural and internal defects. As in the Clitheroe cottage, there was no central heating, simply a gas fire which released enough fumes to anaesthetize a horse. The windows in the winter regularly froze on the inside, a phenomenon Lucy had previously not thought possible, and the toilet, at the slightest dip of temperature, iced over. This was, on a scale of inconvenience, set rather higher than the frozen windows. One could perhaps bear to see the fruits of one's endeavours the first time, but, after two or three people had been, the entire house began to smell like a Turkish lavatory and vacation was imperative. This meant they had to ask each other searching questions like 'Just how desperate are you?' until they all reached morris dancing level. Then they leapt into Nick's ancient Mini and roared off to the nearby leisure centre. This had the added attraction of showers (the taps on the bath were not only frozen but the bath itself was so ringed with dirt it resembled a porcelain panda). Going to the toilet at night had another drawback in that, being situated in the basement and thus very damp, it played host to a small party of convivial slugs who slimed and boogied their way across the floor in the darkness.

Caroline had once visited the house in Manchester, never to return She made a number of fundamental errors – a) opening the fridge (which Lucy had vowed never to do after something moved at the back) and b) trying to light the gas cooker. This had also been banned, since Annie set fire to her hair. Initially there had seemed to be a lack of gas – then they had a surplus, which, on turning the knob, rushed up like a geyser. It made cooking anything exceptionally perilous, so they had all decided that, on balance, it was safer to buy takeaways. The only problem with this was that Lucy seemed to be the only one who cared enough to throw the cartons away. But even then the matter didn't rest, owing to the many stray dogs, who ripped open the bin-liners like a pack of wild hyenas as soon as Lucy put them out. She loved the city, but she was not sorry to leave that house.

Rob now owned an ancient car, which had to be started with a teaspoon and had a windscreen wiper which flipped out too far, so you had to drive with one hand out of the window to catch it and flip it back. He offered to take Peggy and Jack down to Lucy's house, as he knew his mum wasn't confident about driving so far and Jack now never drove. Archie had made repeated attempts to buy Lucy a new car, but she resisted, knowing that Rob would be upset. They couldn't afford the petrol, anyway, for two cars, and Rob had insisted on keeping his awful old bike, so he took that to work on the mornings it elected to start, while Lucy crept towards Blackburn in a series of loud farting noises and alarming leaps forward. There was no first gear, which made setting off from traffic lights on an upward incline a test of true perseverance, involving a great deal of smoke and the smell of burning rubber.

On the drive down – fortunately it didn't rain so Rob could keep his hands inside the car – Lucy kept up a determined stream of bright chatter. She had grown very fond of both Peggy and Jack. At first they'd been incredibly wary of her, and Peggy in particular kept apologizing for everything – 'I'm sorry we have to eat in the front room,' and 'Don't mind Rob's gran, will you,' as the old lady was now approaching eighty and liable to produce a quite startling array of sudden loud noises. The first time it happened when Lucy was there having tea, the dog bolted out of the room and Lucy caught Rob's eye, and thought she would explode with laughter. She'd even got Claire – who was just about to go off to university – on her side, by admitting she'd quite liked the Bay City Rollers too, and letting Claire borrow some of her clothes. Claire loved coming to stay with her and Rob, even though it was only across the valley, because it made her feel grown-up. She thought Lucy was wonderful, so beautiful and ladylike, and continually questioned her about what she saw in her awful brother.

On arrival, Caroline had greeted them effusively – so

effusively, in fact, that Lucy wanted to strangle her. Most of Caroline's dealings with illness fell into the good-works category, and Lucy was terrified she'd start treating Jack like one of her stroke group, which she helped out at every couple of weeks, talking very *loudly* and *slowly*. But, all credit to her, she summed up the situation very quickly and was the first to unobtrusively slip her arm under Jack's to guide him up the steps when he gave a slight stumble, disorientated after so long in the car and Rob's rather erratic driving. Peggy was wrong-footed from the start by Caroline's greeting. As she always did, she leant forward to kiss Peggy on the cheek. Rob's parents never kissed anyone – certainly not in public – and Peggy had blushed bright red, put her face one way, and then very quickly the other, so she and Caroline clashed jawbones. Archie, seeing this, made do with a firm handshake. Lucy, watching all of them, was astonished at how nervous they seemed. Normally her parents were perfectly at ease in all social situations, but they didn't quite know how to cope with Jack and Peggy, as they had little or no experience of meeting people like this on a social basis.

It touched Lucy to see how much trouble Caroline had taken – a fire burned in every grate, and she'd put her huge and elaborate flower arrangements in every room. When they sat down to dinner, Caroline had lit her usual array of candles, the large church ones on the pewter stands at either end of the long vaulted dining room, and the antique brass candle-holders on the wall.

There'd also been a sticky moment before dinner when Archie said, 'Drink?' Peggy looked sharply at Jack, as he wasn't really supposed to drink alcohol. But she supposed that just this once, it would be all right.

She waited for him to say he'd like a beer, and nearly fell out of her chair when he said, 'A gin and tonic would be nice.' Lucy, hearing this and catching Peggy's amazed face, said quickly, 'What a good idea. I'll have one too, Dad.'

Peggy said firmly, 'I'd like a drop of wine.' 'White or red?' Archie said. 'We've got a pretty decent little Chablis here and a lovely smooth Chambertin.' Peggy looked uncertain. 'You'll like the Chablis,' Lucy said.

'That sounds smashing. It's not too sweet, is it?'

'No,' Lucy said. 'Not sweet at all.'

'Anyway,' Archie said, 'we really ought to be popping the champagne, shouldn't we?' Rob and Lucy exchanged a quick, intense glance. Caroline smiled and got up. 'I'll get the champagne flutes,' she said, and went off to delve into the cupboard where she kept her extensive array of crystal. Lucy alarmed herself by a sudden strong urge to cry.

Her parents were being so brilliant, when she knew they were, at heart, unsure about her decision. They both knew Rob so well now, adored his sense of humour, had got used to his dilapidated clothes and complete lack of interest in material possessions, and, as Caroline said, she admired a man with as strong principles as Rob held. But would he make her happy? Could he give her all the things that made life comfortable? Would Lucy have the life they'd always taken for granted would be hers by right? They were fears Caroline and Archie only expressed to each other, privately. Anyone could see how much in love Lucy and Rob were, but would the differences between them cause friction later?

At dinner, Peggy looked in some dismay at the rows of knives and forks in front of her. It seemed like an awful lot of trouble to go to, just for tea. She was also trying hard to stop her stomach from emitting loud rumbles of hunger, because they hadn't sat down to eat until almost nine. She kept looking at Jack anxiously, convinced he was going to faint any moment, because they normally ate at six. Pre-dinner conversation had been a little sticky, despite everyone's best efforts. Perhaps the worst moment came when Archie enquired what line Jack had been in.

'Print,' Jack said.

'Ah,' said Archie, assuming he meant as a journalist. 'How fascinating. Such a good thing the bosses have got tough and broken that *absurd* stranglehold of the unions.' There was a long pause. Lucy wanted to slide off her chair like a character in a Tom and Jerry cartoon and disappear under the carpet.

'I was the father of the print chapel,' Jack said, stiffly.

Archie looked deep into his gin and tonic.

'Ah,' he said. 'I see.' Then they'd sat in silence until Caroline and Peggy returned from a tour around the house to rescue them.

That night, Caroline lay awake. And wished beyond measure that she could control events to make Lucy always happy.

Chapter Fourteen

Rob had asked her to marry him in his own highly individual way. The evening had not begun in a hearts-and flowers kind of way, but then their evenings rarely did.

'If he gives me a bollocking again, I'm going to nut him.'

Rob was pacing angrily around their small living room, made pretty with the flowery lined curtains Caroline had run up for Lucy, along with a couple of matching cushions. 'Just little touches,' she'd said, breezing around the tiny cottage which seemed too small for her, 'but they do make a difference.'

Lucy, who was lying full length on the sofa, was exhausted after a day spent indulging the caprices of the prima-donna presenter for whom she was working as a researcher. It had been made to sound a plum job by the station manager, who fancied Lucy and always pulled his chair just that little bit too close for her liking. Personally, he reminded her of the Fat Controller from *Thomas the Tank Engine*, but she humoured him because she liked her job, most of the time. But then he didn't have to work for the monstrous woman, who made Joan Collins seem unassuming. She was a tiny creature, like a poisonous little dwarf, with eyes constantly darting about looking for someone to blame.

Shirley Cross – It's *The Shirley Cross Show*! (applause) – ate researchers for breakfast. After just a week, they would run, sobbing, into the station manager's office pleading to be transferred to another programme, anything. She'd had her own national radio programme during the Seventies, and was now ungraciously sliding down the ladder of fame. What had once been a bright star was now but a flickering ember. Yet she hung onto the caprices and whims of the truly famous with vice-like talons, blithely unaware of the fact that to everyone else at the station, she was just a bloody nuisance.

Intensely lazy, she swanned in only half an hour before her show was due to start, expecting everything to be handed to her on a plate. Lucy laboriously typed fulsome notes and questions for each of her guests, but these were rarely accepted as all she ever wanted to do was reminisce about the heady days of the Sixties and Seventies. Lucy's fellow researcher, a dour Lancastrian called Bill, who was hanging on for his BBC pension, would say, 'If she mentions the Hollies again I'm personally going to go in there and strangle her.' While the records played she kept a beady eye on them through the glass and if it looked like they were chatting to each other she would bark over the intercom, 'Coffee! Decaff! Now!' or 'I have to have something sweet – I can *feel* my blood sugar falling.' If she felt she had pushed you too far, which she often did, she would turn on the full force of her synthetic charm, which was like being dropped, feet first, into a vat of marshmallow.

She fawned unashamedly over their 'celebrity' guests – situated as they were, only half an hour from

Manchester, they could usually persuade the panto-mime stars from the Opera House to come on, as long as they sent them a car. Lucy often found herself sitting with her head in her hands at eight o'clock in the morning, trying to think of interesting questions to ask someone who had appeared in *Neighbours* five years ago – twice.

'What's the matter now?' she said to Rob, with her eyes closed. Rob moved her legs up, and flopped down. 'I made a bit of a mistake with a caption for a photograph,' he said. His shoulders started to shake. 'They only spotted it on the proofs.' Lucy opened her eyes and looked at him reproachfully. 'What did you do this time?'

'Bit of a balls-up,' he said. 'We had this ludicrous police drawing of a man wearing a monkey mask who robbed the jeweller's in the high street, and the caption should have read, "Have you seen this man?" which I thought was funny enough in itself. But then I also had the story and pic of the new chairwoman of Blackburn Soroptimists and . . .'

'You mixed the two up.'

'An easy mistake to make,' said Rob, tucking his long legs under him. 'She looked like she was wearing a monkey mask.'

'Rob,' said Lucy sternly. 'You must take this job seriously. You're going to get the sack, and then where will we be? Remember what happened with that head-line you tried to slip in? The one about the vicar who scared off his entire congregation by thundering about hell and damnation from the pulpit?'

'"Flock off?"'

'And that other one?' continued Lucy. 'The story about the sculpture of teddy bears whose paws were nailed to a huge piece of wood?'

' "No Picnic for Bears?" ' said Rob. 'I thought that was clever.'

'Not everyone,' said Lucy, 'shares your bizarre sense of humour.'

'I know what'll happen,' said Rob, miserably. 'I'll be condemned to the journalistic equivalent of the rack – an entire week at Blackburn Magistrates Court doing drunk and disorderly and TV-licence dodgers.'

'Just make sure you get the charges right,' said Lucy, wearily. 'Last time you did magistrates you had the wife of the bank manager who'd forgotten to pay her TV licence up for receiving stolen goods.'

'She looked shifty to me.'

Lucy laughed. 'Just remember, we have our entire future ahead of us – what would happen if you did get sacked?'

'On that subject,' Rob said, 'I have something to say.'

After almost two years together, Rob had never aired the subject of their future. Two years of fending off delicate enquiries from her mother, resigned now to the fact that they were inseparable, and far more direct questions from Peggy, who was much more appalled than Caroline at the fact they were openly living together – especially so close to home. 'Over the brush,' she said. 'That's what it was called in my day. I can't see,' she said to Lucy, on one of her visits which both Lucy and Rob loved, because she tidied up the entire house and cooked them delicious hot meals, 'why Rob's so daft he can't see he's got a gem in you, Lucy.'

'Rob, love,' she called out while Rob grumpily washed the dishes in their tiny kitchen. 'Why don't you make an honest woman of Lucy?'

'She's never asked me,' he called back. 'Anyway, why can't I be made an honest man?'

'You and your jokes,' Peggy said, getting out her own darning mushroom to mend Rob's holey socks. Lucy couldn't cope with Rob's socks – weekly, she herded them in a pack into the corner of their bedroom, where they lay, muttering and hissing to themselves, until she eventually captured them in a plastic bag and handed them at arm's length to Rob, who peered inside and wondered aloud if they should be buried or cremated. 'You could wash them,' Lucy pointed out. 'I don't think I could get them in the machine,' Rob said. 'They might make a break for it.' They were silent for a moment, pondering the awful thought of Rob's socks running amok through Clitheroe. 'Burial,' said Lucy, taking them from Rob and placing them firmly in the bin. 'Go and buy some more.' That night she had fearful dreams of the bin lid rising of its own volition.

'Let's go out tonight,' Rob said. 'I haven't been sacked. That's a cause for celebration. Come on. Get your glad rags on, girl, I'm taking you down the pub.'

The old car was once more laid up with a deep and mysterious ailment – the mechanic at the local garage, whom Lucy now knew well, tried the engine, and heard it cough, fart, and die. 'It's bust,' he said. 'I know that,' Lucy said. 'Can you fix it?' 'Parts are worth more than the car,' he said. 'Please,' Lucy said, looking beseechingly at him. Like most men confronted with Lucy's golden beauty, he immediately weakened. 'I'll see what I can do,' he said. 'Thanks,' said Lucy. 'And can you make it as quick as possible,' realizing this now condemned her to getting into work on the back of Rob's ancient bike.

So Rob and Lucy set off on the bike for their favourite country pub. It nestled in a hollow in the undulating hills about five miles from Clitheroe, out into the stunning Trough of Bowland. They'd found the pub quite by accident. Cresting the top of a steep hill, Rob stopped. 'Look at that,' he breathed. It was the most breathtaking scene – a great, wide valley lay before them, densely wooded, with a small glittering river like a silver thread running through the centre. So high up, there was no sound, save the distant bleating of sheep and the occasional sharp bark of a dog.

'Makes you think of Wordsworth,' Lucy said.

'What, the sheep?'

'No,' she said. 'It's like a spot in time.'

'Saves nine?'

'You know exactly what I mean. The grandeur of nature. Wordsworth had it spot on, so to speak. It's like being suddenly humbled by the awesomeness of nature.'

'You may be overcome by the awesomeness of nature,' Rob said, 'but I'm gasping for a pint.'

They climbed back on the bike and sped down into the lush valley. At the bottom of the hill lay an old stone pub. A bench leant drunkenly against the wall, and by the door sat a smiling black and white sheep-dog.

Lucy and Rob pulled off their helmets, parked the bike, and walked in, ducking their heads under the low beam over the door. Both blinked for a while in the unaccustomed gloom. There was no-one else in, apart from a couple of old men playing dominoes. Lucy hitched herself onto a barstool. The pub had a certain air of eccentricity – on every conceivable window ledge stood different stuffed animals, the most arresting of which was a fox's bottom and brush, dis-appearing into the wall.

'I'll give you a game.' Rob settled himself with a full creamy pint on the table, and lit a roll-up. The only sound in the pub was the ticking of the big old clock on the wall. The sheepdog lay panting at their feet. 'You know you want to,' said Rob, shaking out the box.

Lucy beat him. This made him very angry, and they had to play again and again until he won. Carefully standing her dominoes up in front of her and gloating over the ownership of the double six, Lucy said slowly, 'What did you want to say to me?' He looked up from a fervent study of his dominoes. 'I'm going to whack your arse,' he replied, happily.

'Was that all you wanted to say? I'm not sure this is the appropriate place.'

'Ha, ha,' Rob said. 'Actually, there was something.' He lifted his roll-up from the ashtray, studied the glowing end for a moment and then knocked off a small tower of ash.

'I wanted to know . . .' He ran the fingers of his other hand up and down the cracked varnish of the table, making splinters with his bitten nails. 'I just wondered if you'd marry me.'

He raised his head and looked at her, unsmiling. The clock on the wall ticked, and Lucy glanced round the empty pub. They were the only ones there – to attract the attention of the landlord, you had to ring the bell on the bar and he emerged, grumbling, from the back room where he was watching television with his fat wife.

As a child, Lucy had dreamt of whom she'd marry. She used to lie in bed, at the age of about nine, pressing her eyes tight shut and willing herself to visualize the man who would be her husband. She closed her eyes. Then she opened them, and there was Rob. A white collarless shirt, fraying slightly at the edges. Sleeves rolled up over broad, hairy arms. Around one wrist a twisted copper bracelet, around the other a

175

leather shoelace he'd put on one day at university and forgotten ever to take off. Two fingers of his left hand were stained a deep buttercup yellow with nicotine. His dark hair, still long enough to rest on his shoulders, was dark with sweat from the bike helmet.

As he sat, hunched towards her, there was a hollow between his collarbones and his neck, which seemed so fragile she wanted to reach forward and touch it. She studied his face, so familiar now she no longer saw him as good-looking. There were deeper lines, running from the side of his nose past his lips, than there had been when she first met him. She looked into his dark, slanting eyes. Normally they were eyes which implied that any moment something quite unexpected would happen, but that you'd probably like it − at that moment, in the old silent pub, they held a batsqueak of fear. She reached up, and gently ran her hand over his rough, stubbly skin. 'I will,' she said.

'I have a witness.' He looked down at the sheepdog, who smiled back, black and white tail thumping on the wooden floor. 'You can't go back on it.'

'I don't think I want to,' said Lucy, reaching up with the other hand so she held his face cupped in her hands. He leant forward, and they kissed, quietly, under the clock with the deafening tick and the fox's arse. 'Another half to celebrate?' he said, nodding at her empty glass.

'Make it a pint,' she said. 'Let's go completely mad.'

Chapter Fifteen

'For goodness sake, Lucy, sit still!' Caroline, mouth full of hairpins, was trying to fix Lucy's headdress. Lucy had spent all morning alternating between an urge to collapse with laughter, or burst into tears. Her mother had been pinging about the house like a demented bat since seven a.m., working up enough hysterical energy to power a space mission, and her father, who she knew felt deeply emotional about the whole event but had no idea how to express himself, had closeted himself away with his tomatoes, who rarely if ever made emotional demands or asked him if their hem was straight.

Annie, the chief bridesmaid, could not take the day seriously at all and kept wandering about muttering 'This is *so* freaky.' She was currently lying on Lucy's bed, crushing her extremely expensive cream satin bridesmaid's dress, and reading about how to have the perfect multiple orgasm in *Cosmopolitan*. Lucy's youngest bridesmaids, her cousin Sarah's two small daughters who looked like little angels but were in fact hobgoblins in disguise, had already pulled off their tiaras and were jousting with them. A mutinous Helen, who loathed her dress because she thought it made her look fat next to the stick-thin Annie, was mooching about behind her saying, 'I feel a *complete* fool. Why couldn't we wear black?' Claire was the only one being reasonable, but that was primarily because she was rendered speechless with acute social paralysis, brought on by the sheer size and grandeur of Lucy's house and the outrageousness of Annie, who'd said 'fuck' several times in front of Lucy's mother. Caroline tolerated Annie because she'd discovered her father was a friend of one of Archie's friends, and she felt, quite rightly, that most of the outrageous behaviour was attention-seeking, like a petulant toddler. She felt a distinct urge to mother Annie.

'Ow!' Lucy said, sharply, as Caroline jabbed her in the head. 'Darling, *do* be still,' Caroline muttered. 'I knew we should have got a professional hairdresser and make-up artist lady, darling, I don't know why you didn't let me.'

'It was a needless expense,' said Lucy, wincing. 'You've spent so much already, or so you keep telling me.'

'That,' said Caroline, looking at her fiercely, 'is beside the point. This is your big day.' Lucy had to bite back the retort that no, this appeared to be Caroline's big day. She was just a fluffy white accessory. But then she thought that was, perhaps, being unfair. Her mother had put so much effort into the organization of the wedding, as if her entire life depended upon it. Lucy couldn't believe how stressed she was, and could only cope by visiting Planet Wedding when absolutely necessary. Rob had bowed out at an early stage, and refused point-blank to be drawn on any of the vexing questions as to whether they should have a champagne or melon sorbet mid-meal, or whether pale pink or pale yellow silk stripes would look best inside the marquee.

178

'You've got a spot on your chin,' Helen said, peering over her shoulder at Lucy's reflection. 'Thank you, kind sister,' Lucy replied, reaching for her foundation. She'd felt it as soon as she woke, a veritable Belisha beacon, throbbing and pulsating just under the surface. Bloody typical, she thought. She hadn't had spots for two years, and yet on the morning of her wedding – bingo! Zit city. As she drew carefully round her lips with lipliner, she wondered how Rob was this morning. Not hungover, she hoped. He'd elected to spend the night at the B. & B. near to the hotel, with his mum and dad, other relations and Nick. Nick had promised to try to get the green dye out of his hair. The B. & B. was near to the country house hotel where the reception was being held, which had been booked up by Caroline for Archie's clients. She had offered, very delicately, to pay for Peggy and Jack to stay there, but Peggy declined, saying they'd rather be with their other relations who were coming down. A couple of Archie's clients were flying in by helicopter, which Caroline managed to drop into the conversation fairly frequently when chatting to friends. Rob told Lucy that if her mother was so excited about unusual modes of transport he was sure his Uncle Bob could bring his milk float.

Caroline nearly fainted when Rob announced Nick was going to be the best man. Of course she'd met Nick, and knew what a lovely person he was *underneath*, but was he really the best person to be thrust into the spotlight in this way? It was only a tiny suggestion, but she wondered if Rob didn't perhaps have any slightly more *conventional* friends he might ask? Lucy told her mother sharply to be glad Rob had asked Nick, because the alternative choice could have

179

been old schoolfriend Colin, postman by day, Hell's Angel by night. Caroline went very pale, and stopped dropping hints. Lucy then suggested that if Caroline had such a problem with Nick, perhaps Annie could be best man, which Annie was definitely on for, but her mum nearly fainted. 'Could we try not to be *too* way out,' she said, in a voice of barely suppressed hysteria. She then spent ages carefully preparing the ground with her friends by stressing the best man was a *little* unusual, but very *clever*. He was a friend from *university*. Likewise she glossed over Rob's background by stressing where he and Lucy had met, and what a complete original he was. What made her so nervous were Archie's influential clients and their glossy Belgravia wives. In her lowest moments, she silently questioned just *why* Lucy had to choose someone so very different, and why she couldn't have met someone more – well, more like them. Lucy, squinting over Caroline's shoulder at her parents' guest list, said, 'It looks like a business meeting.' 'Think of the presents,' Caroline said, tartly.

Caroline also had a little word about Rob's earring.

'I'm only thinking of the photographs,' she said. 'It will look a bit odd with a top hat. Like a ringmaster.'

Lucy said she would try, but knew he probably wouldn't agree as he hadn't taken it out since he'd had his ear pierced, not even when it got infected. Lucy wondered if perhaps she could remove it when he was asleep, but rejected this idea as she'd have to chloroform him first. It hadn't seemed unusual at all at university, but now, in the world of work, Lucy wondered why he insisted on keeping it. She suspected it was his last relatively harmless way of sticking two fingers up at the Establishment he had now all but joined.

'OK,' said Caroline, sitting back to admire the effect in Lucy's mirror. 'Now stand up slowly.' Lucy gently pushed herself upright, her hands on the dressing table to steady her. It felt like she had a cake on her head. 'I look ridiculous,' she said, crossly. 'No you don't,' said Caroline, a tear glistening in the corner of her eye. 'You look beautiful. Archie, doesn't she look stunning?' Her father, glamorous and dignified in his grey morning suit, had walked into Lucy's bedroom and stood behind them. 'You both do,' he said loyally. 'I'm very proud of my girls.' Caroline simpered. Lucy groaned and caught the twinkle in his eye in the mirror's reflection.

'Just think of all the money you're going to save,' she said to Archie.

'True,' he said, bending to kiss her. 'But I will miss you. So much.'

'Oh Dad,' she said. 'We'll be nearer, now Rob has this new job. It'll be so much easier to see you both.'

'I know,' Archie said. But he knew in his heart of hearts that Rob was not the type who would willingly trot along to have Sunday lunch every week with his in-laws. Without being rude, he'd resisted Archie's blandishments to make him a member at the golf club now he and Lucy would only be living ten miles away, saying, 'There's no point, Archie, I'm useless. Really. I'd get you banned. I let go of clubs. I leave a trail of devastation behind me like a JCB.' Then, mischievously, 'But I'll give you a game of pool in the clubhouse, if you like.' Archie shot him a sharp look. 'We only have snooker.'

Lucy knew it was hard for her father, because he desperately wanted to take Rob under his wing, absorb him into the family, give him a little business advice and perhaps even help out with a few contacts. And Caroline was sure that, with a little effort, he could be made quite presentable, and he was *so* amusing. Things were changing, after all – accents were even becoming quite fashionable. But Rob refused to fit underneath Archie's proffered wing. After the offer to speak to a couple of national newspaper editors had been refused, they'd sat, like two prickly burrs, until Caroline and Lucy came to rescue them.

Lucy looked cautiously down at her stomach in the plain white satin gown. She'd chosen the least fussy dress she could find, because everything about being a bride was so girly and didn't fit in at all with the staunch feminist ideals she'd tried to embrace at university. When she'd told Annie she was getting married, Annie was furious and said, 'Why?'

'Because he asked me,' Lucy replied, lamely. She didn't dare admit that she thought the whole idea of being married to Rob was incredibly sexy, although she felt pretty dodgy on the subject of actually being called Mrs Atkinson. It made her sound like a lollipop lady. Annie said that she and Rollo were never going to get married because getting married made you lose your identity and how could you be taken seriously if you were a wife? No-one needed a bit of paper. 'I hope you're keeping your name,' she said, warningly. 'I'm not going to be friends with you if you're *Mrs Atkinson.*' Lucy said nothing, as she hadn't broached the idea with Rob, who could easily react either way – he'd either say 'fine' or go mad. Lucy was never quite able to predict exactly when his deeply traditional northern roots would poke through. What she was also slowly discovering was that he had quite a puritanical streak and hated wasting money on the small luxuries Lucy thought nothing of buying. Used to the safety net of her father's wealth, she couldn't get worried about money in the same way as Rob. He couldn't see why she couldn't make do with what she had, but 'making do' was hardly Lucy's forte.

Lucy smoothed Annie down by lying and saying that she was going to keep her maiden name at work, if only she could find a new job now Rob was going to settle in Oxford. Yet a tiny part of her wasn't that desperate to work straight away. She was pretty loath to admit this even to herself, in case the Germaine Greer thought police came to get her, but she quite fancied doing nothing for a while and making a home. Goodbye Superwoman, hello Mrs Tiggywinkle.

And – she peered anxiously again at her flat stomach – she'd missed a period. She and Rob weren't very good at birth control. Rob insisted she give up being on the pill because he said it filled your body with vile chemicals and it did make her feel extremely hormonal, so they'd opted instead for the cap. Rob rejected condoms out of hand because he said it felt like wearing a wellington on your willy. But they hadn't got on very well with the cap – Lucy became hysterical with laughter as the round, springy thing shot out of her hand and bounced off the bathroom wall. It took her half an hour of panting to get it in, and then she was terrified she'd never get it out again, or it might migrate through her body and slide down her nose. All in all they were not an advert for the Brook Advisory Clinic and there was a more than remote possibility that she might just be – pregnant. There. She'd said it to herself. Most of her really didn't want to be pregnant, but there was another part of her brain which quite liked the idea. She hadn't told Rob yet, because she knew he would get hopelessly overexcited. He was brilliant with children, which Lucy wasn't. To her they were like little, dangerous aliens and all the babies she knew seemed to be constantly emitting unpleasant substances which they really ought to learn to keep to themselves before they were allowed out in public.

'We *must* get off.' Caroline was beginning to palpitate. She was taking all the bridesmaids to the church, and the two little ones had lost their tiaras and she *wished* Annie wouldn't smoke in her bridesmaid's outfit. She had wanted to hire a fleet of cars, but Lucy said that would make her feel as if she were appearing in a travelling circus. There was quite enough fuss already, without having to pull up in a Rolls-Royce covered in stupid silver horseshoes and ribbons. Lucy and Archie were going in the Range Rover, which Archie had had cleaned and valeted so Ben's hairs wouldn't stick to her dress, for fear of Lucy walking down the aisle wearing what appeared to be a fluffy red bolero.

Caroline fussed about with her veil and train as she heaved herself up into the passenger seat. 'You ought to sit in the back,' Caroline said. 'You'll crush your dress.'

'And drive *slowly*,' she called out to Archie, as they pulled away.

Archie and Lucy smiled nervously at each other. Archie took one hand off the wheel and put it over hers. 'I know you're happy,' he said. 'And that's all I want.' Lucy studied him as he drove, his still-handsome profile, grey hair brushed back from his tanned, freckly forehead, slightly jowly chin, and thought how much she loved him. Would Rob ever come anywhere close?

Near the church, they had to wait until Caroline's car overtook them. As she drove past, Lucy could see her mother's mouth moving incessantly. Thank goodness she'd come with her father. Caroline had also fretted endlessly about her outfit – there was such a fine line to be drawn between extremely expensive and classic without looking showily ostentatious – and had eventually decided upon a scarlet silk shift dress and jacket from Chanel, the cost of which made even Archie blanch and murmur, 'That'll cause a stir in the Burford office,' when he saw the size of the bill. It was teamed with an enormous black hat which Helen said made her look like an animated mushroom. It was almost too wide to fit in the car and was reposing, like a spoilt cat, on tissue paper in the boot. Lucy thought they might have to put cones around her in church.

Once their car pulled up, Caroline leapt forward to help Lucy out. The five bridesmaids were hanging about, the little ones mutinous after having been read the riot act by Caroline in the car. An enormous gust of wind caught Lucy's veil, almost lifting her off her feet. 'I feel like Mary bloody Poppins,' she muttered to Annie.

'Ready?' Archie turned to her, and smiled. Through the open door of the church, Lucy could hear the organist revving up. She tucked her arm through her father's.

'Ready.'

She took a step forward and then realized she wasn't moving. Her head ricocheted backwards. Her youngest niece, Clarissa, was standing firmly on her train. Annie shoved her. 'Get off, beetle,' she hissed, though smiling. Annie had promised the two sisters a water fight later, if they were good.

Lucy wondered quite how she should walk. Brides, in her imagination, glided as if on castors. She was having to take little mincy steps because of the tiny bridesmaids, who would otherwise be propelled forward and hit her smartly on the back. They needed to get a rhythm going, like a pantomime horse. She tugged Archie's arm. 'Slow down,' she whispered as they walked through the heavy oak doors of the church.

The music, inside the church, was deafening. All the guests were sitting very quietly, as if in pain, but when Lucy entered there was a ripple of noise, like a Chinese whisper. As one person, they all turned, apart from her cousin Cassie, who was trying to trap her two-year-old son under a pew before he got to the altar ahead of Lucy. The ushers had been given strict instructions to put the bride's guests on the left, the groom's on the right. But Rob had such a tiny percentage of the guest list, it meant one side was stuffed with smart hatty people and the other side was less than half full. After consultation with the vicar, the ushers had asked some of the bride's guests if they would mind moving to the groom's side. There was hint of polite reluctance, as silk met polyester.

The invitations, issued on thick cream card with twirly embossed black writing, stipulated morning suits. When Jack and Peggy's friends and relations rang to ask what they were and did they have to, Jack said he didn't think it was compulsory. Peggy however said at least he ought to make the effort, and took Jack to Moss Bros to get measured up. But when she saw him in the suit, she could have cried. From being such a well-built man he now resembled a turtle in a grey shell. Eventually she did agree the rest of the family didn't have to bother, as it pushed the cost up no end and they were having to pay for overnight accommodation as well. Most of the men on Rob's side were in suits, apart from Rob's young cousin, Pete, who had mutinied and was wearing jeans. He hadn't wanted to come at all, and had only been bribed by the promise of free beer. Peggy made sure he sat right next to her so she could keep an eye on him. She shifted nervously in her seat. She wished she hadn't chosen a skirt with such a tight waistband, but she'd thought that if she bought the size fourteen it would force her to go on a diet. But she felt so apprehensive about the whole day her only consolation in the run-up were intravenous chocolate eclairs. And, looking down the row, she wished that Rob's eighteen-year-old cousin Kelly hadn't put on such a short, tight skirt. It wasn't as if she had the legs for it – legs like cooling towers, as Rob once very rudely said. Tights would have helped the overall effect, too.

Walking up the aisle, Lucy wasn't sure what to do with her face. She kept catching people's eyes and grinning at them, but then quickly thought that a grin wasn't the appropriate facial expression for a bride. So she tried serene, saying to herself, 'Think Grace Kelly.' She ended up selecting a small, slightly ironic smile to show she knew she looked ridiculous, and responded to the many 'hellos' with minute nods, like the Queen on walkabout. She was trying very hard not to search the crowd on her side for Max, and had spent all morning trying to suppress all conscious thoughts of him. But it kept bubbling up, the idea of seeing him again. It felt extraordinarily like a prize.

He'd amazed her by sending an affirmative letter to the invitation – worded exactly correctly, 'Mr Max Yorke thanks Mr and Mrs Archie Beresford for the kind . . .' unlike most of the telephoned replies from Rob and Lucy's university friends, who just said 'yeah, great'. Caroline told her Max was now living with his Bristol girlfriend in a flat Max's parents – now Sir George and Lady Yorke – had bought for them, after they'd announced their engagement in the *Telegraph*. Archie and Caroline had put Lucy's in too: Mr and Mrs A. Beresford of Burford, Oxfordshire, are happy to announce the engagement of their elder daughter, Lucy, to Mr Rob Atkinson of Darwen, Lancashire. 'Looks like you're marrying a dustman,' said Helen, cruelly.

Caroline had received the news of George's knighthood in the New Year's Honours list with uncharitably mixed feelings and wondered secretly when it would be Archie's turn. When she dropped in the piece of news about the flat, she resisted all temptation to even hint to Lucy *she* could have been living in the splendour of a Chelsea mews.

Lucy and Rob had a big row over who to invite to the wedding. He'd laboriously written a list of about twenty people, Lucy was soon up to at least sixty. She squinted over his shoulder. 'God, you can't invite him. He'll get totally pissed and pick a fight with someone. And definitely not *him*. Rob, are you mad? I don't think he even owns a decent pair of shoes. I'm not having my wedding turned into a knees-up down the pub.'

'Whose wedding?' Rob enquired, gently.

Lucy sat back against the pillows on their bed, sighing, biro behind one ear.

'OK, *our* wedding. Sorry, my *mother's* wedding.'

'Right,' Rob said. 'Let's cop a look at yours.'

Lucy tried to snatch it away, but Rob grabbed it and held it high above his head, before bringing it down, and sitting, with his back to her, to read.

'You must,' he said, 'be bloody *joking*. Half this lot are ex-boyfriends. And look at these,' he said, gesturing at the portion of the list which contained Lucy's friends from home, many of whom Rob had met and weeded out as being shallow and uninteresting. Lucy knew some of them were shallow and uninteresting, but they were a good laugh, and she'd known them all her life. Plus most of their parents were coming too, as they were friends of Caroline and Archie. Rob dismissed them as the 'suitable crowd'. 'At least I keep in touch with my friends,' Lucy retorted. 'You've hardly kept in touch with anyone.'

'They're all in prison,' Rob said, grinning.

'Don't lie,' Lucy said. 'I'd like to meet some of your friends from school. Apart from Colin,' she added hastily. 'Why don't you let me?'

'Don't think you'd like them,' said Rob, rolling over on the bed. 'You wouldn't exactly have a lot in common.'

Rob then ran his finger down the list until he came to Max's name. 'Max and partner,' Lucy had carefully written. 'Not that tosser,' he said.

'I can't not invite him,' Lucy said. 'His mum and dad are coming anyway. Look, it really doesn't matter, does it? OK, you can invite who you want and I'll invite who I want.'

Rob lay back on the bed and closed his eyes.

'But definitely no bikers,' Lucy said.

As she made her way slowly up the aisle, Rob, who'd been standing with his back to her, turned and waved. The vicar looked at him, alarmed. Really, this wasn't what he'd expected at all. He'd imagined it would be such a pleasant wedding when he'd first met Caroline. Doubts had begun to creep in during the wedding rehearsal the day before, when the best man roared up on the back of an awful old motorbike with hair like an unmown lawn.

As she reached the halfway point of the aisle, Lucy's

eyes flicked sideways. There he was. He held her gaze, steadily, curiously, until a sharp tug from a small bridesmaid behind made her turn. As she turned back, she'd passed his row. She had tried to smile at him, but somehow the smile didn't reach her lips. Her hand involuntarily clenched by her side, then she looked up the aisle and saw Rob ahead of her. Relief flooded through her. Of course she was marrying Rob. How could she not?

At the altar, Lucy had to fight back a dreadful urge to laugh. She couldn't catch Rob's eye, because she could sense, just standing next to him, that he was about to burst. Nick was also standing with his lips pressed tight together, staring at something fascinating on the roof of the church, and humming quietly to himself. Lucy turned to make an 'Oh my God' face at Annie, but she was busy lassoing the bridesmaids, who were trying to unpick the flowers hanging at the end of each aisle. One was also clutching her knickers as if needing the loo, although Caroline had made sure they'd both *been* before they left the house.

'Dearly beloved,' intoned the vicar. Rob, looking straight ahead of him, reached down and found Lucy's hand. She glanced up at him through the gauze of the veil. Smiling, she thought how ridiculous he looked. But, she noticed, he had taken out his earring. The lobe was pink and sore. She knew he'd far rather have nipped out to the registry office and then taken everyone down the pub, and had only agreed to this formal rigmarole to please her and her family. She squeezed his hand, and he shot her a wicked grin.

Her stomach lurched slightly. She hadn't been able to eat at all that morning, and now she felt a bit sick, partly due to the unaccustomed glass of champagne when she'd been getting dressed. Her stomach flipped.

190

Maybe there was a baby in there. Maybe it was already swimming around inside her, like a tiny tipsy goldfish. The thought made her smile, and she realized that she wasn't frightened by the thought any more.

After the rings had been exchanged, the vicar sighed with relief. Thank goodness it was almost over. The youngest bridesmaid had remarked, in a loud conversational tone just after the first hymn, that she needed a poo. The other had burst into noisy sobs and had to be carried out by Annie, who tickled her outside the church until she stopped. Annie had then reappeared carrying her on her shoulders, until Caroline made a scary face at her. This had rather less impact than normal because Caroline, despite her best intentions, had cried throughout. Archie silently passed her his handkerchief.

Rob reached down and slowly lifted up the veil. He slid one hand gently under Lucy's chin, and brought his face close to hers. Then he slid his arm around her and kissed her passionately. There was an embarrassed murmuring around the church, and Caroline, mortified, raised her eyebrows at Archie. Lucy and Rob were giving off enough white-hot sexuality to light the altar candles. The vicar coughed. Rob reluctantly put Lucy down. At the back, their university friends cheered.

Outside the church, the photographer took endless pictures, which made Archie rather annoyed as he knew everyone, himself included, was dying for a drink. The wind had got up while they were in the church, and Lucy had to clutch onto her headdress, for fear of appearing in her wedding photographs looking like a peacock. 'Now, let's have the parents,' the photographer called. Caroline, Archie, Jack and Peggy stepped forward. 'Stand nice and close together,' he said. Jack was kept at hat's length from Caroline. Peggy sucked her breath in sharply as the camera clicked. Her suit, which had looked so smart and such a pretty colour on the rail, now looked cheap next to Caroline's silk dress, although Caroline had been lovely, greeting her warmly with, 'What a beautiful outfit. Where *did* you get it?' Peggy didn't want to say, 'a chain store,' so she said, 'just a local shop.' She also wished she hadn't chosen a hat with a little veil, it was like looking through a fishing net, and her high-heeled shoes felt far too tight.

The groups of guests swiftly polarized. Lucy and Rob's university friends stood together, knocking back as much booze as possible, wearing an assortment of inappropriate outfits and desperate to get the boring bit of the meal over. Most of them hadn't seen each other for ages, as they'd nearly all started work – except for Nick, who had managed to wangle a job with the students' union which meant he could put off any meaningful career decisions, as well as get subsidized beer. Two of Rob's biker friends from home, who had been reluctantly deemed by Lucy just about acceptable enough to be invited, stood with Rob's family, like a pair of yetis in suits. The older women among Rob's relatives sat down to take the weight off their feet, refused champagne and asked nervously for orange juice. Aunty Marge had slipped her shoes off, and was massaging her swollen ankles. 'It was that hot in the church,' she said, passing a quivering hand across her face. 'I feel like a boiled 'am.'

A small faction, led by Jack – who had been told very firmly by Peggy he mustn't have more than two pints – had peeled off to try to find a real drink, because they couldn't cope with champagne. 'Too gassy,' Bob, Jack's brother, said. 'It gives me wind something terrible.'

Amongst them but not of them were Caroline and Archie's friends and their children, the women clashing hats, kissing each other effusively on the cheeks and murmuring, 'I haven't seen you for *ages*. Didn't Lucy look stunning?'

Lucy and Rob stood together, holding hands tightly. They hadn't spoken to each other, properly, since emerging from the church, when Rob had whispered, 'Is your mother wearing that hat for a bet?'

'How do you feel, my wife?' he said quietly, against her ear. 'Married,' she said. 'Me too,' he said. 'I can divorce you now.' 'That's comforting,' Lucy said. 'Where's my prenuptial agreement?' 'You can have it all,' Rob said, expansively. 'The bike *and* the guitar.' 'Rob,' she said, hesitantly, her voice barely audible against the hooting of the crowd. 'What?' he said. 'I might be pregnant.' 'You might be what?' he roared, reaching down and lifting her off her feet. 'That's *brilliant*.' 'Is it?' she said, looking down at him nervously. 'Yeah, *ace*,' he said. 'Let's tell everyone.' 'No!' squealed Lucy. 'At least, not yet. I might not be.' Rob patted her stomach. 'No more champagne for you,' he said.

Lucy groaned.

It was at that moment Annabelle and George appeared, as Rob and Lucy were staring at each other in shocked wonder.

'Lucy, darling, you look exquisite. Doesn't she, George?' Annabelle was wearing a hat to rival Caroline's. Lucy's cheek felt slightly bruised from her kiss, and her strong perfume enveloped her like a force field.

'This is Rob. Rob this is Sir George and Lady Annabelle Yorke.'

Rob grinned, and, putting his cigarette in his mouth,

squinting through the smoke, shook Annabelle's hand. '*Lady Yorke,*' he said, charmingly, with much emphasis. 'How *lovely* to meet you.' Lucy looked at him in alarm. Oh Lord. What was he going to say?

Fortunately, Annabelle had just spotted Max. 'Max,' she called into the crowd. 'Do come and say hello! Lucy hasn't met Cat.' Lucy stiffened. Max pushed his way forward, greeting friends as he came. How dare he be so beautiful, Lucy thought. How dare he be so smooth-looking, and so glamorous, and so perfectly at ease. Next to him, Rob looked like an unmade bed. Rough around the edges. A girl in an exquisite cream silk suit was hanging onto Max's arm, wearing what looked like a small cream top hat, large pearl earrings and a pearl choker. She had smooth black hair, which swung in a sharp bob just under her chin. Her lips were scarlet, her skin a smooth alabaster. 'And this is Cat,' Annabelle said, and added, gushingly, 'They're getting married too! We're *so* thrilled.'

'Max,' Annabelle turned to him. 'You *have* invited Lucy, haven't you? At St Mary's, in May.'

'Of course we will,' Cat said. 'And Rob, too.' She smiled at Lucy, with eyes like lasers. Max simply looked at her. Then he reached forward, and kissed her on the cheek.

'It's lovely to see you,' he said. She felt the warmth of his skin, and the smell of his aftershave. Still the same one.

'And you,' she said. They stood awkwardly, so much to say but unable to say anything, marrying different people.

'How are you?'

'Incredibly busy, I—'

'He's been asked to be a partner,' cut in Cat, swiftly. 'The youngest in the *entire* firm. I'm *rarely* proud of him,' she said, opening baby blue eyes wide as if shot in the back.

'But he has to work *so* hard. I hardly see you, kitten, do I?'

Max looked suitably embarrassed. 'And we're moving,too. You must come and see us in the new house.'

'Where do you work?' Lucy said to Cat, quickly, sensing Rob was about to say something deliberately provocative.

'I'm in PR,' she said. 'But Max wants me to give it up, don't you darling? He's positively *Neanderthal* about working women.'

'Quite right too,' George said.

Rob dropped his cigarette on the floor and ground it out with his foot. 'I don't think we've been introduced,' he said, with exaggerated politeness, to Max. Lucy had a sudden vivid mental image of Rob standing bollock-naked in the wardrobe.

'No, I don't think we have,' Max said, pleasantly, taking in Rob's voice, the roll-ups and the protective arm around Lucy. There was something edgy about Rob that made him very uncomfortable. He didn't seem like Lucy's sort at all. A silence fell. Max looked at Rob as if expecting further conversation, but Rob looked about him, as if bored. Lucy, dying inside, longed for an intervention, which arrived in the form of Archie, who kissed Annabelle warmly on the cheek and shook George's hand. Rob tugged Lucy away. 'Come on,' he said, putting on an outrageously upper-class accent. 'You haven't said hello to Aunty Marge yet. She's *longing* to meet you. What a wanker,' he added, under his breath, as they walked off. 'Poncy git.'

'Don't be so bloody rude,' Lucy said, snatching her arm away. He looked at her in surprise. Surely she couldn't be impressed by a phoney tosspot like that?

Lucy seethed. He had made her look foolish.

Just then the black sheep of Rob's family, Uncle Arthur, stumbled past. He held a pint in each hand, and Lucy could see his pockets were stuffed with the cigars Archie had ordered to be put on the bar.

'Look at him,' said Rob's Aunty Marge, embarrassed. 'Owt for nowt and there wi' a bucket.' Cat brushed past on her way to the loo. She bumped slightly into Aunty Marge, who staggered a little. 'Mind out, lass,' she said. Lucy caught her under the elbow. 'So sorry,' Cat drawled, looking her up and down dismissively, as she would a waitress.

Not all of Nick's speech went down well. Caroline sat, with a smile politely stitched to her lips, as he regaled the room with tales of Rob's life at university, describing the flat they shared straight out of *The Young Ones*. Their university friends howled with laughter while everyone else smiled politely, though he had overstepped the mark on a couple of occasions, especially when he referred to the time Rob had been caught in Lucy's room when she was still in halls. Caroline laughed, but stole a reproving glance at Lucy, who pretended not to see her.

The meal almost over, Caroline was finally beginning to relax. It had been such a strain, all the arrangements. Lucy really hadn't appreciated just how much trouble they'd been, the flowers for the marquee, all the little touches which made such a difference. She knew Lucy thought she was fussing, to make the pale pink of the flowers match the silk lining of the marquee exactly – but the result, even if she said it herself, was quite lovely. She just hoped . . . well, she hoped they would be happy. She reached forward for her glass of champagne, to raise a toast to the bridesmaids, and an involuntary shiver ran through her. There must be a draught.

After the meal Lucy did her duty, chatting to ancient aunts and her parents' friends. Rob went to the bar, with his mates from university. Peggy and the female members of Rob's party sat at one table, not dancing, apart from Kelly, who flung herself around the floor with gay abandon. The highlight for Lucy was watching her mum dancing to a rock 'n' roll record with Rob's Uncle Bob, who whipped her about like a top. Caroline kept a fixed smile on her face throughout the entire ordeal, and then gracefully declined a second dance. But there was no other visible sign of mixing. It was like the parting of the Red Sea.

By eleven, Lucy had lost Rob. It was high time they left for their hotel, which had an opulent honeymoon suite. Caroline and Archie were paying, as a special treat. The older relatives were beginning to droop, although the university lot were still going strong. She found Rob at the bar, one hand holding a pint, the other arm round his father, whose arm kept slipping off the bar. Lucy had changed into a simple beige silk trouser suit for going away. In the bedroom Caroline and Archie were to stay in that night, her mother hugged her as she changed. 'We're so very proud of you,' she said.

'You do like him, don't you?' Lucy said, reaching up to smooth away her mother's tears.

'Oh yes. He's a very special young man. A bit different, certainly, but I'm sure he'll make you happy.'

'He really does love me, you know, Mummy.'

'I know he does, darling.'

'Come on,' Lucy said. 'We have to go.' Rob turned. He was quite drunk. 'Do we have to? Now?' he said, almost belligerently.

'You can stay here,' Lucy said crossly. 'But I'm leaving.'

'You'd better go, lad,' Jack said. 'It *is* your wedding night.' Lucy could see he'd had far more than two pints, too.

On the way out, Lucy found Peggy to say goodbye. She was exasperatedly quizzing the two ancient aunts as to the whereabouts of their handbags.

'Have you enjoyed it?' Lucy said, loudly, to Aunty Marge.

'It was lovely,' she said, pressing a hand like a soft cushion against Lucy's face. 'The tent looked *beautiful*.'

Chapter Sixteen

'No,' said Rob. 'No, no, no.'

'What's wrong with Sophie?'

'It's a stupid name. It sounds like sofa. Or soap. What's wrong with Susan? Or Suzanne? Danielle?'

'You are joking?'

'What about Dawn?'

Lucy turned to him crossly. 'Now you *must* be joking.'

'Well, if it's a boy, it has to be Jack. I've always said I would name my son after my dad.'

Lucy mused to herself that she was rather glad the middle classes had annexed that one. 'Jack's OK,' she said. 'Or how about Ben?'

'Benjamin?' Rob howled. 'You want to call the poor little sod after a rabbit?'

'Not Benjamin,' Lucy said. 'Just Ben.'

'Dog's name,' Rob said. 'Stephen, then.' Lucy looked at him sharply. 'Michael, Peter,' he suggested.

'*Dull*. How about Jake?' Lucy said. 'Or Tom. Maybe Daniel. And if it's a girl – Laura.'

'Over my dead body,' Rob said. 'Sounds like that awful old song. Nope, I still fancy the name Dawn.'

'Dawn Atkinson?' Lucy said. 'Oh, *please*. Give the

girl some chance of glamour. Remember she's going to be saddled with Atkinson – ' Rob looked at her warningly – 'so she'd better have a pretty first name.'

They were lying on sunloungers at the side of the hotel swimming pool, trying not to feel intimidated by the large crane hovering above them, like an enormous praying mantis. It was a fine detail which had not appeared in the brochure. None of the happy smiling families had dads with tattoos in the photos, either.

That morning, a home-testing kit bought on the dash to the airport confirmed Lucy's pregnancy. When the pink line appeared, Lucy jumped on Rob's bed. He was fast asleep, and woke with a start.

'Are we being demolished?'

Lucy waved the piece of litmus paper at him.

'Is this the time to be performing scientific experiments?' he said, enquiringly.

'I'm pregnant, you git.'

He stared at her, a slow delighted smile spreading across his face. 'That is *fantastic*,' he said. 'Come here. Wow. Pregnant. A *baby*.'

Lucy snuggled down in the single bed, next to him. They'd got a late deal on the holiday, which Rob had insisted on paying for, alone. Lucy had received quite a lot of money as wedding presents from her close family, but Rob insisted that should be put in a separate account. He didn't want her money. It meant that Lucy couldn't complain about the hotel, although it was situated in exceedingly close proximity to a building site. Not only that, but Rob had managed to book a twin-bedded room. They started off in the two beds pushed together, and then inevitably a yawning gulf appeared between them. Lucy also developed a stomach bug on the second day, which meant she spent most of the honeymoon thundering backward and forward to the loo. Rob said it was like living with a herd of migrating wildebeest.

Rob rang his mum and dad immediately to tell them that Lucy was pregnant. Lucy hesitated. She felt it wasn't the kind of thing she could broach to her mother over the phone. Archie would undoubtedly do rapid mental calculations and work out that unless this baby had a gestation period briefer than that of a rabbit, she must have been pregnant at the wedding. They'd think it had been a *shotgun* wedding. How awful. And it had cost so much. Lucy went hot and cold.

'We could pretend it's premature when it arrives,' Rob said. He knew how much she cared about her parents finding out, although he, frankly, didn't give a toss. What did it matter, now they were married anyway? He was sure that was the line his parents would take, and they did. Peggy didn't turn a hair when he told her, just shrieked down the phone, and then said he'd better get off, this call must be costing him a fortune. Her first grandchild. Rob could almost hear the knitting needles beginning to clack straight away.

Caroline insisted on meeting them at the airport. Archie thought it was a bit of an imposition, and they ought really to be on their own. But they needed a lift back to Lancashire, as they still had to pack up the contents of the house in Clitheroe as well as do battle with the wedding presents, before moving everything down to the cottage they had bought just before the wedding, in a village outside Oxford. Their first real house! Lucy was very excited. Archie had offered to pay a substantial deposit as a wedding present, but Rob wouldn't let him. Archie, although slightly hurt, appreciated the fact that Rob wanted them to stand on their own two feet. Lucy thought Rob was mad. She was well used to accepting handouts from her father, and pointed out to Rob that if his father had offered to give them money, he wouldn't have refused. His dad had paid for his first bike, hadn't he? Rob grudgingly accepted the point, but still wouldn't budge. Lucy was finding out that when Rob made up his mind, it was very hard indeed to shift him.

Peggy was enormously impressed they were buying their own house, so early in the marriage. It had been worth all the sacrifices, she thought, to get Rob through university. The first generation of their family to buy a house, as newly-weds. She and Jack had moved in with their in-laws until the council gave them a house, which they later bought. And she couldn't believe the fact Lucy and Rob were intending to run two cars. In Peggy's eyes, that amounted to an extravagance bordering on the recklessly wanton.

On the plane home, Lucy and Rob rehearsed how they might break the news.

'Ciao Granny! I'm up the duff!' was Rob's less than helpful suggestion. Lucy, who was feeling very sick, glared at him. 'You are not helping,' she said. 'You're not helping at all. It will be the worst thing in the world to them, you'll see,' she added, glumly. 'You just have *no idea*. My mother runs support groups for this kind of thing. If any of her friends find out I was pregnant at the wedding she'll be drummed out of the luncheon club with "daughter is a harlot" stamped on her forehead. In terms of a social crime it's up there with mugging. Please,' she said. 'Stop laughing.'

'Look,' he said, hooting helplessly. 'It's a grandchild, not lupus. I'm sure you're exaggerating.'

'I'm not,' Lucy said vehemently. 'Things like this just don't happen in my family. She will feel like she has failed in her most sacred task as a mother.'

Lucy tried to compose her face into that of a relaxed, happy young wife without a care in the world, as she followed Rob pushing their trolley round the screens into the arrivals hall. She knew she looked awful, tired and thin, and not even very brown, as she couldn't stand lying in the heat, with her gippy tummy and bowels which had clearly led too sedentary a life so far and were now making up for it with moments of frantic aerobic exercise. Rob, who had avoided the tummy bug completely and seemed to have the constitution of a horse, was tanned almost mahogany.

As soon as Lucy saw her parents, so clean, so normal, so *safe*, she burst into tears. Caroline, alarmed, ran up and hugged her.

'What on *earth* is the matter, darling? Are you all right?' Archie and Rob hung back. 'You don't look well at all.'

'I'm not ill,' Lucy sobbed. Then threw caution to the winds. 'I'm pregnant.'

'Goodness,' Caroline said. 'That *was* quick.' Archie looked at Lucy sharply. Quick? It was impossible.

'Come and sit down,' Caroline said, leading Lucy to a small row of plastic chairs.

'I'm so sorry, Mummy,' Lucy said, holding tightly onto Caroline's hand. She decided to refuse to fudge the issue. 'I suspected before the wedding but I didn't really know. I found out on holiday.'

'How long?' Caroline said, gently. 'About three months, I think,' Lucy sniffed.

'Well,' Caroline said, far too calmly. 'It's not the end of the world, is it?'

'We rather hoped,' Rob said, 'you might be pleased.'

'I'm not quite sure how I feel,' Caroline said, slowly. 'It's just rather a shock. Archie, darling, do you think you might get me some water?' Lucy tried to put her arm round her. Caroline, very gently, pushed her hand away. 'Thank you, Lucy. I'll be fine.'

Lucy looked beseechingly at her father. The expression on his face told her she must not say any more. Rob stood on the edge of the group, apart. Archie became very brisk.

'We must get on,' he said. 'The car's this way.' He reached over to take the luggage trolley from Rob, who held tight. 'I can manage,' he said. Almost aggressively. This man had slept with his daughter before marriage, which of course Archie knew had been going on, but now the evidence was being pushed in his face. And he didn't like it one bit.

Speeding up, Archie went on ahead to catch up with Caroline, who was walking very quickly, with her arms folded around herself, as if holding something in. Following them, Rob glanced sideways at Lucy. Tears were running down her cheeks. Rob felt incredibly impatient. Just why did they have to make all this fuss? Christ, what a family. So bloody concerned with how things looked. Why couldn't they be honest with each other instead of all this polite coldness? Why didn't they just have it out, have a good scream and shout if they were angry? He couldn't cope with all this well-bred restrained emotion.

Rob reached out to take Lucy's hand, but she moved slightly away, switching her handbag onto her other shoulder. 'It doesn't matter,' he hissed at Lucy. 'Just ignore them. So what? We're happy. My mum and dad are happy.' Lucy looked at him, her eyes pink. 'You really don't understand, do you?'

*   *   *

In the car, driving home from Lancashire having refused the offer to stay the night at the cottage, Archie pleading pressure of work and Caroline incapable of trusting herself to speak to either of them – the atmosphere in the car on the way up had been so chilly you could have flash-frozen a prawn – Caroline sat with her lips pressed tightly together. Archie reached out to take her hand.

'It really *doesn't* matter so much, darling, does it? It's very different from our day, and they do seem happy together.'

'Lucy isn't happy,' Caroline said quickly.

'I don't think that's fair,' Archie said.

'I know,' Caroline said, her voice breaking, 'she isn't going to cope with this at all. He's responsible. I'm sure she wouldn't have been so silly, but I suppose in his family it isn't quite the issue it is for us,' she added bitterly.

'That isn't fair either,' Archie said. 'They're very decent people.'

'Decent,' Caroline said. 'But hardly the same. Not the same values at all. I'm sorry, but I can't help thinking this whole thing is a terrible mistake.'

'Why now?' Archie said. 'You were quite happy before the wedding.'

'I wasn't really,' Caroline said quickly. 'It was just that Lucy was so adamant he was right for her I was prepared to accept it. But seeing him at the airport, so cocky – not even apologizing or seeming ashamed at all – and he was so proprietorial. I feel we've lost her.' Her voice ended in a sob.

'You're being too dramatic,' Archie said.

'It just seems so *sordid*. I feel like Lucy's been hijacked, and there's nothing we can do.'

'That is unfair. He really loves her, you know. I'm

sure it was just an accident, we won't even think about it once the baby is born. Surely the important thing is that Lucy *is* married?' Caroline looked at him searchingly. 'Is it?' she said.

The next morning, Lucy was very pensive. Rob tried desperately to cheer her up. 'Look, we can sell these for loads of money,' he said, carefully handling two rather hideous large platinum goblets given to them by one of her father's business clients. Lucy was appalled. 'You can't sell wedding presents!' she said, horrified.

Sitting on the floor surrounded by mounds of wrapping paper, Lucy was desperately trying to keep a list, and the thought of having to send out so many thank-you letters as well as move house was profoundly dispiriting. But most of all she felt crushed by the weight of her mother's disapproval. She hadn't rung. Lucy shook herself. She had to concentrate on the matter in hand. She refused to be intimidated by her mother's displeasure. So what? She was a married woman now, not a child. Rob, she knew, was no more likely to send a thank-you letter than take up golf. She unwrapped a small, flowery parcel.

'China egg cups from Aunty Marge,' she said. 'Look, with a little hen on the side.'

'Very useful,' said Rob, daring her to say anything. 'What the hell's this?'

'It's a silver salver,' said Lucy, looking at the card, written in twirly embossed writing. 'From Annabelle and George. Sorry, *Sir* George and *Lady* Annabelle.'

'What's it for?'

'I'm not entirely sure,' Lucy said, turning it over to look at the bottom. 'But it's solid silver.'

'We could melt it down.' Lucy glared at him.

'I'm sure it'll come in handy,' she said, primly.

'What for?'

'Dunno.'

'At least we can give it to someone else for their wedding. Someone we don't like. Oh shit,' he added, unpacking another box. 'Another sodding decanter.'

Chapter Seventeen

'We'd be delighted,' Lucy said. 'It's ages since we've been out for dinner.' On one hip was the baby, in one hand was a bottle she was frantically shaking and, wedged under her ear, was the phone. Laura opened her mouth to scream. Lucy jammed in the bottle, and rocked her. It was a funny thing, this rocking business. As soon as she first held Laura even in the hospital bed, she began to rock gently backward and forward automatically, like a metronome. She had also surprised herself by periodically bursting into song, like a tone-deaf thrush, making up nonsensical rhymes with Laura's name in them. This clearly was what having babies did to you. It sent you potty.

Lucy had been quite unprepared for the amount of love she felt for Laura. Rob, too, was completely besotted, although his initial reaction had been horror at the carnage of birth. When Laura finally emerged after exhausting hours of labour – halfway through Lucy felt like saying, 'Look, this is a really bad idea. Let's just go home and forget all about this baby nonsense,' but it was like being on an aeroplane, you were sure as hell going to have to land somewhere – she was covered in blood, and Rob made rather a faux pas about the baby and the afterbirth. But he was very tired – after all, he'd had to stand up the whole time, while Lucy got to lie down, as he later pointed out. When Laura's head appeared, Rob gasped, 'It's a baby!' Lucy squinted down the length of her heaving body at him. 'What the hell did you think it was going to be?' she asked. 'Trapped wind?' he ventured.

Once it was clear no-one was going to die, at least immediately, he bent to look at the minute scrap nestling in Lucy's exhausted arms. Eyes gummed shut, she was making tiny kitten noises and screwing up little fists. He felt an overwhelming urge to burst into tears or shout with laughter – a feeling like a tidal wave inside him was welling up and seemed as if it might burst from his body. 'Can I . . . ?' Lucy smiled, and gently lifted the baby up.

'Support her head,' she said, warningly. Rob very, very slowly put his arms underneath his daughter and brought her to him. As she felt the warmth of his chest, she mewed slightly and instinctively snuggled into him. Rob looked down at her. A tear slid down his cheek and fell onto the soft baby blanket. He gently placed a finger on her downy cheek. Now he knew what the word 'joy' meant.

When the nurse suggested he had better go – Rob couldn't tear himself away, and would have climbed into bed with both of them – he paused by the door.

'It's the dawn,' he said, 'of a new Dawn,' and, grinning, he ran off down the corridor, leaping into the air and narrowly avoiding colliding with a nurse carrying a stack of sheets.

'Laura,' Lucy yelled after him. 'Laura or you never come near me again!'

*   *   *

209

Lucy had made it very clear she expected Rob to be with her for the birth, which Archie in particular thought was very odd. The last thing he would have wanted to see was Caroline giving birth, and he was sure she wouldn't have wanted him there. What for? It was a woman's thing, surely. He offered to pay for Lucy to have a private room, an offer Rob swiftly refused. 'Thanks very much, Archie,' he said. 'But we'll be fine.' The implication to Archie was clear. Back off, it said. She's mine now. Archie understood Rob's feelings, but it did make him feel rather helpless. An uneasy truce had been drawn halfway through Lucy's pregnancy. After several weeks, Caroline could bear it no longer, and rang Lucy.

'I don't approve,' she said firmly, before Lucy even had a chance to speak. 'I don't approve, and I can't pretend I'm happy about the way this baby is arriving in the world. But it will be my grandchild, and Daddy and I are determined to do all we can to help.'

There was a long pause, and Lucy could feel her bottom lip trembling. She squeaked, 'I'm sorry, Mummy.'

'I know,' Caroline said, in a softer voice. 'But Daddy and I are of the old generation. We never expected anything like this. I've told everyone,' she added, bravely. Lucy went slightly pale and looked at the phone. Had she posted a note in the church newsletter? Announced it in *The Times*? 'And they've been very understanding. I know you think I'm being silly and it doesn't matter these days, but it does, Lucy, to me. Anyway, I'm not going to say another word about it.'

Yippee, thought Lucy.

'Now, have you thought how you're going to decorate the nursery? I saw some adorable fabric in Liberty . . .'

*   *   *

Caroline was horrified to find Lucy and the baby on an open ward when they visited, not realizing that Archie had discreetly offered to pay, and been refused. It didn't help that the woman in the next bed must have weighed twenty stone, and slung her baby about like a slab of fish when she was changing its nappy, saying, 'Shut up, our Ryan, while I change your bum.' Caroline's face was a picture. Archie, too, looked horribly out of place on the ward in his blazer and flannels. He handled Laura as if she might break.

'You are rather gorgeous,' he said, peering into her grumpy little face, wrinkled like a red cabbage.

Caroline and Archie set up a trust fund for Laura. Peggy knitted endless woollen cardigans which she sent down in carefully tied brown-paper parcels. Lucy marvelled at their intricate design and the time she must have taken over them. It broke Peggy's heart that they'd moved before the birth, and Lucy reflected that she probably would have been far more use than Caroline, who was rarely if ever in and made it clear she couldn't be expected to be permanently available for babysitting. Caroline thought that Lucy ought to get an au pair to give her a hand. Lucy pointed out there was hardly room for herself, Rob and the baby in the cottage – they'd never squeeze in an au pair. She'd have to sleep on the roof or perhaps dangle from a window.

'Hurry *up*,' Lucy said to Rob when he finally walked through the door, his face creased with tiredness and carrying a stack of the nationals he hadn't had time to read at work.

'What?' he said.

'We're going out for dinner, remember.'

Rob let out a huge moan.

'No! Not tonight! Oh please, Lucy, my head's throbbing and I have to get through this lot. I haven't had a moment to myself all day. Some gibbon of a junior reporter got a name wrong in a big court case and we're on the verge of being sued. Where are we supposed to be going?'

'Cheryl and David's.'

Rob made an even louder groaning noise and sank to his knees in the tiny hallway.

'Not Cheryl from the National Eating Afterbirth Trust?'

'Don't be silly,' Lucy said sternly. 'She's very nice. And you know it isn't called that.'

'She's *very nice*,' Rob mimicked. 'And she's also very dull. Please, Lucy, don't make me spend the night with the human equivalent of root vegetables.'

'They are *not* vegetables. They are a lovely couple who have a child the same age as Laura, which will come in very handy. And they live nearby. Rob, how long is it since we went out?'

'Two years,' said Rob, walking past her and heading for the shower.

Cheryl was one of those women who was all over you, which Lucy was initially grateful for at the first meeting she attended of the National Childbirth Trust, because all of the other women seemed frankly terrifying and appeared to know exactly what they were doing. Her husband David, Cheryl confided in a breathy whisper while they all lay flat out like railway sleepers concentrating on breathing from their diaphragms, was a senior manager in the planning department of the local council. She had worked there too, she said, but had no intention of going back. Lucy had by now abandoned all thoughts of finding a job

while she was pregnant, and felt that the issue of jug-
gling work and caring for a baby might just be too
complicated. They couldn't afford a nanny, and of
course didn't have room for an au pair, so it was either
a case of Lucy staying put at home or sending Laura to
a childminder's, which Lucy didn't fancy at all.

After they'd both given birth she'd seen Cheryl a
couple of times. It was nice to have someone at exactly
the same stage of chaos and fear as yourself, although
Cheryl appeared to have an extremely supportive
mother-in-law who needed no excuse to whisk into the
house and take over while Cheryl had long baths. Lucy
dreamed of having long baths – whenever she put as
much as one toe in, Laura woke up from what had
appeared to be a deep and satisfying sleep. If Lucy sat
her in her baby bouncer at the side, she had to keep
gawping at Laura over the edge. Nothing seemed relax-
ing any more. Not even sleep.

Truth be told, Cheryl was beginning to irritate Lucy,
but then she hardly knew anyone else in the village
and she couldn't afford to be massively selective. Her
old friends who hadn't moved to London all seemed to
be resolutely single and allergic to babies. They all
wanted wild nights and to get pissed, which Lucy
couldn't manage when she had to be sufficiently conscious at three in the morning to find both Laura and
her own breasts. She chatted to people in shops, but all
the other mothers of young children seemed, well – not
her sort. She was rapidly coming to the conclusion that
Cheryl wasn't her sort either, but she needed someone
to talk to or she really would go bonkers. Caroline
came over as often as she could, but Lucy now had a
chance to see at close hand just how many pleasant
things Caroline packed into her life. Shopping,
lunches with friends, trips to the theatre in London,

going out for dinner with friends, bridge, a little golf – all the things which Lucy had thought were shallow and tedious in her youth now seemed fun and enjoyable. Maybe it *was* time, as Rob said, she got back to work. She couldn't exactly see Rob taking up bridge. The only social event he seemed to enjoy now was going to the pub. Lucy knew he was working incredibly hard and was really good at his job, but there didn't seem to be much of him left over for her. Lucy wanted a bit more jolliness from him, but he wasn't doing jolly at the moment. He was doing grumpy, in great chunks.

Caroline, amazingly, had offered to babysit that evening. She swept up in her new BMW – she'd moved on to something rather more racy now both girls were off her hands – and immediately irritated Lucy intensely by bringing her own tea bags and biscuits in her trusty wicker basket. 'I know you always run out!' she said, playfully, while Lucy felt like clouting her. And, no matter how carefully Lucy tried to tidy up, her mother always homed in on the one thing she had forgotten – the swing bin not emptied, the crumbs left on the draining board, which she'd sweep off with a disdainful hand. Archie rarely came to the cottage, but when he did, he looked ridiculous, its ceilings so low he had to stand bent over like a paper clip.

Lucy felt that Caroline ought to try caring for a baby with next to no money and a grumpy husband. The handful of women who lived near Lucy and didn't look terminally irritating all seemed to work, so there was no cosy network of other young mums to have coffee mornings and chats with, as Caroline had enjoyed when she and Helen were little. Lucy adored Laura, but she did feel as if she was somehow doing time for a crime she didn't even know she'd committed.

* * *

'Could you take off your shoes?'

'What?'

'Your *shoes*,' Cheryl said, patiently.

'Why?' Rob asked irritably, hovering in the glass-fronted porch of Cheryl and David's house. Set on an estate at the back of the village, it was much bigger than Lucy and Rob's cottage, and Lucy saw with a flash of annoyance they had two new cars. Very dull cars though, she thought.

'New carpet,' Cheryl twittered. Rob glanced at Lucy. She was going to owe him, big time.

Perhaps they should have been warned by the musical chimes doorbell. Lucy and Rob obediently took their shoes off, and tiptoed into the hall. 'Lovely carpet,' said Lucy, dutifully, trying not to shield her eyes at the swirling pattern.

'It's a Berber,' Cheryl said, proudly. 'Terribly expensive. Top of the range, almost all wool. We bought it from the carpet centre on the industrial estate. Have you been there yet? It's marvellous. We had a family trip and just fell in love with it.' She put her head on one side, and smiled.

'Now, coats. I'll just pop and hang them in the cloakroom.'

Lucy and Rob lurked in the hall, waiting to be offered a drink. No offer came. Cheryl reappeared, coatless, and led them into a sitting room dominated by a beaten-copper fireplace. Built into one wall was a large fish tank. 'David's hobby,' Cheryl said. 'It keeps him out of mischief.' Lucy did not look at Rob.

'David!' Cheryl called up the stairs. 'Come down and meet the guests. They're here!' Then, in an aside, 'He's just reading Eloise a story. We know she can't understand anything yet, but it's really important, isn't it

215

Lucy, to get them started early? I know you're a one for books, aren't you? Your house – like a library! Now Rob, what can I get you to drink?'

Lucy had a terrible feeling he was going to say 'arsenic'. But he smiled, and said a beer would be great.

'And you, Lucy?'

'Wine,' Lucy said. 'Wine would be lovely.'

Cheryl disappeared, having told them both to take a pew.

Rob looked at her enquiringly. 'You know what this means, don't you?' he said quietly.

'What?' Lucy hissed back.

'Blow jobs for a week.'

'Shush,' Lucy said furiously, as Cheryl reappeared. Rob's beer had been poured into a half-pint glass, which he drained in several swallows. Lucy took a sip of her wine. It was sweet. 'Delicious,' she said. 'Thanks.'

There was the sound of footsteps on the stairs. David, who had glasses and the earnest expression of a Labrador, walked in, carrying a fluffy Eloise. She had an extraordinary amount of hair for a small baby, which always took Lucy rather by surprise.

'Here's a little lady who wants to say goodnight,' David said.

'Give Mummy a big kiss,' Cheryl said. 'Night, night, little lady.'

David advanced on Lucy. 'Kiss, kiss,' he said. Lucy looked at him in horror. Did *he* want *her* to kiss *him*? But he was bending down to bring the baby to Lucy's sitting height. She dutifully kissed her on the cheek. Rob shrank back against the sofa in alarm. David moved towards him. 'And Uncle Rob,' he said. Lucy began to shake with suppressed laughter. 'Come on,

Uncle Rob,' she said. 'Give Eloise a kiss.' Rob gingerly leant forward and peered with distaste at the hairy creature.

'Any history of werewolves in the family?' he said, under his breath. Lucy heard him, snorted and tried to turn it into a cough, but David, thank God, seemed oblivious. Rob looked up at David. 'No thanks, I've just had one.'

David laughed uncertainly, and retreated. Cheryl had warned him Lucy's husband had a rather offbeat sense of humour.

Rob drained his beer, resisting the urge to lick round the edge of his glass, and turned to Lucy. 'You've hardly touched your wine,' he said. 'And you said it was lovely.'

'I'm taking it steady,' Lucy said.

'We do have to, don't we, with little ones! I used to think nothing of drinking half a bottle of wine in one night!' Cheryl laughed.

Cheryl chatted to Lucy about teething and how they were going to tackle potty training, while Rob looked mournfully at his beer and the kitchen door. Cheryl took no notice until Rob stood up and said, 'Can I get another drink?' Lucy looked at him in horror. Cheryl went slightly pink. 'Of course,' she said. 'I didn't realize.'

'I'm so sorry,' Lucy said apologetically, as Rob's back retreated into the kitchen where they could hear the sound of the fridge opening.

When David came back down, rubbing his hands together in front of him, he said, 'Excellent! Time for a beer.' Then he engaged Rob earnestly in conversation, saying, 'Cheryl tells me you're a *journalist*. We'll have to watch what we say, won't we darling?' Cheryl tinkled with laughter. 'Don't want you putting us in the papers!' Rob remarked this was fairly unlikely. Then David leant forward and said, 'Actually, I might have a story for you.' Lucy felt, rather than heard, Rob groan. People were always telling him they had a fabulous story and it was almost always a dud.

'If you ever,' Rob said, lying back in bed with his hands behind his head, 'suggest that we meet either of those two cretins again I will shoot you.'

'I thought you'd thoroughly enjoyed it, Uncle Rob,' said Lucy, snuggling down against his chest. 'It was a *super* meal.'

Rob peered down at her. 'Pâté, coq without the vin and *trifle*?'

'At least we got lots to drink,' said Lucy, laughing.

'Absolutely,' Rob said. 'I for one am as pissed as a rat on four halves of beer and two glasses of wine.'

'At least you drank the wine,' Lucy said. 'I couldn't get it down. Anyway, things could be worse. We could have taken them up on their offer of sharing Cheryl's mum's timeshare in the Canaries.'

'Over my dead body,' Rob said. 'Anyway, remember what you owe me.'

'Oh *no*,' Lucy said.

Chapter Eighteen

'Why are there lots of brochures for skiing holidays on the kitchen table?'

Lucy, who was wiping off her make-up in the upstairs bathroom, started guiltily. She'd meant to put them away and seek an appropriate moment.

'Hang on,' she called. 'I'll be down in a minute.' She tied her dressing gown round her, and went downstairs.

Rob was sitting at the kitchen table, flicking through the glossy brochures. He looked tired, and his skin was sallow. Lucy thought how much he needed a holiday. But not, she told herself fiercely, the Lake District again. On their first holiday together after Laura was born, Rob took them back to a chalet his family had often rented for their holidays there. It was dank, cold, bare and depressing. On their arrival, Lucy had looked about her in despair. They were going to spend a week here? What on earth were they going to do?

'Walk,' Rob said. 'It's wonderful for walking. Great mountains, great scenery, what more could you ask for?'

'A swimming pool?' Lucy said.

'Why on earth do you want a swimming pool?'

'Because,' she said, 'we have a one-year-old child who has to be entertained in some way and is not going to take kindly to being humped over mountains in the freezing cold like a polar-bear cub.'

'You'll love it, won't you Laura?' Rob said.

'You're carrying her,' Lucy said.

'No problem.'

After just one day, Rob's back went. 'Those baby carriers must be really badly designed,' he said, lying in a deep hot bath. Lucy looked at him critically. 'They aren't designed to be worn all day. Who do you think you are? Sherpa Tensing?'

'Your turn tomorrow,' Rob said.

'Not bloody likely,' Lucy said. 'I'll take her shopping in Windermere.'

'Well what kind of holiday would you like?' Rob said, crossly.

'A hotel holiday,' Lucy said. 'A hotel holiday with a crèche and a pool and a health spa so I can lie down and have facials and massage and a room with a huge comfortable double bed and a restaurant serving delicious food and a baby-listening service. *That* kind of holiday. And preferably somewhere hot.'

'Remember Turkey,' Rob said darkly.

'There are other places than Turkey,' Lucy said. 'Be more adventurous.'

'I don't want to be adventurous,' he said. 'I like it here.'

'Well I don't,' Lucy said, and, to her horror, she started to cry.

'Don't be so spoilt,' Rob said. 'I bought you a new Thermos.'

Lucy looked at him in a threatening manner. 'Don't push it,' she said. She thought of all the lovely clothes she'd packed for her and Laura to wear. There was no-one to see them. It wouldn't have mattered if they'd wandered about all day in oilskins. And Rob really didn't see the point in paying huge prices for restaurant meals. He was just as happy eating at home.

'Why on earth,' Rob said, 'would you take a toddler skiing?'

'They're never too young to start,' Lucy said. 'Look, this one has a special mini ski-school. They just do a couple of hours a day, and the rest of the time they play in a crèche. It's wonderful. It means we can ski together, almost all day, and there's a nanny service at night, too.'

'You seem to forget,' Rob said, 'I can't ski. Not all of us popped off to Verbier every five minutes as children.'

'You can learn,' Lucy said. 'Please, Rob. I haven't been skiing for ages. It'll be fun. We could get a party together, hire a chalet. It would be a laugh.'

'I'd rather go back to the Lake District.'

'If you go back there,' Lucy said, gathering up the brochures with a cross sweep of her arm, 'you go alone.'

'I might just do that.'

'Then I'll go with Mum and Dad. They're always offering to take us with them. It would be nice for Laura to stay somewhere decent.'

'Fine,' Rob said, standing up so quickly his chair fell over backwards. 'You go where you want to go – and I'll do what I fucking want.'

'Please,' Lucy said. 'Don't swear in front of Laura.' Rob stomped off up the stairs to sulk. Lucy wondered about going after him, but then thought, 'I can't be bothered.'

Laura was wheeling herself around in her circular

babywalker, bouncing off pieces of furniture like the ball in a pinball machine. She loved it, and could already achieve an impressive velocity. Lucy bent down and scooped her out.

'We'll go on our own,' she said. 'Won't we, darling? We don't need that nasty grumpy man with us, do we?'

'Daddy,' Laura said, keening after Rob.

'Traitor,' Lucy said, slotting her back into the baby-walker. 'What about the sisterhood?'

The brochures lay in the kitchen drawer for several weeks, until Lucy, on one of her periodic tidying-up fits, found them. She stood for a while, running her finger over a front cover depicting a child in a brightly coloured ski suit, skiing at speed down a pristine white mountain, mouth open, cheeks glowing, laughing. She sighed, went over to the bin and dropped them in. Compromise, she thought. Marriage is all about compromise. Only at this very moment she didn't want to reasonably effect a compromise. She wanted to stab him.

Chapter Nineteen

'Mind the boxes!' Martha called down the long passageway. 'What d'you think you're doing, you little shit?'

She aimed a sharp kick at a Jack Russell, who had a full loo roll clenched firmly in his teeth. 'Give it to me!' She grabbed one end and the puppy, Toffee, joyfully galloped off. Soon the entire hallway looked like an Andrex advert.

'I'm going to have that dog stuffed,' Martha said. 'Lucy, just pick your way through. I'm sorry it's such a tip. The girls are in the back garden. God knows what they're doing, but at least they're not in here.'

Lucy's two, who were hanging shyly on her arms, looked hesitantly up at her.

'Go on,' Lucy said. 'You know Emily from riding, girls, and Sophie's five too,' she said to Olivia, who was clutching her skirt as if fearful that if she let go, her mother would balloon into the air and disappear. Lucy gave them a push.

'Laura, take Olivia with you.'

Laura reached out and took her sister's hand. She gave it a tug. 'Come on, creature,' she said. Olivia dug her heels in but Laura's strength was too much for her and she shot forward, yelping. Lucy, free, thankfully flexed her arms. 'It's like having barnacles. Thank God they're growing up. I'm sick of having children stuck all over me.'

'If I got pregnant again,' Martha said, shoving a large cardboard box along the stone-flagged passageway with her foot, 'I'd give birth and do a runner. Let Sebastian see what it's like. I know exactly what he'd do though – employ a sexy Swedish au pair and be much happier.'

Lucy laughed. 'Anyway,' Martha said, pushing open the antique pine kitchen door with some difficulty, 'it would have to be an immaculate conception. We never have sex any more. Mrs Burke – this is Lucy. Lucy, this is my angel, Mrs B. I wouldn't be getting remotely straight without her.'

To Lucy, it didn't look straight at all. Every available surface was crammed with cooking utensils, letters, files, riding crops, hats, plates and saucers. At the Belfast sink stood an elderly woman wearing an apron. She was sweating slightly, her hands plunged into hot soapy water.

'Can you believe,' Martha said, 'the plumber can't come until Tuesday to fix the dishwasher and the washing machine? How am I supposed to manage? Thank goodness Mrs B. said she'd come and tide me over.'

Lucy nodded hello at the human equivalent of dishwasher and washing machine, who didn't seem to mind. Martha had such forceful charm she could con anyone into feeling they were doing her a huge favour. It was a useful skill to have, Lucy thought. Martha put her arm round the woman. 'Mrs Burke is my saviour. We couldn't survive without you, could we, darling? We'd grind to a halt.'

Despite the chaos, Lucy surveyed the kitchen with envy. It was a long room, with thick dark brown beams criss-crossing the low ceiling. In the centre was a long polished refectory table, groaning under boxes and books. The rest of the furniture was a mishmash of wooden cupboards, some antique pine, some oak. Against the far wall was a huge old dresser, with small panes of coloured glass. In the right-hand wall there was a deep stone fireplace, sheltered by a large curved old beam. On the left-hand wall stood a pale blue Aga, all its doors and lids open.

Martha stood in the middle of the room with her hands on her hips. 'What do you think?' she said. 'Should we rip the whole lot out and go totally high-tech, darling, walk-in fridge, Smeg oven, pale oak units – or should I save Sebastian a fortune and keep this heap of old junk?'

'I like it as it is,' Lucy said, decisively.

Martha moved a pile of books. 'Take a seat,' she said. 'Now where the fuck,' she said, 'is that other coffee machine?' She began rooting about in a series of boxes tucked under the table. 'I don't mind instant,' Lucy said.

'Don't be ridiculous.' Martha tucked her thick wavy dark hair behind her ears as she bent down. 'You can't drink that awful crap.' She shivered. 'Aha!' Triumphantly she pulled out a rather dusty-looking Gaggia, with no plug.

'Mrs B.,' she said, 'could you be a darling and find me a plug? Then you must get off. I've kept you far too long.'

Ten minutes later, Lucy and Martha sat opposite each other, hands cupped around mugs of frothy cappuccino. Lucy had been delighted to get Martha's phone call inviting her over, but now she felt a little shy. She looked out of the dusty windows, and saw Olivia and Sophie were playing happily on some rickety-looking swings at the back of the garden. Laura and Emily were standing several feet apart, not looking at each other.

'They'll come round,' Martha said, following her gaze. 'It's lovely they'll have friends so near. Anyway,' she went on, blowing on her coffee, 'tell me about you. I want to know everything. Jobs, affairs, *everything*,' she added, grinning wickedly.

'Well,' said Lucy hesitantly, 'I'm married to Rob. We've been married for almost ten years. We moved here last year, onto the *select housing development* you may have seen at the other end of the village.' She grimaced at Martha, who laughed. 'Before that we lived in a little cottage, in Stanton Harcourt – you know, the tiny ones which look like almshouses. Rob's the editor of the evening paper in Oxford – and I do a couple of mornings a week at the radio station.'

'More,' Martha said. 'Where do your parents live? Are you happy?'

Lucy looked at her sharply. They were not the sort of questions you expected from a new acquaintance. She laughed.

'OK,' she said, spreading her fingers out over the bumps and gnarls of the oak table. 'My parents live about fifteen miles from here, in Burford. That's where I'm from. Rob's from Lancashire. I don't really think he's ever settled here. He'd prefer us to move back north.'

Martha shuddered. 'What does your father do?'

'He's a businessman. Well, he was. He's retired, although he keeps a bit of consultancy work on. He spends his days pottering about the garden, being organized by my mother. Oh, and they've just bought a house in France, in Provence, so they're intending to live half of the year there.' As she said this, a quick flash of pain ran through her. Caroline had rung only that morning to say that she and the girls were very welcome to spend a couple of weeks at the end of the holiday with them, but Lucy had politely declined. Rob would have refused to go, and she couldn't face the row that would ensue if she said she and the girls were going on their own. It was easier to demur, although she knew her mother felt bitterly hurt, not only for herself, but for Archie.

He adored the girls, and was the most wonderfully patient grandfather. Lucy was amazed, because when she and Helen were small he'd treated them like hand grenades. It made Lucy both tearful and happy to see him hugging her girls, and if she analysed the emotion she felt a hint of jealousy, tempered with the joy that they had his influence in their lives. If only Rob would let her parents do more. He seemed to think that if they exposed the girls to her parents' presence too often, they would instantly start demanding to come out as debs and attend a Swiss finishing school. He wanted them to *experience* life, not view ordinary people through a kind of protective glass screen.

'My mother sits on committees, has lunch and shops,' Lucy continued. 'Mostly, she shops. And she helps me out with the children, when she has the time.'

'And your husband's parents?'

'They're still in Lancashire,' Lucy said. 'Well, at least his mother is. His father's dead. He died last year. A stroke, it was very sudden. He'd had one before, but this last one was much, much bigger. It was so sad, he was a lovely man.' It was a waste, she almost added. That was the comment Peggy made to her at the funeral, that he'd wasted his last years, too traumatized by the first stroke to participate fully in life. He had become a spectator at his own life. 'All that hard work,' she said, 'and then nothing. He just petered out, love. I mustn't grumble, though. He was a wonderful husband.'

Rob hadn't cried when his father died. He took the phone call, and Lucy heard him say, 'Mum. Are you OK? When? I see. Yes, we will. Of course. I'll get Lucy to call you.'

Then he'd walked into the back garden of the cottage, and sat down on the bench. Lucy followed him. 'What's the matter?'

'Dad's dead,' Rob said. His face said nothing.

'Oh darling,' Lucy said, putting her arms round his neck. He sat very still. 'I'll call your mum,' she said.

The funeral was held in a small church on top of a rainswept moor. It was like something out of Dickens. The countryside around, in the chill wind, was bleak and forbidding. Rob, standing at the graveside in the black Crombie Lucy had bought him, was impassive. Only Laura had been deemed old enough to come, although both the girls loved Jack, he was brilliant with them, kneeling down on the floor to play horses, and feeding them extra strong mints out of his cardigan pocket. Both he and Peggy adored their visits.

Jack and Peggy had taken the girls away for a seaside holiday two years ago, to Blackpool, and they'd had a wonderful time. Peggy was worried Jack would find it too much, but he insisted he wanted to go. To Lucy it would have been the ultimate torture, but then, children have no taste. They rode on donkeys, built sandcastles, ate candyfloss and went to Madame Tussaud's. They'd come home with their little cases full of pink plastic knick-knacks and cheap jewellery which they hoarded in their bedrooms like precious treasure trove. 'You don't need to spend a fortune,' Peggy said, when Lucy arrived to pick them up. 'Children are always the same. They like the beach and gift shops. They've been no bother at all.' When Lucy emptied Olivia's case she found a plastic bag, carefully tied, full of shiny shells. 'Granny's going to help me make a necklace,' said Olivia, her face radiant. 'All of shells.'

That same summer Archie and Caroline had taken them to stay in a tasteful and hideously expensive little hotel in Provence, where they were looking for a house. The girls ate warm croissants every morning, looking out over the aquamarine sea on a sun-drenched terrace. Archie taught them to swim in the pool, and Caroline bought them French designer clothes. When Lucy asked them which holiday they'd liked best, they had no hesitation. 'Blackpool!' they shrieked. 'The donkeys! Will you come with us next time, Mummy?'

'I'll try my *very best*,' she said. 'I hope so,' said Olivia, putting her hand in Lucy's. 'You'd love it.'

At the funeral, Peggy hadn't broken down. She was calmly efficient, supervising who went to the church in which car, where everyone should sit. At the service, only the vicar spoke, and Peggy remarked afterwards it was as if he'd been talking about a stranger, nothing about the real Jack. Afterwards, she handed round plates of sandwiches and cakes she'd made herself, as their relatives and some of Jack's old work colleagues drank sweet sherry. Lucy found the experience deeply depressing, and wished she hadn't brought Laura.

Rob hardly spoke to any of his relatives. Peggy took

Lucy aside and said quietly, 'Don't worry. Jack would have been just the same. Men like to block it out. He just wants to get it all over with and go home.'

Towards the end of the afternoon, Lucy couldn't find Rob. She left Laura helping her granny clear the plates. Aunty Marge, who was now nearly ninety, tottered out of the front door in front of Lucy, full of unaccustomed sherry, clutching the arm of her son. She turned to give Peggy a hug. 'Thank you, love,' she said. 'It's been a wonderful do. I've right enjoyed myself.' Then, horrified, she pressed her fingers to her lips. 'Whoops.'

'It's all right,' said Peggy, unperturbed. 'It was lovely of you to come. It's a shame we all only seem to meet at funerals.'

'That's the way of it,' said Aunty Marge. 'It'll be me next, you wait.'

Having kissed Aunty Marge goodbye, Lucy walked round to the back of the house, and looked up the garden. At the top, on a raised section of crazy paving, overlooking what had been a field in Rob's youth leading up to the reservoir, but was now a housing estate, stood a bench. Rob was sitting on it with his back to her. Lucy walked up to him. As she got nearer, she saw his arms were folded across his chest. He was crying. She stood for a moment, uncertain. She reached out her hand, and touched him gently on the shoulder. Without looking, he reached up and grasped her fingers. She slid round the bench, and sat next to him. Their hands, entwined, rested in Rob's lap.

'Do you see that tree?' He spoke softly. 'He made me a tree house up there, with planks of wood from the tip over the road. He spent ages on it, hammering away. He wouldn't let me come near until he'd finished. Then he led me to it, covered my eyes. Mum gave me some food for a picnic. My mate Geoff said he had the best tree house, but mine was better. It had a window. I thought I'd take my sons up there,' he said, looking into the bare branches. 'But it fell apart, I suppose. Don't suppose the girls would be very interested, anyway. You know, I thought this garden was the whole world when I was little.' He looked at the small patch of lawn and the carefully tended borders. 'But it isn't much, is it? For a lifetime's achievement.'

He took a long, shuddering breath. 'Jesus, Lucy,' he said. 'He's *gone*.' He slowly dropped his head and Lucy hugged him. 'He was so very proud of you,' she said.

'I did most things for him, you know,' Rob said, turning to her. 'He really wanted me to be a journalist. It was a step up, where the real money was, he said. It isn't good enough, though, is it Lucy?' He looked at her directly. 'It isn't good enough for you, is it? Or your family?'

'Rob,' Lucy said, shocked. 'That's nonsense. We're all really proud of you. I can't believe you've said that.'

'It's true,' he said, turning away. 'To my dad I was a huge success. But to you I'll never be as good as your father.' He looked back at her. 'Will I?'

'But are *you* happy?' Martha said.

'Of course,' Lucy replied, automatically. Then, 'No. No, I don't suppose I am.' She raised her eyes to meet Martha's. 'But it's my own fault.'

'Why?'

'I want too much, I suppose,' Lucy said, trying to smile. 'I thought I knew what I wanted but I don't, any more. I look at my and Rob's relationship and it seems – not the kind of life I thought I'd have. I'm sorry,' she said quickly. 'I shouldn't bore you with all this.'

'No,' Martha said. 'Go on.'

'I married someone,' she said, slowly, 'who seemed to represent everything that was missing from my life when I was growing up – freedom, not living by rules, worrying about little things or what other people might think – who'd challenge me and make me a better person. I thought I wanted a different life to the life I'd known.'

'And?'

'I don't,' she said, shrugging. 'Which I'm sure makes me a very shallow person indeed. Really,' she said, 'we've disappointed each other. Neither of us was quite what we believed. He thought I would be a route to a life he'd seen from afar, and I thought he would make my life so much more *real*. Now he thinks I'm spoilt and shallow and I think he doesn't aim high enough, or try to make our lives together exciting or even pleasant. It's like – ' she traced her finger along a crack of the table – 'it's like all the things we first saw in each other, and what made our relationship different from any other I'd ever had, seem to have disappeared. There are moments when I think I can grasp something, then it's gone. Sometimes I feel like I've married a stranger who doesn't even like me, the person I really am, very much, and that unless I get out, I'll be smothered or simply cease to exist.'

'It often happens,' said Martha, quietly.

'What?'

'That we marry people as an escape. But more often than not it's a dead end.'

'What about you?'

Martha looked about the gloriously chaotic kitchen. 'I should be happy,' she said. 'Two kids, pots of money, thanks to darling Sebastian, no need to work, enough time to go shopping and have manicures – by the way, where's the nearest health club? – but I feel,' she shrugged, 'unloved.' She laughed. 'This is a conversation to have on a Saturday morning! Do you mind?'

'No,' Lucy said. 'I can't tell you how wonderful it is to be able to talk to someone like this.'

'Oh, I know I can make the house look a dream – I will, honestly – but Sebastian takes all that for granted, I don't think he even notices. He certainly doesn't notice me much, unless he's pointing out I haven't put any make-up on or I seem to be gaining weight. He talks to me like he talks to his secretary, as if I'm simply here to receive domestic orders. I run his social life, and make his home comfortable. My only emotional link to him is through the girls – the link between each other has just gone. The worst thing,' she said, leaning towards Lucy, who saw a tear was glistening in the corner of her eye, 'is that I know he doesn't really love me. I could cope with being a social secretary if there was some basic love and respect underneath it but there isn't, certainly not any more. Over the past few years it's become more and more apparent that his primary reaction to me is annoyance. Whatever I say or do is wrong. We don't make each other happy, and there comes a point when you wonder if it's worth being so noble and sticking it out. Somewhere, out there, there might be a person who would really love me.' She laughed. 'Listen to me! I sound like a bad soap opera. Actually, I'm fine. I feel pretty calm about it most of the time, and, as a job, it isn't so bad. The fringe benefits are appealing. We moved here, you know, to see if a change of scenery would make a difference. It hasn't worked so far. And now the girls are growing up, I can't really make them my excuse for staying. Maybe I should have another baby.' She looked down at her flat stomach. 'Or buy one. But the truth is, I'm scared to leave him. I don't have a career, like you. What would I do? The only success I've achieved is through him. It's a terrifying prospect.'

Lucy looked at her, astonished. Most women, on first meeting, tried to trump each other in terms of lifestyle – but here was Martha, prepared to let the barriers down straight away. To Lucy, Martha was the epitome of chic with the Perfect Life. She looked so fabulous, with a sense of style which made even jeans and a white T-shirt, which she was wearing today, look stunning. It helped if your T-shirt was DKNY and your jeans Versace, not that Lucy ever looked at labels, of course. Well, actually, she did. That was a fib. If Laura or Olivia had friends to stay, Lucy found herself peering at the labels in their clothes as she folded them up neatly in their bags, noting if they were designer or Ladybird. Whenever Laura or Olivia went to a sleep-over, she always made sure they took their most expensive clothes.

'But do you love him?'

'Yes,' said Martha. 'That's the awful thing. I do. He just doesn't seem to want it any more.'

'I don't suppose any of us get what we really want,' Lucy said, sadly.

'At least there's dry white wine,' Martha said. 'And shopping,' Lucy added. 'And children. You know what's really made me think it might not be worth just soldiering on?'

'What?'

'I saw someone,' Lucy added, then laughed. 'Well, no, it sounds mad but I probably didn't see someone, I just thought I did. Someone I used to go out with, and it made me feel – well, it made me feel quite different, alive, as if I'd suddenly woken from a long sleep. It was like being jolted back from the present into a time when you really thought you were special and beautiful and all those things you feel when you're eighteen, that everyone fancies you and you could get anyone. Desirable, I guess. And he was so . . .'

'So what?'

'Gorgeous,' Lucy said, grinning.

'How very wicked,' Martha said.

'It's all make-believe,' Lucy said. 'It wasn't him.'

'Mum!' Laura came running into the kitchen, and skidded on a pile of A4 paper. 'Don't worry,' Martha said. 'It's only one of Sebastian's cases.' She scooped up the densely typed notes and dumped them carelessly on an already towering pile of papers on the dresser.

'Olivia and Sophie won't let us play on the swings.'

'Push them off,' said Martha. 'You're bigger than them.'

Laura looked hesitantly at her mother. Lucy always said she wasn't allowed to push, hit, pinch or initiate any remotely violent bodily contact with Olivia. She decided Martha was an ally. 'OK,' she said, and ran off happily.

'Your girls are adorable,' Martha said, watching Laura run out. 'So beautiful. They are lucky, getting your hair.'

'They make it worth it,' Lucy said. 'Whatever balls-ups we may have made, we've made them, which means it can't be a complete failure, can it?'

Lucy, walking home with the girls, felt that her burden had been considerably lightened, and also felt astonished with herself for having been so honest when she hardly knew Martha. But then Martha had a way of getting straight to the heart of the matter, and it would be such bliss to have a real friend, a friend she could be totally honest with, instead of dim Cheryl who was all surface chat and would never in a month of Sundays admit she was having problems. Everything for Cheryl had to be glossily super. Even worse was Jackie, from next door, who'd popped round yesterday specifically to ask Lucy if she'd tried out a marvellous new anti-bacterial spray. Jesus, if that was how exciting your life was, Lucy surmised, it was time for a sharp exit.

Chapter Twenty

Olivia was fast asleep in bed. She had a fierce way of sleeping, her little determined chin pushed forward, balanced against the very edge of her bed. Her yellow and white checked duvet cover, bought by Lucy from the Laura Ashley catalogue, was pushed down to her knees, and she had one tartan pyjama-ed arm wrapped firmly round the neck of her favourite red fox. The fox, for that night's apparel, was sporting a pale pink velvet hairband.

All over the carpet by Olivia's bed were torn-out pages from her new Barbie notebook. She was currently obsessed with practising writing, and the book was full of love letters to Lucy and Rob. 'I lov mumy and dad and Lora and the cats.' The 's' on cats was written backwards. Lucy sighed. All her 's's and 2s were written backwards. Lucy often felt she could educate the girls better at home. Olivia, in particular, didn't seem to be learning anything at school apart from how to skip. Her reading scheme was a complete mystery to Lucy, full of phonetic spelling and strange symbols. When Lucy complained to her teacher that Olivia wasn't being taught how to spell, she was told that spelling was unimportant, and that what was important at this stage was expressing themselves on paper. Olivia was in a reception class of thirty-five other children, and while their young teacher was a pleasant, cheerful soul, they seemed to spend more time doing topics on bullying than writing rows of neat 'a's.

Olivia sat at a round table with four other children, and Lucy suspected all they ever did all day was show each other their knickers and draw on each other's legs with felt-tips. She sighed. Rob said according to the league tables it was the best state primary in the area, but Lucy was not satisfied. It was a long way from her education, and, to prove a point, Caroline had recently produced an essay Lucy had written at the age of nine, which demonstrated how far Laura too was behind. Caroline's campaign at present was to somehow persuade Rob that she and Archie should pay for the children's private education.

Olivia's notes were covered in hearts and houses and flowers drawn in thick, splodgy felt pen. Her fingers, which had been clean after her bath, were now spotted like Dalmatians. Irritated, Lucy saw that her duvet cover also bore the fruits of a busy night with her new pink fluffy zip-up writing kit, a present from Annie, who had amazed Lucy by being a considerate and thoughtful godmother. She and Rollo had four children, and ran a co-operative pottery in Wales. They kept chickens, ducks and a vicious small goat, and seemed as happy as clams in their muddy abode.

When Lucy and Rob went to stay last year, taking Laura and Olivia, they found a dead mouse by their damp bed. The house was heated by solar panels, so it was as cold as ice. Lucy murmured to Rob as they tried to drop off, dodging falling bits of plaster from the ceiling, and listening to the mice scampering about in the thatched roof, 'I think it's great that she's managed to shed all the upper-middle-class inhibitions she hated.'

'Like washing,' Rob said, turning damply over.

Lucy was folding up the clothes Olivia had dropped on the floor when Rob walked silently into the room behind her. Gently, he lifted the duvet up over Olivia's legs, and holding her soft small body in both hands, slid her further back onto the bed. Sensing the movement, she opened one eye, and wrapped a sleepy arm round her father's neck. 'Can I have a drink of water, Daddy?' she asked, eyes closed.

'Yes, love,' Rob said. 'Shush now.' He motioned Lucy to leave them. She gently pushed the drawer in Olivia's pine chest closed, and tiptoed out of the bedroom.

Laura was also firmly asleep – she'd taken two pillows from the spare bedroom and her head was propped up at an impossibly high angle. Lucy slid one out from underneath her, holding Laura's head so she wouldn't bump and wake. Even though a window in the bedroom was open, Laura's thick blonde hair was damp with sweat. Her luscious bee-stung mouth was wide open, and there was a small dribble of spit on her chin. Lucy eased the duvet down a little from her sleeping body to cool her. She loved watching her children when they were asleep. They looked like miracles.

All over Laura's bed lay books – at nine, she was an avid reader, devouring Enid Blyton, her favourite. Lucy felt it was time she moved on to something a bit more challenging, and bought her classics like *Little Women* and *The Lion, The Witch and The Wardrobe*, which Laura pretended to read. She then grabbed the Famous Five as soon as Lucy's back was turned.

Rob, when he read the Enid Blyton stories to her at

night, put on appalling posh accents for Dick and Julian. 'You rotter!' 'You are awful, Julian!' Lucy would hear him bellowing, while Laura thumped him and told him to stop being so silly. Rob, coming downstairs, said it was dreadful that children still read the old snob's books, but Lucy replied it was harmless, and at least Laura was reading. She used to love the Mallory Towers and St Clare's books when she was Laura's age.

'It made me long to go to boarding school,' she said.

'Exactly,' Rob said. 'And neither of them are going to boarding school.' Lucy bit her lip. She drove Rob mad by constantly correcting the girls' grammar, and saying '"baath", darling, not "bath".' She did mind the accents they were picking up from school, and both had quickly learned to develop two voices – one for school, and one for home. Caroline winced when she heard them, and had a little word with Lucy about elocution lessons. Laura said, 'But Daddy says "bath". And he says bloody and bugger too,' she added naughtily. 'That doesn't mean you can,' Lucy said, sharply. 'Is he a naughty daddy?' Laura said.

'Sometimes,' Lucy said, absent-mindedly.

'Why don't you and Daddy laugh any more?'

'What?'

'I used to hear you laughing when I was in bed. You don't do it now.'

'You grow out of laughing, a bit,' Lucy said, tucking her in.

'I hope I don't,' Laura said, sleepily.

Having checked the children, they both flopped down on the sofa. Lucy thought that if Rob dared to call it a settee again, she would definitely have to leave him. He picked up the newspaper. He was wearing an old blue denim shirt, sleeves rolled up, and a pair of jeans. His feet were bare. In front of him on the low coffee table lay an ashtray and the Marlborough Lites he now smoked, having finally given up the roll-ups. He had promised to give up smoking when Laura was born, but it hadn't happened, nor had he kept his promise to cut down on beer. Lucy made two cups of tea and placed one in front of him. She perched on a corner of the table.

'Rob?'

'What?'

'I saw Mum today.'

'How is my excellent mother-in-law? Still biting the heads off chickens?'

'Very funny. She's fine. She — mentioned something that I think we ought to talk about.'

'Lucy.' Rob put down his newspaper and looked at her with his piercing dark eyes. 'If this is about France again, I'm off. Why can't your mother realize that we're just happy to see her, that she doesn't have to give us things all the time? We've had a holiday. I don't want her offers. I'm more than happy to see her and Archie, but I do resent being treated like one of her charities.'

'It's about Olivia,' Lucy said. 'And Laura.'

'What?'

'I'm not happy about their school.'

'Jesus, Lucy, not that again? You're forever falling out with their poor teachers and demanding this and that. They're getting the same education as everyone else and if they aren't doing well it's because they're not very bright.'

'You know they're bright!' Lucy said, shocked.

'Well, you think they're bright and I think they're bright, but who's to know?'

'Mum offered to pay for them to go to private school.' It came out in a rush.

'And you said?' Rob's voice was dangerously quiet.

'I said I'd talk to you.'

'The answer,' he said calmly, 'as you know, is no. Private education is a complete waste of time. All it is is showing off There's no difference in what they're actually taught. End of argument.'

Lucy got angrily to her feet. 'No, it isn't the end of the argument! Just because you think it's a silly, snobby thing to want to do which won't make a blind bit of difference to them, we have to give up an offer like this. It's a godsend. Why can't you see what a head start it would give them? The facilities at Radlett are fantastic – Martha's been telling me all the extra activities they do – they even do Latin, and there's a swimming pool and they can board and . . . It's like being a member of an exclusive club. It'll set them up for life.'

Rob stood up, and, without a word, pushed past Lucy. At the door, he turned. His face was tense with fury.

'Our children,' he said, 'will have the education *we* give them. Not your parents. And if you are an example of how people grow up from private school then I definitely don't want it for our children. I'm going to the pub.'

Lucy sat, after he'd gone, shaking. How *dare* he? Why did he think he was completely in charge, that he made all the big decisions? She took a gulp of tea. Then she stood up and walked deliberately towards the phone on the table in the hall. She dialled her mother's number, her hands trembling.

'Darling,' Caroline sounded slightly out of breath. 'We were just sitting in the garden. Isn't it a lovely night? Darling, have you tried Bombay gin? Apparently it's all the rage and it's delicious. I'll get you a bottle – oh, Rob doesn't drink gin, does he?'

'Mum,' Lucy cut in. 'Would you still be prepared to pay for the children's school? If you would, we'd love you to help.'

There was a long pause, then Caroline said, 'That is *wonderful* news. Archie – ' Lucy could hear her mother calling out through the open stable door in the kitchen, and pictured Archie sitting, puffing on the cigar he wasn't supposed to smoke any more because of his blood pressure – 'Lucy and Rob have said yes to school fees. Isn't that super? Lucy, I'll put your father on.' Lucy heard her father's heavy tread towards the phone. He was panting slightly – Lucy had noticed it took him a while these days to get his breath, and the fact that he was really getting quite old, sixty-five, often brought her up with a start. To her, he would always be the age he was when she was a child.

'Lucy, that's marvellous. I'm so pleased. And you must let us help with uniform. We'd be delighted, you know that? Now are you sure Rob's happy, because he did seem rather anti the idea last time we talked?'

'Oh yes,' Lucy said, quickly. 'He's fine about it. Bye. I love you too, of course I'll tell the girls.'

Having said goodbye, she put down the phone carefully. What on earth had she done? Rob was going to be livid. Then she shook herself. It was about time Rob realized that he couldn't jackboot about the house all the time, deciding what happened and who did what. He had become so critical of everything she did, from tiny things like the way she stacked the dishwasher, to the food she bought in the supermarket and the way she was bringing up the girls without what he called 'real values'. He even went through the fridge saying, 'Organic crap. Lucy, we can't afford all this kind of stuff. Anyway, it's all bollocks. A few pesticides won't do you any harm.' But most of all Lucy resented the fact that he didn't talk to her. In the pub, he'd chat away quite happily to vague acquaintances. At home, it was like trying to extract a tooth to get him to talk. He seemed to save his amusing stories for strangers, as if trying to make her laugh was no longer important.

Lying in bed, she waited for the sound of his key in the door. Half of her dreaded it, the other half longed for the sound. That was what was so frustrating about their relationship, which she'd hardly touched on in her heart-to-heart with Martha. Even though she felt she was drowning in a sea of making-do, she still longed to see him. When he did walk in, her heart skipped a beat – until he found the latest thing to criticize, when it sank to her boots. Would they just carry on, she wondered, like this for ever and ever, treading water, accepting a relationship in stalemate? Or was the real Lucy Beresford still in there, somewhere? The girl who thought she'd have a golden life?

When he came home, eventually, at two in the morning, she turned over and pretended to be asleep. She heard him open and close the doors of the girls' rooms. Then he pushed open their door, and quietly took off his clothes, dropping them on the floor. There was a pause while he set the clock for the morning, and then slid into bed. They lay like bookends on either side of the bed, the space between them a no-man's-land of hurt. Lucy fell into an uneasy sleep. At about four, she woke and went to the loo. Getting back into bed, she turned towards him and tried to snuggle up. His skin was cold, and even in his sleep he pulled away from her.

That morning she woke early, suddenly, jolted into consciousness from a sleep that had brought no benefit. She'd have to tell him – if she didn't the girls were bound to, although Lucy had bribed them with chocolate to keep the little secret to themselves, just for now. It was more than likely he'd force her to ring her parents and admit she'd lied about him being in favour of Radlett. She turned over. She'd look such a fool. But then, she admitted to herself, it had been a terrible thing to do, when Rob felt so strongly about the idea. They were his children too. What had he said, after Jack's funeral? That, in Lucy's eyes, he would never match her father? This was, she admitted, a pretty brutal way of making him feel inadequate. She lay awake for over an hour until she had to get up with the girls for school, trying to work out how she could sell the idea to Rob. She went through endless mental conversations, all of which ended up with her in tears. There was no way round it, he would say no. How much easier, she thought, life would be if she was on her own.

Chapter Twenty-One

'Tell me about Radlett,' Laura said for the ninetieth time. Lucy was driving towards the school, in a car especially cleaned and valeted – it had taken her over an hour to get rid of all the sticky ice-lolly wrappers, Coke tins, bits of shredded McDonald's wrappings and straws from Happy Meals, not to mention odd shoes and bits of Lego – to buy their uniform from the shop within the school. In her pocket was a blank signed cheque from Caroline. She still hadn't had the nerve to tell Rob what was happening, and there were only four weeks until the end of term. Just thinking about it made her go cold all over.

'I've told you,' Lucy said patiently. 'I've told you all about it and I've shown you the brochure.'

'Will Emily be there?'

'You know she will.'

'Will she be in my class?'

'I think so,' Lucy said, snappily.

'Mum,' Olivia said from the back. 'How many days until we go there?'

'Lots and lots.'

'How many days in a week?'

'Seven,' Lucy said through gritted teeth.

'How many numbers is that?'

'Seven,' Lucy said. 'Do listen.'

'How many days in a year?'

'Three hundred and sixty-five.'

'How many days till my birthday?'

'Olivia,' Lucy said, twisting round in her seat, 'shut up.'

'It's rude to say shut up,' Laura said.

'Why did Granny say my new pyjamas were aged six?'

'Because they're special big ones.' Lucy's head was beginning to throb.

'Are my legs six years long?' Olivia said. There was a long pause. 'What happens when the tooth fairy loses a tooth?'

The presenter on *Woman's Hour* said, caringly, 'So do you think we should be actively encouraging more black women to become members of the European Parliament?'

'And you can shut up,' Lucy said, switching the radio off.

In the back, Olivia began to sob. 'You told me to shut up again. Everybody hates me today. No-one's being nice and my tummy hurts.'

'I didn't mean you,' Lucy said.

'You did! You did!'

'Here we are,' Lucy said, turning thankfully into the drive.

It was a very long drive. Either side was bordered with ash trees, like sentinels. Ahead of them loomed a gracious large stone house, turreted and eagled to the point of ostentation. Lucy drew the car up directly in front of the school, then thought better of it, drove round the grass circle and found a space at the back, by two large green bins.

There seemed to be no-one about. Lucy knocked hesitantly with the big brass knocker on the imposing front door, then, holding onto both girls' hands, pushed it open. They walked through into a black-and-white tiled corridor. At the end was a large chair, like a medieval throne. On it sat a complacent-looking grey cat. Laura and Olivia ran forward to stroke it, but as they got near it raised a sheathed paw warningly, and sat there staring at them, swishing its fat grey tail.

There was the noise of a phone being put down behind a white-painted door, which said 'School Secretary'. Lucy knocked hesitantly.

'Come!'

Lucy found herself in a long narrow room, bordered by shelves holding numerous files. At the end sat a tall thin woman with greying brown hair pulled back in a bun.

'Yes?' she said, pulling half-rim glasses to the end of her nose.

'Mrs Atkinson,' Lucy said. Her voice sounded squeaky. She coughed. 'Lucy Atkinson. These are Laura and Olivia – ' the two girls retreated round her back at the sight of this gorgon, as if they were all about to dance the conga. Lucy fished them out from behind her. 'We were told to come and enquire about the school uniform?'

'Ah,' the woman said. Lucy remembered her name was Miss Beatty, she'd signed one of the letters from the school. 'Second-hand cupboard?'

'No,' said Lucy, coolly. 'New.'

The woman rose reluctantly. 'I'll get the key.'

They followed her in a long line – Lucy had a terrible urge to grab her waist and sing 'na, na, na, n-nar nar na' but managed to resist – until eventually she unlocked a room at the far end of the building. It was awfully big, Lucy thought, and very like Tom Brown's schooldays. In the centre of the main school was a huge echoing hall, with a stone central staircase. There was lots of wood panelling which made you want to tap it for secret passages, and small unexplained doors. It would be an ace place for hide and seek, Lucy thought.

When she and the girls had been shown round – they'd gone while Rob was out at work – she was struck by how quiet the children were, and how polite. The noise at the girls' previous school was deafening, like that of a football crowd. Everything here was hushed. Laura and Olivia, normally so voluble, were awed into silence by their surroundings. Driving home, Lucy said, 'Well girls, what do you think?'

'It's very big,' ventured Laura.

'I don't like it,' Olivia said. 'It smells.'

'No it doesn't!' Lucy said, thinking of the strong smell of wee which emanated from the boys' loos at their present school.

'It does. It smells old.'

'Old is good,' Lucy said firmly. 'I'm a great believer in old.'

In the uniform shop, Lucy held stiff maroon blazers up against both girls. The right age drowned Laura, but, for Olivia's age, was too tight. 'Make sure there's plenty of room for growth,' Miss Beatty said. 'It makes much more sense,' she said, 'financially.' She knows, Lucy thought, horrified. She knows we're not paying the fees. The children will be marked out like scholarship kids. Then she shook herself. Lots of grandparents would be helping out. They couldn't be the only ones. Who the hell could afford almost ten thousand pounds a year out of income? It was more than a second mortgage.

*   *   *

That night, she steeled herself to tell Rob. She couldn't let the lie continue like this, it was ballooning and threatening to get completely out of hand. The door slammed at just after seven. Lucy was lifting Olivia out of the bath, Laura was still lying in it, practising her breathing underwater. Lucy felt very snappy because she hadn't wanted either of them to get their hair wet as she couldn't be bothered to dry it, but they had.

She heard Rob dropping his briefcase, and then his heavy tread on the stairs.

'Good evening, mermaids,' he said. He seemed in an unusually good mood. He bent to kiss them, without looking at Lucy.

'Hi,' she said, and reached up to kiss him. He glanced down at her in surprise. He felt as if it was a long time since Lucy had seemed even remotely pleased or interested to see him.

'You seem happy,' she said.

'You,' he said, 'are looking at the editor of the regional newspaper of the year!'

'That's *fantastic*,' Lucy said, standing up. She wanted to throw her arms round him, but she had lost the habit. So she reached up again and gave him an embarrassed peck on the cheek.

'It is, isn't it? Maybe all the aggro is worth it after all. Come on, try and find a babysitter. Let's go out.'

In the restaurant, Lucy leant her chin on her hands as Rob studied the wine list.

'Rob?'

'Yes?' he said, looking up.

'I've got something to tell you.'

'Is it bad?'

'Pretty bad.'

'Then I don't want to know tonight,' he said, shutting the wine list with a snap.

'I have to,' Lucy said. He looked at her steadily. 'Why do you manage to spoil almost anything?'

Lucy clenched her fist under the table. Keep calm, she thought. He does have a point.

'I know this is a really bad time but I can't keep it to myself. It's going to get horribly out of hand.'

'Go on.'

'You know the – suggestion – Mum made. Please,' she said, 'don't say anything yet. That night, I was so angry with you, I did something really awful. I rang Mum and said we'd accept their paying for school fees.' The last words came out in a rush and she sat back, waiting for the inevitable explosion. None came.

'I know,' he said.

'*What?*'

'I found a letter from some school secretary bird in the kitchen drawer.'

'And you didn't say anything?'

'I've reached the stage,' he said, very quietly, 'of feeling it isn't worth trying to change things any more. If you think going behind my back to please your parents is a valid thing to do to our relationship, then I cannot even find the energy to react.'

Lucy bowed her head. 'I'm sorry,' she whispered.

'It's OK,' he said. 'You go ahead. I think that's the best way, don't you? You live your life, I'll live mine.'

'I don't want to live like that,' Lucy said, feeling tears rising in her eyes.

'We already are,' he said. Then he looked at her, quite calmly. 'Now. What would you like to order?'

*   *   *

On the girls' first morning of school, Lucy was awake by six. She lay in bed, feeling anxious, and not quite sure what was causing it. Then she remembered. First day at school. All their bags lay neatly packed at the bottom of the stairs – they seemed to need an inordinate amount of things, from PE kit to hockey boots to schoolbags, neatly marked, with their own pencil cases and protractor sets and a St James's Bible each. Lucy had spent an unhappy evening sewing Cash's nametapes onto all their clothes, stabbing herself repeatedly in the finger. She wouldn't need acupuncture for stress – just sew on a few nametapes. She then had a panic about their shoes not being polished. She found herself remedying this at midnight. Rob stuck his head round the door, saw what she was doing, and retreated wordlessly.

Olivia refused to eat her breakfast. Laura spilt milk on the floor, and Lucy shouted. Rob hadn't said anything, just kissed and hugged the girls goodbye.

'Don't hit any teachers, will you? he said. 'They're allowed to hit back at private school.' Both Laura and Olivia looked traumatized. 'He's teasing,' Lucy said, quickly.

Lucy found herself in a phalanx of four-wheel drive cars on the drive up to the school. It was like being trapped in the middle of a panzer division. When she eventually found a parking space, she saw thankfully Martha's Discovery was only two cars away. She could see Martha helping Sophie down, while fending Toffee off with the other hand. Her mouth was moving constantly, and, getting out of the car, Lucy could hear, 'I have no idea where your ballet things are! How the hell would I know? Toffee, if you bite me again I'm having you stuffed. Mind that hockey stick! Jesus Christ, Emily, look at your hair.'

Lucy helped her two out of the car, and lifted all their bags out of the boot. She staggered slightly under their weight.

'You'll get used to it!' Martha called out. 'It's like a bloody Everest expedition every Monday. Hello girls. It's so lovely you're here. Emily and Sophie are so excited.'

Laura ran forward to catch up with Emily. Olivia held back, clutching Lucy's hand tightly. She felt very apprehensive. The building was so very big compared to her previous school, and instead of having a packed lunch, they had to have a school dinner. Olivia was very worried about the food. Some food was positively dangerous. Just thinking about semolina made her feel seriously ill.

Martha and Lucy walked to the front door together. Lucy, despite her own schooling, felt conspicuous. Martha sensed this and tried to put her at ease. 'She's a tart,' Martha hissed, as a very made-up mother brushed past them in tight black leather trousers, clutching the hand of a pink-faced small boy. 'Second wife. Groom.' A terrifyingly beautiful woman was emerging from a Mercedes sports car next to them. 'Amusement arcades,' Martha whispered. Lucy snorted. 'Look,' she said quietly to Martha, 'there's a car worse than ours.' An ancient Escort chugged up the drive. 'Nanny,' Martha said. 'I'm sorry, Lucy, but you're going to have to buy a Discovery.'

Lucy laughed. 'And how much off-roading would I do? Accidentally mounting the kerb at Sainsbury's?'

'You could run Rob over with it,' Martha pointed out.

'True,' Lucy said.

Sophie was in the class above Olivia, but she walked with her to her classroom, and showed her in, before kissing her goodbye. Lucy smiled at the teacher. 'This is Olivia Atkinson.' Olivia's face was crimson with embarrassment and fear. 'Olivia. How lovely to see you. We're all very excited, aren't we, that Olivia's joining us?' The teacher looked round the class of fifteen children. 'Freddie, show Olivia where she puts her coat and her games bag. Now,' she said, turning to Lucy. 'If Mummy says goodbye, we can show Olivia how we say good morning.' Olivia ran from the back of the classroom, and buried her face in Lucy's legs. Lucy gently prised her off, and lifted her up.

'You'll have a lovely day,' she whispered into Olivia's buried blonde head. 'It'll go very quickly, just like that, and then I'll be there.' She put Olivia down. Freddie came up to her, and took her hand. 'We have to sit down,' he said, kindly.

Lucy slid out of the door. Martha was waiting for her. She smiled when she saw Lucy's tears. 'She'll be fine. Come and have a coffee. You're not rushing off, are you?' Lucy shook her head dumbly. 'Good,' said Martha. 'Unless I can offload on someone what a complete bastard Sebastian is I will have to ring him up and tell him so myself. Which would be not only imprudent but financially disastrous. So I'll tell you instead. Oh – ' she added. 'I've something else to tell you. I met someone who knows you the other day.'

Chapter Twenty-Two

'His name,' Martha said, warming her hands on a steaming cup of coffee in her now immaculate kitchen, every gleaming copper pan in place. 'Oh God, what was his name? Sebastian met him through some work do and we all ended up having lunch, he's lovely – stunning actually – very Chelsea wife, absolutely beautiful. Three children and as slim as a wand, the cow. They used to live in Notting Hill but they're moving here – they're buying the Rectory.'

Lucy's heart was beating unnaturally fast. It must be a coincidence, it hadn't been Max. Martha would give her the name of someone else she used to know vaguely, maybe someone she was at school with. Her parents' house was only fifteen miles away, there were still odd pockets of people she'd grown up with who hadn't decamped to London, and there were bound to be those who'd decided this was a wonderful place to move back to, to bring up their own families, away from the smog and temptations of London. But then . . . and thinking she might have seen him at Sainsbury's . . .

'I know,' said Martha, triumphantly. 'Max. That's it. Max and Catrina Yorke. His father used to be a Tory

Minister, remember? I think it's Sir George, now.'

'It is,' Lucy said, without thinking. Martha looked at her sharply.

'Well, they've put an offer in on the Rectory – almost a million, so my spies tell me. We'll have to get an invite, I'd love to have a snoop around. You're very quiet. What's the matter?'

Lucy made a swipe at Toffee, who was attempting to unravel her skirt, which had a thread hanging down from the hem. She'd tried to dress the part for the girls' first morning, and had agonized about what she should wear. Should one be ultra casual, with jeans, a shirt and sunglasses on the top of one's head, or should one go the whole hog with skirt, tights and lipstick? In the end she'd found an uneasy truce with a raspberry-pink short wool skirt which she thought made her look slimmer, black opaque tights and a black polo-neck jumper. Harmless, but smart, she thought, putting on a light smear of pink lipstick and just mascara, no eye-liner. Apart from the skirt, she decided she looked like Emma Peel. Ka-pow! She could floor anyone who laughed at her car.

'I do know him,' Lucy said, slowly, taking a long drink of her coffee. God it was strong, like drinking neat adrenaline. 'I know him very well indeed. Or I did. He's an old boyfriend. He's— I saw him, Martha. Do you remember? I told you I thought I'd seen some-one that first time I came round for coffee, someone I used to know. It must have been *him*.' They grinned delightedly at each other, like schoolgirls.

'*Really?*' Martha's face was flushed with excitement. 'Wow. You lucky thing. He's *stunning*. So glamorous – that hair, fabulous clothes, and a body to die for. Honestly, when he kissed me hello I felt like rolling over and waving my legs in the air. It was all I could do not to stare, darling, all the way through lunch. But she's very possessive, keeps touching him all the time, very darling this and darling that – ' Lucy made a wry face, Martha was one to talk – 'and killer looks if he talked to you for more than five minutes. Well, well,' Martha said, leaning back in her chair and looking at Lucy, who had gone bright crimson. 'This could be fun.'

'Oh don't,' Lucy said, putting her head in her hands. 'Things are bad enough between me and Rob at the moment without Max hoving into view. You may think it's funny,' she said, raising weary eyes to Martha's delighted face, 'but it's going to be hell for me.'

'Stop lying,' Martha said, wickedly, 'you're thrilled.'

Driving home, Lucy forced herself to stop peering at the line of people waiting in the butcher's, and had to swerve to avoid a young mother with a pushchair. She waved apologies. Every car that went past made her heart beat a little faster – was that him? She knew she shouldn't but she just couldn't help herself – she drove very slowly up to the Rectory. At its stone gates, she stopped the car. There was no-one about. Hesitantly, she got out. The house was being sold off by the Anglican Church, who reckoned it was far too valuable an asset simply to house their new young vicar and his family. Far more convenient, the diocese decided, to find him a nice new house on one of the estates, much easier for a young wife with two small children than having to run this draughty old place. And it was in a bit of a state, Lucy could see, the front pillars crumbling, and the garden a wilderness of briars and tall thistles. But it was beautiful, in that calm, graceful way old houses are, surrounded by an aura of timeless peace and dignity new homes, however large, could never achieve, no matter how much Virginia creeper or wisteria was grown up them.

Lucy breathed in the smell of new-mown grass, and could faintly hear the sound of a lawnmower on the back lawn. Probably a handyman brought in by the estate agent – it had been on the market for almost six months, prospective buyers put off by the scale of the renovations needed and the fact that it needed completely rewiring, damp-proofing and a new boiler. She tramped forward, stepping sideways to avoid the nettles and tall weeds growing up through the white gravel of the drive. It really was magnificent, Lucy thought, looking up at the facade – a central white door with a huge black wrought-iron knocker, two tall sash windows either side, three above, and then the roof, at the end of which two stone eagles spread their wings.

She was so lost in thought she didn't hear footsteps, until they were by her side. 'Can I help you?' She turned to see a whiskery old man, clutching an electric strimmer. 'I'm just having a nosey,' she said, smiling. 'I live in the village.'

'Grand old place, ain't it?' he said, following Lucy's gaze up the facade. 'Sold now, I hear. They've asked me to try and knock the grounds into shape, big bloody old job, I can tell you.' He rubbed his back.

'It's definitely sold then?' Lucy said.

'So they tell me,' he said, his voice tailing away as he walked off, still gently rubbing the centre of his back.

Lucy found her hands were trembling. She knew she'd better go, but couldn't resist peering in the window of one of the downstairs rooms. Shading her eyes with her hand, she looked in through the dusty glass. 'Gosh,' she murmured. It was a huge room, a real old-fashioned drawing room, with a high carved white plaster ceiling, and a central chandelier. Against the far wall was a grand speckled black and white marble fireplace. The floor was wooden, covered in dust, but clearly saveable. Lucy sighed. What would she give for a house like that? She heard the strimmer start up. Reluctantly, she turned away.

At home, she stopped the car on their tarmac drive. She stepped out, and heard someone calling her name. She turned, and saw Jackie appearing, holding out a leaflet.

'It's a quiz night,' she said. 'Not really our thing, but we thought it might just be fun. Do you think Rob would be interested? It's next Saturday in the Palmer's Alms. We could make a team.' She smiled expectantly at Lucy. 'I'll ask him,' Lucy said. 'But he's very busy at the moment.' Jackie followed her to the door. Lucy turned, pointedly. 'I'm sorry, I have to do some work at home.'

'Of course. See you!'

In the kitchen, she put down her purse and car keys, and looked around her. The white Formica fitted units needed a good wipe. The metal sink was splattered with milk, and bowls of half-eaten Rice Krispies still lay there, the top one tilting slightly so the milk and cereal had run out, clogging the plughole. On the yellow pine breakfast bar sat three plates of half-eaten toast, crumbs littering the surface. Rob's newspaper was propped up against the wall, and his coffee cup was half-drunk. The milk was congealing slightly halfway up the side. Lucy would need to scrub that, the dishwasher wouldn't get it clean.

There were no messages on the answerphone. She'd had to give the front door a shove – the post had come. One electricity bill, which they paid by direct debit, one circular pleading with them to take out a new credit card, a garishly coloured leaflet offering amazing

259

discounts on double glazing and a clothing catalogue.

Turning her back on the mess, she walked to the hall table and looked at herself in the mirror above it. The face that looked back at her *was* still pretty, she thought. For her age. But, in repose, there was a tiredness, an age that made Lucy shudder. If she put her hands over the bags under her eyes she looked the same, the same as the image she carried in her head. But take away her fingers and there were two deep lines under her eyes. How awful to think she had had the best of herself. That she would never again really turn heads, draw whistles, make other women envious. She placed her hands against the cold, steely surface of the mirror. She couldn't just give up. She couldn't give up on wanting to be loved, to be desired, to be *valued*, to see the future as a place where the best of life was still to come. It was time to stop going relentlessly downhill.

She looked at herself steadily. What would Max think if he met her now? Would he see the Lucy he had always known, or would he think that she was no longer desirable, a middle-aged woman, unremarkable? She smiled at herself. And, for the first time in several years, a tiny piece of the old Lucy smiled back.

Chapter Twenty-Three

One Saturday morning, a month later, Lucy was sitting at the wooden table in their tiny back garden, drinking a much-needed cup of coffee. She'd been up since the middle of the night with Olivia, who'd contracted some awful tummy bug and had been throwing up all night. The first she and Rob knew about it was when Olivia wandered into their bedroom, sobbing, clutching a dejected-looking fox by the paw. 'Mummy,' she wailed, 'I feel—' And then it came out, projectile vomit, like *The Exorcist*. Rob groaned loudly, and put his pillow over his head. 'You deal with it,' he said, muffled. 'You know sick always makes me be sick.'

'How very convenient.' Lucy climbed wearily out of bed, and, clutching Olivia's hand, led her to the bathroom. 'Now sit there,' she said. 'Don't move. If you feel it coming, into the loo. Or Mummy will be very cross.'

As Olivia bent over the loo, Lucy peeled off her vomit-stained pyjamas, tugging the top over her head. They couldn't even go in the wash basket, as they'd make everything else smell. She wandered into Olivia's room, and surveyed the sheets. Thank goodness she hadn't been sick on them. She trailed downstairs, and, eyes half shut, bunged the pyjamas into the washing machine. They could sit and pong to themselves until morning.

Olivia wailed again. 'It's coming!' she shouted. 'Loo!' Lucy yelled, taking the stairs two at a time. Laura now appeared, sleepily, on the landing.

'What?' she said.

'Olivia's being sick.'

'My head itches,' Laura said.

Oh brilliant, Lucy thought, thousands of pounds in school fees, and Laura's got nits. Didn't nits realize there was a social divide?

'I'll have a look in the morning,' she said.

It took her an hour to get a shaking, heaving Olivia back into bed, and she was woken again, twice. The first time she made it to the loo, the second it was all over the covers. Lucy stripped the bed, feeling like an extra in *Cell Block H*. Outside, the pale morning sun was beginning to rise. It was a time of day she hadn't seen since she was breastfeeding. She gave up thoughts of remaking the bed and let Olivia climb in beside her, and immediately she fell asleep, her hot little body moulded round Lucy. Lucy lay awake, unable to move – if she turned over she'd push Olivia out of bed, and Rob was sprawled across the bed as usual, taking up most of the room. Lucy lay, feeling like the ham in a ham sandwich.

Carrying the morning paper, she headed out for a bit of peace and quiet. The air was chilly now, in late autumn, and the back garden was full of leaves, russet, lemon and a deep fiery red. She really ought to rake them up, but what was the point, when more would only fall again? Anyway, she quite liked them. It was like having a carpet outside. She still couldn't evoke any interest from Rob in gardening – he declared that it was on a par with driving a Volvo. Boring. Middle class. Bourgeois. 'But don't you care?' Lucy said desperately. 'Surely you want it to look nice?' 'I like it how it is,' Rob said. 'It's natural. You're always going on about how dull everyone else's garden is, why can't you appreciate the fact that we are refusing to bow to the social convention of tidying up your garden as if it was some kind of housework?' It was a logic with which Lucy couldn't argue, but she still had a hankering for at least some kind of order. But then she peered over the fence at Jackie's garden and actually felt quite glad that hers was such a mess. Jackie must nip out with nail scissors. Lucy had a sudden vision of her spraying Dettox over the flower beds.

She stirred a pile of leaves with her foot, and, sitting down, thankfully took a sip of coffee and opened the local paper. A headline caught her eye. 'Rectory Sold to Former Minister's Son,' Lucy read. 'After six months,' the copy ran, 'a buyer has finally been found for The Rectory, a grade two listed Georgian building in Lower Winchborough. Thirty-seven-year-old Max Yorke and his wife Catrina, 36, will be moving in shortly. Max, a banker from London and the son of the well-known former Tory Minister Sir George Yorke and his wife Lady Annabelle, of Casterton Hall, said, "It's a wonderful old house and we can't wait to start work on it. It will be the perfect place for our three young children to grow up."' Lucy squinted at the picture. Max was standing in front of the house, his arm round Cat. Lucy surveyed her. She didn't look any older than she had at the wedding. Skinny, too. In Max's arms was an adorable dark-haired little girl, about three, grimacing at the camera. Lucy examined her face for traces of Max. She looked more like Catrina. In front of them were two bigger children, a boy and a girl. Both were dressed smartly, looking self-conscious. The boy was the image of Max, but with his mother's dark hair. Without knowing what she was doing, Lucy let her fingers gently trace the outline of Max's face. He looked just the same, maybe a little tubbier round the middle, and there were deep lines around his eyes, but he was unmistakably Max. Closing her eyes, she could hear his voice, picture the way he wrinkled his nose when he laughed, imagine him in bed with her. She shivered. God. This must be a midlife crisis. She'd be waking up with hot sweats and shoplifting next.

'Mum!' Laura shouted. 'Come and get this clip out of Barbie's hair.' She stood by the patio doors of the living room, holding up a Barbie doll with a pink glittery clip hopelessly tangled in the doll's long synthetic blonde hair.

'Not now!' Lucy snapped, crossly. 'Just give me five minutes without asking me to *do* something.'

'OK,' said Laura, hurt. 'I'll ask Daddy.'

An hour later, Lucy was pushing her trolley around Sainsbury's in the usual Saturday morning crush. Olivia staging a remarkable recovery, had insisted on coming, because she thought it might be possible to catch Lucy at a weak moment and persuade her to buy sweets. Lucy, who'd rushed out of the house without bothering with make-up, just wanted to get the whole ghastly ordeal over so she could get off to take the girls riding.

'You can sit in the trolley,' Lucy said.

'I'm too big. I want to walk.'

'You either go in the trolley, or you stay in the car.'

'Someone might take me,' Olivia said, piteously.

'Good.'

Lucy heaved her up, and stuffed her legs with some

difficulty into the spaces more designed for two-year-old than five-year-old legs. At least in the trolley she wouldn't be able to veer off and grab sweets, not to mention slide aboard small goodies like chocolate chips and hundreds and thousands, which Lucy wouldn't discover until she was at the checkout with a huge queue behind her.

Rob said they had to be on yet another economy drive as the latest credit-card bill had been far more than usual, so Lucy couldn't even cheer herself up with some expensive moisturizer or aromatherapy bath oil. Defiantly, she put in a budget pack of three pairs of black opaque tights. A necessity, now the colder weather had come. Lucy wondered how she'd ever managed without them.

Economy drive meant no asparagus or rocket – green beans and iceberg instead.

'Yawn, yawn,' Lucy said to Olivia. 'Let's hope it doesn't last, this little phase of Daddy's.'

'Can I have some peaches?' Olivia said, making a cute smiley face. 'Please, Mummy.'

'OK,' Lucy said, relenting. 'As long as you eat them all, don't just take a bite and put them back into the fruit bowl.'

'I won't. Honestly.'

Lucy refused to look at the delicious French bread and resolutely pulled three-for-the-price-of-two sliced white loaves off the shelf. Yuck. But then if she did buy lovely pain rustique, she scoffed the whole lot in one go, anyway, which wasn't good for the hips – and she'd given up trying to entice Rob with the delights of whole-wheat granary.

'Tuna,' she thought. 'Must get tuna.'

She was just pushing her trolley round the corner into the canned section when she saw him. He was meandering slowly down the aisle, looking at the Italian extra-virgin olive oil. Blonde, gorgeous, tanned, Max.

'Shit fuck and bugger!' Lucy hissed under her breath, desperately going into reverse and scooting back up the other aisle.

'What's the matter Mummy?' said a deeply alarmed Olivia, whose head was practically whipped off in the G-force.

'Shush,' Lucy said, crouching down over her trolley and peering round the corner.

'WHY are you hunched over like that?' demanded Olivia, loudly.

'There's someone I don't want to see.'

'Why?'

'Just because. Now be quiet.'

Why hadn't she put on any make-up? Why hadn't she washed her hair? Why was she wearing an old jumper she'd shrunk of Rob's with a hole in the bottom? Why was she wearing a pair of trousers which were too tight around the thighs and which weren't quite long enough for the old black loafers she'd pulled on? And, oh no, she thought, looking down – navy blue socks with black suede shoes. Desperately, she tried to fluff up her greasy hair with her fingers, and rub out any old mascara under her eyes, attempting to catch her reflection in the metal trolley handle.

'What are you doing, Mummy?' Olivia said.

'Nothing,' Lucy said, 'I'm just . . .' Oh Lord. He was walking directly towards her. She buried her head in the fridge containing the fresh pasta and ready-made sauces. Surely he wouldn't recognize her bottom? Just how interested could you be in carbonara? Olivia tugged her jumper. 'Can we get some pizza?'

'OK,' hissed Lucy into the pasta.

He must have gone by now, thank God, she thought, straightening up, and whirling her trolley round to set off in the opposite direction.

There was a loud metallic bang, and Olivia jumped six inches in her seat. 'OW!' she yelled loudly, rubbing her bottom.

'I'm so sorry . . . Good heavens. *Lucy.*'

'Max.'

The first thing she took in was the contents of his trolley. Grappelli extra-virgin olive oil which cost well over six pounds. A packet of gravadlax, fresh coriander, smoked duck breasts, olive ciabatta, fresh figs and a weird knobbly green fruit Lucy had never seen before which looked like a sex aid. Her eyes travelled upward. Chocolate brown suede brogues, moss-green corduroys, a duck-egg blue shirt which looked pure cotton, soft to the touch. It was open at the neck. His hands, resting on the trolley bar, were tanned, the blond hairs bleached and glistening. His nails were neatly cut, clean. Rob, to Lucy's continued annoyance, still bit his nails as well as the skin around them.

He was smiling, his eyes more crinkly now at the corners, and there were deep lines running down the centre of his cheeks. His hair was shorter, smarter, but still thick and wavy. If she'd seen him, as a stranger, she would have thought, what an attractive man, and wondered about his life, was he married, did he have children, what kind of car did he drive, where did he live? What would her life have been with him?

Olivia was regarding him solemnly.

'I'm Olivia,' she said.

'How do you do,' Max said, reaching over and shaking her small hand. 'I'm Max. I know your mummy.'

'How?'

'A long time ago,' he said.

'Before I was born?' Olivia asked, a concept with which she rather struggled.

'Yes.'

'Do you know my daddy?' she said.

'Not really,' he said.

'My daddy's very tall,' Olivia said. 'And he shouts sometimes.'

'Olivia!' Lucy said.

'Well, he does. Come on Mummy. I want to check out the pizzas.'

'Hang on,' Lucy said, as Olivia tried to lever the trolley away by pushing against Lucy's thighs with her strong little legs. 'Ow,' she yelped. 'Stop it, Olivia. Just wait. How are you?' Lucy said to Max, unable to meet his eyes.

'Fine,' he said. Why wouldn't she look at him? He examined her carefully. She looked rather less glamorous than he remembered, but she was still head-turning, slim, her blonde hair shoulder-length. But not as shiny as he remembered.

'How's the house?' said Lucy, rather desperately.

'Complete chaos,' Max said. 'It's driving Cat mad. It was in a terrible state. And you? Where do you live?'

'Um, at the other end of the village, on an . . .' she tried but failed to get the word 'estate' out. 'It's a new house,' she said, 'I really hate it but it was Rob's choice.' Then, aware of how rude this sounded, she said, 'But it's fine, really.' Oh Lord. She was not making any sense at all. He must think she was now completely mad. Not only old and ugly, but mad too. She pushed Olivia and the trolley away from him.

'I must be . . . um, I take the girls riding this afternoon and we're a bit . . .'

'Where do they go?' Max said, quickly. 'Cat's desperate for ours to start – one of the pleasures of the country. There are some old stables at the Rectory, so we might even go the whole hog. You used to ride, didn't you?'

'Yes,' Lucy said. 'But I don't, now. No time.'

'That's a shame,' Max said, easily. 'Cat's really keen to take it up again and it would be lovely for her to have someone to ride with.'

'Yes,' Lucy said. 'What a shame.'

She began to move away, but Max said, 'Where do your girls go to school?'

Lucy sighed thankfully. 'Radlett,' she said, casually.

'Really? Ours are starting there too. Isn't that lovely? Look, you and Rob must come to dinner. We're still in a hell of a state, but I know Cat would love to meet you properly. I met a couple you know, Martha and Sebastian? We bumped into them through a friend in London, amazing coincidence they live here too. They seem good fun Are they close friends?'

'I know Martha fairly well,' Lucy said.

'Great. Cat certainly took to her – I think Martha's cooking up some scheme to make them members of some health club or other. Bloody huge expense, no doubt.' He laughed.

'Really?' Lucy said. After all Martha had said about Cat. Hmmm. Traitor. 'I really must go,' she said.

'Give me your number,' he said, 'and we'll sort out dates.'

Lucy fished about in her bag.

'It's OK,' Max said. 'I have a card. Write it on the back of this.' Lucy saw he'd already had cards with his address printed on, and email. How efficient. He handed her a beautiful Parker rollerball.

'Lucy Atkinson,' she wrote, and the number. Max looked at it for a moment.

'I can't think of you as that,' he said, looking at her.

'How weird.' Her heart did two beats for the price of one, and she realized one hand was shaking slightly on the handle of the trolley.

'Neither can I, sometimes,' she said. 'Bye. Good luck with the house.'

'We'll call. Goodbye, Olivia.'

Olivia said nothing, just waved a regal pink hand. 'Was he a boyfriend, Mummy?' she said loudly, for the benefit of the entire aisle.

'Hush,' Lucy said, terrified he'd hear. But he had gone. 'You are awful,' she said, laying her cheek against the top of Olivia's glossy blonde head. Olivia absent-mindedly reached up and, taking a strand of Lucy's hair, put it in her mouth. 'Can I have some picamix?' she said.

'Go on, then,' Lucy said, wheeling her round. And suddenly felt she wanted to laugh out loud. Holding onto the trolley, she did a little hoppity-skip.

Chapter Twenty-Four

'Hullo,' Lucy said, grimacing at herself in the mirror above the phone. She had a bit of toast stuck between her front teeth. It would be her mother, ringing to see if she needed anything because she was just popping out to Waitrose.

There was a short pause.

'Is that Lucy?' said a clear, bell-like and imperious voice.

Lucy thought swiftly about saying no, this was the cleaner. But thought better of it.

'Yes, it is.'

'Hi,' said the voice. 'This is Cat – Cat Yorke?'

'Oh – hello,' Lucy said, unconsciously straightening and putting on what Laura called her telephone voice. She did a wicked imitation of Lucy's answerphone message, and Rob often re-recorded it in his broadest Lancashire accent just to annoy her. His version started, 'Howdo . . .'

'I'm so pleased I've caught you in. Max said he bumped into you and your adorable daughter in the supermarket, I can't tell you how thrilled I am to find somebody we know – well, Max knows – in this little village. You and your husband – Bob, isn't it? must both come to dinner. I'm already great chums with Martha and they're coming too. Isn't Sebastian a poppet? Martha is lucky.'

Really? Lucy thought. Martha obviously hadn't enlightened her, then.

'Rob,' Lucy said. 'Not Bob. We'd love to,' she said in a precious voice which made even her feel slightly sick. She made a face at herself in the mirror.

'I have seen you at school, but everything's such a tizz at the moment, I haven't popped over to say hello. Ghastly builders, everything is *such* a mess. You'll have to excuse us, the place is a tip. But do come. Saturday? Fabulous. About eight? You know where we are, don't you?'

'Yes,' Lucy said. 'Thank you—' But Cat had rung off, leaving Lucy standing, looking into the receiver, feeling incredibly foolish. How could someone make you feel fat and insecure, just over the phone? She just knew she'd put on the wrong clothes that morning. She resolved immediately to go upstairs, change into a jumper that suited her, put on make-up and paint her nails. And how much weight *could* you lose in four days? Nothing but pine kernels and bananas will pass my lips until Saturday, Lucy vowed. There was just one slight problem. How was she going to persuade Rob?

'You must be bloody joking.'

Rob, on a chair, hands above his head, was trying to mend the curtain pole in Laura's bedroom. He'd said at the time he put it up the screws were too short, and Lucy said it was his fault for buying a cheap one from a local DIY superstore, when she would far rather have spent more and got a lovely solid wooden one with acorns on the end from John Lewis, never mind the fact that it was three times the price. Rob had been about to concur until he found out you had to pay for each individual curtain ring.

'It's just a pole,' he said. 'No-one will see it.'

'I'll see it,' Lucy said. 'My mother will see it. It *says* something.'

Rob groaned and rolled his eyes. 'Well, this one will say "cheap – but functional" OK?'

And now, predictably, it had fallen, brought down by the heaviness of the lined curtains Caroline had had made for them, as she knew a little woman who did a super job, combined with Laura swinging on them.

Rob, his arms going numb, looked down angrily at Lucy, who'd put off asking him until Friday, knowing they had nothing else planned. She'd already booked a babysitter. 'Why the hell,' he said, 'do you think I want to voluntarily spend a night in the company of that complete wanker and his snobby wife?'

'Shush,' Lucy said. 'Laura.'

'I don't care. We're not going.'

'Martha and Sebastian will be there too. You like Martha,' she pointed out, slyly. He had, surprisingly, taken to Martha, and Martha too had been amazed at how very attractive he was, far more attractive than Lucy had intimated. They had begun flirting immediately, Rob taking the mickey out of her voice and Martha reacting instinctively to such a gorgeous man. She didn't mind his accent and blunt observations, because this made him a character, and Martha collected characters, to bring out at dinner parties like little novelty gifts. Lucy did mind this relationship a bit, as it made it much harder for Martha to be truly understanding when she wanted to go on about how vile Rob was. At least she could nod completely

273

truthfully when Martha said that Sebastian was a selfish bastard, because he was. In fact Martha found Rob so attractive Lucy was rather loath to leave them alone together for any length of time – not for fear of what Rob might do, as he was so trustworthy on that front, but for fear of what Martha might, when pissed, attempt to initiate. But all moves to make Rob get on with Sebastian had failed dismally. The one time they had been round for dinner Rob had become so desperate to avoid his patronizing remarks he'd even got up to help clear the plates. Left alone, there was a serious danger he might just punch him. Things had gone badly wrong from the moment Sebastian had asked Rob where he had gone to school.

'Please,' Lucy said.

'We'll talk about it later,' he said.

That night, over supper – Lucy had fought a long and hard campaign to stop him calling it tea, and explained that dinner usually involved more than two people – she said quietly, 'Why can't we go?'

'Because I don't like him. Look, Lucy, they aren't our sort, what would be the point?'

Lucy looked at him in amazement. 'What do you mean?' she said.

'That wanky London commuter set,' he said. 'Yah, yah, I've bought a farmhouse – sorry, *Rectory* – and isn't it wonderful bringing up one's children in the fresh air . . . all that bollocks.'

'I'm so pleased you now decide who should be my friends,' she said, icily, secretly acknowledging that was pretty well how the conversation would go.

'Remember Martha's going,' she said.

Rob grinned at her. 'Stop trying to tempt me with Martha. And if she's going Sebastian will be going. He

274

is a complete pillock. I'd rather spend an evening with Michael Howard.'

'Don't be silly,' Lucy said, sternly. 'Please,' she wheedled. 'Just come. It'll be OK.'

'I'll come,' Rob said, putting down his fork filled with fresh pasta, 'as long as no-one mentions their income, private school, the stock market or the price of property outside London. Oh – and horses too. Complete no-no.'

'What about politics?' Lucy said, innocently.

'I would relish,' Rob said, 'an honest political discussion with Max and Sebastian. Positively relish it.' Lucy cringed inside.

'Just come,' she said, smiling winningly. 'It'll be fun.'

In the car, they had a row about the wine. 'Why the hell,' Rob said, 'did you have to buy Gevrey Chambertin? And Montrachet? It must have cost a fortune. What's wrong with Chardonnay like we always have?'

Lucy sat heavily on a rising bout of temper. She knew he was spoiling for a fight, ever since he'd deliberately put on his most disreputable shiny trousers and a shirt he knew she hated, ignoring the nice navy and white striped one she'd laid out for him on the bed. They'd also had a brief tussle with a hanger containing a pair of jeans. 'Does it matter?' she said. 'Why shouldn't we buy decent wine occasionally?'

'Just a little something for you,' he said, in his most annoying mimicking-Lucy voice. 'Montrachet! We drink it all the time!'

'Don't be pathetic,' she said.

'Stop being so pretentious, then,' he said.

'I'm not.'

As they swung into the smoothly gravelled circular drive, the large front door was wide open, despite the cold, letting out a pool of light. Lucy wished heartily they had a better car. Martha's Discovery was parked next to Max's Range Rover, and Lucy saw Cat had a Mercedes estate with a personalized number plate. She tried to slide the Fiesta in at the furthest point from the door, but Max was already advancing across the drive and could see them.

Lucy slid out of the car as quickly as she could, so he wouldn't notice the side pocket stuffed with sweet papers and Ribena cartons. He took her hand.

'Lucy, how *lovely* to see you.' He bent down and kissed her on the cheek. She felt the hair by his ear against her skin, and slid her hand up, almost involuntarily, to touch his face. He smelt of expensive aftershave, and his stripy shirt was crisp and clean. Her fingers were cool against his skin. Rob slammed the car door. Walking round the car, he put his arm firmly round Lucy's waist.

'Rob,' Max said, holding out his hand.

'Hi,' Rob said. He made no move to shake Max's hand, forcing him to drop it to his side, embarrassed. Lucy sensed Rob smile to himself in the darkness.

Max turned and led them inside. 'Cat!' he called as they walked through the door. 'Rob and Lucy are here.' He pulled the old door closed behind him, with a great satisfying thud.

They stood looking about them in the black-and-white tiled hall. Rob took in the large oak staircase, sweeping up to the galleried landing, the heavy chandelier which hung in the hall, the oil paintings Cat had placed on the floor, beneath the spot she wanted them to be hung. Even the building work, still in evidence from buckets and ladders, was tidied neatly away into a corner. Cat emerged from a door at the far end of the oak-panelled hall.

'How lovely of you to come,' she said, advancing, and kissed them both silkily on the cheeks. 'You'll have to excuse me – I'm just at a delicate moment with the hollandaise. Isn't it hopeless?' she said to Lucy. 'Thank God I've Fajita.'

'The housekeeper,' Max explained. 'Thick as a brick but a wonder in the kitchen. We were really worried she might not move out of London, but we bribed her with more cash.' He smiled at Rob. 'Always works.'

'Really?' Rob said.

'Do give me your coats. Come on Max, darling, *host*.'

Lucy tried to shrug off her coat, but got her arm stuck. The lining was slightly ripped under the arm, and, putting it on, she often went down a couple of blind alleys before finding the hole. 'Let me help,' Max said. They had a brief struggle, until Max extracted her. 'It didn't want to let you go,' he said.

'What a lovely coat,' Cat said. 'MaxMara?'

'Principles,' Lucy muttered.

'Here's mine,' said Rob, holding out his jacket. Lucy sighed. Why had he put on that awful anoraky thing? He had a perfectly good Barbour at home, which she'd bought him for Christmas. But he refused to wear it as a matter of principle. When they were first married she'd gone through his wardrobe like a tornado, chucking out anything which looked cheap, too woolly or too polyester. She now tried to impose a style offensive by buying all of his clothes, but occasionally something slipped through the net. Like this kagoul.

Max led them into a vast drawing room. In the hearth, a huge fire blazed. Martha, her black satin shoes half off her feet, long slim legs in sheer black tights, was tucking into a glass of champagne, lounging seductively on a large squashy burgundy sofa.

Sebastian was standing with his back to them, looking into the fire. Lucy sensed immediately they'd just had a row. The atmosphere was so chilly it could have given you a nasty nip. Martha slipped on her shoes, and rose. Sebastian didn't look round.

'Lucy, darling.' Martha gave Lucy a hug and looked at her quizzically. Lucy made a small grimace indicating Rob was in a bad mood.

'And Rob.' She reached up to give him a smoochy kiss. Rob's face lightened. 'Hello, Martha, *darling*,' he said. 'And how many of those have you had?'

'Only two,' she said. 'Don't be awful.'

'I better catch up,' Rob said, and taking a glass proffered by Max, he downed it in one. Lucy stared at him. Was he going to be like this all night?

'Hello, Sebastian,' she said, which forced him to turn.

'Lucy, Rob. How are you both?' he said, in his deep, clipped voice, without the slightest hint of actual interest. Rob eyed him with loathing.

'No doubt all the better for seeing your cheerful face,' Martha, said, quickly. He shot her a furious look. Max caught Lucy's eye, and they flashed a swift understanding smile.

'That's a lovely picture,' Lucy lied, walking over to inspect a swirling modern painting above the fireplace, which looked rather like projectile vomit. 'Isn't it?' Max said. 'He's a young artist, I've bought quite a few of his. A marvellous investment, isn't it, art? I'm really just getting into it. Don't you think, Rob?'

'Absolutely. No doubt about it *whatsoever*. I was just saying to Lucy the other day—'

'And how are the renovations going?' Lucy said, swiftly.

'Bloody awful,' Max said. 'It's so hard to get reliable workmen these days.'

'*Isn't it*,' Rob said. 'I couldn't agree more. Feckless and irresponsible, I've found. But that's the working class for you.' He smiled openly at Max, and swallowed another glass of champagne.

Just then, a little face peered round the door. Max smiled indulgently. 'Cosima. Come in. Come and say hello.'

An exquisite dark-haired girl appeared, about eight, wearing a long white nightgown, swiftly followed by a much younger girl, the daughter Max had been holding in the photograph, in pyjamas. 'Jessica. Where's Bruno?' 'He's here,' Cosima said. A younger version of Max sauntered into the room, wearing baggy combat trousers and a huge T-shirt, swiftly followed by a harassed-looking but pretty au pair. 'I'm so sorry,' she said, in a strong German accent. 'They did insist on coming down.' 'That's OK,' Max said, picking up Jessica and kissing her gently on the cheek. 'Now say goodnight, children – and then off to bed. You too, Bruno. No sitting up all night at the PlayStation.'

'Goodnight,' they chorused, like the Von Trapp family, looking about them, the girls shyly, Bruno belligerently. Max ruffled his hair, and hugged him. 'Off you go, champ,' he said.

'I'm sorry they disturbed you,' the au pair said, gazing adoringly at Max.

'No problem. But keep them in the nursery, from now on, won't you?'

'Of course, Mr Yorke.' Lucy wondered if she might curtsey, but she didn't. There was more than a hint of sway in her hips as she departed, and Lucy noted Max's eyes followed her out of the room.

*   *   *

At the table, stunningly laid out with silver cutlery, candelabra and two enormous fresh-flower arrangements, which Lucy had to peer round as if playing hide-and-seek, Cat had put Rob next to Martha, which cheered him up. They were both rapidly reaching Planet Pissed. Lucy was next to Sebastian. Immediately, across her, Max and Sebastian began to talk about the state of the stock market, and how their investments were doing. Lucy avoided Rob's eyes, but he was being chatted up by Martha, who, Lucy saw, kept putting her hand on his arm. Then they started on about wine, and Max told them at length about the wonderful cellar Cat was due to inherit, and the incredible vintages her parents had given them for a wedding present. From wine they moved swiftly to house prices in London compared to the country, whether they should take up hunting, and then back to wine.

'And what do you think of Radlett?' Cat said suddenly to Lucy.

'Um,' she said, and before she could think of anything interesting, Martha was off about how marvellous it was, which amazed Lucy as Martha was usually so rude about all the other parents. Then Cat and Martha started on about the benefits of boarding, and should they/shouldn't they send their children away. Rob raised his eyebrows at Lucy. She ignored him.

Because she'd put on a skintight black velvet dress, she could hardly eat any of Cat's amazing food. They began with exquisite pan-fried scallops, then a rocket salad with warm pigeon breasts, and, for the main course, linguine with squid ink and Parmesan. It looked like slimy seaweed covered in sawdust. Rob stared at it suspiciously, and Lucy hoped against hope he wouldn't ask what it was. At least he was eating it, but then, Lucy thought, by now he was so pissed he would have eaten his way through his own tie, if he'd been wearing one. When they first went out to restaurants he wouldn't try anything he hadn't eaten before, and Lucy banned him from ordering steak, well done. She remembered one awful moment in a restaurant when they'd just moved up to Clitheroe. Rob had ordered lamb and the waiter, who was very sniffy, asked him how he'd like it. 'Cooked,' he said. 'Not pink,' Lucy butted in, quickly. It had also taken an age to stop him ordering the house wines and persuade him to branch out a little.

Finally there was a sliver of delicious onion tart, chocolate mousse and cheese. Cat ate practically nothing, and was constantly leaping up from the table to harangue Fajita, while Max uncorked more and more bottles of wine. Halfway through the meal, Lucy realized she desperately needed the loo. Standing up, she felt her head swim. Thank God they'd said they would get a taxi – they could collect the car tomorrow. There was no way she could drive.

'Where's the . . .'

'Just across the hall,' Cat said, smoothly. 'Or any number upstairs.' She laughed. 'But I can't guarantee the plumbing! Honestly, Martha, can you find a decent plumber round here?'

Lucy caught Max's eye. She'd been aware of his gaze all evening, from the scallops through to the heavily-laced chocolate brandy mousse. Whenever she looked up, she felt his eyes had been on her. Whatever she said, she was aware of how it would sound to him, and every gesture, every movement, she made with him in mind. She hadn't felt so conscious of herself for ages. It was probably the copious champagne, but she felt witty, lively – and desirable. If only Rob would join in and show Max how funny and interesting he could be. He was now pretty well past the point of making any kind of articulate contribution to the discussion anyway, and only seemed prepared to talk to Martha. Lucy felt ashamed of him.

She walked slowly to the door, concentrating very hard on not weaving, and grasped the door handle firmly. Out in the hall, she took several deep breaths. She must not have any more to drink, or she'd say something regrettable, or fall off her chair. She headed off across the hall, but there were so many doors she couldn't find the loo. After opening several doors, one of which revealed a library, she gave up, and tottered up the wide staircase. There was a large mirror at the end of the landing, and she was alarmed to see just how red her face was. She veered off and found herself in an opulent sea-green bedroom. Obviously Max and Cat's, judging from the silky garments over the back of a chair and a pair of Max's brogues, in shoe trees, by the wardrobe. On the bedside table was an array of photographs. Lucy, who knew she was being appallingly nosy but couldn't help herself, wandered over and peered at them.

Oh, how perfect. How absolutely perfect. Max, laughing, at the wheel of a boat, his hair blowing romantically away from his face in the wind. Max with Cosima on his shoulders on a deserted windswept beach, both wearing identical blue and white stripy jerseys. Max and Cat, arms round each other, he in black tie, she wearing a cowl-necked silk dress, smiling into each other's eyes. The two girls, wearing swimming costumes and too-big panama hats, shielding their eyes from the sun. Max with his arm round Cosima, holding skis, grinning with tanned faces, goggles pushed up on their heads. How *lovely*. The record of a lovely family life. Not her life. To her horror, she felt tears welling in her eyes. She hastily brushed them away. Turning, she saw a door and pushed it open. Thank God, she was in the adjoining bathroom.

Locking the door, she sank down. Then she looked at herself in the mirror on the door. Oh dear. Pink in the face, running mascara, no lipstick. She looked about her. There was a hairbrush, and Cat's make-up bag. Full of Estée Lauder and Chanel lipsticks. She helped herself to eyeliner and lipstick – far more scarlet than she would normally wear – and sprayed on a good deal of expensive perfume. That was better. Quite presentable, now. She gulped down some water from the tap out of her cupped hand. She must not drink any more champagne.

Slowly, she pushed the bathroom door open, and, in the darkness, walked hesitantly across the room. There was a movement by the door. Oh no. She was going to be found by one of the children, or the au pair, or, worst, Cat.

'Lucy?'

It was Max's voice, hushed, slightly drunk.

'Yes?'

'I just wondered where you'd gone,' he said, smoothly. 'Are you OK?'

'I'm sorry,' she whispered back. 'I didn't mean to end up here. I got a bit lost.' She moved forward, and saw he'd pulled the door almost closed behind him. She reached out for the handle. 'We'd better go down,' she said. 'They'll . . .' 'Shh,' he said. And, sliding his arm round her, he pulled her gently towards him. Lucy, frantic, could only think that her mouth would taste of cheese. Her eyes, now more accustomed to the dim

283

light, saw how serious he looked. As if he was going to kiss her.

Her heart was banging against her ribs, and a thin trickle of sweat ran from under her arm into the tight velvet of her dress. Surely not. Surely not here, not with his children only yards away, the au pair . . .

'Lucy,' he said, reaching down to lift her face to his. Their eyes met in the dimness.

'I've missed you,' he said.

'Why?' Lucy said, and then paused, thinking how rude she sounded. She wasn't very adept, she realized, at this kind of situation. What should she do? Here he was, hideously attractive, sexy, practised – yes, she reckoned, he was quite practised at this kind of thing – and all she could think about was cheese.

'Why do you think?' he said, quietly. 'I never stopped loving you.'

Lucy looked hard at him. This was pretty obviously a lie, but his gaze never flickered. With his other hand, he began to make circles on her bare arm. It felt wonderfully sensual. Lucy felt her resolve weaken. Rob had been so foul . . .

'You're so . . . ' His mouth began to descend on hers, and Lucy felt the pit of her stomach swoop and dip like a swallow in spring. On the bobsleigh run to adultery. Then, suddenly, there was a sharp click. Max lurched back slightly, as the door he'd been leaning on banged shut. The noise seemed to reverberate around the landing, and Lucy looked at Max in horror. He reached for her again, but it had broken the spell. She turned away, her heart thudding.

'We'd better go down,' she said, her voice sounding amazingly calm considering that her insides felt like a washing machine on full spin.

'Don't,' he said, quietly.

'We have to,' Lucy said, firmly. 'This is crazy. Let me out.' He stood aside, silently, and she turned the handle. On the landing, as she closed the door, she put her hand to her chest. Her breath seemed to be coming in short gasps, and she had to consciously slow her heart-rate down. In the mirror, she checked she hadn't smudged Cat's lipstick. Her eyes were unnaturally bright. You wicked woman, she said sternly to herself. Don't even think it for *one moment*. Then she walked, unsteadily, down the stairs. There was no sign of Max.

Lucy slid as unobtrusively as she could into the dining room. Cat was soberly trying to press espresso on Martha and Rob, which they were both refusing. Cat thought that this dinner party had got away from her, rather, and where was Max? Martha, who felt she'd been amazingly witty and gorgeous all night, now felt an enormous urge to cry. Rob was so lovely. Why didn't he fancy her? No-one seemed to fancy her any more. And, pissed or not pissed, she'd seen the way Max looked at Lucy. There was big trouble brewing there, and, even in her state, she'd noticed the way he'd slipped out of his chair when Lucy set off for the loo. Thank goodness Cat had been out of the room at the time, it was so obvious. Lucy, Martha thought, would be like a lamb to the slaughter. Max – and she had a pretty sharp eye for this kind of thing – was clearly a serial adulterer. So why didn't he fancy *her*?

'Come on, you old trollop,' Rob said to Martha. 'Have some coffee.'

'You're so bloody charming,' Martha said. 'I don't want any coffee.' She sloshed some more champagne into her glass, red nails gripping the stem.

'I think we'd better go,' Lucy said, looking at Cat's frosty expression.

They stood in the hall, as Cat went to fetch their

coats, leaving Martha with Sebastian. Through the open door they could hear him saying, furiously, 'You are completely drunk.'

'Fuck off,' Martha said, distinctly. Rob grinned.

Lucy kissed Cat on the cheek, holding with the other hand onto Rob, who was gambolling sideways. 'Thank you so much. The food was delicious. It was lovely.' Rob abruptly lunged forward and kissed Cat full on the mouth. 'Great do,' he said. 'Smashing food. Specially the worms.' Cat, completely taken by surprise, stepped back. He smiled down at her, eyes glinting. Having ignored him all evening, as being not her sort at all, she suddenly thought, what an attractive man. A blush shot up her cheeks. An attractive man, but not one she could handle. Lucy bundled Rob out of the door.

Outside in the cold night air, their breath smoking, she rounded on him. 'What a display!' she said. 'You were *completely* out of it.'

'And where did you shoot off to?' Rob said, his voice suddenly far more sober.

Lucy's heart skipped a beat.

'What do you mean?'

'You disappeared,' he said. 'For ages.'

'I got lost,' Lucy said, hurriedly. 'I took a wrong turning and then I had a good nosy around the house. That's all. Anyway, you were nose-to-nose with Martha all night.'

Rob looked at her long and hard.

'I don't believe you,' he said.

Lucy stared at him in horror. 'Don't be so silly,' she said. 'That's ridiculous! Come on, let's ring for a taxi on the mobile.'

'You can get a taxi,' Rob said, swinging towards her so his face was only inches from hers. 'But I'm fucking well going to walk.' He turned and began to stride swiftly away. 'Rob!' she called after him. 'Don't be so daft. Wait. It's freezing.'

'Fuck off,' he said loudly. 'Ask your pal Max for a lift.' Then he disappeared into the darkness.

Lucy stood for a moment, hugging her coat around herself. She felt a sob rising in her throat. Brilliant. He could just walk off and leave her like this. What could she do? Knock on Max's door and ask to make a phone call because Rob had left her? Ring herself from outside, and risk being picked up by some lunatic rapist operating under the guise of a minicab driver? Sighing, she began to walk the mile or so home. Alone.

Chapter Twenty-Five

'Just treat yourself, darling,' Caroline said. 'It really won't hurt to let Rob pick the children up from school just for once. Come on, we'll have a lovely shop and I can buy you a few things. You deserve a treat. You've been rather down lately.'

'OK, Mum,' Lucy said, doodling hearts on the yellow pad she kept by the phone. Caroline was spending the week in London in an opulent hotel with Archie, who was doing some consultancy work.

'I'll come on the train,' she said.

'Well, make it first-class, darling. I'll pay.'

'If you force me,' Lucy said.

At the station, she paid for her ticket, declining the tube option as she'd decided she would also splash out on taxis. Why not? She needed something to take her mind off the awful coldness between her and Rob, which had spread out since the dinner party like the dawn of a new ice age. Caroline was taking her for an expensive lunch, and with shopping at Harvey Nicks and Peter Jones, today stretched out like an oasis of bliss. She'd even painted her fingernails and put conditioner on her hair. Small luxuries, but they made her feel so much better. Cat, bumping into her at school, was polite, but distant. She had obviously decided since the dinner party and Rob's drunken behaviour that Lucy was not suitable to be a friend. This was the conscious reason in the front of her mind – lurking round the back was the real reason, that Max clearly still fancied Lucy. Cat would put up with the odd au pair here and there, secretary even, but a fellow parent at private school – *that* would be an infidelity too far. But she had swooped on Martha as a chum, which made Lucy very pissed off indeed. What price loyalty?

On the platform, Lucy bought a newspaper and a cup of cappuccino, with a white plastic lid which didn't quite fit. The train arrived on time, and as she was climbing into the first-class carriage, she caught sight of a blond man running hell for leather over the bridge which linked the two platforms. She watched him for a few moments, amused, and then realized, with a lurching heart, that it was Max.

He jumped onto the train. Lucy looked determinedly out of the window. He probably wouldn't see her, and, anyway, what could she say to him? But she'd thought of so little else since that evening. Just that feeling, that lurchy feeling, of being close to a man who was not Rob. Gorgeous, yes, but also grumpy, fractious Rob, who made life so difficult at the moment. Max was so smooth, so sure of himself, so – so non-contentious, just effortlessly charming and confidently sexy. In quiet moments, driving home after dropping the children off at school, Lucy allowed herself a small but wicked private fantasy. A fantasy of sleeping with Max, preferably in a large, luxurious hotel room, with pale satin sheets and champagne and hot radiators – Rob never let her turn the central heating up high enough – and just the sheer abandonment of glorious sex for sex's sake, not as a thank-you, or a bribe, or mere habit, but the real animalistic passion so often lost in marriage. Max would still be good at that, she was pretty darn sure. In fact, so seductive was this particular fantasy Lucy often lapsed into it driving the children *to* school, and images of herself and Max, golden bodies on silken sheets entwined, would be interrupted by a stern little voice saying, 'Have you remembered my recorder?'

'Lucy?'

She looked up. His face registered pleasure. Lucy took in the thick blond hair brushed back from his forehead, gorgeous charcoal grey cashmere coat with the collar turned up, chestnut leather briefcase and – looking down – suede brogues. She noticed the woman in the seat opposite covertly watching him. His voice was loud and confident. The palms of her hands suddenly felt sweaty and she was very glad about the conditioner.

'Can I?' he said, sliding into the seat next to her.

'Of course,' she said, hastily moving *Hello!* – she only read it on trains – and the *Daily Telegraph*. After he'd stood up and taken off his coat, Lucy saw he was wearing a dark grey suit, beautifully cut, immaculate white shirt, with a glint of cufflinks. Her father always wore cufflinks. Rob didn't even know what they were when she first met him.

'Where are you off to?'

'Lunch with Mum in London,' Lucy said. 'She's treating me.'

There was a long pause, and then Max said, 'We haven't seen you for ages.'

'No,' she said, as if surprised. 'So we haven't.' She allowed herself a small note of irritation in her voice. 'I'm sure you've been very busy.'

Max looked at her sharply. 'What do you mean?'

'With the house and everything.'

'Oh that,' he said, dismissively. 'Cat's sorting that out. Her job.'

'And you're settling in well?'

'Lucy,' Max said. 'Why are you cross with me?'

Lucy swung round. 'Why should I be cross with you?'

'I have no idea,' he said, examining his immaculate fingernails. Then looked up at her with a sly sideways glance. 'Because I tried to kiss you?'

'Shush!' Lucy said, horrified, looking about her.

'Did you mind?' he said. 'You seemed very shocked.'

'You may go about kissing people,' Lucy said, furiously, 'but I certainly don't. Yes, I was shocked.'

'You won't come to a hotel with me now, then?'

'Max!' she said, torn between a desire to laugh and to be appalled. 'You are *terrible*.'

'I'm not terrible,' he said. And reached down to hold the hand not clutched around the polystyrene cup of coffee. 'I just think there's a chance for us to pick up where we left off.'

'Max,' Lucy said, putting down the cup on a narrow grey ledge with a slightly trembling hand. 'That was more than fifteen years ago. We can't just carry on as if we're teenagers.'

'Why not?'

'You're completely amoral,' she said. 'Have you always been like this?'

'No,' he said, raising Lucy's fingers to his mouth. 'Only with you.' The girl opposite eyed them with wonder. Lucky cow.

Lucy pulled away her hand and looked furiously out of the window. She sensed that Max was laughing at her. 'You're still very earnest, aren't you?' he said.

'Don't patronize me,' Lucy said. 'And stop that.'

Very gently, he was stroking her thigh through her skirt.

'Please,' she said, lifting his hand and placing it firmly in his lap. Abruptly, he turned.

'Would you like another coffee? That one looks like crap.'

A tired-looking woman was trundling a trolley towards them. She brightened at Max's voice. 'Two coffees,' he said, dropping pound coins into the woman's hand. She blushed scarlet as he smiled at her. God, thought Lucy. I can't cope with this.

He handed her the steaming cup. 'Sugar?'

'One.'

'Very naughty,' he commented, ripping open the sachet and pouring it in. He stirred it for her, as if for a child, and then, reaching across, he put it onto the ledge, taking the old one away and handing it to the trolley woman who was still standing there with her mouth open.

'Are you happy?'

'What?' Why did everyone ask her if she was happy, these days? Did she look miserable?

'Are you happy,' he repeated, dropping his voice, 'with Rob?'

'I don't think that's any of your business.'

'I know it isn't,' he said. 'But are you?'

'Yes,' Lucy said, defiantly. Max looked at her quizzically. 'Really?'

'Why shouldn't I be?' Lucy said. 'We've got a lovely home – OK, maybe not lovely but it's fine really – two children, Rob has a good job, why shouldn't we be happy?'

'Doesn't sound like much to me,' he said.

'Don't be so *patronizing*. Just because you married

Little Miss Heiress and live in a whopping great rectory doesn't mean you're the one who's got their life sorted out.'

'I don't mean that at all,' he said. 'It's just that Rob doesn't quite seem the kind of guy I thought you'd end up with.'

'And who did you think I'd end up with?' she said.

'Me.'

Lucy looked out of the window and stirred her coffee. She desperately wanted to get up and brush her hair in the loo, but couldn't face the thought of squeezing past him. Far too dangerous. After a moment, she turned to look at him.

He was staring steadily at her. The handsome face she knew so well, every line, every freckle, and now there were more lines, more creases to know. But underneath it was exactly the same person, just deeper, more rounded, more complete. He has total confidence in himself, she thought. He has become the kind of man who would not believe it if I turned him down. And she realized with a flick of alarm that very few women were likely to turn him down. If she was going to have an affair with anyone, it would be him, she thought. He was so successful, so confident, so known – but under that smooth, easy exterior, somehow she sensed that sharks lurked. He was very used to having his own way. And he wants his way with me, she thought, shuddering, partly with pleasure. And partly with fear.

'Anyway,' she said. 'Are you happy?'

'With Cat?'

'Yes,' said Lucy, patiently.

'Not really,' he said.

'You're very spoilt, you know.'

'Am, I' Max sounded amused. 'Why?'

'Because you have practically the perfect wife and the perfect home and the perfect children and even a perfect housekeeper, and you have the cheek to sit there and say you aren't happy.'

'But I haven't got you,' he said.

'You'd forgotten I existed until a few months ago!' Lucy pointed out.

'No I hadn't.'

'Really?' said Lucy, turning to him. 'And what visible sign was there that you were pining for me, all those years, carving out the perfect life in your lovely home in wherever-it-was?'

'Belgravia,' Max said, smugly. 'Of course I didn't get in touch. I didn't know what I'd find. You might have gone to seed.'

'You are awful,' Lucy said, scandalized. 'So you're only interested because I haven't turned into a dumpy little woman with housemaid's knee?'

'Yes,' he said, laughing. Lucy, despite herself, laughed too.

'I suppose I should be flattered that I'm still considered remotely attractive.'

'Of course you should,' he said. 'Deeply.'

'I'll think about it.' Lucy snuggled down into her first-class seat. 'A little.'

'When will I know?'

'What?'

'When you've reconsidered?'

'Reconsidered what?'

'My offer,' he said. 'My offer to make a fallen woman of you.'

'I'll let you know,' Lucy said, grinning. 'In due course.'

*　　*　　*

As the train pulled in, Max picked Lucy's bag up for her. It was mock leather and a little scuffed. 'Not a very nice bag,' he said, dismissively. 'I'll buy you one.'

'No you won't,' Lucy said. 'How could I explain it to Rob?'

'Say it's a gift from an admirer.'

'He's not very hot on admirers,' Lucy said.

'Well,' said Max, handing Lucy her coat in a manner which made her go hot and cold. 'We just won't have to tell him then, will we?'

After they had both shown their tickets and passed through the barrier, Max paused.

'Send my love to your mother,' he said.

'I will.' She grinned. 'Creep. You'll be late for your important appointment.' Max made a face. 'I want to stay with you.'

'Well you can't,' Lucy said sternly. 'Now go away and be a grown-up.'

'Don't want to.'

'Just bugger off,' Lucy said, smiling.

'OK,' he said. He turned, and walked away. Lucy was determined not to stare after him, and squinted up at the board. Where was the taxi rank? Then she felt a tap on her shoulder.

'What?'

'I fancy you rotten,' he said. And, bending down, he kissed her hard on the mouth. Putting her down, gasping, he smiled wolfishly. 'Will you go out with me?'

'Unless you stop bothering me,' Lucy said, 'I'll call the police.'

'Too late,' he said, confidently. 'The damage has been done.'

And walked away, whistling loudly.

Chapter Twenty-Six

Every time the phone rang after that day, Lucy jumped. Max had carefully written down her number again in his neat leather-bound diary, under 'B' for Beresford. But he didn't ring.

She met him at school three days later. She saw his car, with a pounding heart, as she turned into the drive. Pausing behind a dithery mother in a Volvo, she gently rested her chin on the steering wheel and watched him. He was carrying Jessica in his arms, Cosima swung on one hand and Bruno looked up at him adoringly. Putting Jessica down, he patiently lifted all their paraphernalia out of the boot of the Range Rover, and herded them towards the big old door. How right he looked here, Lucy mused. She noted how several of the mothers stopped to chat, how charmingly he smiled at them, and she saw, once he passed, how two of them smiled in the conspiratorial way of women smitten. Rob loathed dropping the girls off at school as he didn't know many of the other parents and hadn't made the effort to attend any but the most essential of events, like parents' evenings. He literally pushed the girls out of the car and sped off down the drive, back to known territory. Lucy knew that most of the other parents, with the wealth and success they carried so comfortably, made him edgy. Funny how all the parents sorted themselves out, Lucy mused. They formed into distinct cliques – the new-money lot with their tight, designer clothes and convertibles, the old inherited-money set with ripped jeans, Hunters wellies, hair like thicket hedges and muddy old Land Rovers, and the smooth successful nearly-theres with their new Range Rovers and very clean Barbours. Lucy didn't know where she fitted in, with her old car, usually scruffy clothes but odd flashes of glamour. A foot in all three camps, she guessed. Tart *and* old money.

Once she'd parked the car, she peered in the tiny car mirror. Not too bad. At least she'd put on lipstick, and her hair was newly washed. She fluffed it up a bit, and smiled at herself in the mirror.

'What are you doing, Mummy?' said Olivia's crystal clear voice. Their accents had improved a lot since coming to Radlett. 'You're going to make me awfully late for assembly.'

She hustled them both through the door and down the corridor, just as the assembly bell rang. 'Oh bugger,' Laura said loudly. 'I'm going to be late.'

'Hush, Laura!' Lucy said, giving her blazered shoulder a shove towards her classroom. Someone laughed behind her.

'What a charming expression.'

'Max!' Lucy squeaked. 'This is Laura.'

'Hello,' Laura said, eyeing him warily.

'This is Max Yorke – he's Cosima and Jessica's daddy.'

'I don't like Cosima,' Laura said. 'She's very spoilt.'

'Shush, Laura.' Lucy laughed nervously. 'Do excuse my charming children.'

'Don't be so bloody rude,' she hissed to Laura as she ushered her into the classroom.

'Well, she is,' Laura said. 'They both are. And Bruno beats people up.'

'I'm sure he doesn't,' Lucy said. 'Give me a kiss.'

'Tara,' Laura said. Lucy sighed.

Having taken Olivia to her teacher, Lucy retreated towards her car. As she got nearer, she saw that someone was leaning against it. It was Max.

'Thought you'd never come,' he said. 'I've had some very funny looks.'

'I'm not surprised,' Lucy said. 'It's hardly your car, is it?'

'Our cleaner had a Fiesta,' he said musingly. Lucy looked at him crossly. 'If you're going to be patronizing again you can sod off. And take your horrible Range Rover with you.'

'You're just jealous,' Max said. 'Would you like to come for a walk?'

'Why?'

'It's a nice day. Don't be so belligerent all the time.'

'I'm just suspicious of your motives.'

Max held his hands out in front of him. 'It's a lovely crisp day. I'm suggesting a walk. What could be more harmless?'

'Hmm,' Lucy said. 'I'll follow you. Now go.'

She waited a minute or two until Max's car had moved off smoothly down the drive. He indicated left, and Lucy followed him. They drove for about a mile, until Max pulled up by a public footpath sign, high on a hill. There were wonderful sweeping views down to the school.

He slammed the car door shut, and walked over to her. From the back of the car Lucy could hear a muffled squeaking sound. 'We've got a puppy,' he said, opening up the boot. A small black Labrador jumped up and down in a shiny metal cage.

'Oh,' Lucy said, her heart melting. 'Isn't he gorgeous?'

'You can hold him if you like,' Max said, unhooking the door of the cage. The puppy leapt into her arms, and she cooed with pleasure as it squirmed about, trying to lick her face. She buried it in his thick black fur and smelt his fabulous puppy smell. Much nicer than babies.

'Rob doesn't like dogs,' Lucy said. 'Or I'd have five.'

'Really? But you used to love them. What happened to Ben?'

'Died. Great Red Setter home in the sky. He's probably up there now, scaring the hell out of St Peter and flattening all newcomers.'

Max laughed. 'I can't imagine you without a dog,' he said.

'Why?' Lucy said. 'You don't really know me at all, now.'

'Don't I?'

He clipped on a new lead. 'Come on William,' he said. He looked at Lucy. 'I insisted. He died soon after that holiday, you know. Awful.'

Walking up the muddy track, Lucy pushed her hands deep into her pockets. Max had let William off the lead, and he charged backward and forward, his tail a blur. They walked in silence, until Max said, 'Have you missed me?'

'Is there no end,' Lucy said, 'to your self-esteem? No, I haven't missed you. I haven't thought about you at all,' she lied.

'Liar.'

'Max,' Lucy said, patiently, turning to face him. 'We

can't carry on like this. We're not seventeen, or eighteen, or whatever. We're old now – really quite old,' Max smiled, 'and we can't mess about like this, flirting and being silly. It isn't as easy as that.' She scuffed the muddy ground with the toe of her welling-ton. 'Anyway,' she said, looking shyly at him. 'What's the point?'

'The point,' Max said, advancing towards her, and gently taking hold of the ends of her grey cashmere scarf – a present from her mother last Christmas – 'is that I'm so delighted to have found you again. And found you just as you were. Do you know what that means to me? For years and years I've carried around in my head a fictionalized portrait of you, Lucy Beresford, the girl I loved most in the world, who dumped me in the cruellest way imaginable and wrecked my life' – Lucy laughed – 'and now I've found you again and you're exactly the same and it's made me feel like I did then. Do you see? I've never felt like that since, not about Cat, not about anyone. You,' he said, winding Lucy in, 'were the perfect girl for me. In every way. I wanted to marry you. Don't you remem-ber? I meant it, Lucy, I really meant it that day on the beach, although I presume you didn't, from the way you cast me so brutally aside. All these years I feel like I've been sleepwalking – I know Cat is fabulous in lots of ways but really, Lucy, she's bloody boring to be with, and I was just starting to think there was never going to be anything remotely exciting in my life and then there you were. Just the same. Or nearly the same. Do you see?' he said, earnestly. 'Do you see what you mean? You mean that I can feel like that again and it makes me feel – happy.' He paused, and took a great deep breath. 'Did any of that make sense?'

'A little,' Lucy said, slowly. 'But we aren't the same

people, are we? We're grown-ups with families and partners and houses and mortgages.' Max looked at her quizzically. 'Well,' she continued crossly, 'I have a mortgage and I can't let myself fall in love with someone just because it would make me feel *happy*.'

'Why?' said Max, reasonably.

'Because life isn't like that,' Lucy said angrily, pulling away from him and beginning to walk towards the wood. 'Come on. We're going to lose William. You can't just say yippee I've met someone I fancy, and jump into bed with them. That's what marriage is about, isn't it? Denying yourself things?'

'What a puritan you've become,' Max said.

'No I haven't,' Lucy said, crossly. 'I just see marriage differently from you.'

'You mean you don't want me?'

He stood, shoulders hunched against the wind, hands now driven deep into the pockets of his brown Nubuck coat, chocolate brown scarf wrapped round his neck, hair lifting in the breeze, looking like an advertisement for country clothing. 'Come on, Lucy-Luce. I don't believe you.'

Lucy looked at him. And started to laugh. 'You're just *awful*,' she said. 'I've trundled along with my life, getting on with it, and then here you come upsetting everything. Stop being so smooth and so sure of yourself. I'm *not* going to sleep with you.'

'Not even if I say please nicely?'

'Especially then,' she said. He walked back towards her. 'I'll accept no for now,' he said. 'But you've got a tiger by the tail, you know.' Lucy shivered.

'I can handle you, Max Yorke,' she said. 'Just remember how well I know you.'

'Exactly,' he said. 'That's why you'll give in.'

*　　*　　*

'*Why* won't you let me make love to you?' Lucy had been in the middle of grilling fish fingers when the phone rang. He was on the train, coming home. It was the fifth time he'd asked her in three days. He had decided that persistence was the best course of action.

'Because I can't,' she said.

'Why?'

'Too scared,' she said.

'I'm scared too. But I'm more scared that all this will just end if we don't.'

'All *what* will end?' Lucy said.

'The fact that I've found you again.' Lucy looked at the phone and made a small face. 'And I love you.' Then they lost the signal. Gently, she replaced the receiver. 'I love you.' No he didn't, she thought, shaking herself as she headed back towards fish fingers and reality. He just thinks he does. He likes the drama. He likes all the subterfuge. I'm just a diversion, she thought. Something exciting in his life. I can't allow myself to be sucked in because I don't know if he means it.

'Who was that?' Olivia called from the kitchen.

'Daddy,' Lucy said. 'He'll be home soon.'

Rob, walking through the door while the girls were in the bath, resolved that tonight he would tell Lucy. He would tell her the big thing he'd been hiding, the thing which had been eating away at him for the past few months and had made him so distracted. He felt guilty he'd paid her so little attention, and he knew he had been rather bad-tempered. But he'd make it up to her.

He'd been offered a job in London, a good job, on one of the nationals. It would mean more money, and a big step up, but he just— Sitting at his desk in the office that afternoon, staring blankly at his computer screen, he rubbed his fingers over his eyes. He wasn't sure if Lucy would go with him. The thought terrified him. She always said she hated London, how sorry she felt for people trying to bring up children in the city, and how lucky they were to live in a rural village. But his hours would be so unpredictable, he'd need to be within easy distance of the office. For the past month, he'd been stalling. But he couldn't stall any longer. They needed an answer, and he would have to speak to Lucy about it tonight. Thank God she seemed so happy at the moment. He had an odd feeling at the back of his mind, as if there was something he needed to tackle. But he was so busy at work, there was so little energy left for anything in the evenings beyond sitting down, eating a meal, and falling into bed. They hadn't slept together for ages, and he was sure that was partly his fault. And she hadn't brought up the subject, which was unusual for her. Normally if they had a row, she was the one who would bring things round. But they'd just let their life drift – since the dinner party, in fact. It was odd she hadn't brought the issue to a head.

Lucy read Olivia's bedtime story, and thought about Max.

'Love me, love me, say that you love me . . .' Laura's tape was playing in her bedroom, her favourite CD of the moment, from Baz Luhrmann's *Romeo and Juliet*. Leonardo DiCaprio was Laura's idol. Lucy wouldn't let her watch the film, because of all the snogging, but had bought her the tape. Lucy also fancied him rotten, which made her depressed, as she was old enough to be his mother and he was unlikely to fancy her back. At least when she'd fancied Bryan Ferry or Sting, there was a remote possibility they *might* fancy her, if she could ever engineer a meeting. That was the funny thing about age, she thought. In her teens, she couldn't have believed it ever possible to be physically attracted to a man over forty. But now when Lucy saw Sting on the telly, she didn't think, well over forty, yuk. She thought, cor!

Rob was home earlier than usual, Lucy thought, hearing the door. She had put on make-up, washed her hair. When she smiled at her reflection, she was pleased. Not young, of course, but . . . OK. Desirable. She must be desirable, because Max desired her. She felt as if she had learned to like herself again, because someone claimed to love her. This was not someone who just lived with her, and tolerated her, and raised children with her, but someone for whom she was special, who wanted her, who talked to her and listened and laughed at what she said. There was no harm in it. He was just – a good friend. It wouldn't get out of hand. She knew Max of old, and she couldn't let herself be – in love. She gingerly rubbed her chest. Of course she wasn't in love with him.

'Let's have some wine.'

Lucy looked surprised. Rob had been on a go-slow, drinking-wise, for several weeks, having admitted to her that he probably did drink too much. Lucy had asked him on what comparable scale. 'A fish,' he said.

'Are you sure?'

'Sure. There's some in the cupboard in the dining room.'

'The Fleurie?' Lucy said. 'I thought we were saving that for a special occasion.'

'This is a special occasion,' he said. Lucy's heart beat a little faster.

'There's something I have to ask you.'

304

Lucy's stomach dropped like a stone. He had found out about Max, somehow. Maybe someone had seen them on the train, or at school – or – Martha. Lord. She'd kept Martha pretty much in the dark about Max, as she was so close to Cat, but she was no fool. She knew Max was agitating for an affair. Rob would leave her. No, he would kill her and then he would leave her. But she hadn't done anything. Hardly anything – just one brief snog at the station, a couple of near misses – totally harmless. But none of that excused the way she felt, and the adultery in her heart. She sensed a blush beginning to rise from her shoulders, and her pulse raced. She tried to arrange her features in a portrayal of outraged innocence. She looked nervously at him, as if for the first time, in months. He looked tired, and distracted, and – he ran his hand through his dark, thick, long hair, just touched at the temples with grey – very attractive. Yes, really very attractive. He stretched, so the tails of his shirt were pulled out of his trousers, showing just a hint of hairy, flat, pale stomach. For the first time in what seemed like ages, Lucy felt a stirring of desire for him, mixed in with fear.

'What?'

'Nothing,' Lucy said, quickly.

'I've been offered a new job.'

Lucy let out her breath with a gasp.

'Where?'

'London.'

'Oh.'

Lucy looked at her left hand, at her wedding and engagement rings. Then her eyes flicked to the large square sapphire she'd inherited from her grandmother which she wore on her middle finger, a big, expensive ring. It put Rob's to shame and he hated her wearing it, like a badge of her past life, better than his.

'What do you want us to do?' she asked quietly. 'I know we've . . .'

'I don't know,' he said, dropping his head into his hands. 'Christ, Lucy, I've been in such a muddle. I really want to go but I know you'd hate it. You've been so much happier lately – ' Lucy winced – 'I can't bear to put you through it. And I know the girls love their school.'

Lucy looked at him. The phone rang. 'I'll go,' she said.

'No,' he said, pressing her down in her seat. 'I'll go. It'll be work.'

There was a long pause after he picked up the phone. Then he said, 'I see. Yes, we'll come right away. Where? The girls? We'll find someone.'

His voice scared Lucy. What? What could it be? She thanked God that everyone she loved most was here in this house, apart from Max of course, she knew they were safe, only her parents – oh Lord.

Oh dear Lord. Her parents. A stabbing pain went through her, so sharply it made her gasp out loud. It was her father, she knew, even before Rob came in and said something to her, it was her father, she'd known something was wrong from all the brief comments, breathlessness, pains in his chest, dizzy spells, little symptoms Caroline was worried about, which her father brushed aside. They were so busy at the moment, getting the new French house sorted out, he had no time for illness.

Rob walked over and, bending down, put his arms round her. She raised her head to him, and stared deep into his eyes. Rob said, 'It's your father. He's had a heart attack. They've taken him to hospital, he's still breathing but it doesn't look good. Your mother's there already, she went in the ambulance. Hang on.'

She heard him walk back to the phone, dial, and speak to Martha. 'Thank you. We'll drop them off now.'

The girls were asleep, and opened their eyes in amazement as Rob and Lucy lifted them up, in their duvets, carried them downstairs and out into the cold winter air. 'What's happened?' Laura mumbled. 'Nothing, darling,' Lucy said. 'Grandpa's just a bit ill, Daddy and I are going to see him, it'll be fine, I'll be back in the morning to take you to school.' Laura kissed her sleepily. 'OK.'

At the hospital, Lucy followed Rob down endless harshly-lit corridors until they reached the cardiac ward. Caroline was sitting by two double doors, bent over, crying. Lucy ran to her. 'Mum?' she said. Caroline raised her face. Lucy had never seen her like this, terrified, lost. Her eyes weren't made up, her face was naked, laid bare. 'I can't, you know,' she sobbed. 'I can't live without him.' Rob knelt beside her, gently took away Lucy's arms. 'You go and see him,' he said quietly. He put his arms tightly round Caroline, who rested her head on his shoulder.

Lucy pushed open the swing doors. A young junior doctor walked towards her. 'Miss Beresford?' 'Mrs Atkinson,' Lucy said. 'I'm his daughter. Where is he?'

'Over here,' he said. 'I must tell you,' he ran his hand wearily through greasy hair, his face pale with tiredness. 'It isn't looking optimistic, I'm afraid. He's had a massive coronary, his blood pressure is through the roof. We're trying to stabilize him, but,' he gently touched Lucy's arm, 'you should prepare for the worst.' Lucy stopped, and stood quite still. She breathed in, held her breath, then let it out again. The pressure was so intense, she understood now the weight of grief, she wanted to lie on the floor, as if standing was too much, she wanted to be as small as possible, so it wouldn't hurt so much.

'Would you like to see him?'

She followed him to a pair of screens, which he pulled back. Her father was lying there, his big frame bulky and yet fragile on the narrow hospital bed. Tubes ran into his throat and his chest, his mouth was covered by an oxygen mask. His chest was rising and falling very slowly. His chin, when she got near, was covered with an awful yellow liquid. 'Bile,' the doctor said. 'We'll clear that up.'

Lucy reached out and touched his fingers. They were pale, but freckled, his strong hands. 'Can he hear me?' she said. 'I don't know,' he said. 'It's possible.'

'Is he conscious?'

'There is brain activity. But it's too early to tell.' Lucy stood, helplessly, holding his fingers. 'Daddy?' she said, 'we're here, we're all here.' She felt embarrassed, standing in this open room, having a one-sided conversation with the man she did love best in the world, who had given her so much, and now she couldn't do anything for him. He'd always made it better for her, and now she was making a mess of it, not helping, didn't even know what to say. 'I love you,' she said, the tears running down her face. 'Please, please,' she whispered.

Holding his hand, she ceased to be Lucy Atkinson, married, mother of two, a grown-up – her hand shrank, softened, and she was five again, she'd had a bad dream, the monsters were coming. He was holding her, rocking her, making everything all better. Only now the monsters had come.

'Please don't go.' There was a high-pitched whine.

'Excuse me,' the doctor said. 'Could you leave us a second?'

Lucy was pushed back, the screens went round him, people rushed in. Lucy turned and ran. 'What?' Her mother jumped up in the corridor, staring at Lucy's stricken face. 'I don't know,' she said. 'I think he's died.'

Her mother, who'd been holding onto Rob, buckled. Rob caught her. 'No,' she wailed. 'No, no, no.' Rob, his arm firmly round her shoulders, led her away. Lucy sank into the chair. The next moment the young doctor appeared. 'He's dead,' Lucy said.

'I'm afraid so.'

Lucy wanted to scream. How could he be dead? She'd spoken to him on the phone yesterday, he'd teased her about getting lost on the way to their house because she hadn't been for a while, he'd asked what Laura wanted for her birthday, he'd talked to Olivia and made her laugh, he'd promised her a rabbit, never mind what her mother said. How, Lucy thought, how could she tell them their grandpa was dead? How could there be so much life, so much of a person one minute, and it be not there the next? How could so much character and forcefulness just *end*?

Rob walked back down the corridor. Her mother had stopped sobbing, was glassy-eyed with shock. 'He is dead,' Lucy said. Her mother just stared at her. Rob said, 'We'll take you home.'

Caroline said, very clearly, 'I want to see him.'

Lucy led her inside the ward. All the fuss, all the activity, had stopped. The staff parted before them. On the bed, he was lying, his eyes closed. Lucy thanked God. She couldn't have faced seeing his open sightless eyes, couldn't bear to touch him where there was no life. He'd ceased to be her father. He was a body. Her father now was in her mind, in her thoughts, in her memory. She turned away.

She heard Rob talking to the doctors. 'I'll take them home, then come back. Yes, I know, there are many things to deal with, of course.'

In the car, they drove in silence. Lucy helped her mother into the house, shushed a cowed Hamish, who looked for Archie, couldn't see him, whined. Lucy led her mother up to her bedroom, and, silently, helped her undress, and put her into bed. 'Don't leave me,' Caroline said. 'I won't. I'll be back in a sec.' Lucy walked downstairs. She couldn't bear to be without Rob. She wanted him to hold her, to keep her standing, remind her that she had a family, her own life. In the kitchen, she put on the kettle. On the top of the wooden table was a birthday card. It was open. He'd written, 'To Laura . . .' Lucy sat down. He'd written it that evening. So little drama before a death. She walked into the laundry room, searching for Hamish, the red setter they'd bought to replace Ben. He was lying in his basket, his tail down, moaning. She knelt beside him, and buried her fingers in his deep glossy red coat. On his fur, she smelt her father. And she sobbed, and sobbed, against the silky smooth ears, while he pressed his face against hers.

Rob made everything happen. He organized the death notice, he spoke to undertakers, he rang Lucy's work to say she wouldn't be coming in for several weeks. He arranged with Martha to keep the girls and take them to school. He told Laura and Olivia their grandpa had died. Martha had brought them to the house. Caroline said she wanted to see them. She'd hardly moved since his death, lying in bed, sedated by the doctor, holding onto the pillow on his side of the bed. Laura walked up and gently put her arms round her granny. 'It's all right,' she said, 'he's in heaven. You'll be there soon.' Lucy, for the first time in two days, laughed. 'Oh, Laura,' she said. Caroline smiled, and stroked her hair. 'Thank goodness I have you two,' she said. 'And you,' she said, reaching out for Lucy. 'And you,' she added, holding tightly onto Rob's hand. Helen, who was away travelling, was due to fly back later in the week. Lucy, looking at Rob's face, wanted to cry. She couldn't have coped with this without him; the night after her father died, Rob had made love to her for the first time in months. Silently, wordlessly, as if somehow real life needed to continue, the possibility of new life from death. Afterwards, Lucy slept in the crook of his arm.

The worst thing for Lucy were Archie's clothes. They smelt so strongly of him, were so imprinted with not just his smell but his personality, she couldn't bear to get rid of them. Caroline wanted Rob to have the jackets and shoes, they were the same size, although Archie was much bigger round the middle. Rob took a handful, to please her. There were a couple of items Caroline couldn't part with – his favourite pair of shoes. Lucy kept his handkerchiefs. She'd always used them as a child, to make herself go to sleep, pouching them into a little ball and holding them against her face, because they smelt of him and she felt safe. Now she held them to her, and breathed in, and sensed again that she was not alone. Rob stood behind her, and she leant against him.

In the ensuing weeks, especially during the funeral, Lucy felt Archie was there. A sudden noise, a gust of wind, and she would feel him, beside her. When the grief became too much, as it occasionally did, she would reach out her hand, and clasp his broad palm, feel the warmth of his solid fingers wrapped around hers. She held it tightly for a few minutes, then let go, and the pain was bearable again.

Four days after he died, the phone rang. It was Max. 'I'm so sorry,' he said. 'I would have rung, straight away, but I was too worried . . . you poor darling.'

'Of course,' Lucy said. 'It's very kind of you to ring. I'll tell my mother. Would you like to come to the funeral? It's on Thursday. You can't? No, really, it doesn't matter.'

Rob stood behind her.

'Who is it?' Lucy shushed him with a hand that was shaking slightly.

'Rob and I really appreciate it. And tell your parents, the flowers were wonderful. Mum will reply, she's just too . . .'

'I know,' Max said swiftly. Then, very quietly, 'Can I see you?'

'I don't think that's possible, just now. But thank you for the thought. I'll tell her. I have to go,' Lucy said. 'Yes Cat, I might see you tomorrow. I'm shopping too. Waitrose? After school? Perhaps I'll see you. Thanks. You're so kind.'

She put the phone down.

'Who was that?'

'Max and Cat,' Lucy said. 'They send their love.'

'Strange they'd bother.'

'Max knew Dad quite well, remember?'

'Oh yes,' Rob said. 'So he did.'

Lucy pushed the trolley towards the big automatic doors. Her hands shook slightly on the handle. Everything felt such a trial at the moment. All around her, normal life went on, and yet her normal life had had a huge hole ripped in it, a hole that she was not sure she would ever fill. All the time, everywhere she went, people asked her how Caroline was, said how sorry they were, how was the family coping? Lucy longed to hear a normal voice, not one tinged with pity and embarrassment. Rob had been the only one to keep her going. She'd even laughed the day after Archie died, when Rob enquired, in a deeply sensitive voice, if Archie's new car *had* to go back.

She saw Max straight away. He was standing with his back to her, flicking through *Horse and Hound*. 'What do you want that for?' Lucy said, over his shoulder. 'Buying horses now, are you?' He turned. 'Cat is,' he said. 'For the girls. Maybe I will. I fancy a big hunter.'

'Quite the country squire,' Lucy said.

'Don't take the piss. How are you?'

'Sick of being asked how I am,' she said. 'How are you?'

'Missing you,' he said.

'Are you?' Lucy said. 'Are you really?'

'Of course,' Max said, defensively. Lucy looked at him as if with new eyes. Yes, he was so good-looking – but was there something a little studied about his appearance, all that careful glamour and the perfect clothes for every occasion, even shopping?

'You didn't call very soon.'

'Christ, Lucy, how could I? Rob would have answered the phone, and he would have thought it was very odd. Anyway, I had a really big deal on. Serious money involved too. I couldn't drop everything.'

'Of course,' Lucy said. 'We're moving.'

'What?'

'We're moving – much nearer to London. Rob has a new job.' Lucy stood to one side to let a harassed-looking mother with a squealing baby push past. She glanced about her. 'What do you want me to do?' she asked. Max looked worried. 'What do you mean?' 'Should I leave Rob? Stay here? Do you *really* love me,

Max?' His face now bore a look of pure terror, and he glanced nervously about him.

'Of course I do,' he said, quietly. 'But we can't rush into anything. There's the children, the house . . .'

Lucy laughed. 'I had you so worried,' she said. 'I had you so worried that I might proposition you and force you into a decision you have absolutely no intention of making. You haven't changed, have you? You still want everything, don't you? You can't have *everything*, Max. It doesn't end nicely. This wouldn't end *nicely*.'

A woman reached up to take a magazine behind them. 'Excuse me . . .'

'Sorry,' Lucy said, stepping back.

'Maybe we could meet . . .'

'Max,' Lucy said, patiently. 'Maybe we couldn't do anything. Yes, I could have slept with you. I could have fallen in love with you again – and I probably would have done. You could have told me how marvellous I was, how much you still loved me, we could maybe have snuck off for weekends in lovely five-star hotels and, who knows – perhaps even abroad if we could have lied to everyone convincingly enough. The only future we would have, Max Yorke, would be if I left Rob and you left Cat and we moved my children into your life and you became a weekend father. Would you like that? Would you like my children?' Max looked at her in horror. 'That's not what I meant at all,' he said. 'Of course it isn't,' Lucy said. 'You wanted romance, didn't you? You wanted us to flirt and have great sex and make each other feel eighteen again. You can't do that. You can't go around creating drama and expecting other people not to get hurt. You'd never leave Cat, would you?' Max looked pained. 'I . . .'

'Would you heck,' Lucy said. 'And threaten your comfortable life? It would just be a grand passion, a secret spice that would leave your heart untouched.'

'That isn't fair,' Max said quickly. 'You've become very hard, Lucy.'

'No, I haven't,' she said. 'I'm just not soft enough to fall for the fantasy you were offering.'

'I do love you,' he said, moving towards her, taking her arm. 'It's real, how I feel, honestly.'

'Maybe it is, and maybe it isn't,' Lucy said. 'But over the past week I think I've been shown just what real love is. Sorry, Max,' she said, wheeling her trolley away. 'Time for you to move on to a new diversion.'

She walked swiftly away from him, so swiftly that only a handful of fellow shoppers noticed the tears running down her cheeks. It wasn't just Max who had been shown the folly of a dream.

At home, she struggled into the kitchen with heavy bags of shopping. Rob was standing looking out of the window. When he heard her, he turned. Lucy looked at him in surprise. 'Are you not going to work today? I thought they needed you.'

'They can wait,' he said. 'Lucy, there's something I have to ask you.'

Lucy put down the bags, carefully, so she didn't break the Ribena bottle. One of the plastic handles had wrapped tightly around her wrist, and she rubbed it. She didn't look at him. 'What?'

'Have you stopped loving me?'

Lucy stared at him aghast. 'Of course not,' she said. 'Why would you think that?'

'I haven't been what you want, have I?' He rubbed one hand over his eyes, and then turned away from her. 'We don't have to move together, you know. I could go on my own. If you'd rather stay here.'

Lucy walked towards him and slowly ran her hand

up his back, feeling the boniness of his spine through his cotton shirt. Despite his height and strength, he seemed vulnerable, defenceless. She let her hand move up into his hair, feeling the warmth of his neck, and she slid her other hand round his waist. Gently, she rested her head against his back. He held himself slightly away from her, and Lucy thought, I'm losing him. I could lose the most precious thing in the world, and for something so worthless, so intangible that to breathe on it would break it.

'No,' she said. 'I will be with you.'

THE END

Homing Instinct

Diana Appleyard

When having it all just isn't enough . . .

It's time to start thinking the unthinkable . . .

Carrie Adams, successful television producer, mother
and wife, is about to return to work. Baby Tom has
fallen in love with the new nanny; six-year-old
Rebecca isn't too keen, but hopes the nanny will at
least be better organized than Mummy. Carrie
meanwhile is desperate to reinvent herself from
housewife to svelte career woman.

Because this is what today's women do, don't they?
They're smart, successful, glamorous wives and
perfect part-time mothers. They can be brilliant at
work *and* brilliant in bed. Carrie lives by the maxim
that working full-time is no problem as long as she has
the right child-care, and has never doubted for a
moment that this is her path in life – until reality
begins to hit home. She isn't happy, the children aren't
happy, and husband Mike – until recently trying
desperately to be a New Man – is now becoming more
and more detached from family life. She beings to
think the unthinkable. Perhaps, just perhaps, she
doesn't *have* to do all this . . .

' A FABULOUS, FUNNY NOVEL . . . THIS
WONDERFUL BOOK IS ESSENTIAL READING FOR
MOTHERS TRYING TO DO IT ALL'
Daily Mail

'RUTHLESSLY AND HILARIOUSLY FRANK'
New Woman

'A BRILLIANTLY FUNNY READ'
Woman's Realm

0 552 99821 4

BLACK SWAN

Love is a Four Letter Word

Claire Calman

Sex. Yes. She remembered that.

Wasn't that the thing that happened somewhere
between the talking-and-going-out-to-dinner bit
and the sobbing-and-eating-too-many-biscuits bit?
Still, Bella was sure she could handle some –
preferably before her as yet unopened packet of
condoms reached their expiry date. She must be
practically a virgin again now, all sealed over like
pierced ears if you don't wear earrrings for too
long.

But the 'L' word? Uh-huh. No way. She never
wanted to hear it again. There were things in her
past which needed to be put well away, like the 27
boxes of clutter she'd brought from her old flat.
And having changed her job, her town, her entire
life – the one thing she wasn't about to change was
her mind.

'SIMPLY WONDERFUL! I WAS TOTALLY
ENCHANTED'
Fiona Walker

0 552 99853 2

BLACK SWAN

Excess Baggage

Judy Astley

A Proper Family Holiday was the last thing Lucy
was expecting to have. But as a penniless and
partnerless house-painter with an expired lease on
her flat and a twelve-year-old daughter, she could
hardly turn down her parents' offer to take them on
a once-in-a-lifetime trip to the Caribbean. She'd
just have to put up with her sister Theresa (making
no secret of preferring Tuscany as a holiday
destination) and brother Simon (worrying that
there might be some sinister agenda behind their
parents' wish to take them all away) with their
various spouses, teenagers, young children and
au pair.

In a luxury hotel, with bright sunshine, swimming,
diving, glorious food and friendly locals, any
family tensions should have melted away in the
fabulous heat. The children should have been
angelic, the teenagers cheerful, the adults relaxed
and happy. But . . . some problems just refuse to be
left at home.

0 552 99842 7

BLACK SWAN

A SELECTED LIST OF FINE WRITING
AVAILABLE FROM BLACK SWAN